Elemental.

In the world of Kayan, it is a word full of implication.

Three-hundred years ago, it was an epithet. A curse.

Today it is a description. A title. Another word among many.

Elementals are wizards, born with the power of creation, set to inherit the rule, the responsibility, the very fate of a country. They are the most dangerous creatures in Kayan, including the gods themselves.

They are the carefully trained, accounted for, numbered, humbled, kept in check.

Any one of them could doom the world.

Or save it.

And the most powerful among them has disappeared.

Elemental

ELEMENTAL

By Tam Chronin

Cover designed by Noelle Barcelo

This book is a work of fiction. Names, characters, places, and incidents either are products of the author's imagination or are used fictitiously. Any resemblance to actual persons, living or dead, events, or locales is entirely coincidental.

Tam Chronin
Visit my website at www.tamchronin.com

Independently published

To Sabrina,
You were there from the moment I started writing this
book,
You've been here, asking for more
As I struggled with every word.
There were days I only kept writing this
Because of you.
Friends who stay friends as long as we have been
Become family.

To Grandpa Alan,
For the art, for the stories, and for all the things.
I miss you every day.

Elemental

Elemental

CONTENTS

PART ONE

I am human.

Let no words you find here or elsewhere convince you otherwise. No myths, legends, rumors, or tales should cloud your thinking. No matter what the other wizards or elementals say, I am human.

I entered into this world from my mother's womb just as naked and helpless as any other babe. My parents loved me while they still lived. While that and other things may make me more fortunate than most, it reinforced in my heart the knowledge that so many other elementals lack. The knowledge that we all enter the world the same. Naked and afraid.

"Agrad!"

My fears didn't have a face until I was nine years old.

"Agrad, wait up!"

Until a wizard visited our small town.

"Mother sent me with an extra apple today." My friend, Garim, hurried to catch up with me that morning.

He was round faced and friendly, nearly always smiling. His hair was a light shade of brown, almost blond, which was unusual in our town. Most people in Lesser Stonegore looked more like me, with dark hair and brown eyes. Garim stood out.

"Thank you," I said, taking the apple. I put it into my lunch sack and handed Garim a candy I found inside. Garim loved sweets, but I preferred fruit. Candy was a little too sweet, I thought. We traded like this most days.

That morning was a typical morning. It was summer, and I remember the air was heavy and warm. I wasn't sweating yet, but my hair was getting warm in the sun. I remember wondering if Garim's hair got this warm when something else caught my attention. A mother was scolding her small daughter for throwing a fit. "Stop crying so loud, you'll call a wizard's wrath down on us all by making such a noise."

The little girl just cried harder, of course. How many times had my own parents said the same thing to me when I was that small?

Garim and I exchanged a look of mutual exasperation with the mother before us. Her girl was crying harder now, of course. She was obviously scared, because now a wizard was going to come and take her away and gobble her up, just like in the stories.

It was the fate of disobedient children in nearly every tale we'd heard. We grew up thinking a wizard was twenty feet tall and had skin of smoke and flame. They ate babies for breakfast, when they weren't too busy with destroying villages or blighting crops for fun. We learned better in school, but it was an image I'd had that was hard to shake off.

"Yes, scare her to death, that'll get her to be quiet," Garim said in a hushed tone, rolling his eyes.

I nodded. "If I ever have kids, I'll never say that. Ever."

These were thoughts and opinions we'd shared before. We walked past the mom and her girl, convinced of our superiority.

"Oh," Garim stopped me before we reached the scribe's office. "Denie taught me a new spell last night. I'll show you later, right?"

I grinned, excited. "I'll see if I can go play tonight. See you later."

He nodded and continued on to the common classes. As for me, I had an aptitude for magic and had a private tutor. I opened the door and slipped in quietly, setting down my things. "Good morning, Master Kavidrian."

"Agrad," he said. "Your practice work is on the slate."

It was all so very routine. I did my work silently until Master

Kavidrian completed whatever he was in the middle of. About half the morning passed with the usual work, assessment, and discussion. I can remember that day so much clearer than I can remember every other lesson I've ever had. We were discussing the Arcane Wars and the ascension of wizards to power. Before then the human world had been run by priests. Mages had rebelled against the priests and had declared war on the gods over three hundred years before. Seventeen of them survived the war and became wizards.

"They were powerful enough that they killed seventeen gods in the battle and took their power," Master Kavidrian explained.

"How do you kill a god?"

"There are three wizards left who know how, since they're the ones who did it," he said. "You could ask one of them if you want, but I have never plucked up the courage to do so myself." There was a twinkle in his eye that invited levity in response, and I grinned at him obligingly. "The rest of the wizards who rule today are just as powerful as the original wizards, but they're called elementals. Do you remember why, from last night's reading?"

I nodded. "They have the element of a god's power when they're born, but they didn't do the spell themselves. So, when a wizard is killed that element goes to a baby, and the baby gets to rule the wizard's country." I paused for a moment. "But, if the wizard is as powerful as a god, they should be just as impossible to kill. So, if someone kills a wizard, shouldn't they be the next wizard?"

"It doesn't work that way," Master Kavidrian said. "So far, the only people who have been able to kill wizards are other wizards or elementals. You might--"

He was interrupted by a messenger. It was a common enough occurrence that I paid it no mind, opening my history text to read silently. Master Kavidrian was frequently given correspondence for farmers or other laborers who had better things to do than read for themselves. Their literacy was limited to simple spells that were necessary to their labor.

This time was different, though. He did not say, "I will be visiting with Farmer Tarrinus for a few minutes," or "I'll be wasting another lunch, so you had better enjoy yours thoroughly." I looked up curiously and silently to see him watching me with a thoughtful frown.

"Sir?" I said.

He shook his head and folded the note. "This town needed some excitement anyway," Master Kavidrian said as he dismissed the messenger with a coin.

I waited expectantly, but he turned his attention to something on his desk and began writing. He didn't even look up when he spoke. "Our lessons the rest of the week will be canceled. An old acquaintance will be arriving tonight. Let your parents know."

"Yes, sir," I said, grabbing my things and leaving. It was clear we were done for the day, as well.

Curiosity tagged along with me, whispering questions and inspiring a string of what-ifs. What sort of acquaintance would he have, that I wouldn't know? Hadn't he lived here his whole life, like everyone else? At that age, I still had a difficult time imagining any adult had a past at all, let alone one I didn't know about. He was my tutor. He was the town scribe. He served as a mediator when necessary. That's who he was, just as my parents were spellsmiths. Garim was the son of the only store's owners, and he would own the store when they were done with it. My friend Natali would likewise succeed his parents as farmers. Everyone had a place, and everyone's place was decided since long before I was born. No one left who didn't come back. No one arrived, except temporarily. Messengers and traveling merchants were the only ones who weren't a permanent fixture upon my life, and even they were familiar faces in their comings and goings.

I was stopped no less than ten times on the way home. At first I expected to be stopped for not being at my lessons, but I was surprised. The news that there had been a messenger had already hit the town and painted it with wild speculation.

"Master Kavidrian had a messenger today," I said. "That is all I know."

"You probably know more than I do," many of them would say, or words similar enough to mean the same thing as they turned to share the news with someone else.

Even Wydram Longbar, our local enforcer, stopped me in passing. "Messenger, huh?"

I just nodded, trying to make my way home and yet not turn my back on him disrespectfully.

"Agrad, you know--" he began, but stopped himself with a shake of his head. "Never you mind that right now. You just keep a low profile, hear me? There's whisperings of a wizard on the move, and your tutor used to be friends with their like. Get me?"

"Yes," I said quietly.

"Don't 'yes' me just because you think you should," he grumbled darkly.

"Sorry, sir."

"It can't be Verwyn," I heard someone nearby say, and I recognized the name of a country from maps I had seen in my lessons.

I turned, trying to see who had said it. When I looked back at Enforcer Longbar, he had already turned and walked away. I crept closer to the couple who were talking.

"Lorwyn," the other said. That was the name of our country, and the name of the wizard that ruled us.

The man beside her shook his head. "Our Lord would invite

Master Kavidrian to visit his castle, not come here. He's done so before. More likely Ceolwyn or Kaelwyn. They're more active and have ears everyw--" He caught sight of me listening in on them and closed his mouth abruptly. It was Garim's father, Master Dayle, I realized as I saw his face. He was talking to Mistress Cesana, his sister. I hurried along home, shamed to have been caught eavesdropping by people who would probably give my parents an earful about it.

By the time I made it home my father was fixing lunch while my mother was in the midst of repairing some charm.

"Aren't you early?" Mother said. There was a sparkle in her eye as she saw me, despite her tone of admonition. There always was when I walked into the room.

"Master Kavidrian sent me home," I said, setting my bag on the table and taking out my lunch sack. "There was a messenger, and Master Kavidrian told me classes are canceled for the rest of the week."

"A messenger?" Father asked. He took my lunch sack, setting the apple aside and putting the rest in the preserver. It was like an icebox, but it worked with magic since ice could be hard to find this time of year. It also kept things at the temperature you put it in at, instead of making everything cold. I thought that was just one of the perks of having spellsmiths as parents, since preservers were so rare that I didn't know anyone else who had one.

"Master Kavidrian said a guest is arriving tonight," I said, giving my mother a tight hug. "Enforcer Longbar said a wizard's on the move, and that Master Kavidrian was friends with wizards. Is that true? And I overheard Garim's dad talking about it, too. He said it couldn't be Lorwyn, because then Master Kavidrian would just go there. Do you think a wizard is really coming here? Or an elemental?"

My mother's arms had gone stiff around me. She held me

tight, holding her breath, looking over at my father. I couldn't see their faces, but I just knew they were looking at each other.

"Agrad," Father said stiffly. "We don't gossip in this house. It is none of our business what sort of friends your tutor has, or who might be visiting. Come and eat."

"Yes, sir," I said, feeling small from his rebuke. Lunch was eaten in almost perfect silence.

It made me anxious. They were tense all day, finding busywork and chores for me the rest of the day. When I asked to go play with Garim they said no. They looked scared by the question. We had a handful of guests, and most were immediately turned away. Only Mistress Cesana wouldn't be turned away. My mother stepped outside to talk with her, and I stayed glued to the window the entire time.

I expected Mistress Cesana to point to me and yell about my indiscretion earlier, but that's not what happened. They talked quietly and calmly, at length. I had nearly given up when I saw that my mother had started crying. Mistress Cesana gave her a hug, patting her back, and they stood there until my mother had calmed.

The thought was a disquieting one. Was my mother crying because a wizard was coming? Perhaps they were more terrifying than I realized. The image of a monster of smoke and flame, gobbling babies and destroying everything in their path, returned for a moment. I shook it off and returned to putting away the dishes to keep myself occupied rather than dwell on those thoughts.

Raised voices kept me awake that night, though I couldn't make out the words they exchanged with such impassioned urgency. It worried me so much that I pulled the covers tight over my head. Their silence held me awake even longer, when it finally came.

The next morning my mother was cleaning furiously. I

quietly ate the apple I had forgotten the day before. It bothered me as much as her crying had. She never cleaned like this. Most of the time she was creating messes with her wild experiments, meaning to clean and never finding the time or attention. It fell on my father to tidy up after her, until the calm after the storm broke and she would laughingly declare a few days off to catch up.

"Stay near the house," Mother told me, putting the last of the books neatly away on freshly-dusted shelves.

"Let the child have fun," Father said. "Agrad will be fine, and it will draw attention if--"

"It's a little late for that!" Mother threw her hands in the air in frustration.

"I'll stay out of sight," I promised meekly as I slipped out the door to let them argue some more. There wasn't much I could do, anyway. My friends were all with their own tutors or in the common classes, like Garim. Those were held for all the children between the ages of seven and twelve. After twelve it was widely held that a general education was unnecessary, since everyone needed to focus on what they'd be doing the rest of their lives. It wouldn't make sense for me, for example, to learn more than the very basics of harvesting or carpentry, since I had no aptitude for growing things or using hammers and chisels and other such tools. My gift was for magic. I'd be much more helpful if I made spells to sharpen plows than I would be trying to guide one through the soil.

The weather that day was perfect. I spent time hiding alone by the stream near my house, or in the clearing a bit upstream. I grew bored quickly on my own, and despite my promise to stay hidden I crept closer to town. From the top of a hill I climbed a tree and watched from a distance, looking at the carriage in front of Master Kavidrian's house and thinking I'd never seen anything so fancy in my life.

I watched people come and go. A couple of them were well-dressed strangers, and I wondered which one was the wizard. Was it the girl with the golden hair and scarlet dress? The man who simpered around and avoided the mud holes with such obvious distaste that I could see it even from my distant vantage? Would wizards fear getting dirty, or would they just dry up the mud with magic? I thought a moment and decided that's what I would do, if I didn't want to get dirty. Zip, and the earth would be dry until I was past it, and then it could be muddy again at my will.

I smiled and climbed down the tree, heading back to safety again. There was nothing to worry about, there. The wizard couldn't be worth a thing if he was afraid of mud holes, or if she showed off her prettiest dress when there wasn't even anything going on.

I came back the next day, emboldened by my success in watching the visitors from afar. I came closer this time, still hiding, but determined to get close enough to see their faces if they walked out. I'd brought a peach with me and ate it slowly as I walked, pretending to be too wrapped up in eating it to notice where it was I was going if anyone asked. I suppose it was child logic that told me that it was a good excuse to be so close to the strangers, but I did not need it. I saw no one that day, but I thought for a moment that I felt eyes peering at me from the darkness of Master Kavidrian's house. I took a step closer, curiously, nearly taking a step from the patch of tall grass I'd hidden myself behind.

"Agrad!"

I jumped, turning to see Master Kavidrian behind me, carrying a bread basket and a handful of other items from the general store.

"Get home before they see you out here," he muttered, walking past me without looking at me.

I stared after him, watching as he walked into the house and light spilled into the empty parlor. The door shut quickly and I hesitated only a moment more before I dashed home. That was close enough to get to a wizard, I decided as I walked. If they made even a powerful man like Master Kavidrian act so jumpy, I wanted nothing more to do with them.

I did stay close to home the next day, staving off boredom by enchanting rocks into a row of toy soldiers and letting them loose to fight each other. I was supposed to be too young to do magic like that by myself yet, but that didn't stop me and my friends from doing this when we were together. Tychel's brother hand taught him the spell once, and we all learned it and kept it a secret. I wondered if the spell Garim had talked about the other day would have made things more exciting, but I hadn't been allowed to see him so I could learn it.

We'd usually fight one at a time, but since I was alone I'd needed at least two. That got boring rather quickly, and soon I'd built an entire army. I pitted them against each other, like they were in training for a real battle.

The spell itself was almost ridiculously simple. I'd never had trouble bringing forth the power I needed, and that was half the work of being a mage. Next came the image within my mind to show the power what form it should take. Finally the words, "N tasiado en ardre." I couldn't figure out why there had to be words, or what they had to do with the spell I was doing, but saying the words finally made it all either come together and work, or just fizzle out. Maybe it was like saying "the end" at the end of a bedtime tale, to let the magic know that's all you wanted and it was time to make it happen.

"N tasiado en ardre," I said under my breath. Another miniature soldier would unfold from the rock and begin to walk around.

I was nearly caught at least half a dozen times that day, so the day that followed I went further, away from town this time, following the stream until I reached a clearing that my friends and I had discovered the year before. I rebuilt my stone army quickly and almost missed the sound of someone approaching. I turned quickly, cringing and looking sufficiently guilty in case it was an adult who would be upset at my blatant misuse of magic.

The one who approached was a stranger, so I knew it must be one of Master Kavidrian's guests I hadn't seen before. His skin was pale in the same way my tutor had pale skin, from spending too much time indoors. Shock white hair topped his head and framed his face like a mane, and he wasn't all that much taller than me. I relaxed and offered a hesitant smile. "Hello." My tone and stance changed, offering a greeting of equals since I thought he must be a child like me.

He nodded and found a tree stump nearby. "Hello," he answered in a deep voice that disproved my first impression. "What have we here?"

I crossed my arms over my chest. "Just playing soldiers," I said, defensive once again. I willed the other soldiers to stand at attention instead of fighting, but they looked as uneasy and restless as I suddenly felt.

"I've never seen such an army," he grinned, picking one up and looking it over. The tiny soldier yelped when he was turned upside down. "Not an army of such small men, that is." He looked at me, and his smile was both cheerful and kind. "I didn't know girls liked to play soldiers. What's your name?"

I didn't bother correcting him, but it struck me as absurd that he'd think I was a girl. I was told I was a pretty child, but everyone knew I was a boy. Was it my long hair? My mother was distracted most of the time and forgot to cut it, so perhaps that was it. It didn't matter either way. I relaxed and sat back down on a patch of grass in the face of his absurdity. "I'm Agrad," I said. "What's yours?"

He almost looked surprised for a moment, but he smiled and said, "Krecek."

"Do you play soldiers, Krecek?"

"All the time," he said, sitting down next to me and setting down the toy soldier he'd picked up before. "Not like this, though. What spell did you use?"

He was delighted when I taught it to him, picking up five rocks and changing them instantly. They had tabards and armor of bright blue and silver, while mine were still slate gray. I was both surprised and delighted. "That's wonderful! I didn't even think about making them look so real." I concentrated a moment, closing my eyes so I wouldn't mess up as I whispered the words as quickly as I could. When I opened my eyes again, a miniature army in gold and green surrounded me. They began milling about, looking each other over in surprise.

Krecek grinned and began making more soldiers of his own. "When we're even, shall we battle?"

"Can you make soldiers that fast?" I frowned a bit, thinking. "I could give you some of mine."

"I think I can manage," he said. "You look like you're…about ten? I'd say I have a few years of doing magic on you."

Well, if he was part of the wizard's entourage, he was probably right. "I'm nine," I told him, concentrating on bringing all of my soldiers into a line. "I've only fought with one soldier at a time before, though. We're not supposed to do magic without a grown up."

"I think I'm grown up enough that you shouldn't get in trouble," Krecek said lightly. "Now, since you have more experience with these particular soldiers than I do, I hope you'll go easy on me." His eyes sparkled as he matched my number of soldiers in an instant. He hadn't uttered a word or moved his lips.

I grinned and we talked over simple rules. He tucked his hair behind one ear, absently, as he listened to me. His ears came to a small point, I noted curiously. Was he an elf? I couldn't be sure because I'd never seen one before, but drawings I'd seen made me think they were slenderer, more delicate, and somehow more exotic. However, if he was an elf it might make it harder to beat him because there was no telling how old he might be.

It wasn't much longer before we set our magical toys to fighting, and I could tell right away that he was the one going easy on me. My face was scrunched up in concentration while his was vaguely thoughtful and amused. To add insult to injury, he easily defeated me and I almost didn't catch how he had won. It wasn't his unnumbered years of experience that had brought about my downfall, I realized.

"You cheated!" I protested, grabbing my last intact soldier as I figured out his trick. "Y-you made more while we were fighting!"

"You did so well." Krecek shook his head, still looking amused in the face of my anger. "I forgot I was fighting a child, honestly. Give it a few years and I think you will be a dangerous opponent."

"You broke my soldiers!"

He waved a hand, and they returned to their natural state as mere rocks. Again, he used no words to end the spell. I tried very hard to remain more angry than impressed. "And now they are returned to their natural state, unbroken and waiting to be enchanted again. I won, yes, but you should be proud in your defeat. You did well, for your age."

"You cheated," I insisted, dropping the lifeless rock in my hand and placing my fists firmly on my hips.

"Yes, that's right," Krecek smiled. "I cheat."

I stared in awe. He admitted it! He admitted to cheating! I wasn't prepared to deal with someone who would state it so boldly. "But, Mother says nobody likes a cheater and nobody plays with cheaters," I finally growled darkly.

"Yet I predict," Krecek said, "that you'll play with me again. Even knowing I'm a cheater, you'll want to keep playing until you can defeat me."

"It's no fun if I know I can't win," I muttered. I crossed my arms over my chest, glaring.

"Who said you'll never win?" His expression was too confident, too smug. "The only way to be certain you'll never beat me, cheater or not, is if you stop trying."

He had a point.

I stormed off without another word. Still, before I walked into the house I picked up a rock. That night, instead of going straight to sleep, I practiced changing it into a soldier faster and faster, until I finally couldn't keep my eyes open at all.

"Are you sure you're only nine?" Krecek asked a few days later. We'd continued our battles, of course. We met every day, spending hours playing and talking about strategy and old wars and all sorts of games. Every battle had been a resounding victory--for him.

"Nine and a half," I said shortly, scowling as I tried infusing life into ten soldiers at once. No matter how I'd tried I couldn't figure out his trick of casting spells silently. Converting so many at once with total silence was growing unnerving. Krecek had done so during our last battle, and had made it look effortless. I had to learn to do the same or I'd never beat him.

Every fight he did something new and more difficult, but I wasn't going to let that hold me back. I redoubled my resolve to defeat him with every underhanded trick he pulled.

"So, you're almost old enough to be apprenticed," he mused, looking thoughtful. "Too bad we have to leave so soon."

"You're trying to distract me," I said. "It won't work." I made an effort, trying to force a wedge through his front line, but his soldiers allowed the break and closed in behind my forward advance, cutting them down from behind where they were vulnerable. I hadn't committed enough of my soldiers to the offense, and they were finished off.

Still, I'd done more damage than before.

"That wasn't my intent," Krecek said as if he hadn't all but beaten me at my own game. Again. "We're leaving tomorrow, and hopefully taking a friend of mine with us. However, that will leave you without a tutor."

"You're taking Master Kavidrian away?" In an instant my soldiers stopped fighting, reacting to my surprise.

Krecek halted his own attack. "His only concern was that you should still have a teacher. You are what is holding him back from returning with us to Anogrin. It's an amazing city, full of magic, libraries, history--"

"I couldn't," I shook my head, cutting off whatever other temptations he wanted to offer. "My parents would never let me."

"I'm sure they would agree if you told them I requested it," he said.

"I'm only nine."

"Agrad," Krecek said softly, catching my eyes and holding my gaze as if to mesmerize me into going along with what he said. "You'd be apprenticed soon anyway. What's a year and a half, between friends?"

"They'll still say I'm too young. And they'd never let me go so far away, especially not with a wizard."

"There's no sense in waiting to begin your apprenticeship," he said with a proud smile. "You've clearly got all the talent you'd need for any sort of magic you could dream of crafting. Don't worry about rules or what's expected; where a wizard is involved exceptions can always be made."

It's just what I'd wanted to hear all my life. I'd craved this sort of attention and being told I was special and deserving of an exception. Still, I hesitated, almost convinced but not quite. "I'd miss everyone. I wouldn't know anybody there and I'd be lonely."

"I'd be there, and your tutor would be there."

Rather than answer him I turned away, scared that I'd tell him yes if he asked one more time. I had to talk to Mother. I had to ask her. She would know what to do and what to say.

Krecek grabbed my arm, and as soon as his fingers brushed my skin a shiver went down my spine. I'd felt something, but I didn't know what. From his gasp I realized he'd felt something as well.

"I've found you," Krecek whispered so softly I almost couldn't be sure of what he'd said. "If you come with me I can offer you anything. Everything. Whatever you wish."

I took a step back. My heart was pounding with fear that I just couldn't understand. "I have everything I want. If it's all the same, I'd just like to stay right here."

"You're telling me no?" Krecek paused with a strange expression on his face. It made me think he was not used to being denied anything.

"Yes," I said. "I mean no. I mean, yes, I'm telling you no. I don't want to go anywhere with a wizard. They're scary, and they do bad things, and I don't want to leave my family and my

Elemental

friends and my everybody here."

"Do I scare you?" he asked gently.

"Well, no," I said. He was starting to, but he hadn't been until a few moments ago. "You're my friend."

Krecek hesitated just a moment, as if he'd been about to say something and changed his mind. "If we're friends, won't you miss me when I have to leave?"

"But you can come back!"

Silence fell for a time, and I started backing away toward home.

"I won't be back here," he finally said, halting my backward motion. "They need me in Anogrin, and I can't come or go as I please."

"But you have friends at home. Don't you?"

"Not many. Not really." Krecek smiled sadly, seeming very old for a moment. "Most of my truest friends are gone."

He meant dead. I knew he meant dead. I felt so bad for him, and I wanted to be his only real friend so badly, but there was some part of me that was yelling that if I gave in to him I would be swallowed whole and never return. There was something wrong with him. I had to leave. Now. It was almost like another voice inside me, telling me to run or I'd never be free.

"I can't!" I yelled. "My parents would never allow me near a wizard, or his friends!"

I turned away, intent on running home.

He was already standing in front of me, and I could feel a rush of air and smell the tang of magic in the air. "I could make you come with me," he spoke just above a whisper. "It is my right."

"No!" I screamed as I tried to push past him. "Then I'd never be your friend!" My heart was pounding, and something within me started to swell and build. It felt like magic, only much bigger. I wanted to use it to push him away, but I was afraid to

25

touch it somehow. Like it was too big for me.

"I won't kidnap you." Krecek grabbed my shoulders, and he started to smile kindly. "Don't worry. You're right. You have too many reasons to stay here. Of course you wouldn't want to leave everything you've ever known behind."

I believed him, and I started to calm down. I chided myself for my irrational fear. He was an adult, after all. And I'd just said some rather unflattering things about him and those he associated with. It was time to placate him, before he set the wizard on my family and me. "It's not that I don't want to go. You've been a great friend. I just, I can't leave. This is home. This is where I belong."

"I see," he said with a wry twist of a smile. "I understand. I would still like you to come, though. I can't stay here."

"I'm sorry," I said, slumping a bit as he let go of my shoulders.

"If you change your mind," Krecek said, "I'll be leaving tomorrow."

I nodded and just walked home.

I wish I could remember more of the rest of that day. I was quiet that evening, but my parents were even quieter. I was a little scared still about the conversation I'd had with Krecek, but I hadn't really entertained the thought of them being afraid. They didn't know what had happened to me. I didn't know why they were quiet, but it didn't occur to me to wonder at the time because I was so wrapped up in my own worries.

I eventually fell asleep, though I don't remember it. I had to have been asleep though, because I woke up to the smell of smoke and the sound of fire roaring in my ears. I might have heard screams, or I might have imagined them and embellished the memory over time.

I may have been the one screaming.

I ran through the house, through the center of the

conflagration consuming my home. I heard laughter, recognized it, and ran toward it.

"Even magic flames cannot touch me. Don't you know who I am?"

I turned the corner, feeling suddenly like time had slowed down. My parents were standing when I saw them. They didn't see me. Their hands were up, both of them casting a spell, chanting in unison, and I thought they were both taking a breath at the same time.

Their chests didn't expand. Their eyes didn't blink. They just fell, and there was a thud, and my mother's head bounced against the floor. Bounced. One moment they were casting a spell, and the next they were lifeless things that couldn't even keep their heads from bouncing when they hit the ground.

The air shimmered from the heat, but I didn't feel a thing. Not heat. Not grief. I just stared.

It wasn't the fire that ended them, though it was hot enough that it should have. The fire would destroy their bodies and remove the evidence of what had killed them, but I knew.

I could feel it.

This was the work of a wizard.

PART TWO

Krecek stood in the center of the burning room, as untouched as I was. He turned to look at me, eyes meeting mine. He took a deep breath and his eyes went wide momentarily and his jaw went slack. He may have winced, but the air was warping, shimmering between us.

Finally, his mouth set in a grim line. "Come with me, Agrad."

Krecek's hand moved forward, toward me, but it fell short, faltered, and returned to his side.

"There's nothing holding you here now."

He was right. There was nothing.

But, I couldn't. Not with him.

"NO!" I screamed.

He opened his mouth to say something more, but the feeling that had built within me earlier had returned, bigger and more immediate and terribly sudden.

There was a flash of light brighter than the flames, and then the feeling died just as suddenly as it had arrived.

The cold air shocked me back to myself and I gasped. I felt the ground rush up to hit my knees and slam into the arms I'd tried to brace myself with at the last moment. Then I felt nothing at all.

I was aware of sunlight on my skin, feeling it before seeing it. The warmth of it made me flinch, made me afraid for just a moment that I'd never really left my burning home. I whimpered like a hurt pup as I opened my eyes, terrified of what I would see.

Everything was green. The loam beneath me, the moss on the trees, the leaves that rustled in the breeze; the green was transcendent in that moment of relief. There was no fire. It was the warmth of the summer sun and brightness of day.

"Over here!"

It was a woman's voice, close by.

"It's a child, a little girl."

I was still in my nightshirt. Soot stained and singed, but modestly covered in all the important spots. That was the second time someone called me a girl. I didn't fight it. I just looked down at myself and wondered if I should care.

"I'm here, I'm here," grumbled a man, crashing through the woods toward us.

"Come and pick her up," the woman said. "The poor dear looks exhausted."

I was. I could fall asleep again and just not care if I lived or died.

The man picked me up and he carried me, fussing over me. "She reminds me so much of--"

"I know," the woman interrupted him excitedly. "Like a gift from the Old Gods. She looks so much like Eria did."

The man nodded, looking me over. "I'm Brinn," he told me gently.

The woman stepped on something that made a loud snap, probably a twig. She made a loud hissing sound, interrupting his introduction.

"Goriath Brinn," he continued. "She is my wife, Rhada. Don't worry, we'll keep you safe, get you cleaned up, and take care of you until you're better."

I nodded, leaning against his bushy brown beard. It was bouncy, like a pillow, but a little scratchy. My father hadn't had a beard, and his hair had been black, not brown. Goriath sounded a little like my father had, though. Not exactly like him, but enough that I liked the sound of his voice.

"Is she hurt anywhere?" Rhada asked.

I shook my head.

"She says no," Goriath said.

"Good," Rhada said. "I'm going to hurry ahead and start a bath. Take your time and don't jostle her around too much. She's tiny, and you're a huge bear of a man."

It almost made me want to smile. It was such an apt description. Huge bear of a man. His arms were as big around as my head. I couldn't smile, though. I watched Rhada walk ahead of us and I didn't know if I liked her. She had black hair, like my mother. She was darker, and her eyes had almost looked red when I first saw her, and it had made me think of fire. She was a little bossy, I thought. They weren't like my mother and father at all.

Except, her confidence already reminded me of my mother, and his kindness already reminded me of my father.

"You were in a fire?" Goriath asked gently.

I nodded.

"I'm glad you escaped," he said. "Fires can be very dangerous. What about the rest of your family?"

I froze, holding my breath even. I couldn't answer that.

"I see," Goriath said, as if I had answered. "Don't worry. You don't have to talk about it."

That was a good thing, I thought, because I wasn't going to talk about it. I lost track of how long he carried me, but he didn't ask me any more questions after that and I was grateful for it. The trees eventually thinned and I saw a town, larger than Lesser Stonegore. The road I saw was paved in stone all the way up to the edge of the forest. It looked cleaner. There were more red brick homes and fewer wooden ones than there had been at home.

I decided right away that I didn't like it. I didn't like anything about the town. It was too different. It was at least twice as big as home, and maybe bigger. There were rolling hills everywhere, I noticed as we reached the top of one hill. And there, at the apex of the closest hill, was a tidy two story house that overlooked both forest and town. There was a cute little fence around it that served no practical purpose at all. I noticed as we walked past it that it wasn't even warded with spells to keep intruders, or even wildlife, away.

They gave me privacy to bathe. The water intensified the smoke scent that clung to me. I almost obsessively scrubbed at myself, needing to be rid of the scent. I scrubbed until my skin was raw, and still I could smell it. Frantic scrubbing gave way to utter hopelessness. I cried as quietly as I could. I didn't want them to come in on me and see me cry. If they saw me cry they'd know something bad had happened. They'd ask their questions again. Questions that I couldn't answer, because if I opened my mouth it would all be real.

My tears just stopped coming out eventually. The smell washed out eventually. Numbly, heavily, I put on the dress that had been left for me.

"You're so pretty," Rhada said when I opened the door. She was looking at me with the sort of adoration my mother had. There was a sparkle in her eye that was only for me.

I looked down at myself in the dress. Frills and lace and soft colors, and in my heart I decided to be the little girl who made her eye sparkle. That girl had parents still. That girl wasn't being chased by a wizard. That girl wasn't homesick, because she was home.

Rhada brushed my hair and soothed me, telling me that everything was fine now. Everything would work out just fine. She kept telling me how pretty I was, how stunning even my eyelashes were because they were so long and lush.

"Now, my pretty child, can you tell me your name and where

you came from?"

I opened my mouth to answer and nearly choked on a sob. Oh no, oh no, I couldn't cry. I was wearing a dress. It didn't happen to me. I was wearing a dress.

"It's okay," Rhada said softly. "You can take all the time you need. Can I call you Eria? It's what I called my little girl, before she was taken from us."

It seemed weird, but I nodded. No weirder than thinking if I wore dresses then my parents wouldn't be dead, I supposed. Or that it hadn't happened to me. I knew that these trivial things made no difference. I knew I was just telling myself lies. If Rhada needed to lie, too, because losing Eria still hurt, it was okay. I just gave her a hug, because I felt like I understood, and a hug made everything better.

"You're a good child," she whispered in my ear, and it felt so sincere that I wanted to do anything to make it true, for both of us.

Dawnsday, the summer solstice, arrived faster than I'd expected. So many things had happened that I'd forgotten all about the holiday and how soon it was. A new dress was made for me, and I was surprised with it as a gift. It matched the soft brown of my eyes, and it had a sash as black as my hair. It was the first dress that was made only for me. I cried when they handed it to me.

They showed me off at Dawnsday like a little doll, with red ribbons in my hair and a black ribbon around my neck like a choker. I was the center of attention at first.

"I hope you like it here in Myrenfeld," a man said to me, leaning down to my level. "Are you from Verwyn, or another country?" He barely waited for me to answer before he went on. "What is your name? Did you get lost?"

"She's terribly shy," Goriath said. "Doesn't say a word, poor thing. We've been calling her Eria."

The man looked uncomfortable for a moment before he nodded. "So long as you remember she's not Eria. Even the Old Gods never brought a child back to life." He made a strange gesture and turned away quickly.

"One does not question a gift from the gods," Rhada said, shaking her head.

"It is a new era," Goriath murmured, placing a hand on her shoulder as if to hold her back from something.

"Even still," Rhada said. She dropped the subject though, because the revelry began to truly take shape.

The celebration took a more pagan tone than the celebrations at home ever had. There were drums and bonfires that filled my heart with terror and reminded me of everything I'd wanted to forget. The drums were the pounding of my own fearful heart, and the flames were magic that would take everything away. People danced with wild abandon, and every moment I expected them to all fall to the ground like broken marionettes.

Rhada and Goriath spoke and chanted and gave blessings to couples who would disappear into shady patches in the woods around us. Their blasphemous words were sought out by everyone in the town, blessings given openly, praises to the Old Gods being given with enthusiasm instead of fear. Things that were unspeakable in Lesser Stonegore were celebrated here, on this night. Were all their holidays the same?

Clothes disappeared from the adults a piece at a time until only the barest preservation of modesty was observed. Everything about the evening scared me or worried me or filled me with confusion that Dawnsday never had before. What was expected of me? What was I supposed to do? Even the other children had their own circle with more drums and dancing, and I couldn't even bring myself to ask what was going on, or if I could join them. I didn't have the words to ask.

I hid under a banquet table and stared at the strange sight of bare ankles until I finally fell asleep.

"Agrad!"

My mother was calling me through the crowd. The sun was bright and the breeze kept the day from being miserable. I was running around in just my pants, hair in a wild tangle of curls that flew everywhere.

"Agrad!"

It was the best Dawnsday ever. Mother was chasing me through the streets, trying to get me to put my shirt back on.

"You look like a pagan savage! Get over here!"

I laughed. I was looking for my friends. Natali, with his straight hair that always looked like silk. Garim, so chubby and pale. I had to introduce them to Krecek, because we were going to play soldiers, and we were going to teach them how to make great armies.

"Agrad, they'll know you're a boy!"

I tripped over the hem of my skirt. Goriath picked me up and dusted me off.

"Don't worry, Fadal," Goriath turned to my mother. "I'll make sure they think he's a girl. No one will ever find him in that dress."

I looked around. Where were my friends?

"Torba will be upset with me if anything happens to our little baby," Mother said, wringing her hands. "He's so protective."

I was still holding Krecek's hand, running, trying to find my friends. "I'm sorry," he kept saying. "I'm so sorry, Agrad."

"They're just over there," I said. "There's Natali and Garim now!" I ran harder, calling their names, but they didn't hear me. The drums of the Dawnsday revelers were getting too loud.

"I'm so sorry, Agrad."

I couldn't hear him. I let go of his hand so I could run faster, and a woman picked me up. She held me at length, like I was a viper. Her eyes like fire and ice at once, and somewhere within lurked secrets even she did not want to see. I started to say hello.

I woke up in bed with the sun streaming through my window, still wearing my Dawnsday dress. I fought a moment of panic when the dream I'd had seemed too real, and I wanted to claw off my dress. I hurried to the bathroom and washed and changed into fresh clothes. I played silently with my dolls.

Inspired by my dream, they were all given names of the people at home I'd never see again. I couldn't go back. It was safer if I stayed away. So I brought my home with me, in my heart, and pretended that their lives went on in my doll house. I was pretending that they were having their own Dawnsday, just like the ones I remembered.

Rhada came in and interrupted. "You've seen what we are now," she said softly.

"Priests," I said reluctantly, quietly.

"Close enough," Goriath said from the doorway.

"Indeed," Rhada agreed softly. "So, you can speak. Well then."

I could, but I didn't want to. I shrugged and returned to my dolls, making them exchange gifts of food and clothing. That was the tradition I knew.

"There are things we can teach you," she said. "Things you won't learn anywhere else or from anyone else."

I looked up at her. Curiosity prompted me to nod. I didn't understand the concept of blasphemy, I'd just heard people say it when they talked about the Old Gods. But, if it was something that went against the wizards, maybe it's what I needed.

I thought they would teach me magic. They started out by teaching me names.

"The names of the gods weren't known by most people," Rhada said. "Only the priests were taught them all because knowing their names gives you power."

I frowned.

"Even the names of the dead ones have power in them still," she said. "It's not the same kind of magic you were taught before, so it's going to feel strange."

Feeling strange wasn't what bothered me, though. Knowing the names made them seem more real, and less like stories from the past. It bothered me in ways I didn't understand. A part of me resonated with these teachings as much as shied away from it all. I thought it was because I'd met a wizard, someone who had killed a god. As I learned the stories of all of the gods along with the names, it became more personal. I wondered which god it had been. The idea became less abstract as the lessons continued, until I started having dreams that the gods all knew me and blamed me for what the wizards had done.

The names of the fallen gods, the dead ones, stuck in my mind with a particular resonance, and I squirmed when they were spoken out loud. I began looking forward to mundane lessons, like sewing and cooking. It didn't get any less frustrating when they taught me their faith-dependent version of magic. It was frustratingly weak, like filling a pillow by blowing feathers across the room into the fabric instead of grabbing handfuls of down and stuffing it in. I wanted to grab the power within my mind and bend it to my will. I wanted to command the power with words of a real spell, not coax it about like a scared wildling. Supplication seemed ridiculous when I'd been taught to demand.

I couldn't express it, though. Rhada knew I was frustrated, but I still couldn't bring myself to talk. I couldn't tell her what was wrong even if I were talking. I'd have to tell her about Krecek. I'd have to tell her that I'd met a wizard, that for a few days he'd been my friend. That I'd thought of him as a kindred spirit, not a murderer. She worshipped the gods he had murdered.

"You're learning quickly," Rhada assured me every day. "Just keep trying. Nalia, Fotar, Bogradan, Atherva, Egridaea. They were the first."

Their names made my skin itch the most. They were names I'd never forget.

"Deyson, Brennan, Ashvra, Baedrogan, Thebram, Saedral, Kaskal, Vaederan, Dacet, Agruet, Wirudel, Ceraan. They fell in the Arcane wars, along with the first ones."

I knew their names. I knew them like I knew my own.

"Hastriva, Kedaran, Garatara, Luriel, Chevonich, Beyla, Esier, Velana, Sadrath, Melura, Kerad. Thar and Brin. These are all gods that are still around, though they hide. They keep their secrets as well as they can, now that the keeper of secrets is dead."

I nodded. Those were names that didn't stick in my mind as clearly or burn as bright.

"Those are the gods whose power you can call on directly,

but doing so will call their attention to you. You can use those names in your spells. Think the names with all the focus of your mind and their powers will be yours."

I couldn't remember which ones had what powers, though. At the end of her recitations my head was full of a distracting magical hum.

"Don't worry, you'll get it. It will come to you, you just need to keep trying."

I thought she was wrong, but I stayed there for more than a year, and for her sake I did keep trying.

It didn't take that long before I started to feel safe and secure in my anonymity there. Their dangerous beliefs worried me, especially considering the position I would put them in if I were found here. I was nearly eleven when I started noticing the world around me enough to realize I really wasn't safe. Since I hadn't spoken much at all, others took me for an idiot and began talking as if I weren't there when we would travel as a family to community gatherings. There were many such gatherings here, and they relied on the priests, my foster parents, to help them organize it all.

I kept hearing the same rumors over and over again, with increasing frequency over time. Krecek Ceolwyn, wizard of the country of Ceolwyn, was looking for me and offered riches in an amount I couldn't dream of for whoever found the child that had escaped Lesser Stonegore alive. Someone, probably Master Kavidrian, had corrected him about my sex. In larger cities, it was posted that a young boy, pretty as any girl, had been orphaned in an accidental fire set that night, and because it had happened while the wizard slept he was concerned for the welfare of the child and wanted to set it right.

No one in Myrenfeld believed his motives were at all altruistic, and I was grateful. No one gave me any significant glances when they talked about new details, but I still worried that someday someone would. Some people had defiance and outrage in their eyes, but still others reeked of greed as they expressed a wish to find the child in question and get their reward.

"It's cruel," one of our neighbors, Master Denbro, said at the resurgence of the rumors one day.

Rhada and Goriath were helping our hosts in the kitchen and I was still seated at the table, picking at the last of my food while some of the more influential members of the town met.

"He's a wizard," Master Denbro continued. "If he wanted to find the child, he would just do it. He's playing games and offering false hope to the populace that they might get a reward for—"

"I'll bet the boy is an elemental," Mayor Stalay interjected. "It explains why Ceolwyn can't find him. The Verwyn castle has sat empty long enough, and he seems to be concentrating on our lands. But you didn't hear that last bit from me."

A lady at the table nodded fervently and also leaned in. "Wizards kill elemental children that aren't raised by them, the way the wizards want. Ever since the Elemental War, and how bloody that got. Can't risk it, you know. Too dangerous."

"That's rubbish," the old man next to me said. "It would incite the people to revolt."

Mayor Stalay shook his head. "Ceolwyn has held stewardship over the Verwyn lands for over a decade. I'd be willing to bet he's not too keen to give up control, if you know what I mean."

I looked away, bothered by their theory. I wasn't an elemental. The very thought was absurd. If I'd been an elemental, my parents would still be alive. Wouldn't they? I'd have saved them automatically with my god-like powers, or at the very least I'd have been able to better defend myself and avenge their deaths. I wouldn't have just run away.

But I hadn't run. I'd disappeared. I'd had an aptitude for magic. I'd felt something as I left everything behind. A surge of sorts had filled me, and if I thought about it I could feel it build within me again.

No. That didn't make me an elemental.

I could have been a mage or a spellsmith like my parents. They'd been very powerful, after all. The most powerful spellsmiths in the whole town. They probably could have been mages if they'd tried, but they didn't have any desire to work so closely or directly for wizards. I could have just gotten my potential from them, not from being a wizard reborn.

Mayor Stalay stood abruptly, shaking his head. "I'm not saying Ceolwyn will kill the boy. Not if he can turn the child to his side, at least. But the smart thing for the boy to do is to hide, and keep hiding, until there's nothing any wizard can do to stop him." He looked me in the eyes at that moment, and I nodded despite myself, understanding and agreeing.

"They've already destroyed a town to find that boy," the lady at the table said. "Staying in one place would be too dangerous. I'd stay on the run, if I were him."

"And you'd be condemning the boy to death," the old man scoffed. "A mere child, out in the wilderness alone? Sit down. Think about what you're saying."

"Would you have an escaped elemental hiding in our town?" Mayor Stalay shook his head, but he sat down slowly, reluctantly.

"It would be a good place to hide." The old man's voice quavered. "And it could do us some good to have someone that powerful around to help. No one would tell the other wizards that the boy was here. We're still loyal to Verwyn in these lands, even if he doesn't know who he is yet. We'd protect him."

"I know that no one would turn him in for the reward." His expression was grave, and he wasn't even glancing in my direction anymore. "Not here. But that doesn't mean this is a safe place to hide. Unless you think we could escape the same fate as Lesser Stonegore."

I left, unable to listen to one more word. I waited on the porch for Rhada and Goriath to finished, but Mayor Stalay came outside first. He kneeled in front of me and spoke in a hushed voice.

"I don't know if you're really that Agrad boy, or if you're really an elemental," he said. "Nobody's said anything about a little mute girl, but the timing would be right. Some people are going to start looking closer at little girls soon, because of the description that's out there, to make sure they're actually girls. They've been looking at only pretty boys for too long without finding anything. I don't want to tell you that you have to run away right now, if you're him. Just get ready to run if you need to. These are Verwyn lands, but we still have to answer to other wizards when our own isn't here to lead us.

"If I'm right, and if you're Lord Verwyn, I hope you'll come back and let me know. And remembered that I warned you before anyone else did."

Mayor Stalay patted me on the shoulder and left without another word.

The next time the door opened it was Rhada and Goriath, relieved to find me and ready to leave. I felt exhausted by the time we arrived home and I made my way to bed.

Was I really a missing elemental? What would it mean?

No town I stayed at would be safe, if I were. The mayor was right about that. It would mean that Krecek would never give up trying to find me, even if he had to visit every small town on the continent himself. The rewards for my capture would increase until someone who needed it desperately enough decided to turn me in, and then Myrenfeld would be wiped from the map as thoroughly as Lesser Stonegore had been.

If I did have that sort of innate power, it also meant I didn't dare use it. I could feel magic being used around me, and that meant that surely Krecek could as well. He'd know if I used it, since he'd watched and felt me use magic in front of him before, and he was much more powerful than I was. Even practicing to strengthen my ability and control was too risky, in case he was near.

I'd need to find a wizard or elemental ally if I hoped to learn anything at all, but what if the rest of them were just as bad as Krecek? What if they'd use me for their own ends, or decide I was too useless and simply dispose of me quietly while the rest of the world thought I was simply missing? And then, what if I really wasn't an elemental, and they mocked me and put me away for my arrogance?

The ideas raced through my mind all night, keeping me awake despite how tired I was. Finally I curled up with my pillow in my lap and cried for only the second time since my parents had died. I cried alone all night, from silent tears to sobs and keening, until the sun came up in the morning and the tears had run dry. At some point in my seemingly endless grief I had come to the decision to leave, to protect the people who had taken me in from the same fate my parents had suffered.

My plan was to leave a fortnight after that night. I planned to gather a few necessities, and then two days before I left I could spirit away some bread, cheese, and other food that would not spoil too quickly. I packed with me two books, hidden first with two dresses and my winter cloak. One was a simple book of stories and the other was an old sacred text that they had given to me specifically and quite deliberately. I thought of leaving it behind, but it had been such a precious gift that I could not bring myself to dishonor them by rejecting it or leaving it behind.

I was out pumping water when the carriage trundled past. It slowed just past our yard and I felt panic rise within. It wasn't Krecek's carriage, but it was similar in style and the elegant design. The horses that pulled it were gigantic, three times or more as tall as me, and dark as the midnight sky itself, dark eyes glittering the same hue. The driver stood, dressed in gray and black, motioning for me to approach.

"Girl! Is there a tavern in this speck of a town?"

I walked forward slowly, reluctantly, nodding ever so slightly. Speck of a town? It was so much larger than where I'd been raised.

"A blacksmith as well?"

I nodded again and pointed down the road.

"Don't be shy, girl! How far? I've coin if you're helpful enough."

That would be very helpful for when I left, I thought, but though I tried to speak I'd been silent so long that the words stuck in my throat. I licked my lips, stepping closer again until I was nearly up to the passenger compartment of the carriage, working my mouth to try to speak.

"Bring her with us," a deep voice from within the carriage said, sounding bored or tired.

The driver hopped down from his seat and shrugged. "Can you point us where we need to go?" At my nod he picked me up by the waist and hoisted me up to his seat, then scrambled nimbly up to sit beside me. "That's a good lass. Polite, cooperative, and quiet. Good to see these days. So, we follow this road into town, first?"

I nodded, relaxing a bit and smiling in return. The driver urged the horses into motion again with a quick motion of the reigns, and I pointed him to the tavern first and the blacksmith after. He handed me a small coin purse for my troubles, and I looked in shock as I heard coins within strike against each other. Not many from the weight of it, but for such a simple task I'd seen others given a simple bronze nub for their troubles. I opened the pouch and found three silver wheels and a silver star. Enough to buy, well, I couldn't think of a toy I'd ever wanted that would have cost so much. There were 25 nubs to a wheel, and I'd seen my mother buy a sack of flour for two or three nubs, depending. And at ten wheels to a star, this was a fortune.

He must have given me the wrong sack. He'd set me down and started opening the carriage door when I tugged on his sleeve, open pouch showing him what was within. I shook my head almost violently.

The driver shrugged me off, muttering, "Can't keep my Lord waiting." He swung open the door and bowed low.

"Too much," I said, voice cracking with the effort to make myself speak.

They hadn't heard me. The man from inside the carriage was stepping down, looking toward the tavern. The driver was speaking to him about how they'd wait there until the blacksmith repaired the wobble in the wheels or something like that. I frowned, frustrated that I was trying to do the right thing and being so completely ignored. There were others along the road, in wagons and on horseback, and a bit of foot traffic, going about the business of a normal day, and I felt so terribly small surrounded by it all. Diminished and insignificant.

I'd finally spoken after all this time and no one had noticed or

Elemental

cared.

PART THREE

The man from inside the carriage turned to me suddenly, kneeling, giving me his complete and undivided attention. His eyes were as dark as night with flecks of gray that reminded me of stars. His hair was black, wavy, and hung just below his shoulders. Despite looking weary from a long journey, there was something more vibrant and alive about him than I'd seen in anyone before.

"You're troubled," he said gently.

I nodded, frowning a bit. I started to hold the coin pouch out once again.

"As am I," he went on, setting his hands on mine, closing my fingers around the pouch. I felt power, tremendous power, as he made contact. "Tell me. Have you seen any new children around here in the last two years? Someone that's been adopted, perhaps? He would be around your age, black hair about like yours. Light brown eyes, not unlike your own."

I shook my head, heart pounding. "Why?" I asked, still just a hoarse whisper. I took a step back, pulling away from his hands. "Are you a wizard?"

"I am," he said. The corners of his eyes were crinkled like he was on the verge of a smile. He leaned forward and winked as if we were co-conspirators. "My friends are looking for this boy, you see. A young boy named Agrad. If you see him--"

His words were drowned out by a voiceless word that thundered through my head. RUN!

"If I see him," I whispered in return, starting to back away as I drew the strings of the coin purse tight. "Yes. I will."

Before another word could be said, I ran.

Elemental

I didn't run far. I'd thought about simply running blind, never to return, but I turned a corner and caught my breath instead. I heard laughter and talking, but I didn't hear him chasing after me.

Why would he make chase? He was a wizard and he knew who I was. He would be able to find me wherever I was. No matter how I tried to catch my breath, fear kept me breathless. I closed my eyes and gathered my courage. I ran home.

Home. I nearly tripped as I thought the word, realizing I'd applied it to Rhada and Goriath's house. It was home and I had to protect it, the way I had not protected my last home. There was a wizard in town, and this time I would not let my home be destroyed because I was here.

I opened the door and ran inside. Rhada and Goriath were gone for the day, or I'm not sure I'd have been able to leave so easily. I threw a few belongings, some bread, some cheese, extra shoes, a book, and two dresses into my winter cloak and tied it up in a bundle. Every sound made me jump, scared that the wizard had come for me after all. I kept imagining Rhada and Goriath returning, trying to protect me, and falling to the ground the way my parents had.

I couldn't let that happen. Not to anyone. Not ever again.

I wrote them a simple note. "Thank you. I am leaving to protect you. I am Agrad Leyfraiin. They think I am a wizard. I don't know. Don't look for me. I love you." The last was the hardest for me to write. I wasn't sure if I did, but I knew they'd want me to. I wanted to believe that I did. Why else would I want to protect them so fiercely? Why else would I give up everything for the uncertainty of running away?

Like a wildling, I slipped into the forest and did my best to disappear.

I didn't stray too far from the road, though I avoided it the rest of the day as I walked. I kept it to my left, darting behind trees or crouching behind shrubs whenever I heard someone approach. It bothered me that so soon after I'd planned on departing, so close to the date I'd chosen to run, my choice had been taken from me.

I hiked all day, relentlessly, ignoring hunger pangs and sore feet until the shadows grew long and the sky began to grow dark. I sat down to eat beneath a tree as the stars and moon grew bold overhead. I portioned my food out, just a bit for tonight and a bit for tomorrow. I thought of the stone soldiers I'd once played with as toys and set a run of six or so around me to warn off any animals while I slept.

In the morning I was awoken by the rumble of a carriage on the nearby road, and I held my breath until the sound faded. Beside one of my small stone soldiers was a book bound in green leather with gold leaf. Inside the front cover was a note. "Keep running." It was signed, Lorwyn. The words disappeared as soon as they were read.

It should have scared me, but it soothed me instead. Lorwyn was trying to help me, against the rest. I had one secret ally. It must have been his voice, telling me to run. Perhaps he found me just in time to keep me safe from the others. I held the book to my chest before packing it away beside the others I had taken with me.

After a few days I made my way to a road and followed it, just traveling from town to town, sometimes staying a night, and sometimes staying a few. When I had a chance I looked at the book from Lorwyn and discovered that it was a book of simple spells, some familiar, others new. Whenever I found a few moments alone I would read them all, over and over, though I didn't dare practice. I could feel it when others cast spells nearby. I had to assume that other wizards were the same.

I didn't go through the coins I'd been given very fast. Especially in the rural areas I always found a family willing to take me in for the night against the dangers outside. I didn't talk much, and that may have prompted some of the generosity I was shown. I was willing to help out with anything they needed, and perhaps that was enough. I even obtained a leather rucksack from an old lady in exchange for a few simple chores that she couldn't do herself as easily as she used to. It was a relief to have somewhere to put my belongings other than in a large bundle.

One night I couldn't find an inn or anyone to stay with, and I found an abandoned chapel that was so small it would only hold six people, maybe. It smelled of earth and dust, but the door still opened and closed with some effort. I carried in some tree branches that were thick with leaves and made myself a little bed up off the cold floor.

There were several roadside shrines and statues around. There was almost always a bench, a stool, or at least a stump beside them so I could rest my weary feet. Midday I would find one and eat berries, or fruit, or something I'd been given for the road, and I would read my books and enjoy a chance to rest.

I'm sure the locals knew what the story behind each shrine was, but for me they were curiosities. Landmarks on a long road. They would inspire my imagination as I walked. Some were surely to honor the old gods, but I could not tell those from markers of ancient battles, or memorials for loved ones who died in tragedy. Some were crumbling and falling apart, old and overgrown and neglected. Some were well tended and had flowers and candles scattered at their bases. They were all fascinating pieces of the past.

I curled up on my bed of branches and leaves, pulling my

cloak over me as I heard the wind pick up outside. It was such a small chapel, I thought as I held my eyes shut tight. No one would think to find me, or anyone else, within.

I was awoken to the sound of growling and an uneasy feeling in the pit of my stomach.

The door was being pushed open, slowly. The hinges were old and rusted, making the same loud groan it had given when I opened and closed it before. Within the nominal security of a small shelter I hadn't thought to use my little magical soldiers to guard me. I don't know what almost came through the door after me. I slammed into the door, holding it shut until the morning light, long after the creature had left. There were claw marks in the old wood, and my right shoulder was bruised, but I was alive.

I never again slept without setting up some sort of protection spell around me.

I'd been traveling for weeks when I came upon a town obviously suffering hardship, and a young mother with a baby and a child of maybe two, invited me to stay. She had rosy cheeks and fair skin, reminding me of Garim's mother in her roundness and infectious smile. She introduced herself as Eleneh, and she didn't stop talking long enough that my long silences ever grew awkward. She had an odd accent I'd never heard before, but it was melodic and soothing, and I found myself warming to her faster than usual.

She had her back turned to me as she added a log to the fire and moved the large cauldron closer to the center of the heat in the fireplace. "There's been a bite in the air. Winter'll be here soon," she was saying. "D'yeh have a ken as to what ye'll be doing then?"

"The city," I said simply. After so long of not speaking I still found myself short with my replies. I was trying, but it was a difficult transition to make.

"Aye, they might have a place for a young girl there," she said with distaste. "Ye'll not be knowin' the sort of place I mean, and I'd hope ye'll never have to find out. Unless ye've been promised schooling there, I'd avoid cities."

I sat at the large oak table, staring at the grain and frowning. I kept my hands folded in my lap as I thought about what she'd said. Maybe it was time to set my disguise aside.

"I'm not a girl," I finally admitted while she bustled around the room. I think it was the first time I'd ever said that, though it wouldn't be the last.

Eleneh hummed noncommittally and looked me over before punctuating the sound with a nod. "Couldn't be sure," she said as she picked out a dozen apples from the basket next to the door and placed them in her apron. "Ye're pretty enough it won't matter to most, and that's no way to live." She tossed a final apple out the window and murmured a quick prosperity spell. "Dadrae sa niasaveh." It wasn't the most effective spell out there, but most rural magic of that sort wasn't. It didn't really have to be. I think it was more superstition than magic, or a rough blend of prayer and spell, but you couldn't convince them of that.

It wasn't her rudimentary spell that worried me, though. "What's--" I frowned, not sure even how to frame the question. I had no idea what sort of concerns she had about the city.

"An ye don't know that much, it's all the more reason not to go there, an ye ask me." Eleneh handed me an apple and a carving knife, grabbed one for herself, and we started peeling them. "Nobody's thought to tell ye much about what life is like out there, eh? Ye poor thing..."

I absently healed a bruise I'd found beneath the peel as I'd seen my mother do a thousand times. I hesitated a moment and internally chided myself for doing useless magic. I could have just cut the blemish out and tossed it with the skins, the way

Eleneh was doing. I could even have left it, since these were going to be baked into dessert. Krecek, or any other wizard or elemental, would find me for sure if I didn't watch what I did. Especially for the incidental, casual little conveniences.

"Don't know as it's my place to tell ye," she said, picking up a second apple. "Wait a few years. Abide with us a while; we've got room. I'll be having another babe soon enough, I'm sure, with how fertile our families both are. It's the longevity we lack, me and mine. Unlucky lot, we are," and she laughed despite her words, "but we get by and we do it with a great deal o' love and caring. Being as me parents can't be here to help me with the little ones ye could stay an' learn a bit more, grow a bit more, an' help me out. It gets lonely with Dagran away so much."

I frowned a little and set the pile of peel to one side as I picked up my own second apple.

"Ye have a look about you," she said, slowing in her work for the first time since I'd arrived. "There's a reason ye'll not be staying, eh?"

"Yes," I said.

"I'll be working at convincing ye otherwise, ye know. Ye're barely past being a wee one. What could make ye flee safety so readily?"

I looked up at her, trying to say it, but I couldn't force it out. I'd kept everything to myself so long that I couldn't put any of it into words to share with another.

"Ye've been hurt," she said slowly, reading it from my expression. Eleneh leaned forward and patted my arm compassionately. Her fingers were moist and slightly sticky with apple juice. "Are ye running from yer parents? We'll hide ye, if need be."

I shook my head quickly; I was shocked that anyone could think that.

"Something else then? But, who would hurt a child like

yerself?"

Perhaps it was her resemblance to Mistress Dayle, Garim's mother, that prompted me to honesty. Her last kindness to me had been to send Garim with an extra apple for me, and perhaps I made the connection on a subconscious level. It made me momentarily trust this woman, this stranger, with my life.

I tried again, and the barest whisper came out. "A wizard."

Understanding flooded her countenance, and I felt a chill as I wondered if she'd turn me in to Krecek then and there. She wasn't my best friend's mother, no matter what string of coincidences had reminded me of her. "Ye're the child that Ceolwyn is looking fer!"

I didn't have to answer her. She knew as surely as if I'd spelled it out for her in detail. My fear must have been plain upon my face, for she patted me again and clucked her tongue as if I were some sort of pathetic thing.

She picked up her knife again, and we finished peeling and coring the apples in silence while she thought. We arranged them on a baking tray and set them on the rack above the kettle with spices and berries, and washed off our hands in a basin of cold water. The knives were washed and set to dry next, and I returned to my seat with my hands placed patiently in my lap, or so I hoped it seemed. On the inside I was trying to muster the power to disappear just in case there was a need.

The toddler awoke from his nap and she placed the little boy in my lap. "Ye've good reason to run," she said as she leaned in to do so. "Stay the night and in the morn' I'll give ye what food we can spare that will travel well. I'm turning ye in for the reward, so see to it ye won't be caught. And next time, lie."

"Is there anything I can do to repay you for your kindness?"

"An ye mean magic, keep it to yerself," she said gruffly. "I'll be taking no favors from someone I've got to hand in."

"You don't have to," I said in a plaintive, petulant tone. She'd been so nice right up until then!

"Ye know nothing of wizards an ye think that." Eleneh was busy stirring the stew she'd had cooking all day, and adding herbs to it for flavor. Her son was still drowsy and snuggled up against me as if he'd known me all his life. "I'm taking a great risk not turning ye in right away. Hiding ye entire would be the ruin of us!"

"Fine! I'll leave right now," I said hotly, eyes stinging at the corners. "I'm sorry to have bothered you." I stood and set the little boy down on his feet. He started crying immediately and reached for me to pick him back up again, arms upraised as he pressed his face into my skirt.

Eleneh whirled, brandishing her wooden spoon like a sword, and I covered my head with my arms reflexively.

"Ye'll be sitting down, eating, and then having a good night's sleep is what ye'll be doing! D'ye think me hospitality so poor that I'd be running ye out with night closing in like this? Set yer arse down, boy."

I sat back down quickly, eyes wide. She was barely taller than I was, but she was a mother and I was not nearly old enough to argue against that sort of authority.

The rest of the evening she talked about her husband's business as a carpenter, among other things. His skill was enough that he was kept busy and even traveled at times to install cabinets or other things he'd made for people in more prosperous towns. They had plans to move some day, but not while the children were so small.

More importantly, she talked of things she'd heard about wizards. I didn't listen much about the others, but when she mentioned Krecek I paid complete attention.

"I heard he had another name, afore he became Krecek Ceolwyn. They say his mother was human and his father is an elf, but he gave up his father's name long ago. My mother was a friend of elves, so she told me about that when I was little. It was a huge scandal among their kind, especially after the Arcane War. But, his elven blood is what made him the oldest of the wizards, feared even afore they gained their power.

"His short stature," she added, shaking her head slightly, "living among humans, I wonder if it made him ruthless. Short men are seen as weak. He must have felt he had somewhat to prove."

Her words went on, and my thoughts spun faster. Who was Krecek? How was he anything like the person I had met? How was he anything like the wizard who had killed my parents?

Eleneh tucked me into bed as if I were her own, and her son curled up beside me. The hearth was banked and the candles snuffed, leaving the faint remains of smoke in the air to slowly dissipate. She snored softly from the loft, and her words still circled in my mind. I was awake too long, full of too many thoughts. Even from the perspective of time, Eleneh had as much impact on me as Rhada and Goriath had. She was the first person I'd been myself in front of since my parents had died, and the first person to see me as an individual in my own right.

Before the sun rose she woke me and prepared me the luxury of a bath. The small wooden tub was cramped, but the water was warm and inviting. I hurried out of necessity, but it was difficult to force myself out of it. I thanked her profusely and departed into the misty autumn morning as the sun rose. I could feel moments passing and wondered how long I had before Krecek would be after me again. I wondered what would happen to this kind lady and her small family just starting out. Had I brought ruin upon them with my visit and "escape"? Or would they be rewarded for bearing news to my enemy? I was uncomfortable with either idea.

I hid in the woods once again, thinking to stay there a while this time. I cut away from the road deliberately, making my way across the small river it ran near. The spot I crossed was rocky, making it easy to go from one slick and rounded boulder to the next until I was across. I followed it downstream a way, across two creeks that met up with it. I was doing more climbing than walking, which was difficult in a dress, but not impossible.

When I'd left I'd been able to count on the foliage to hide me from view if I stayed close to the road, but autumn was nigh. Squirrels and other small scurrying animals dashed about, filling the landscape with a cacophony of sounds as they prepared themselves. They gathered anything, even coming up to me when I would stop to eat. They'd take any crumb I dropped, any morsel I would give them. Some would even scurry right into my open rucksack, smelling the food I'd kept there, hoping to take the treasure therein for themselves. They were better company than the many people I saw on the road, of that I was certain. It was a relief to have company that didn't try to talk to me, to get me to open up, when I just wanted to nod and continue on my way. I liked this side of the river, away from the road, much better despite the harsher terrain.

I slept only when my body would not allow me to do otherwise, though sometimes the terrain forced me to stop until I had daylight again. The sides of hills and sheer drops were littered with rain-slicked autumn leaves. The weather had turned from fair to foul rather quickly, but instead of cursing my discomfort I was grateful for the hindrance it would bring to anyone trying to track me. I had to be careful, but I would look behind me and see fresh leaves covering my trail, sticking to the wet soil like they'd been there for days.

It was a great relief when I found a cave large enough for me to stand and move about in. I made it my own, wondering after a few days if I'd lucked upon the den of an animal that had been killed by a hunter preparing for winter. I'd almost been too scared to use it after my experience in the small chapel, but it proved to be the perfect shelter to weather the storm. I lived on the food Eleneh had given me, but I couldn't be sure the storm would pass before I ran out. My breath had started to come out in puffy white clouds in the mornings, and I started to wonder if I'd be able to leave the cave before winter struck. Would I have a chance to forage before the storm blew over?

There were no entries in the book Lorwyn had left me about using magic to create food. I was far enough from people that I thought that trying a couple of spells wouldn't be too risky. First I cast a spell from the book to light a fire.

"Sh'kash a nve ah."

It was so easy. I laughed at how simple it was. Despite the damp, the fire was instantly bright and warm. It made me giddy, both at the risk and at my accomplishment of casting a new spell with such facility without anyone to guide me.

To make food I had to get creative, and I was still excited by my success with fire. I didn't know what words to use, so I tried the words for a conjuration spell.

"T dava reah."

Despite thoroughly visualizing what I was trying to end up with, the food completely lacked flavor or aroma of any kind. It was filling for a moment, but before long I was more ravenous than ever. I wouldn't have tried again even if it had been filling, though. I felt a shift in the air as magic stirred and searched for the spell I'd cast.

It was subtle at first. I was distracted by pulling the last of my real food from my rucksack. My skin rose in goose bumps and it felt like I itched beneath my skin, deep in my bones. I held still, barely daring to breathe.

Something intangible was coming closer. I could feel it, like eyes upon the wind, or a bodiless nose searching me out. A shadow seemed to move within the clouds, dimming the world around me as something sought the magic I had cast. The air was heavy with power.

The world had gone silent. I was used to the silence that a large predator could bring. Small things hid when they scented approaching danger.

This was bigger. Even the distant sound of the river had muted. The trees and their leaves had stopped whispering. The air was completely still as the darkness drew closer.

The silence was destroyed by the sound of rain suddenly rushing in a torrent to the ground. It stirred a chill wind within my cave, nearly extinguishing my fire with its force and the heavy mist that it carried. Minutes later lightning arced across the sky. I began to breathe again, relaxing as the storm began to seem more natural. It was inconvenient, but it was just rain. It soothed me and eventually lulled me to sleep.

When the rain let up at last I looked for berries and familiar fruits to carry me through a few more days. It was still windy and I didn't want to travel in such unsafe weather, but the idea of fresh food was irresistible. I was more thankful than ever that Rhada and Goriath had thought I was a girl, since skirts were so easily used to carry fruit.

I gathered a handful of my hem and walked around, freely picking the best fruits in reach. Rain had enhanced every smell, and I reveled in the scent of the fruits I brought to my nose. There was enough low hanging fruit around that I didn't have to climb much, just pick whatever I could reach. Some were leaning toward overripe, but it didn't matter to me. I just wanted enough to regain my energy. Tomorrow I would replenish my stores and grab more nuts than fruits. They didn't have to last long. They just had to last for one night.

Upon my return I found a new fire blazing in my cave. My imagination went wild, suspecting a deep dwarf searching from the stone countries that may be deep beneath my little cave, or perhaps an elf from the distant wildlands. My heart skipped a beat, for I'd never seen an elf or a dwarf in person, and what business would a human have with a cave in weather like this? They'd know I didn't belong there.

Furtively I crept to the opening to look inside, one hand clutching my skirts and holding my food within, the other hand clutching the stick I'd found. Whoever the stranger was, he was not human, but also I was certain he was neither an elf nor a dwarf. Not if what I'd heard of them could be at all true, at least.

He shivered, looking impossibly cold as he pulled a leg of his pants up. His skin had a blue cast, but I couldn't be sure if that was from the chill or for the same reason his hair and eyes were the deep color of a clear blue lake. I'd never seen anything like it before, nor heard of anyone like that.

I stared as he began dressing a rather messy wound in his leg, and I looked around to notice a bloody and broken arrow on the cave floor beside him. His blood was as red as my own, at least. I flinched sympathetically as he cried out in pain from pouring something on the wound. The arrow had to have gone through his calf and gotten stuck halfway, so that he had to break off the head to remove the shaft. At least, that's the assumption I made.

He was shirtless, and I think what he had tied around his thigh was part of his shirt. The rest of his shirt was set to the side, probably so he could use it as a bandage later. He covered the wound clumsily but tightly, with an increasing tremble to his fingers. He took a long drink from the flask of liquid he'd poured over his wound, and I realized it was some sort of strong alcohol. No wonder he'd cried out in pain! He didn't even cap it before passing out, spilling the liquid over the stone floor beside the fire.

I tossed aside the stick I'd picked up for my defense, and the stranger didn't even flinch in his unconscious state from the clatter it made. Whoever this injured person was, he was in my home no matter how temporary a home it was. I had to help him. I'd bought a blanket my first week on the road, and I pulled it from where I'd hidden my meager possessions. I checked him for weapons or anything he could hurt me with as I draped the blanket carefully over him. He had nothing but a small utility knife that I confiscated carefully and set near the fire. He'd be able to see it but not reach it before I could defend myself.

He remained asleep, so I began cleaning up, taking a trip to a nearby stream for extra water to splash at the entrance and wash away some of the fresh blood smell. I was afraid of predators looking for an easy meal in the middle of the night more than anything else. Predators would mean using magic in self-defense, which would mean more dangerous predators being able to find me.

I kept the fire stoked, and I stayed awake all night just in case he awoke. It was a long night, and in the middle of it the wind died down and the rain began anew. He stirred a few times, but it wasn't until nearly dawn that he opened his eyes. He stared at me for a while with a sleepy and confused expression, hand searching where his knife had been. He looked more bewildered than afraid, but after a while understanding began to dawn in his eyes. When I saw that he wasn't going to attack I finally moved, tossing more wood into the fire and stirring some of the coals.

"Hello," he finally said, pulling my blanket tighter around himself and curling up a bit.

I nodded and sat back down, watching him closely.

"Do you speak?" he asked.

I nodded again, and after an expectant look I finally shrugged. "When I choose to."

He waited a moment more before he said, "Is this your, uh, cave?"

"For now," I said.

He thrust his hand out of the comforting warmth of the blanket and offered it to me. "I'm Ysili. Ysili Ronar." Now that his face was a bit more animated, and he seemed in less pain, I guessed he was close to my age. Well, maybe a year or so older. "Do you have a name?"

"Agrad," I said, reaching out quickly to brush his fingers with my own, not offering a full handshake. Even that much was enough to feel a residue of magic upon him, and I was not surprised at that. I fully expected him to be able to tell from that small amount of contact that I was touched by magic as well.

He just grinned and settled back down. "I suppose it's bad form to nearly die in someone else's cave, and I'm sorry for it. I'll just have to do my best to live, if you don't mind."

I nodded, wondering if it was really appropriate to laugh. "Can I get you anything?" I asked instead.

"I don't suppose you've secreted away any bandages, or anything for pain? I've got to keep this clean, and it won't exactly be easy or painless, all things considered."

I'd bought a few things for emergencies, and been given other things by concerned families I'd stayed a night with, but I hadn't had need of any of it yet. In the night I'd pulled out linen bandages, and now I reached beside me and handed him the sack I'd kept them in.

"There's enough there to dress a dozen wounds, and I've only got the one," he said with a wide eyes, examining the contents. "There's ointment in here as well. Wow. Are you an angel, or am I just lucky?"

"An angel would have healed you by now," I said, poking at the fire and avoiding his eyes. "My apologies."

He chuckled a little and nodded, sitting up and carefully moving closer to the fire. He was still shaky and pale, but somehow kept his humor even while stripping off the bloodied remains of his shirt and tossing them in the fire. "An angel probably would have shot me a second time, just to be sure. I'll take my chances with ordinary folks, thank you."

"I'm ordinary?" I gave him a funny look.

"I guess you're right," Ysili said. "It's not exactly common to be hiding away in a cave like this." How he managed such a conversational tone while putting ointment on his leg and then wrapping it was beyond me. It looked gruesome, and it had to be very painful, but he looked almost like he wanted to poke at it to see how it worked. It was like his leg was an experiment to be examined rather than a part of his own body. "That makes neither of us exactly ordinary, but I already knew that about me."

"You do magic," I said, staring down at my skirt and scowling a little. The words had come out suddenly, without any real thought, and with a lot more accusation than I thought I'd ever use toward someone in so much pain and at my mercy.

"Well, yes, and I'll admit I've got more talent with it than most," he said, brow furrowed. "It's not like you aren't a wellspring of the arcane, yourself. I can tell these things, you know."

"Are you going to heal yourself and just go?" I glanced at him without lifting my head to look at him properly. The thought made me nervous and angry all at once.

"I'm no wizard," Ysili grinned, shaking his head. "It'll be a while before I can walk, I'm afraid. Sorry to intrude."

"I just don't want to be here too long," I said, finding a loose string and tugging at it lightly. "I wanted to be in the city before winter hits properly."

"Well, if you want to heal it yourself, by all means--"

"No!" I shook my head violently. "I-I don't heal! I don't know how, either."

"I never said I didn't know how," Ysili gave me a funny look and then tied off the fresh bandage he'd applied. The cave pulsed with a wave of magical energy as he healed as much as he could. It wasn't enough that the energy would be felt much beyond the area, but with the magical storm still raging I cringed a bit. "It just won't be enough to get me on my feet for a while. That's okay, though. You'll get to look after me that much longer. To make sure I don't die."

I nodded and looked away, scanning for anyone approaching from outside of the cave. I could feel his eyes upon me, feel him grinning at me, right up until he fell back to sleep.

"At least it's not raining now," Ysili said a few days later.

I just nodded, staring out the mouth of the cave. I had been watching the weather myself before he had spoken. I found it annoying that he was remarking on something I was observing myself.

"I think it's warming a bit, too. When I hopped out to piss I didn't see my breath get as foggy as it had been. It will be good traveling weather again soon."

I looked at him, frowning. I'd done the same, noticed the same. He wasn't unique, and I wasn't stupid.

"I even heard birds earlier. Did you hear them?"

"Yes."

"I've always loved the sound of birds. They'll be leaving, soon. It's going to be too cold, and those might have been the last birds of the season. They've probably got the right idea, about leaving soon."

"I'm not healing you," I said, for the fifth time that day.

"I didn't ask," he said, sounding hurt. "Honestly, Agrad. I can take a hint."

"You drop more than you take," I said.

He went on as if I hadn't spoken. "You know, I didn't think I would like humans. When I woke up here and I saw a human I thought to myself that this could be a problem. I thought you would kill me, or just leave to let the arrow wound finish the job. You're nicer than any human I've ever met before."

That clearly said more about his previous company than it did about humans in general, at least in my opinion. I didn't say that, though. I just kept looking outside.

"Am I getting on your nerves?"

"Yes," I said. It had been days of this mindless chatter, until it all began to blend together into one long monologue.

Ysili just laughed. "Every other human I've known would have lied to me. Too polite to admit the truth. I like you, Agrad." He was inching closer to me, until he put a hand on my shoulder. "The other humans I've met would have just left." He was so serious now. "They'd have lied to my face and then done what suits them."

"I'm not going anywhere," I said. It seemed like an important thing to say, like the right thing to say. I put my hand over his cold fingers. "I'm just not used to so much talking. It's been a long time."

"You're so sincere!" He grinned. Ysili then reached over and grabbed something. "You have to go, though. We're out of water." He thrust his water skin into my hands.

If I'd yelled at him for this little game of his, I'd have wasted time I could have spent away. I grabbed the water skin from him and glared for just a moment before I began my trek to a nearby spring. I took my time filling it, too, because it was such a relief to have my ears unassaulted in those brief moments of solitude.

As soon as I was finished I hurried back, though. His chatter was incessant, unnecessary, and at times inane, but it felt good to have someone around. I was annoyed, but at least I wasn't alone.

Once the weather cleared I gave in and asked him to teach me how to heal. I couldn't be sure, but I still thought the rain had been part of a wizard's attempt to find me. It may have felt natural after the onset of the downpour, but the clouds could have been hiding more. Clear skies gave me more courage, though not recklessness. I attempted it with the lightest touches of magic I could bear so I wouldn't call attention to myself once again.

"You're not exactly putting your all into it," Ysili complained, flexing his leg and wiggling his toes. "You could be rid of me in half an hour if you really tried."

"I got used to your face," I muttered, concentrating even harder on not putting too much energy into the spell and giving myself away. "You can stick around a bit longer."

Ysili grinned, but he didn't press his luck by saying anything else about it. "So, when we get to the city, what do you think you want to do?"

All I'd really thought of doing was hiding. With so many people, I just wanted to blend in and go unnoticed. I shrugged and sat back, trying to think. I didn't even really know what people did in the city. What could I do? Beg?

"I guess we'll figure out something when we get there," Ysili said after a long pause. "I can read and write, so that should be worth something at least."

"I can, too."

Ysili looked me over thoughtfully. "You'd make more if you apprenticed to a mage or a spellsmith. Scribes are rare enough, but--"

I shook my head. "No magic."

Silence fell between us again, Ysili staring at me while I got up to tidy the cave and avoid meeting his eyes.

"We'll think of something," he finally said with a frustrated sigh. "I just don't want to attract too much attention, you know?"

"Me too," I said softly. Then I lifted my head and looked at him directly. "Is that how you got shot?"

He looked at me with an expression devoid of emotion. "Is that why you won't use magic?" he countered instead.

I was sure he didn't expect an answer, but instead I simply said, "Yes." I then walked out of the cave without another word.

Ysili and I left the cave behind as soon as he was well enough, following the roads and offering services for a night's lodging when we could. Sometimes we walked through the night, if neither of us were tired. He was surprised that I was up to it, because he said I looked so frail and girly. I was surprised that he was up to it, because of his injury.

"Just working it out," he explained, pausing to flex his legs and show off a bit.

"You know by now I'm not a girl, right?"

"Well, yeah. Girls don't generally relieve themselves from a perfectly vertical position, so you could say I've noticed. You still don't look up to walking a day and a night straight through."

I sighed and just kept walking. I didn't get tired the way I used to, just like I'd grown used to the cold. Was it from pushing myself, or was it related to the magic I felt growing more powerful within me by the day?

Still, it was nice to stop when we could. When we started our journey together the houses we were invited into were small and private, like Eleneh's. There was space between neighbors, and plenty of forest to forage in. This led to plenty of chores Ysili and I were happy to do in exchange for a night's rest. As we grew closer to the city the nature of the houses gradually changed. There were occasional small hovels and lean-tos, but they had a makeshift and temporary look. Most of what we saw were larger houses, and the space between them shrank. Carriages became a common sight, and we were forced to the bumpy edge of the road to avoid mud, muck, and ruts.

We were still a few days away when I slipped on a particularly wet patch of mud. It was a humiliating and dispiriting experience, finding myself suddenly coated in the stinking muck of the road, with my hands stinging from catching myself. Ysili stoically held out a hand to help me up, looking me over without expression.

"If you laugh at me I'll push you in," I muttered.

"Wouldn't dream of it," Ysili said. His face was a little too composed, however, and his eyes were squinting with the effort of holding amusement back.

I tried to wipe my hand off, but it and my dress were both too sullied to do so effectively. Finally I sighed and took his hand. "Thank you," I said as I stood.

"I'm not sure how far the river diverged from the road here," Ysili said, looking to the north where we'd seen the river last. "You might have a while to walk before you can wash up."

Elemental

"Oh! You poor thing!"

PART FOUR

I hadn't even noticed anyone around us, so wrapped up in my own misfortune.

A girl, a bit taller than I was, was running up to us. She was unclasping her own cloak as she ran, and before I knew what she intended I was wrapped up in its warmth. Ysili looked just as surprised and confused as I felt as the girl began ushering us to a path between some hedges.

"Come along, it's right through here. We must get you warm and clean."

We hadn't seen the house tucked behind the hedges from the road. It was the largest I'd ever seen to that point. "This is your house?" I was beginning to doubt my senses, wondering how I could have missed it, when I felt a background hum of magic. They had a spell to mask the place, and it was quite well crafted.

"My father's house," the girl said. "He is in Cairnborough for the week, conducting business. Don't worry, though. Even out this far from the city we are safe. I have servants and spells to keep evildoers away. A brigand has never set foot on these grounds."

Her dark hair was in a long braid, and tiny white flowers had been woven in for contrast. I wanted to do the same to my own hair, to be as pretty as she was, instead of itchy and damp and covered in mud and road muck. She ordered her servants to draw me a bath. It was the most natural thing, it seemed, for her to order others around.

"I'm sorry you'll have to wait while the water warms," she said, handing me a plush robe. "But tell me, what are the two of you doing, traveling on the road alone?"

This was where Ysili took over. "It is a tragic tale," he began, and she was immediately hooked. "Until a month ago, the two of us were betrothed. We grew up as friends, knowing that our future was decided for us, and we were content with our lot."

"Oh!" she cried, hands coming to her throat with a look of delight. "How romantic! It's just like my favorite book!"

"My parents lost their fortune," he said, bowing his head humbly. "I do not know how it was lost, but because of that misfortune the betrothal was called off and my love here, Emowi, was going to be given to another man. We couldn't stand the thought of being parted, so we ran away. We're traveling to Cairnborough, and maybe beyond, where our parents will never find us. We don't care if we're poor, as long as we can be together."

"You poor things," she said with genuine tears in her eyes.

I took Ysili's hand and smiled up at him, trying to pretend his story was true. It was hard, since I didn't know the first thing about being in love, but the girl loved the story so much that she invited us to stay the night. Servants came and told us that the bath was ready. As soon as I was in the water they took my befouled clothes and I leaned into the tub, thinking over his story. Everywhere we'd stopped Ysili had come up with some new tale of why we traveled.

I dried my hair and put on some of the girl's old clothes, a dress she'd given me that was now too small. It fit me well enough, though there was a fraying hem on one of the sleeves. I tucked the end under and walked out with a smile. Ysili was still telling her tall tales from his imagined past. I didn't know how he kept track of his lies so well, but it was a sight to behold. He had told the tale of us being in love before, though the details changed from place to place. Sometimes we were cousins traveling to visit a sick grandmother. Sometimes we were on our way to be apprenticed, and he had delayed his travels so that he could go with me and keep me safe. Once we were orphans seeking an opportunity in the city, and tears sprang to my eyes. I suppose it made the story more convincing, but when we left I told him never to say it again.

The bath was an amazing indulgence. I savored every moment of it, scrubbing every inch with care. Bathing in the increasingly cold river was enough to keep from smelling bad, but warm water indoors with privacy felt like heaven. A new bathrobe had been set aside for me for when I was done, and it was so plush and warm that I felt a stab of envy when I put it on.

"We should leave as soon as her dress is clean. Visandra, you have been too kind and generous already, and we don't want to be any trouble," Ysili was saying as I returned to their company. So, her name was Visandra. That was good to know.

"Don't be silly," she said to him. "Stay the night, eat your fill. Traveling always makes me so hungry, and I've been lonely in this house with only servants. They're wonderful people, but they're adults and they're constantly busy even when I ask them to treat me like a friend. They won't do it. I'm sure you understand."

"Indeed," I said, trying to pretend, trying to live the lie that Ysili had given our lives. I sat down in a way that imitated how she had sat before, graceful and slow. "We can stay until morning. I would appreciate a place to sleep without rocks in my spine." My pout was a match to one she had given as well.

"My lady has spoken," Ysili conceded, but he nodded to me with a satisfied smile.

Visandra and Ysili did most of the talking. It was about inconsequential things like weather, the latest romance tale Visandra had read, or some silly notion that Ysili helped her spin into an even more outlandish fantasy. For my part, I watched her carefully and tried to match my manners to hers.

Once we reached the city I wanted to be mistaken for someone I could never be. From a common boy to a poised young lady seemed to me the greatest leap I could make.

It was something I'd been working at. Mothers and other girls who took us in became my models for behavior. With Visandra I tried to mimic her hand flutters, but I stopped when it became too distracting. Instead, I concentrated on how poised she was, even when excited. When she leaned forward she bent from the hip, keeping her back straight and her shoulders squared. It made her look so confident. I wanted to be a confident girl like her.

The bed she offered me was so comfortable I fell asleep immediately. I couldn't remember the last time I'd had such a deep rest. Ysili woke me some time before dawn and we snuck out into the frigid late autumn air. The mud and muck from yesterday had crusted over with ice and I stepped more carefully this time.

"Did you find my dress?" I asked. Visandra had assured me that her maid would have it for me by morning, and I hadn't seen it before I went to bed.

Ysili nodded. "Better than that," he said. He held out his own rucksack with a smirk. "The room she put me in had what looked like all of her old clothes. Never thought to sell one of them, apparently. I took three, and I doubt they'll be missed."

I looked inside. We stood to the side of the road and I held the dresses against me. One was too small, but it was beautiful and would probably sell for a few nubs at least. The other two looked like they would fit me, though I wasn't sure the blue one would be very flattering. Ysili probably picked that one out because it was the color of his hair.

My dress was at the bottom, gold and brown and looking road worn the way my other dresses were. "Thank you. I think I'll need to replace everything by the time we get to the city.

This is a good start."

"I grabbed a couple of things for myself, but her father must be very successful," he said, rolling his eyes as he held up some very large pants.

"We'll find a tailor and get them taken in," I said, putting the dresses in my own pack. It was getting full, but we couldn't afford to get rid of anything. If fabric ripped or hems frayed, we'd have rags for other uses than clothes. Every scrap was valuable in some way.

As we continued our journey the road conditions improved. The day before we reached Cairnborough the roads were cobblestone, and we met with the first snow of the season. It was light and fluffy, drifting from the sky like individual tiny flower petals. Fellow travelers paused to smile, to reach out their hands, and to enjoy the beauty of the moment.

In Lesser Stonegore, winters had been a time of quiet reflection and rest, and that didn't change much in Myrenfeld. When the snows came everyone retired to their homes, keeping in contact with neighbors through spells more often than traveling to visit. Spellsmiths were in high demand, of course. My parents would bundle me up to go with them when I was tiny while they shored up wards against hungry predators or helped with warming spells upon firewood. When I started lessons with my tutor I'd spend half days or entire days cooped up indoors with him, learning and yearning to be playing in the snow.

As we walked along the road to Cairnborough my eyes stung as the memories filled me. First snow was always such an occasion, but as the snow grew heavier Ysili and I were simply doing our best to keep one foot going in front of the other. I dug my fingernails into my palms, trying to banish thoughts of the past and concentrate on my footing. I did not want to fall down at the side of the road again.

I could see the outline of the city as we walked through a mountain pass, and it was enormous. Smoke poured from more chimneys than I'd ever seen, making the air hazy and dark as we approached, blurring the view of the further parts of the city. At some point while we were walking the road had changed from cobblestone to brick, and instead of being shoved into dirt and mud as carriages or wagons pressed past, sidewalks became more common. They were a darker color than the roads, mostly free from the filth that was also becoming more common. The crisp smell of fresh snow could not completely mask the odor of civilization.

Our final night of travel before reaching Cairnborough I stared at the mass of lights from our vantage. We were still high enough that the view was only slightly obstructed by some of the closer trees. We set our camp on an outcropping despite the snow. There were warm, yellow lights from fireplaces or candles. Multicolored and twinkling lights danced from window to window from spells. There were so many people. I hadn't imagined that a city could be quite that full, quite that big, or nearly that densely packed.

"You sure this is where you want to hide?" Ysili murmured in my ear.

I nodded quickly, grinning at him as I pulled our shared blanket closer. It was perfect, really. With so many people it would be easy to lose myself among them.

Sleep was elusive that night. I'd wanted to keep going, but Ysili said we should walk into the town rested. It was easy for him to say since he fell asleep easily and stayed that way while I tossed and turned with anticipation. By morning I was glad for it, however. We were still at a high enough vantage that at dawn I could see the whole of the city come to life. I was so entranced that Ysili had to nudge me to get moving.

The air seemed more biting with its first snow than any other first snow I could remember, and the road less inviting as snow was trampled to slush and frozen into ice. I learned later that it was the sea that incited the weather to more intensity than the sleepy valley where I'd lived with my parents, or the prosperous town with spellsmiths enough to keep extreme weather from our doors in Myrenfeld. Despite the frigid weather, people of Cairnborough hurried about their business, buying and selling and rushing to and fro for reasons I couldn't fathom. Within minutes of entering the city we were just part of the masses of people all in too much hurry to even look at one another's faces.

"This might work. It's just like any other city, I suppose." Ysili looked around with less awe and distraction than I felt, wrapping an arm around my shoulders as was his wont when we played at being a young couple in need.

"I like it already," I said softly, leaning into him. "I feel like I can get lost here."

"Just don't get lost without me." Ysili smiled softly and guided me down a small street where we began our search for shelter and income.

Without Ysili I would have been hopeless in the city, trying to find income and a place to stay. The money I'd been given sustained us for a mere three days at the hotel I had found. I'd assumed I would have no problem finding work as a scribe's assistant, or find apprenticeship somewhere. Without someone to sponsor me an apprenticeship was out of the question, and no one wanted to hire me for legitimate work. I'd never given much thought to money before, since I hadn't had to spend much while traveling and surviving off the land. My great fortune had been provided by the kindness of strangers. That kindness dried up as the specter of scarcity reared its head, and we had no one to turn to. I'm not sure how many times I was tempted to turn to magic, but wizards and elementals were known to haunt cities and I was sure I would be caught and maybe killed if I attempted anything.

While I was wasting our coin and looking for legitimate work, Ysili was smarter than I was and had made connections with other orphans and outsiders. I'm not sure how he did it, but as I began to panic over our situation, he invited me to meet one of his new friends. Everything about the area made me nervous. Things were rundown and people were leaner and looked more suspicious.

He brought me to a large building that, from the outside, looked more like a warehouse than a place anyone would live. A large chimney belied that first impression, but I did not expect the warmth that greeted us when we walked in. The solid double doors opened to a common room that was oddly inviting despite its ramshackle state.

Someone waved us over, recognizing Ysili right away.

He was stout, solid. That was the first thing I thought of upon seeing him. "Ysili, is this your girl?"

I wasn't sure how to react. Ysili hurried me over and sat down beside his friend. "This is Agrad," he said, neither denying nor agreeing that I was a girl, or that I was somehow his. "Agrad, this is Bledig. He's been showing me around town and giving me some advice."

"First bit of advice is, you're staying in the wrong part of town," Bledig said, looking me over. "Ysili tells me you're both runaways, both orphans. You're not going to find any sympathy in Cairnborough. Trust me, I've looked. Lot of shit, no sympathy."

My cheeks warmed for shame, hearing him use coarse

words. I'd been scolded and swatted the only time I'd used a crude word.

"How cute, she blushes," Bledig said. "That won't last long. You'll hear that and worse, the longer you're here."

"I'll survive," I muttered, finally sitting down. I hated feeling so flustered, feeling more uncomfortable with this meeting by the moment.

He nodded to me and then turned back to Ysili. "I can introduce you to Mistress Relata. There's a room open, but there are more orphans than she has rooms. It will go fast. You can bet on the cold bringing disease and death, but if you don't have anywhere to stay you'll probably succumb sooner than anyone staying here."

Ysili nodded once, firmly. "I'll take care of it," he said to me. "Just wait here. I don't want to be sleeping under the sky when the snow and the sick hit."

I nodded and handed him my last silver wheel. "If this will help, use it." We would sell the smallest of the dresses we took from the merchant's daughter for food, and that would be everything we had. How long would that last us? My stomach hurt, just thinking about it.

I sat quietly while Ysili spoke with Mistress Relata. She was a tall, thin, severe woman with what seemed to be a permanent frown on her face. Her voice was strident and carried, though I couldn't make out the words through the din of the other boarders in the room. I looked around, in a daze. Was this mass of chaos about to become my home for a time? It was completely unlike anything I'd ever known before.

Ysili motioned me over. Mistress Relata looked me over before handing me a key. "Evenings are quiet around here, even if you are awake. Strictly enforced. Everyone takes a turn either cooking or cleaning up after a meal. There's a list to sign up. If you don't pull your weight you'll hear from the others and from me. Shifts can be bought and sold, but I wouldn't count on either one while you're new here."

I nodded.

"Keep your own room clean. There's a basin and a line for laundry just past the kitchen. The line's enchanted so it'll dry in rain or snow, but it takes some time. Other than that, your business is your own. I run this place because I was an orphan once, and the actual orphanages are nightmare prisons that'll rob you. Count your blessings, children. I'm not your mother, and I'll kick you out if you can't pay, but you've got a home where you can be your own person."

"Thank you," I murmured.

"Oh, also, it's a right den of thieves here, so keep your room locked. You're kicked out if you're caught lifting something that belongs to someone under this roof, but that's no reason to tempt fate. Or anyone else who happens by."

It all seemed fair to me. Lawless and crazy, but fair. I could survive like this.

At first I did not understand what Ysili did to keep us in that place. The friends he had made who told him about it were thieves and scoundrels, earning money through various dishonest means. He was helping them, though I did not ask for details. I didn't want details. The amount of risk he was undertaking set me on edge from the moment I realized what he was doing.

"We can't trust them," I growled in a low voice. "Why can't we just do what we've been doing? We'll survive."

"You honestly think that?" he looked at me with round eyes in exaggerated astonishment, and then sneered at me in disdain.

"It's not a matter of trust. It's a matter of not freezing to death before Nightwatch at this rate. What do you know of what we've been doing, anyway? You look for legitimate work that just doesn't exist! You think you'll ever get it? Open your eyes! It's your little girl act coming back to haunt you. In a city like this it doesn't matter how well you read or write or know your spells if you can't do magic. MEN read, to provide for their families. You're just a little runaway to them, and they'd be happier if you go home to your loving parents so they'd stop worrying about you being raped and left for dead on the streets. GROW UP, Agrad!"

"I'd be happy to go back if I could," I glared. "Or did you forget my parents are dead?"

"You don't walk around with a sign proclaiming you're an orphan. 'Oh, look at me, orphaned and alone, my whole town erased overnight, and I'm really a boy so you shouldn't worry so much.' Please." He gave me a look of disdain. "All they see when they look at you is their own worst fears for their daughters or sisters. They're not looking at you at all."

"That's not fair!" Something about what he'd said bothered me, almost nagging me, but I was too angry to think of what it might be.

Ysili nodded. "You're right. It's not fair. Welcome to the actual world we live in, where things just aren't fair. At all. Ever."

"Well, something's got to go right!" I was frustrated nearly to the point of tears. "I can't just--"

I was interrupted by a somewhat loud and impatient knock at the door. The door swung open immediately following that. "If you're too good to pay your rent, children, then I'm too good to let you stay while you're raising a ruckus."

Ysili produced a bronze nub for Mistress Relata, promising the rest soon and assuring her that we would be quiet from that point onward. As he talked the landlady looked over at me and I could see in her eyes exactly what Ysili had been lecturing me about. It was as if her thoughts leapt out at me and I could feel the mix of concern and condemnation she had for a runaway girl like me. Even in this hovel, where we weren't even the youngest thieves and pickpockets housed within the walls, I was singled out for being too good for this life. It made me want to scream, and I stormed out without a word.

PART FIVE

Mistress Relata had been about to deliver a lecture on top of everything Ysili had just said, and I couldn't bear to hear it. I could feel her intent to set me straight about the harsh realities of the world as if it pressed against my skin. If her words were anything like the intrusive thoughts that surrounded me I didn't want anything to do with any of it. Ysili was right that I wouldn't be able to find legitimate work at my age; I'd figured that out already.

The gods had decreed long ago that childhood was for learning, and apprenticeship was the closest a child was supposed to come to earning their keep. Every race on Kayan followed it, even now after most of the gods had been dead for hundreds of years. Rhada had taught that to me and I hadn't thought a thing about it until now, in the city, where it worked against me at every turn.

"Well, it's the pretty little lady," one of Ysili's new friends mocked as I reached the bottom of the stairs. "Tired of fighting with your boyfriend? We could hear the yelling all the way down here!"

It was one of the older boys, and again I could feel his thoughts shoving their way into my head, telling me that I should just go home. That this was no life for someone as spoiled as me. I hurried faster, picking up my skirts as I rushed out the door. Is that all anyone thought when they looked at me? I found it exhausting, realizing that because of my disguise I was so diminished in the eyes of others. I hurried out of the building to wander the streets aimlessly until I could calm down.

I had left behind my new winter cloak, and I frowned

because it had cost me ten nubs two days ago, and now I had nothing left. What point was there in buying it if I left it behind? The cold itself didn't actually concern me, just the recklessness of my spending. The chill had served to clear my mind and make me more aware, but it did not discomfort me. I walked slowly, listening to every conversation around me. Many sounded excited about the coming of Nightwatch and were talking enthusiastically about buying gifts for it.

Buying Nightwatch gifts. I shook my head at the thought of it as I turned onto a different street. Every Nightwatch gift I'd ever received had been made by hand. How decadent those who lived in the city must be, to buy gifts for others instead of spending the time to make them.

Down this street the conversations turned to business, and I heard one person swearing another to secrecy as they repeated a rumor they'd heard somewhere else. No one paid me any mind as I wandered, losing my own concerns as I overheard the concerns of others. The emotions they wore on their faces were self-absorbed and animated, and I relaxed in the face of so many others who had not an ounce of condemnation for me in their bearing. I was nothing to them, and it was a relief.

I reached the waterfront and sat down on a bench next to a large pier. It was bustling with activity, but still somehow scenic and attractive. I wasn't the only well-dressed person relaxing in this place. It seemed a perfect spot to try to put my thoughts in order.

Ysili was right, of course. It would be so much easier to look like myself, dress like a boy, and hope that the sheer volume of people would keep me from being found. Anxiety welled up at the thought, however. In my memory, I could clearly hear the man in the carriage who had paid me so much for so little. He gave me a description of myself, saying I was a boy that was as pretty as a girl. The only way I thought I could stay hidden from that was to keep pretending. No one was looking for a girl. Still, it handicapped us. I was a liability. Ysili would be better off without me holding him back, now that we were here. What would I do without him, though?

I could follow him, go along with whatever scheme he had in mind for us, or I could reveal myself and stop running. I wasn't ready to stop running, though. Would they kill me? Would they keep me trapped and locked away for my own good? I'd seen what Krecek had done to my parents. Would that fate be mine, or would I face something worse? I couldn't defend myself against wizards. They were older than I was. More powerful. In my mind they were still larger than life. I had to keep hiding until I was ready. Until I was strong enough. I had no choice but to do whatever Ysili said we had to do in order to survive the winter.

I placed my face in my hands, hunched over and defeated. They were terrible choices to be faced with. A life of petty crime just to survive, or giving myself up to the mercy of the wizards for whatever they had planned. It was all too much for me, and I gave in to my feelings and took advantage of my disguise to cry, publicly. It was a short-lived indulgence, not more than a few tears, but one I was certain would go unnoticed in this alien society of self-centered hurry.

When I finally wiped my tears away and looked up I noticed a man sitting a bit of a distance away. He was lean and lanky, sitting with a board propped at an angle in his lap and a stick of charcoal swiping furiously across the paper clipped to it. A lock of his wavy blond hair fell into his face, and in one swift and smooth motion he tucked it behind his ear and glanced up at me. His eyes widened as they met mine. I stood quickly and remembered to rub my arms as if the cold bothered me as I began to hurry away.

"Hello!" His voice carried as he called out to me. "Excuse me, hello, could you please wait?"

I hesitated, turning slowly and looking back, but poised to run if I had to.

The man rushed up to me, smiling disarmingly. "Thank you. I wasn't sure you would stop."

"I wasn't sure I would, either," I said.

"I'm an artist," he said. "Naran Tennival, you've heard of me, yes? No. Well. I'm sure you noticed me sketching before you jumped up as if I were going to rob or something of the sort." His smile remained in place, and he showed me the tablet of paper, revealing very detailed sketches of me hunched over on the bench, crying. "I saw you and I had to draw you, but this is simply not enough for me. Please. Not many boys of your age are so beautiful, and fewer still are comfortable wearing such fetching dresses. I must have you pose for me."

I took a step back. "How did you know? No one else has ever--"

"I'm an artist." They were the same words, but more deliberate and emphatic this time. It was an answer, not an introduction. "Small things, small differences in the proportions of your body that are subtle but those with a good eye can spot. Nothing to be alarmed about, and nothing that would give you away to the layman. The length of your arms and where your elbows fall in relation to your waist, for example. Only someone who has studied anatomy extensively would notice it."

He offered his arm and we began walking as he went on in greater detail about proportion and frame and color and shading, empty space and implied action, and various other things while he guided me to a teahouse. We were sipping something rich and cloying before I fully realized we'd arrived. The drink was akin to hot apple cider, but with less of a tang. There was some lingering taste to it that I eventually decided I liked. He hadn't paused in his art lesson to order a thing, and he placed a silver wheel and a few nubs change casually on the table without hesitating over a single word. It was a somewhat dizzying experience, and it ended with him pressing a coin and a slip of paper into my hand.

"Think on it," Master Tennival said. "I could use a good model who can sit still this long and listen to me ramble so patiently. I'll pay you well, and even teach you whatever you'd like, if you're inclined. Show up at any time. Only, please let me know."

I nodded, still overwhelmed. He left and I looked at the coin he had offered. An entire silver star. That was worth ten wheels. 250 nubs. Just for considering the idea of modeling for this man. I hurried back to the room Ysili and I shared, thinking to tell him we could find a better place to stay now, having forgotten entirely about our argument.

"Where have you been?" Ysili demanded as soon as I opened the door. "I've been worried. I'm sorry. I didn't mean to drive you away."

"I'm fine," I said. "I just needed to clear my head."

He walked over and placed a hand on my shoulder. "No. It's my fault. I'm just worried, and I'm hungry, and it made me say things I didn't mean." He hesitated and took a step back. "You're so pretty, and that doesn't help. Sometimes I forget you're not a girl, and that I don't always have to take care of you and protect you. And it angers me a bit when I do remember."

I clutched the paper and the coin in my hand, keeping them to myself for now. Some things were more important, and more immediate. "Do you wish I really was a girl?"

He nodded, suddenly becoming the taciturn one.

"Why?"

Ysili never answered me, but I thought I understood. He slept on the floor that night, and the next day a cot appeared in our room. I made a point of telling him that he was silly for it, but he was stubborn and we never slept in the same bed after that. When his breath settled at night I would take out the coin and the paper, looking over the map upon it, wondering if I should go. During the day I would look at street signs and landmarks, thinking to myself that if I only turned here, or walked down that street there, I could find my way to his house, as I searched for more honest and traditional employment. Nightwatch was coming closer, and at every door I was turned away. They stopped hiding their opinions of how a child my age should be at home for the holiday rather than seeking something more permanent in a distant city. I began to feel I had no choice.

I paid our rent for half a year with that coin, and every day it became harder to resist the promise of more for simply sitting around in my dress. I was shocked when I finally walked up to the grand home the artist lived within, thinking there must surely be a mistake. There was an imposing wrought iron gate surrounding the property. A brick path went straight from the gate to the stamped cement steps before the door. The design on the steps was elegant as well as practical in the snow and ice. The house was the largest building in sight on this street, elegant, looking like a candy house with the snow on top and the icicles hanging from the edges of the roof. I stared, thinking of how I'd heard whispers among the prettier girls about what demands some artists made upon them, asking them to undress for the poses they did, and sometimes even more. He wouldn't ask that of me, would he? He knew I was a boy. Still, he was offering so much simply to pose for him. That could not be all.

I hurried away, but I kept finding myself at the gate outside, thinking harder and harder about going within and doing whatever he asked of me. The quiet neighborhood and large house lent an air of respectability to the offer. Master Tennival had treated his money like it was of little consequence, so he was either incredibly successful with wealthy clients, or he had some other source of income. Throwing money around and offering so much for so little may have had less to do with iniquity and more to do with just not being aware of the value of what he offered. I finally took strength in that thought, and in the thought that I would be keeping Ysili safe from a more serious life of dishonesty and crime. I opened the gate and walked up to the door, knocking before my resolve could fail.

An old man opened the door and looked me over with an expectant expression upon his wrinkled face.

"Master Tennival invited me," I said in a small voice.

"This way, Miss," he said formally. He ushered me into a room that smelled like paint and turpentine and dust. There were three easels of different sizes, each with a different sized canvas resting upon them. There were vials and shallow dishes of paints of different sorts, pallets stained with a multitude of colors, and dried flowers hanging upside down against the far wall that I assumed were for rare pigments.

The room seemed to be divided in half. In the half with the paints and pallets and cubby holes full of various things there sat an old couch with paint stains and spills, and a tattered drop cloth draped unceremoniously across it. On the other half of the room were stiff-looking but beautiful chairs that appeared mostly spotless. There was a curtain rod on that side of the room, with curtains of various colors hanging from it. Various items from lutes and violins to vases and silk flowers were strewn on shelves and giant wooden blocks and ornate plaster columns throughout both halves of the room. Thankfully there were many cushions of different sizes as well. Long swaths of fabric were draped over objects or hung from the ceiling as some sort of backdrop that could be changed with a tug. I nearly backed into table covered to overflowing with ancient-looking books. It was very clear that one side of the room was strictly for models and objects that would inspire art, while the other half was a glorious clutter that grew from the frenzied work of an artist absorbed in his work.

I was left alone in the room to wait, and I kept my hands clasped behind my back so I would not be tempted to touch a thing. When I found a jar of paintbrushes I couldn't imagine why he'd need so many brushes of so many different sizes and shapes. There were fat ones with fat handles that splayed out like a part of a puff ball. There were long and skinny ones that came down to a tip that looked like one hair sticking out barely above the rest. And, the ones that fascinated me the most looked like a small lady's fan, like a flattened half-circle of bristle. So many of them looked alike, just slightly smaller or wider, or exactly the same but the brush hairs themselves might be a different color or slightly thicker, or the handles were of a slightly different shape. I found out later that this was a small selection of the brushes he owned, and he used them all for different purposes, and some were just gifts from people who did not know what else to get an artist.

There were several sticks of charcoal on a tray, and similar sticks with different colors and textures. There were pencils of every color of the rainbow and beyond, and there were huge sheets of paper as well as rolls of plain canvas and wooden frames. Next to that he had canvas stretched over the wooden frames and painted pure white. There were flat boards of wood sanded down carefully and also painted white sitting next to the canvas. I hadn't imagined the need for so many things, or that there could be so much preparation needed to simply make art.

I heard the door click open and startled a bit, bumping into a hat rack with a variety of hats, capes, and cloaks resting upon it. A large floppy red hat with several feathers sticking out of it began to slide its way down to the floor and I caught it, blushing.

"I knew you would be here, sooner or later," Master Tennival said, grinning as he strode across the room to take the hat out of my hands. He returned it casually to its spot and winked. I felt a flare of magic, and the room brightened to outdoor daylight levels in an instant. "I've been looking forward to immortalizing you on canvas, just the way you are now."

I bowed to him, cheeks still burning. "Master Tennival."

He patted me on the head and smiled. "You don't need to bow. I just want you to answer one question for me. Are you ready to begin right away, or are you here simply to state your intent to accept my offer?"

"I'm not sure," I said slowly as I straightened. "I wanted to ask you some questions."

"Did you, now?" His eyes sparkled and he sat casually on the paint-stained couch. He gestured for me to join him, and I sat gingerly on the other side. "By all means, tell me what is on your mind."

"Well, what would I have to do? It seems like quite a bit of money to just sit still for a few hours."

"Does it?" Tennival asked, looking surprised. "It doesn't seem like so much to me, but you might be surprised by how tedious sitting still becomes after a time. It truly is a trifle, and I expected you to try to ask for more."

"More?" I was completely shocked. "No, sir, I wouldn't risk it. You might change your mind!"

"What, and risk you leaving without a chance to paint your pretty face before puberty changes it and erases what nature has done? Not to mention, not many boys will sit still for as long as you do. I think that I shall have to raise what I pay you, now that I think of fairness. A golden favor, once the painting is done."

I'd never seen such a coin in my entire life. Gold? Real gold? For me? "No, no! I couldn't accept that much. I'd have to move or they'd kill me and rob me in my sleep for having so much wealth."

Master Tennival laughed, though I was completely serious. "How much will you accept from me?"

"Three stars?" That should be a good wage for an entire painting, without being too greedy.

"Five. Per week. And not a nub less."

I thought that over, feeling suddenly nervous. "That's…a lot. What if I'm not good enough?"

"Let me worry about that," Master Tennival said, smiling and rising to his feet. "You just sit as still as you can, and relax. I'll worry about what's good enough or not."

It was all I got before he pulled me like a doll into the center of the room and began to pose me to suit his artistic eye.

I returned home exhausted, feeling almost as if I'd earned the coins I'd been given. I dropped a silver wheel on the table and told Ysili to buy whatever food or other extras we needed, and his eyes grew large in shock. With the rest I went to a public bath and ordered a private room to indulge myself and then I found a tailor and bought myself a new dress.

The tailor didn't bat an eye at the amount I was willing to spend on one dress, but the rich and beautiful textiles he brought out for my approval were taken from the back, and felt like nothing I'd ever touched before. Without a question or a sly look the tailor then suggested a scarf or a choker when I matured, to hide the tell-tale bump at my throat that would someday give me away as a boy. I blushed furiously and thanked him for the advice, and still he was unflappable. At that moment he gained my loyalty for as long as I lived in Cairnborough.

The next time I was paid I bought presents for Nightwatch, giving them out proudly to Ysili and his new friends. I felt so sophisticated, and a touch decadent, picking out trinkets of no practical use at all, just things that looked nice or might be fun. It was an interesting night spent getting to know the people who lived near us just a bit better. There was Bledig, of course, the stocky lad who had invited us into this den of thieves. He claimed his great-grandfather was a dwarf. About the mid of the night he told us of treasures his mother had once hoarded, before the tornado that had made him a penniless orphan. There was the girl from the room next to us, Tanyai, who spent the entire night either silent or stammering, looking at Ysili as if he were a hero of legend. There was the elf, Paelloret, oldest of all of Ysili's friends, who was still but a child by his people's standards.

"Don't worry," Paelloret said to Tanyai at one point. "Ysili's lady will leave him some day, once she realizes she's too good for such a lowlife. Then you can console him, and I shall swoop in and show Mistress Agrad that any elf is higher born than any human, and keep her for myself."

I wasn't the only one to blush and stammer at this statement, even though his tone implied jest.

"I-I'm hardly high born," I protested. "I've never claimed to be!"

"Dressed in your finery? With such a pretty face?" He laughed and went so far as to bow before me, taking my hand and placing a kiss upon the back of it. "You'd make even the courtesans of the old elven court die of shame that a human could outshine them."

"You are a horrible tease," I said, striking Paelloret lightly on the shoulder. "And your flattery is so blatant as to shame all of your kind."

"Be that as it may," Ysili said, rescuing my hand from that of his elven friend's, "I don't think there's a one of us worthy of my lady's radiance. Given a few years I'm sure your predictions will be true." He looked so sad, and his hold upon my hand lingered long enough that I wondered if he'd forgotten I was actually a boy. Or, had that stopped mattering to him, had it stopped being part of our charade?

We continued telling tales until the dawn as tradition dictated. The quality of their company on that longest Nightwatch night was perhaps the friendliest I was ever to know. I kept looking throughout the night at Tanyai, as she continued to look at Ysili, and I can still recall her face and the self-doubt she inspired. Should I encourage the two of them to know each other better? No. I selfishly decided that night that, as long as we lived in Cairnborough, I needed him more than any true girl could. I inched closer to Ysili, and Tanyai looked hurt when he absently wrapped an arm around my shoulders.

PART SIX

A fter the holiday parties had died down and normal life began to reassert itself, I sat in Master Tennival's parlor before my modeling session.

"He knows I'm a boy," I was explaining, telling Master Tennival the details of our Nightwatch celebration. "It's just that, more and more, he treats me like I really am a girl."

"Does it bother you?" He looked mildly curious as he set his teacup down and waited for me to formulate a reply.

"I'm not sure," I murmured as I played with the thought. "When we arrived here he treated me like just another friend, and we shared a bed, and it didn't matter to either of us. The closer we came to the city the more we had to act like a runaway couple to get anything, like food or shelter. He would hold my hand and stroke my hair for effect, or wrap an arm around my shoulders to protect me from the cold when we were trying to look particularly pitiful. Ysili said he started thinking of me as a girl at times, and the easy comfort we shared has disappeared. His gallantry in front of others doesn't make me feel like he's pretending anymore. It makes me feel strange, and I don't know what to think of it."

Tennival nodded thoughtfully and ran a finger over the rim of his teacup. "You're both so young still. Everything is confusing at your age. It's one of those things that will work out when you get older, I think. Don't be in too much of a hurry to figure it out."

"That's easy for you to say," I grumbled, finishing my tea and pushing the cup aside.

"It seems so, doesn't it?" He just laughed and stood, ending the conversation by guiding me back to his studio for another exhausting session. Never let it be said that sitting still is not hard work.

That winter was one of the worst in memory according to some of Ysili's friends. Mistress Relata had the fire downstairs going day and night, adding it to the list of chores we all had to do. Thanks to the money I made modeling for Master Tennival we all ate well, though I begged Mistress Relata not to mention where the extra food had come from. Ysili had put spell wards on the door, but I did not want to tempt anyone to break Mistress Relata's rules against stealing from housemates. I heard rumors of hardships and shortages in parts of the city, but everyone in the boarding house had uncommon luck for our lot.

When spring arrived it was sudden. There were snow drifts against some buildings that loomed over me one day, and the next there were melting patches huddled in the shade. The cold may not have made me suffer, but the warmth of the sun was a welcome feeling the day it finally came.

I arrived at Master Tennival's house to find paintings stacked carefully, leaning against the walls of the foyer. The drapes were thrown wide open to let the sun stream in, and Master Tennival greeted me personally at the door. "No painting today," he said with a sparkle in his eye as he ushered me in. "It's too beautiful to let the day go to waste."

I smiled up at him and shook my head. "Now how am I going to spend the day? Ysili will call me a slacker, and I'll have to sell my body just to make ends meet." I was learning the art of teasing, and was somewhat proud of being able to so boldly make such a jest.

He laughed outright and patted me on the head. "Oh dear!

You might decide you enjoy sex better than spending all day cooped up with an old man like me, and then where would I find such a patient and entertaining model?"

I blushed and shook my head, but followed through with the banter. "Ew, no, I'm still too young for that, thank you." I pretended to pause in thought a moment. "Though, I have to admit, girls don't seem as vapid and useless to me as they used to. You might be right." It struck me, in saying such things, how much more open people were in the city. I wouldn't have entertained such thoughts before coming here, let alone have spoken them aloud. I was changing just by being here and trying to fit in. The thought didn't sit entirely well with me. "Besides," I said, hoping to change the subject, "you are not old."

"I'm much older than I look," he said, drawing himself up straight and looking for the moment every inch of the aristocrat he was. "Don't let appearances fool you, little girl."

We both laughed loudly, drawing disapproving glances from the maids who were washing the walls and hanging up new sets of paintings for the new season. I waved shyly at them and they returned to their work. I wondered if they just wished they could be enjoying themselves as well, or if they genuinely disapproved of mirth.

That's when I saw the portrait about to be placed beside the door.

My blood went cold and my ears seemed to fill with cotton, muffling all sound around me. I nearly ran out the door, but my feet rebelled and only stumbled a few paces toward the portrait. I was entranced, terrified. I couldn't mistake the boyish face and the hair as white as newly fallen snow, nor could I fail to recognize the green eyes that glowed like emeralds set in marble. Irrationally I thought I was caught and now I would be killed, untried and untrained.

"Krecek Ceolwyn," Tennival said directly behind me. "Nearly

as enigmatic a subject as you are, Agrad."

In the painting Krecek was holding a small kitten. He wore an expression of pure joy. I'd seen that very smile before, when we had played. Whenever he had triumphed. I didn't know such a monster could express joy for things other than besting a weaker opponent.

"I'm nothing like him," I whispered, partly in protest to what Tennival had said; partly to reassure myself.

"You know him?" Master Tennival placed a gentle hand on my shoulder.

"We've met," I said, stepping away from Master Tennival and turning my back upon the painting that had trapped my gaze for so long.

Turning my back did not help lock out the memories, nor the sight of my adversary. Another painting was being hung above the mantle, and it disturbed me just as much as the other one had. I vaguely remembered a panoramic landscape scene of golden grasses and crimson flowers being there over the winter, but now it was replaced by a large group of people sitting together, somehow both unassuming and powerful. It was posed to look candid, to show humanity where I suspected no one would ever have thought to find it. They wore scholarly robes and were surrounded by books. Seated upon a pillar of books was Krecek again, elbows on his knees as he leaned forward. He gazed upon the face of a beautiful young woman with a bored expression on her face. Had it been anyone else I might have laughed.

"Agrad?"

I remembered to breathe.

I felt as if I knew the rest of them, somehow. The faces were almost familiar, but I also knew I'd never seen them before. Perfect strangers, but their names rested on the tip of my tongue, tantalizingly close to being recalled from somewhere deep within. My eyes darted all over the canvas until they rested upon the bored woman that had Krecek's attention. I knew why she looked more familiar than the rest. Her dark blond curls and unusually bright blue eyes were the same as the artist beside me, and their faces shared a similar structure that told me they must be related, though even so they were not the same person.

"Are you okay, Agrad?"

Was I? I couldn't tear my gaze away from the cozy scene that somehow pained me to look at. "Are they all wizards? Or only *him?*"

"You mean Krecek?"

I nodded, taking a step closer, drawn to it by what felt almost to be a physical force.

"They're the original seventeen," Tennival said. "It was painted the year after their rise to power."

"You know them?" I asked, pointing. I did not mean all of the original wizards, of course. That would have been hundreds of years ago. But why else would he have this painting? Why would he look so much like one of them if he was not at least distantly related to one of them? "You've met wizards before?"

"I am an artist," he said. "I meet many people."

"Why is it being put up now?" I looked around the room and realized that the portraits being hung upon the walls around me were all wizards and I nearly felt crushed beneath the weight of their combined gazes. "Why is all of this here?" I was terrified that he would tell me that wizards and elementals were on their way to visit, and he was a friend to them all, and would like to introduce them to me that very minute.

Instead he looked at me thoughtfully. "In a few days it will be Memory Day." When I continued to look nonplussed he shook his head and continued. "Sometimes I forget that you have not been here for long. You don't know the history of

Cairnborough, do you?"

"Well, no," I shifted from one foot to another, uncomfortable with the intensity in his eyes suddenly.

"Continue without me," Tennival instructed his servants as he grabbed my hand and pulled me out the front door. "Honestly, Agrad. I thought the name would have at least made you curious."

"It did," I said. "I've just been busy surviving since I arrived." And hiding, of course. "I didn't know where to begin."

"I have perhaps the most extensive private library in the whole city," he shook his head and slowed his pace a bit. "From now on, I want you to spend time in it, do you understand? You're far too smart to be uneducated."

I nodded and we lapsed into silence as we walked through the streets to the outskirts of town. I had too many questions to decide which to ask as we walked, and he showed no sign of wishing to speak until we reached an expanse of land at the edge of town that seemed forgotten and unattended. I saw the stone cairns among the barren ground and nearly planted my heels, wanting none of what he pulled me toward. At the first sign of hesitation his grip on my hand tightened firmly and his pace did not slow. I did not want to be here, but I could not pull away from him either.

The small decorative fence on the city side of it was as impenetrable to the city as a solid wall would have been – nothing of Cairnborough went beyond that point. The piles of stone looked both ancient and recently placed at the same time. Age had weathered the stones, but they looked clean and untouched by dirt or leaves or any growing thing. It was an entire field of graves, and Master Tennival pulled me along a well-worn path to the center where the largest stone mounds were found. Three cairns surrounded by a ring of seventeen that still pulsed with unimaginable power. Before Master Tennival even opened his mouth, I knew where this was.

"This is Cairnfeld, the place where the battle was waged. Where the dead were buried. Where mortals wrested power from the Old Gods and triumphed more completely than any of them imagined they could."

I shivered, wrapping my arms around myself. "I didn't expect there to be so much power, even still. The Old Gods are dead, and yet..." I reached forward, touching the stones upon the closest one of their graves. In a flash I knew this was once Fotar, god of fire. The names that had been drilled into me in my years of silence and grieving flooded into my head and I fell to my knees, clutching my head in my hands.

"That one is particularly volatile," Master Tennival said, helping me up and guiding me away. "They were gods, Agrad. Do you think so much power could be erased even after their deaths?"

"Wait," I said, pulling away and standing unsteadily. "After my parents died, the people who took me in were, well, they claimed to be priests. I don't know if it's some sort of blasphemy, but I feel like I owe it to them, to — " I made a vague gesture toward the cairns.

"It's fine," he said. "I understand. Do what you feel you must."

I smiled gratefully and then turned back to their graves. My reason for wanting to walk among them was a lie, but I couldn't have explained it to him any more than I really understood the urge myself. I walked to each cairn, knowing each one as I came to it, and the names I'd learned finally meant something to me. There was Kaskal, god of luck and fortune; Dacet, god of nightmares; Ceraan, goddess of memory; Baedrogan, god of death; Atherva, goddess of water. Wirudel, Agruet, Ashvra, Vaederan, Egridaea, Saedral, Thebram, Brennan, Deyson, and Bogradan. I hesitated before I reached the next and final cairn. It had been drawing me in as much as it had repulsed me, from the moment I'd first glanced at it. Nalia, goddess of magic. I'd read that she was the first to fall in battle, and that Baedrogan had been the last. Being here and touching the remains of their energy, I knew for myself that the account had been correct.

"These three," I finally called to Master Tennival when I just couldn't take the haunted and eerie feeling that had been steadily overwhelming me. "The three in the middle. Are these the wizards who fell in battle?" I walked over to one of them and placed my hands on the nearest stone. There was energy there, too. It just wasn't as overwhelming, or as personal.

"Mages," he corrected me as he approached. "Yes. They faced the god of death, and he took them before he tasted death of his own, they say."

I nodded, feeling bad for them, but not overwhelmingly so. "Did they return as elementals, too?"

"They may have returned," Tennival said, stroking his chin. "Not as elementals, though. They didn't defeat the gods; they were among the defeated."

"What are the rest of the cairns for?" I asked, rushing from the inner circle as soon as I had an excuse to.

"It was a large battle, Agrad. Gods and wizards weren't the only ones fighting, and nearly everyone present perished from the backlash."

"Everyone except for the wizards? I read that once."

Tennival just nodded, falling into silent thought.

I understood the urge. Being surrounded by all these thousands of smaller stone piles gave a significant weight to what remained of the greatest battle in history. I knelt by one of the small cairns, wondering which side they'd fought for. There was no real energy to speak of. Their graves were as lifeless as the stone left to commemorate them.

"It will have been three-hundred and twenty-eight years, this spring," Master Tennival said, kneeling beside me. "And only three of the original wizards are still alive."

"They're the most powerful, right? I mean, they're immortal, aren't they?" I don't know why I searched for the answer in his eyes, but what I found there was sad.

"We're all immortal," he said, "until the day we aren't."

I had a dream that night. I was wandering through Cairnfeld, looking at the sea of graves once again, and a woman was watching me from among the center stones. I ran to her, needing to be near her, needing to say hello, to say I loved her, to say I was sorry that she was dead.

Go away, she cried with rage and anguish, holding her hands out to stop me.

I stopped, confused. For a moment I had thought of her like a mother, but I knew she was not my mother. She looked nothing like my mother. But, she was someone's mother. She was beautiful, wise, and powerful. She knew so much, her eyes held stories beyond telling.

You're just a child. Her words were like a revelation, and I felt how very young I was. She hugged me and held me and whispered in my ear, *I hate you. I'll hate you forever. You should have died, not me.*

I woke up crying. Ysili was across the room in his cot, fast asleep. I wiped away my tears, trembling from the intensity of the emotion held in that dream, deeply sad and yet terrified by the words that woman had said. I stared into the darkness that enveloped the room until dawn, unable to move, to sleep, to do anything but play the dream over and over in my mind.

I returned to Cairnfeld about once a month after that. I think I was searching for myself in those piles of stone. I was coming to terms with the thought that I really was an elemental. Part of me was one with the gods in that field, and part of me was one with one of their murderers. I wasn't sure what I should be doing out there. Apologizing? Gloating? Giving thanks for the cursed power I'd been given? Even still, without knowing what I was doing, I couldn't stay away.

I breathed a sigh of relief when the paintings were changed again to more natural scenes and I didn't walk in to see Krecek's face every day. I no longer modeled every day, growing to be more of a friend and an assistant to Master Tennival. When he had another model I cleaned brushes or pallets or changed out props and furniture. In turn he began to teach me how to turn dried herbs into pigment, and then to paint. True to his word, he gave me a great deal of time to myself in his library. Master Tennival was surprised at how voraciously I read. He joked that he should set up a cot in the room so that I wouldn't have to leave my beloved written word.

Ysili complained about the hours I was keeping, not knowing how any of them were spent, or that most of them were my own while I ravaged Master Tennival's library.

"I'm going to forget what you look like by anything but candlelight," he complained, while I laughed and patted his cheek.

"I've steady employ, and we are moving to nicer quarters as soon as a room is open, and you complain about my hours?"

"We're supposed to be friends," he said, sitting on the edge of his cot.

"We are!" I was feeling a bit exasperated. "You're the best friend I've got."

"How can I be, when I barely know a thing about you? I don't even know who you are."

"Of course you do." I smiled. "I'm Agrad. You know that. Everything else, well, I guess it doesn't matter, or we'll both have to find out. It's like I'm a completely new person now that we're here, and that's how I prefer it."

Ysili was starting to look agitated, shaking his head abruptly. "Who you were is still part of who you are and who you will be, and I don't know any of it. I mean, I know who I am. I'm a boy, I'm half water spirit and a failed magical experiment, formerly a wizard's slave. I'm the only one of my kind, an outcast, a thief. I live for the day, I seize every opportunity with both hands. I live a life of comfort, thanks to you, but I could get by on my own if I have to."

"A wizard's slave?" I asked with wide eyes. "Whose?"

"That's not the point!" Ysili's hands balled into fists and his lips pursed. "This isn't about me, so stop changing the subject! You're always gone these days, and I barely know anything about you or what you're doing. Every time we do talk, you turn it around and ask about me and don't tell me anything! I want to get to know you."

"I'm sorry." I cast my eyes downward demurely while my mind raced to find a way out of answering. Could I outright lie to my closest friend? Could I find a way out of answering? I wanted a normal life. I wanted to live. I wanted to keep him safe. I couldn't be sure I'd have any of those things if he knew who I was. "I don't know what to say."

"All I know about you is that you're a boy, you dress like a girl, and you're an orphan. Oh, and for some reason you put up with me."

"You know more than that," I said gently, but inwardly I was cheering. I knew how I could get out of this. "You know my favorite color is green. You know that I love apples. You know I don't like wizards any more than you do. You know I've been modeling because being a thief just isn't for me. You know better than I do if I snore or not. That's something no one else in the whole world knows about me. Just like I know that you do snore softly, you love peaches, your hair shines like the ocean and your eyes are like a tempest. And you blush when you look at me sometimes."

"I do not," Ysili said, proving himself a liar. "Why do you dress like a girl, anyway?"

"Does it matter that much?" I took off my bonnet and gloves and threw them on the simple wooden table. "I don't know why I prefer these things. I'm not a girl and I know it. I don't even want to be one. I just feel safe, dressed like this."

"Safe?" He pounced on the word. "So you're afraid of something. What is it?"

"I told you. Wizards. I would think you'd understand that much, considering what you just told me."

"Hey," he said, leaning forward, "no fair bringing that up now. It's personal, and it's in the past."

"Exactly," I tried to interrupt.

"Just tell me. How is wearing a dress going to protect you?"

I rolled my eyes and stood to strip off my dress. I knew it would distract him no matter how casually I did it, or how much I set aside my usual girlish mannerisms. "It won't. I'm not stupid. If a wizard showed up here no amount of frills would save me from whatever it is they'd do to me. I know that. I said it makes me feel safe, not that I would be safe." I pulled the dress off over my head and tossed it casually upon the bed.

My ploy worked. "You shouldn't strip so casually in front of guys," he said gruffly and stalked out of the room.

He was safer not knowing. And I was safer by holding the

knowledge deep inside where no one would ever know.

Days went by.

You'll always be alone, she said, caressing my cheek almost kindly. Her eyes were endless, like the night sky above us. I was laying on my own grave. *I'll make sure of it.*

It must be sad, having nothing but hate. She said I would be alone, but I knew, somehow, it was her fate that she was wishing upon me.

Don't flatter yourself. She slapped me across the face, but in the way of dreams I felt no pain. I just looked at her and forgave her.

Everyone you ever love will die before you. You will be alone. You will be alone.

I woke up crying again. The idea of being alone scared me so much. I'd already lost everyone I loved once. I knew just how painful a wish that was to put on someone, and perhaps that's why I had that dream. A book I'd read at Master Tennival's had talked about how dreams were how we learned to cope with the waking world, and I knew I still had a lot to cope with.

I took a deep breath and walked across the room. "Ysili?" I shook his arm gently.

He shifted, shrugging me off at first, but he sat up. "It's dark," he grumbled.

"I had a bad dream," I said. He pulled me down next to him and held me, and I started to cry again. "I watched my parents die," I sobbed into his shoulder. It wasn't what my dream was about, but it was something I hadn't told him about me before. "I don't like to think about my past because it was wonderful once, but now everything's terrible and if I don't talk about it maybe I won't have to think about it. They burned to death.

105

Magic saved me, but it couldn't save them. Nothing could save them."

"I'm sorry," he said, stroking my hair. "You don't have to tell me. Just be who you are now."

The tears were already slowing. I breathed slowly, deeply, still holding onto him for a while, until I felt like my voice wouldn't crack and the tears wouldn't fall if I spoke again.

"I took a job as an artist's model," I said quietly. "He's been taking care of me, teaching me, and letting me read his books. The books are the reason I've been staying late, because I lose track of time. I can't believe all the books he has. History and magic and mathematics. I didn't know books about mathematics could be so interesting. It was always the thing I hated the most before, and now I can't get enough of playing around with numbers and figuring things out."

"Modeling and reading," he said, eyes sparkling in the scant light that crept in beneath our door. "Well, it's better than what I was afraid you'd fallen into."

"Much better than what I was afraid I'd have to resort to." I hesitated a second. "While I was making up my mind to accept Master Tennival's offer, one of the girls downstairs offered to teach me and introduce me to a client she had."

"Tennival?" he asked. "He does have a reputation."

"He hasn't laid a finger on me," I said, pulling away. "He wouldn't dream of it. He knows I'm a boy, and that's why he hired me, but not for anything nude or unsavory."

"Not that sort of reputation," Ysili chuckled. "I've heard he's rich."

"Don't you dare," I said. "If you or any of your friends think about hitting him, stop right there. There's some odd magic in his house. And don't you even think about asking me to help or to take anything. He's not merely my employer, he's become a friend and mentor. I'm not risking that for anything."

"I promise," he said. "I won't do a thing to him. If it means so much to you, I won't even entertain the thought."

"Good," I said, leaning against him once again. "I think he might have met a wizard or two in his time. He put up paintings of wizards in the spring, and I think he painted some of them, and that might be why he's got so much money."

"Doesn't that worry you?" he asked. "I thought you were running from them."

"It scares me so much," I said softly. "When I think about it I can't breathe. I knew that going to a city, any city, would be a risk. I have to survive somehow, though. This, with you, is much nicer than a cave."

"Wizards are very busy," Ysili said. "You should be fine, even if he's one of their closest friends."

"Are you sure?"

He took my hands and looked into my eyes sincerely. "I hate my past as much as you hate yours, but yes. I am sure they're busy. He always was, when I was young."

"Who was it?"

Ysili just shook his head.

I didn't need to know. There were questions I would not answer. I had to respect his wish not to answer the same.

"Would you like to meet Master Tennival?"

He hesitated a moment before he nodded. "Okay."

I got up and walked over to my bed. "Good. You can come with me tomorrow." I yawned, finally tired again. "Thank you, Ysili. I'm glad you're here."

"Go to sleep," he said gruffly, but I could tell he appreciated it.

I could finally drift off, secure in the knowledge that I was not alone.

When they met they each assured me later that they approved, as if I needed someone's consent to have a friend. It wasn't a terrible thing that they cared, of course, but it was a bit exasperating that they'd both felt the need to tell me the same thing about each other.

"Are all friends overprotective like this?" I asked Paelloret one evening. We were doing chores together. I had signed up to scrub floors and he was doing the same.

"Only the good ones," he said, pausing to rinse out his sponge. "Ysili warned me away from you, I'll have you know. He must really like you."

"He did?" I was confused. "Why would he do that?"

"There are many reasons," Paelloret said. "He clearly cares about you and does not want to see you hurt. Elves and humans, well, it always ends tragically. You are a beautiful lady, but he was right to say that you and I should not be close."

"Is this because you were flirting on Nightwatch?"

He nodded and began to scrub the floor again. "Friends I had when I came to Cairnborough are grown and have children your age. It will be nearly a human lifetime before I will be old enough to entertain thoughts of a family of my own. I will still be a child when you are old."

"That's no reason to not be friends," I said.

"Perhaps not," Paelloret said, but his eyes twinkled. "Being a rogue and an outlaw, with a bad reputation and no wish to better myself, on the other hand..."

I laughed. "Someday you'll be king of the thieves, and on that day I'll say you are a friend of mine."

"And I'll visit you as you lay dying, old and decrepit, and I won't even recognize you because getting old does weird things to a human's face." He was laughing as well.

"Just as long as you're there," I said.

He nodded and we got back to work. The scoundrels here were good people, as long as you were one of their own. I knew that Ysili and I could afford now to live somewhere nicer, but we had friends here, and smaller children who were starting to look up to us.

The dream was peaceful this time. The lady was tired, worn down by things unfathomable to me. *The future is always in motion, and it doesn't even slow down for gods and immortals.*

I hugged her, wanting to cheer her up. "I don't know why that makes you sad. Things are supposed to change, aren't they? It would be boring if nothing changed."

It's supposed to follow a plan. She held me, and I wanted to stay like this forever. It was such a relief that she wasn't yelling at me, or cursing me, or wishing death upon me. *There was an order to things, and now it's gone. We didn't have a contingency because this path was supposed to be impossible.*

"Make another plan."

In the way of dreams it felt right, both as advice to someone distraught and to myself. My life had had order, once. I'd known what I was going to do. I was going to be the best spellsmith in the world, learning from my parents, taking what they'd started and perfecting it. I would live my days in Lesser Stonegore, until I died quietly of old age, surrounded by my children, and their children, and perhaps even their children.

Make another plan.

And if that one did not work, do it again.

Time passed and as puberty hit my voice strained to destroy my disguise. Ysili was walking with me to Master Tennival's house, talking lightly of the coming winter, and the bounty the farmers had brought that summer to our shore. It was then that my voice betrayed me and I stopped in my tracks, hand at my throat. "Oh no," I whispered. "Oh no."

Ysili just laughed, amused since he had been through it nearly a year before. "It's not that bad."

I didn't utter a word the rest of the way while Ysili teased me. Master Tennival was standing outside that day and smiled as I arrived. "What's troubling you?" he asked as I stepped up to the gate.

I frowned, reluctant to speak.

"It's Agrad's voice," Ysili explained with quiet amusement.

"Are you sick?" Master Tennival opened the gate for me and placed a hand on my forehead.

I backed off, shaking my head.

"It's changing."

Tennival immediately understood. "So soon? Oh, don't keep quiet or it will take your voice longer to adjust."

"It's true," Ysili agreed. "Just get it over with and then you can figure everything out from there. Bye!"

He left, and the rest of the day Master Tennival did not paint me, but relentlessly questioned me about anything and everything just to get me to keep talking. I was embarrassed at first. When he didn't laugh or even smile at my plight I eventually relaxed. I realized that the root of my anxiety was less about being embarrassed and more about maintaining my disguise, my new lifestyle. Would my voice be too deep?

What I strained most at during this transition was keeping

the sound soft. I don't know if it was my effort or the nature of my body, but my voice did not end up so far changed that it would have been ridiculous to maintain my mode of dress. It simply took more awareness of how I spoke than it did before.

That was not the only change puberty brought, of course. I did not grow facial hair, thankfully. Ysili didn't either, which saved us a bit of effort having to shave. It was a great relief to me since my hair was black and I was sure stubble would have been very visible very fast if it had grown in. Every other physical change I went through I could hide or at least disguise with the cut of my dress, accessories, and a slight use of cosmetics. Master Tennival helped me with that, with the aid of one of his maids.

"You're going to keep wearing dresses?" Ysili asked one day in the midst of all this growing up.

I nodded, giving it just a bit of thought.

"Oh, lucky for you, pretty boy. Here I thought you wouldn't be able to, but--" He broke off with a shrug.

"I've thought about buying a suit," I admitted reluctantly.

"I don't know if I'd even recognize you," Ysili laughed.

I smiled to myself. That, of course, was the idea. Not Ysili specifically. I just hoped that if I did wear a suit someday, no one would recognize me at all, and I'd be completely free once again.

It was a thought I only toyed with but never acted upon. I could never bring myself to speak up to my tailor about my potential request. What would he think, after all this time? It was an idea I played with every few months still, especially in the spring. At that time I would look at the painting of the wizards with less trepidation and more longing. Their robes may now be dated, but something like that would neatly solve my dilemma.

"You don't look so scared anymore," Master Tennival observed as he straightened the last painting in the foyer after they'd all been replaced. I was seventeen and very nearly his apprentice except that I hadn't drawn or painted a thing for myself.

"It's just paint," I said. "Pigment and oil. What's to fear?"

"That's what I've wondered," he smiled, walking over to me. He was still slightly taller than me, but not by all that much. "You were so very afraid of these. Of Krecek, specifically. Are you still?"

I thought about it and started to nod, but I held myself in check after a moment. "Not as much as I used to be. I guess that means I've grown up a bit."

"I suppose so," Master Tennival said with a gentle smile. "But would you still think the same if you saw him today?"

My blood ran cold just contemplating it. "Me? Meeting a wizard, face to face?"

He just nodded.

How could I answer without giving myself away? "In the town where I was born everyone was afraid of wizards. It would probably be hard to overcome entirely." That was safe, wasn't it?

"They've never scared me," Master Tennival said with a faraway look in his eyes. "In fact, Krecek once laughed at my fearlessness. Many of them did. It was the subject of an amusing discussion while I painted this scene."

Hadn't he said that this painting was over three hundred years old? My eyes grew wide in wonder at what he was telling me. I could see a similarity in technique, but it was so primitive next to what he did these days. Humans simply did not live for hundreds of years, and I knew he was not a wizard. What was he?

"I'm just an artist, of course." He was smiling, keeping a hand on my shoulder, gentle but firm. "They like what I do and appreciate my talent. As long as they do, I'm safe."

"Oh, I don't know about that," a woman's voice drawled behind us, and a shiver went down my spine. I'd felt her presence a moment before I'd heard her voice. "Some of us are getting a bit unpredictable in our old age."

There was a wizard in the room. I tried with all my power, every bit of magic I could call upon, muttering what little charms I could remember, to be unnoticed. To be small and insignificant. It was impossible. Just as I knew she was a wizard at this proximity, she had to know I was an elemental.

"Agrad, this is my sister, Aral Kaelwyn."

PART SEVEN

I couldn't breathe.

My heart was pounding and my tongue felt too large in my mouth suddenly. I thought I should say something, but it was impossible. I wasn't ready for this. I had no defenses. No skill. No practice. No hope.

She could do anything to me. Anything at all. Enslave me. Kill me. My imagination was vague on the details, but dread didn't need details to make me tremble.

I forced a deep breath in. Smile. Turn. Curtsey…deeper. She was a wizard, after all.

"My apologies," I said. My voice wavered, but there was nothing I could do for that. "I am not sure how to properly address someone of your stature."

She replied with a soft laugh. "Naran, you're right. He makes an adorable young lady, doesn't he?"

Master Tennival let me go to take a step toward her. "Aral, you promised to behave. He's terribly shy and still fragile. You haven't given me a chance to talk to him or prepare him for this." He turned to me with a pained look. "I'm sorry, Agrad. My sister has her moods and thinks that since she's all powerful she can do anything she likes, including being rude."

"Of course I can do anything I want," she said, pouting. "It's been quite some time since I could not."

"Aral," he said. Master Tennival's tone was very serious in counterpoint to her playfulness.

"Mind your tone with me," Aral said. "I am still nine years your elder and the ruler of an entire country, after all."

"You do not rule here," he said, staring her down as if he were the one with the power.

They bantered back and forth while I twisted a finger of my gloves behind my back, staring at the floor as I hoped my mind would find something useful in its frightened scrambling. I continued trying to project an image of myself as small and insignificant, but without much hope. There was a pause and I looked up to notice them looking expectantly at me.

"To what do I owe the honor of your presence?" I asked, though my tongue was like clay and my throat like desert sand.

"I wanted to meet my brother's favorite new toy, of course," Aral said. "It's rare I'm not disappointed, but this time he shows good taste."

I frowned, shooting a glance at Master Tennival before I looked back at Aral. "Am I supposed to be flattered to be thought of as a plaything?"

"Oh, don't sound so irritated, little mouse," Aral said. "A plaything is more than most will ever rate, after all."

Master Tennival walked over to me and put a hand on my arm and looked at me intently until I met his eyes. "She's teasing," he said. "She's just trying to pull out some sort of reaction."

"And succeeding," she smirked. "Look at the both of you. I can't remember the last time I saw you so protective of anyone, Naran."

I squirmed away from Master Tennival. "I should leave," I murmured, casting my eyes to the floor again. My heart was still pounding and my emotions were running a bit high, but I'd been a model all these years and I knew how to still myself outwardly while my mind raced in other directions. "This is family business. I should not intrude."

Aral giggled childishly and I cringed. Before either of them could say a word I gathered up my skirts and rushed out the front door and into the cool spring air.

The perfume of flowers assaulted me in a cacophony of scent

as soon as I pulled the door open. The brightness of the sun pierced my eyes. Everything felt so much more vivid than ever. I realized it was from the magic I'd woven around myself to make me seem insignificant to Aral.

The world in its natural state of being seemed too strong for me to handle, to the point that even a gentle breeze threatened to choke me. I did nothing, defeated even by my thoughts. A great tide of sound washed over me and I held my hands to my ears as an ornate carriage drove past. The power of those within overwhelmed me and I fell to my knees, but no one paid any notice. They were wizards. I began to suspect myself of childish hubris that I'd ever thought I was an elemental. They were so overwhelmingly powerful.

I slipped further down, hands splayed on the ground once the painful hum of their magic had passed. Someone nearly walked into me, stepping casually on my finger and the hem of my dress. I was beneath their notice. I was beneath any notice at all. The pain roused me enough to run, finally. I rushed to my apartment. Ysili was seated in my favorite chair, but he didn't raise his head to acknowledge my return. He didn't see me at all as I gathered my favorite belongings and threw half of the money I'd saved on the table beside him.

I knew only as I did so that I was leaving, abandoning all of my belongings so that I could run far and fast. It was time to run away again, and I didn't know if I'd ever see him again. I kissed him on the cheek as my last act of farewell, and I whispered words to him that I'd never dreamed I would say. I don't know if he'd heard them at all. There was no reaction from him. I backed away from him, watching for anything at all, until I could stand it no more. I ran from the room and I didn't look back.

I thought I was just running away. I thought it didn't matter beyond that. The city was infested with wizards and elementals, and I needed to be gone. I needed to be somewhere. I needed to hide and wait for my insignificance to fade away or to destroy me and swallow me whole or something. Unfortunately, the spell I'd cast upon myself sublimated my own self-will and I felt drawn and unable to fight.

Three hundred and thirty-three years.

It was the voice of the woman who haunted my dreams. It was as clear as if she'd stood at my shoulder and spoken directly in my ear. I shivered and wrapped my shawl tighter around me, quickening my pace away from home. I wasn't sure where I was being drawn to yet. As long as it was away from Master Tennival, and Ysili, and all the things that had tied me down and given me a false sense of safety, it didn't matter where I went. I was just thankful that the ones who meant the most to me were gone. Behind me. Safe.

There's a special power in repetition and pattern, Agrad. There's power in those numbers.

I couldn't even address the voice. It overwhelmed me as much as the presence of the other wizards had. It was inside of me and I couldn't fight it. I couldn't think beyond a growing panic that this wasn't the freedom I'd looked forward to. It was a prison and I'd locked the doors me.

Why else would the others gather upon the place of our deaths? The place of their ascension? Three hundred and thirty-three years ago, today. This place. This hour.

I was coming to Cairnfeld, and the cairns of the gods were glowing bright red. I felt anger and smelled death. I trembled and wanted to collapse onto the ground and weep, but my body was a marionette and a goddess was pulling my strings. I'd given up my free will for an attempt at escape and anonymity.

Thank you, Agrad.

What had I done?

Thank you, for your sacrifice.

Oh no. No. This was all wrong.

For giving your life, that I may live again.

"No," I whispered aloud, struggling with all of my will just to do that much. "No, they'll just kill you again. This is all wrong." I became a gibbering mess, spent as my will drained from me. "All wrong," I said again. "All wrong."

I saw things.

Glimpses of war.

A feeling of jealousy.

Betrayal.

Terror.

A great spell.

Summoning.

Devouring.

The blood of the gods was bitter.

The pain of death was immense.

Couldn't stop.

Don't stop.

This is it.

The end.

Suicide.

End of the world.

End of all.

End...

"Agrad!"

The voice was familiar and nearly jolted me from my stupor, but I was too small, too hollowed out at that point. I didn't have the strength to turn and look. I barely had the strength to recognize that it was my own name. The visions grew into an overwhelming jumble playing in my mind, drowning out the real world as I walked through the graveyard.

"Stop," I mumbled out loud. It took as much will as it would have to scream. "Won't work."

The voice in my head didn't say a word. She was intent on one thing and couldn't see beyond the past. I tried to stop, to shut my eyes, to sit down and catch my breath or something, anything, to delay the disaster to come.

I couldn't.

"Agrad!"

Something hit me in the stomach and I fell to the ground. I couldn't breathe. There were two worlds, and in one of them I was walking to my doom.

In the other, I gasped for breath. "Help!" I rasped, grabbing the person who had tackled me.

"I'm trying," he grunted, pushing me pack down, pinning me to the ground.

That's when I realized how I knew that voice.

"Krecek," I hissed with hatred. The hatred I held for him was nothing to the inferno of rage that came from the one who was taking over me. I very nearly lost myself in that moment, clinging to my own reasons to hate him as if they were driftwood on an impossible expanse of ocean.

Others were grabbing my ankles and wrists, and Krecek was kneeling next to me. His emerald eyes burned into me with anger of his own, and he backhanded me across the face, stunning me.

"I name thee, Agrad Verwyn!" he shouted intently. "I behold thee for who thou art! Know thyself and return to the destiny and power thou hast been born unto!"

"Nalia," I heard myself say, struggling against them all. "*I am Nalia...*"

He hit me again and my head rocked against the ground.

"Agrad Verwyn! Nalia is dead!"

I had no idea he could look so enraged. I stared at him and forgot to be scared. *"Gods…cannot die…"*

Krecek stood up and gestured for the others to carry me. With another gesture from him, they tossed me roughly onto the pile of stones that was my grave. Her grave. Nalia's grave.

Nalia's.

"Taste of your own death, bitch," he growled, pushing me harder against the stones, crushing my back into whatever sharp edges were there. I felt the light spring fabric of my gown tear easily, and I knew my blood spilled upon those stones. "Now return Verwyn to us!"

I screamed and struggled, but the magic that chained me snapped and I was finally myself again. The force of the spell finally ending left me limp, drained. "It's me," I said at last. "I'm me. Agrad." As soon as I was let go I slid to the ground against the rough stones, ruining my gown further and adding to my abrasions. Every inch of me throbbed in pain, but that was nothing next to the sudden emptiness I felt. "She's quiet…so quiet…"

Krecek kicked me in the ribs, hard, and bent down to grab me by the hair. "Stop it," he said inches from my face. I tried to protest, but it hurt to breathe. "If you lose control like that again, I'll kill you myself. It's about time I get a turn, Verwyn."

Someone pulled him off of me, chiding him gently for losing control. Someone else, someone I vaguely recognized, picked me up and I am afraid I coughed up blood on his soft gray shirt, ruining it. I could feel myself healing already. It took more than that to kill an elemental.

This stranger carried me as easily as if I were a baby, humiliating me, and I struggled to free myself.

He let me fall.

I passed out, barely registering the landing through the rest of my pain.

I was told much later that I was kept there for the ritual that followed, despite my unconscious state. I slept fitfully for days while I healed and recovered my strength. I was alone each time I awoke to take care of necessities such as eating, and I fell back to sleep entirely too easily when I was done. On the third day I finally caught someone taking away my empty plate and tried to say hello, but he hurried out without a word. Moments later, Master Tennival and Aral Kaelwyn entered with twin expressions of frustration and scorn.

"Good morning?" I ventured, unsure what time of day it actually was.

Master Tennival sat down beside me on the bed while Aral chose a chair nearby.

"Are you recovered?" Master Tennival asked, even while he looked me over.

"I think so," I said. "I'm still a bit weak. What happened?"

"You were there," Aral said with an edge to her voice. "Why don't you tell us?"

I blushed. I'm certain that I did. It wasn't a teasing, playful, or in any way coy sort of blush, either. It stemmed from a deep pain and embarrassment at thinking of what I had done and what I had almost unleashed upon the world. "I lost control."

"It's almost vulgar in its understatement," she said, eyes flashing. Aral leaned closer to me, trembling. "Lost control. You child. You utter imbecile."

Master Tennival held up a hand and, surprisingly, Aral went still. "That's enough," was all he said.

I sat up fully, hugging my knees to my chest protectively.

This was my doom. This was my hell.

"Agrad, you should have stayed and listened. I thought you trusted me by now."

I stared hard at the sheets so I wouldn't have to look at Master Tennival, feeling guilty that I couldn't bring myself to trust him, or anyone, that far. It was too much to ask though, especially after springing such a huge surprise upon me. What did he expect from me when he introduced a wizard into my life so suddenly, without explanation or warning.

Suddenly the question in my mind went from rhetorical to something I almost desperately wanted to know. What had he expected from me?

"How long have you known?" I finally asked when I realized he wasn't going to expound upon the trust issue, or explain why I should have stayed.

"From the moment I laid eyes on you. How could I not?" Master Tennival said, hands spread in an almost questioning gesture. "I've known every Verwyn since Davri, and we all knew your parents."

"So I've been a bug under glass the entire time I've been here?" The corners of my eyes stung and my stomach knotted around the meal I'd just eaten. "And you think you deserve my trust?"

Aral made a scoffing sound of disbelief and exasperation. "You've been given a normal life the entire time you've been here. We've stayed back to give you the space and security you need and let you flourish under my brother's care. We left you alone to grieve, to grow, so that you would heal after Krecek's unfortunate mistake--"

"He murdered my parents." My tone was as dead as they were, flattened by my weakened state.

"I am well aware," Aral said. "Killing them in front of you was a grave error on his part. He should have known how volatile that would have left your emotional state. Believe me when I say we know, more intimately than you could imagine, just how dangerous and stupid that was of him."

I glared at her. "So that's it? His big mistake was in making me upset? Not murdering two innocents who were just trying to protect their child?"

Naran flinched as if he'd been hit, then stood up and strode over to the window, staring outward and divorcing himself from the conversation.

Aral watched him with sad eyes before turning to me. "I will not discuss their guilt or innocence at this moment. What I will discuss, and what I need you to understand more importantly than anything in your life, is your need to maintain control. You could have died. You could have killed us all. Not just those of us standing there, not just Cairnborough. All, as in the entirety of Kayan, every living soul in this gods-forsaken world. So, yes, his big mistake was in upsetting you. It was as stupid as my own mistake of startling you the other day. We each contain the power of a god! Honestly, Verwyn, how could you not realize what the stakes are? What we all could have lost?"

It sounded as if she were talking through me, to someone layers beneath it all. Whoever she spoke to, he wasn't there. It was just me, and this goddess power burning within me, laying in wait for me to falter again. Just me to hold back the rising tide...

"I didn't know," I said. "I still don't know how I lost control like that. All I wanted was to hide, to make myself insignificant so that you wouldn't notice me, and it just got out of hand. That's all."

"Oh, that's all," Aral mocked me. "A wizard with the power of creation handed to you by birth, and you just wanted to be insignificant, that's all. You need to stop dying, Verwyn. It addles you."

"Stop that," I said. "I'm just Agrad. This Verwyn person isn't here."

"Oh, he's there, and he's you," she said, walking over and flopping down on the bed beside me. "Somewhere in there Davri Verwyn, the first of your line, is still a part of you and your fate. After that there were many more. All of them, instigating wars, sowing the seeds of chaos, finding different ways to die so heroically before **she** breaks free and has her way. Sure, you're Agrad, but you've inherited the problems of Davri and all his successors. Give it time and you'll see that I'm most certainly talking to him as well as you."

I wrapped my arms around myself tightly, feeling an invisible weight upon my shoulders. Was this my destiny? Was this my new fate?

PART EIGHT

A ral," Master Tennival said, still gazing out the window. "It's not all as bad as you've made it look; it's not all horror, death, weight and responsibility. It's not all sacrifice."

Aral said nothing, but her silence was far more eloquent than his words. There was pain in that silence, pain she did not want to share with her brother.

"What shall happen now?" I asked, needing to end that silence and the strange and alien empathy that had risen within me.

"You have seventeen years of learning to catch up on," Aral said, patting my shoulder and standing to leave. "I would suggest you don't waste a second of it. There is a carriage awaiting your presence as we speak. Go home, Verwyn. You've overstayed your welcome here."

Master Tennival walked over to me. "You'll be fine," he said softly, patting me on the back, but he wouldn't meet my eyes. "I'm glad you've recovered."

They both left and I heard their voices as soon as the door was shut, but I could not make out what they were saying. Too soon I was left with silence and an empty room and no idea what was ahead of me. I hesitated a bit as I stood, shaky upon my feet for a moment. I found a beautiful dress I knew Master Tennival had to have picked out himself, but I pushed it aside. There was no point. I could wear suits now, just like any other man my age.

I could.

Yet...I didn't want to.

I didn't want anything.

My masquerade was over, but what else did I have? Who was I, beneath all the hiding and being afraid? I had no idea anymore.

"What do I do now?" I whispered to myself.

Put on the dress.

The voice of the goddess had returned. I shivered. "No. I can't do this."

Just wear the thing.

I found myself fingering the lace longingly, but I shook my head. "Well, I can't wear it now that you've told me to. It would be the first step to me losing control again. You tell me what I want to do, and I do it? No. I won't."

You'd rather establish the sort of relationship where you deny yourself just to spite me?

"No?" I was so confused, and I felt manipulated, but now there was nothing I could do that wouldn't be giving in to her suggestions. Getting dressed should never be such a moral dilemma. I was too tired still to worry about what it might lead to down the road, if anything.

I closed my eyes and waited for more commentary from Nalia, but she had gone silent. I sighed and dressed myself, embellishing as necessary for someone of my status. When my worries or doubts over my new status began to overwhelm me I would apply rouge or pull on my gloves or one of a thousand things to busy myself with. When I ran out of things do complete my look I simply walked out the door.

"Lord Verwyn," a handsome man stood on the other side of the door, waiting for me. He bowed formally and then held out his arm like a proper gentleman.

"Thank you, sir," I said in my softest voice as I took his arm.

"I am your servant, sir," he said rather pointedly. "Not the other way around."

"S-sorry," I stumbled.

"Wizards need not apologize to anyone, sir," he said, frowning.

"I'm sorry," I said. It was just an automatic response to criticism, and I cringed when I realized what I'd done.

"I am here to take you home, sir." He guided me down the hall rather forcefully before I could say another word. I was virtually dragged to the awaiting carriage.

I was surprised at first when we headed in what I thought of as the wrong direction. My home, the small room I shared with Ysili, was in the heart of the city. We were clearly driving away from it entirely. The realization that I would never see that room or Ysili again hit me like a punch to the gut. That was no longer home.

All the travel I'd done with Ysili when we'd met was undone by the swiftly turning wheels, carrying me backward along the same road we had traveled. In a mere week's time we passed through Myrenfeld. It had been a much longer journey by foot while trying to hide. And, mere days after that, I was taken to the hill upon which sprawled the castle that was to be my new home.

It's impossible to describe the feeling I had as we crested the final hill and I first saw the Verwyn estate. It was a castle, a palace, a clear and unmistakable seat of government, with people walking around, fixing things, talking in groups and staring at my carriage while trying to appear as if they weren't staring. It was beautiful and it was large and sprawling, with gardens that took up twice as much room as the palace itself. I felt a shiver go through me as we passed through the gate. There was a great deal of magic invested in what looked like a simple fence of wrought iron and hedges.

"Welcome home, Lord Verwyn," the carriage driver called down to me as we approached the courtyard.

My legs were tired and my bottom was sore from sitting so long and from inevitable bumps in the road. The ride had been bouncing and jarring, despite a lush cushioned bench within. Even my shoulders were sore as we came to a stop, and I was so eager to stand again that I threw open the door myself. The footman made a softly disapproving noise as he set a stool down for me. His disapproval was of little consequence; I was on my own feet again.

A man walked up to me, stately and stuffy. "Lord Verwyn, I am Waithe Burdan. I shall be your valet until such time as you see fit to replace me."

"Replace?" I was surprised to hear something like that as part of an introduction. "Why would I--"

"Lord Verwyn!"

I was interrupted by another man approaching, calling out to me as he lithely skipped down the steps toward me. He was an elf, I noticed first of all. He was unlike the northern elves I'd seen in Cairnborough. His hair was straight and dark, like mine, and he was taller than most humans.

"Waithe," the elf said to my valet, "we will discuss this later. Dresses are not that much different from suits, and it would be inappropriate to ask a young woman--"

"I can dress myself if it's such a problem," I said hurriedly.

Waithe's shoulders somehow managed to grow more squared, and he inhaled sharply as if slapped.

"Let the boy learn how the household is run," the elf said, looking strained. "He's not threatening you, and he hardly has call to criticize your job as he's only just arrived."

I was flustered and confused, and I hadn't even taken five steps onto the property. "I'm not sure what the problem is, but we can fix it. If you want to stay, then stay. If you want to leave, then leave."

"Sir," Waithe said, as if I were the most impossible creature to have ever crossed his path. He bowed as if a metal rod had at some point replaced his spine. He turned smartly and stalked away.

"Will he be okay?" I asked the elf.

"For Waithe, that was akin to an armed rebellion," the elf said with something between a grimace and a grin. "It's not much of a welcome, I'm afraid, but welcome home Lord Verwyn."

"Am I ever going to hear my own name again?"

"Eventually." He looked me over and finally nodded as if I'd met some expectation. "I am Byrek Arsat. I have been the regent in the absence of a wizard here, and I will be your instructor." He paused a moment. "Until such time as you see fit to replace me."

I paled. Did everyone here want to leave that much, now that I was here?

"That last bit was a joke," Byrek said, leaning in almost conspiratorially. "You are my ward, technically, until the other wizards are satisfied that you can perform your duties adequately."

I finally took his hand and shook it. "I'll do my best," I said quickly. "Thank you for looking after me."

Byrek didn't smile. He showed me around personally, telling me what each room was for, and his demeanor changed on occasion. Whatever inspired those changes, though, he kept to himself. Still, I could tell there must be a lifetime of memories hiding behind his eyes as he showed me what had been his home. What would now be my home.

I didn't have the courage to ask him if he resented me for it. Instead I simply tried to remember everything he said, until he finally showed me to my own suite and said a bath had been drawn as soon as I'd arrived. He left without another word, and I wondered if I'd ever be able to find my way out of this maze of halls and chambers again.

I needn't have worried. There was always someone around to take me from one place to the next, always someone to tell me where to go and what to do. It took time, but within a week I was being followed to the more important places I had to visit, rather than being led.

Sadly, Waithe did not stay on as my valet. I'm not certain what happened to him. I overheard that what he'd said to me was considered quite the scandal, so I assume that was why he did not remain. I was not consulted on the matter in any way. No other member of the household staff said another personal word in my presence if they knew I was listening. No introductions were made except by job title. Over time I concluded that they were afraid to end up like Waithe. It made every day lonely after the bustle of the boarding house Ysili and I had called home.

"Dear Ysili," I wrote. "I'm so sorry to have disappeared. I am alive. I am fine. Please do not worry about me. I will come back for you some day, when I can, and explain it all. Don't look for me if you still fear the wizards. I am in their hands."

I paid an entire gold favor to the courier to deliver that letter and to bring me a reply. He returned with nothing. The room had been rented to someone else. Ysili had vanished shortly after I had, the room emptied and a tip left to the landlady for her service. That was all I was told.

I wrote to Master Tennival as well, speaking more freely, but his replies were curt and a long time in coming. After the first year I stopped writing anything but official correspondence to other wizards.

"I don't see why I can't just delegate it to you," I complained once, when I was in one of my worse moods.

"Too many things are delegated already," Byrek frowned, giving me a disapproving look that made me squirm. "Wizard business is never to be delegated. Also, you need the practice."

"It's just Requiwyn asking about the weather. Again. Is he obsessed with a little rain?"

"I am not the wizard here, Verwyn." His lips curled into something between a smirk and a smile. "If you would like to try his patience instead of mine, perhaps you should ask him."

Out of sheer frustrated boredom I considered the idea. I tapped my finger on the side of the ink well, considering, but in the end I kept my reply short and to the point. It might be seen as disrespectful, and I'd had lectures enough about formality and tone already. Perhaps wizards would be my equal someday, but for now I was little more than an errant child in their eyes.

Byrek stepped close as I wrote, putting his hand on my shoulder. "Requiwyn has a reason in asking. I'm not sure what it is, but I have answered similar queries in the past."

"You never asked why?"

He shook his head. "I have had other concerns. We all take on our own projects to fill the time."

I nodded, finishing the letter. "What sorts of projects are you working on?"

"Running your country, for one." There was a hint of humor in Byrek's tone, as if he were teasing me about something. "Most of them are of a personal nature. The rest, well, I will tell you when the time is right. For now it is time for you to show me your progress in casting silent spells."

I quailed at the thought. If it had been merely about subvocalization or concentration, I would have figured the trick out on my own before I'd even met Byrek. It was a completely different process from traditional magic, more unwieldy, and requiring a strict control over your thoughts and intentions while casting the spell. After that, the desire for the outcome of the spell had to be intense and driven, letting no other desire become a distraction. And, finally, the spell had to be set aside entirely once cast, or it would linger and take on a life of its own.

"I don't think I can do it," I finally told Byrek in a small voice.

He sat down across the desk from me, looking me in the eyes. "You have already done it poorly, which is why you need to learn to do it correctly."

I knew what he was talking about. The spell that had taken me over when I'd met Aral Kaelwyn. "That wasn't me, though. It was mostly Na--" I stopped myself from saying Nalia's name out loud. "It was the one who gives me my power."

Byrek reached across the desk and took my hands in his. "It was you. You took her power and created a spell to make yourself insignificant, and you kept working the spell until she ended it for you. Agrad, you have to master this so that you do not make such a mistake again."

I looked at his hands. I hadn't noticed that his skin was just a bit darker than mine. Most people in Cairnborough had been pale, and I'd wondered if it had been some sort of a fashion choice to show that they were city dwellers who did not have to toil in the sun. Master Tennival had finally set me straight that skin color was inherited, and he taught me about geography, and how skin color was a gift from the ancient gods depending on how much sun your ancestors had in their homelands. Master Tennival's ancestors had come from cold areas like Anogrin and further north. I wasn't sure where my ancestors had come, but I knew that southern elves came from lands of sand and desert. Southern elves wandered, never burning beneath the sun because of their dark skin, speaking to the spirits of water and growing things so that they could find plenty in a land of scarcity. They were tall and willowy where northern elves were short and angular, dark to trick the sun into mercy on their already darkened skin where their cousins were pale to invite as much warmth as the sun would grace them.

That is a simplistic way of viewing our gifts. Your mind would boggle at the reality behind it.

"Agrad?"

I snatched my hands away and folded them on my lap. "She talks to me," I nearly whispered my confession. "Just now, she...my mind wandered, and I was thinking about skin color. She said I was stupid for how I made the concept so simple. She hates me, Byrek. She hates me. I'm so tired of how little she thinks of me."

"You're still a child," he told me gently. "The way you understand the world will be simple next to a mind like hers for a very long time. It's how they made us. The gods did not create us with a full understanding of their creation at birth, and she just has to deal with that and accept it. You will learn over time."

"She'll just learn more over that time," I said. The idea filled me with gloom over the prospect of continuing with this life while Nalia watched me stumble through it, always a child from her point of view.

"She won't," Byrek said. "She's dead. It's very difficult for the dead to grow or change. In order for her to learn at all, she will have to cooperate with you."

"That'll never happen," I said. "She wants me dead."

"That is why some day you will be greater than she is," Byrek said. "You just have to live long enough to reach that day."

Such an impossible task. Even if Nalia stopped actively seeking my death, and I somehow lived for a very long time, I couldn't imagine a moment I would surpass one of the gods. I dismissed the idea as hyperbole on Byrek's part.

"Did any of the others?" I blurted the question suddenly, as soon as I thought of it, before I lost courage.

Byrek looked at me as if he'd been startled from a daydream.

"Which others? Do what?"

I was twisting the fingers of my gloves, not sure if I wanted to know the answer after all. "Did any other Verwyn hear her voice? Did she talk to the others? Do you know?"

He pursed his lips and stood. "That's enough distraction for today. Last night I asked you to practice turning pages in a book without touching it, and while keeping your tongue still. Show me. If your mouth so much as twitches that's all you'll be doing the rest of today."

Years passed in this manner. Uncomfortable questions were sidestepped. Every day that wasn't a holiday was a day full of lessons about one thing or another. Even days we had to travel to a town here or there, there were lessons to learn and spells to practice on the way and back again. I met with mayors and town councils, shook hands, cast spells, and returned to my carriage for a long ride home. I saw new faces, met new people, but they were there and gone. My only constant companion was Byrek, and the continuous lessons he had to teach.

When Byrek finally said to expect a guest after so long I entertained a sense of giddy excitement despite myself.

"Who?" I demanded eagerly, leaning forward and clutching my hands to my chest.

"Ceolwyn," Byrek said. "He needs to speak with you over formalities of your position and his stewardship over your lands."

I didn't care. It was a break in the monotony. A chance, at last, to socialize. "When?"

"Within the hour, I believe. His herald just arrived and said the rest of the entourage was not far behind. He will want some time to rest from the trip and clean up, I'm sure. You have time."

An hour? Or, perhaps, less than an hour? It was short notice for guests from far off lands, wasn't it? "How long have you known he was planning on coming here?"

Byrek gave me a slightly amused look. "I have known for a few months. I did not want to distract you from your studies and concentration. He will need to see how far you have come."

My stomach churned with nervous excitement, which made me think that perhaps Byrek had been wise to keep such a potential distraction from me. "Fine. I forgive you. This time." I smiled sweetly as I dashed from the room to prepare myself for a guest.

Should I wear a suit this time to show off how far I had come, how much I had changed? No, I decided. It would look artificial and I would be uncomfortable. I still preferred dresses, though I did wear pants when the occasion called for it. I had done so for a week when I arrived before deciding I missed the feel of skirts against my legs and how nice they made me feel. I was comfortable in dresses. Before I even reached my room I had decided upon a formal gown that trailed to the floor even with the high-heeled slippers that so perfectly matched. It didn't matter who was visiting, I told myself. This was a chance to show someone, anyone, how much more beautiful I'd grown over the years of isolation.

You preen for him?

Nalia's voice within my mind scoffed at my choice as I sat to style my long black hair just so. A golden barrette to keep it from my face, with green and aqua ribbons to match my dress.

"I've wanted a reason to wear this dress since the first time I saw it," I murmured into the mirror as I added a few loose braids for texture. "Even you said it makes me look more beautiful than any man has a right to. I'm tired of trying it on for ten minutes, sighing, and putting it away."

Oh, I see. It gives you a sense of power, does it?

I frowned, pausing with my fingers tangled around a braid in progress. "No..."

He still makes you feel powerless. He's a full wizard and you're just the weak link among their ranks. You can't even keep me in check, but you don't want him to beat you to within an inch of your life again. Pretending to be confident, when you're anything but...

I didn't say another word, but I could feel her smug satisfaction as my own doubts grew. When I left my room to formally meet Krecek and invite him to my estate, I was much more subdued. Byrek caught my eye with a concerned frown, but I shook my head and squared my shoulders and strode forward with slow formality.

"Welcome, Ceolwyn," I said with a betraying quaver to my voice as I curtseyed. Krecek looked so tiny, now that I was fully grown. Had he always been so small and fragile looking? He had inspired so much fear that he had towered over me in my memories. How had I not realized he would remain so small? He was still the only half elf I had met, and somehow the blend of elf and human made him seem, well, oddly more delicate than a full-blooded elf. I cleared my throat and continued with false confidence. "I do hope your journey was pleasant."

"Verwyn," he said with a nod to acknowledge my deference without offering one of his own. "I hope you'll pardon my intrusion." He spoke with a subtle ironic undertone to his voice and just a twist of humor. "I'll do my best not to abuse your hospitality."

"I--" I broke off and gestured, stumbling over my thoughts and ideas of what to say. "Please, make yourself at home. Did you find your chambers to your taste?"

"They are exactly how I left them the last time I visited, so yes." His eyes sparkled. "That was before your time, so perhaps I should extend my gratitude to Byrek instead?"

"Perhaps," I said, the sinking ship that was my confidence sprang another hole. "Honestly, I don't even know how many rooms there are, or where any specific chambers might be. I'm not sure five years would be enough to learn where all the doors lead even if I'd had time to try to find them."

When he laughed I thought I saw Byrek visibly relax from the corner of my eye. "I have kept Lord Verwyn busy, I'm afraid. I'm surprised he didn't leave a trail of breadcrumbs to find his way back to his room the first year. Davri was very whimsical when he..." Byrek trailed off and then shook his head as if to dispel an unpleasant memory.

"Yes, he was," Krecek replied softly, looking kind and understanding while I looked on in discomfort at the exchange between the two. They had such a shared history. I had nothing.

"Dinner will be served in an hour," Byrek said, pulling himself straight and resurrecting the formality of the meeting. "I will leave the two of you to renew your acquaintance."

I stood there nervously, watching Byrek walk down the hall away from us. I fought with myself for a moment over calling out to him to come back and act as a buffer between the two of us, but Byrek rarely did anything without purpose, or at least reason, and I knew I'd have to confront Krecek on my own sooner or later.

"How have you been, Agrad?"

"Busy." The first word that had come to me was lonely, but it seemed far too personal to say to him. "Master Arsat really has kept my time well occupied."

"I had no doubt that he would," Krecek said easily, smiling a touch. "He is very practiced with the art of teaching. You are fortunate he has agreed to stay here for so long."

"I am?" I didn't understand what he meant by that. I realized I didn't know much about Byrek's past, or why he had been placed as regent in my lands. "Why is that?"

"Byrek is an old friend," Krecek said with a distance in his eyes. "He taught magic long before the idea of rebellion against the gods had been conceived. Only circumstance kept him from becoming a wizard like the rest of us, but I truly don't think he regrets his absence on that day." As he spoke he guided us to the sitting room, his pace slow and thoughtful. "He taught most of us. The original wizards, I mean. Didn't he tell you?"

I shook my head. "He doesn't talk much about himself or the past. So, does he travel from country to country, teaching and helping out?"

"No," Krecek said, looking me over before continuing. "He will assist with training the new wizards if we find it necessary, but this is his home." His voice went soft and his eyes were thoughtful. "This is not idle gossip to be spread about, but since this is your palace you should understand. Byrek and Davri were very close. Essentially, Davri had all of this constructed for Byrek. If you had any thoughts of removing him from this place, though it is your right, there could be repercussions."

I had stopped as well, taking those words very seriously. "There is no need to threaten me. If this is his home, this is his home. I'll only rule here. Some day. Perhaps. If you find me worthy."

I let the bitterness I felt creep into my voice with those last few words and resumed walking, sitting down upon the nearest chair and crossing my arms before me.

Oh, yes, that is certain to convince him that you are ready.

I scowled, nearly telling Nalia to shut up, but Krecek was suddenly in front of me, hand on my arm, looking quite concerned.

"What is it?" he asked, so much closer to me than I could stand.

"I don't know," I said, pulling away from his touch. "I suppose I just don't see the point in this. You have some connection to a past that doesn't belong to me, and you look at me as if you expect me to be like every Verwyn before me. I'm not. I never will be. They may have been your friends, but we could never be. Every memory you evoke in me is an unpleasant one."

His emerald eyes narrowed, but he nodded and backed away. "I'm only concerned with the control you have over your powers, of course. After last time--"

"What happened in Cairnfeld will never happen again."

"Can you be certain?" He sat down too near me, examining me closely. "I could feel it, when--"

I cut him off with a glare. "Yes, fine! Her presence is strong. She speaks to me. I don't think that could ever be reversed. However, I am dealing with it, and we have reached a sort of a truce, and that is the best I can do about it."

"You sound insane," Krecek said. "I've never heard a voice from within. None of us have. I control the magic; it does not control me. You are the only one who has ever been like this."

He's wrong. Nalia projected the thought within my mind, and I echoed her words and the further knowledge she gave me. "You're wrong," I said. "Davri heard the voice of the goddess. Every Verwyn has. She says that it drove some of them mad, and some of them even welcomed death to silence her, just as you must have suspected. They kept the truth from you to keep you from thinking less of them, or to keep you from being afraid. I suppose that's an advantage I have over them. I don't particularly care enough of your opinion of me to feel the need to lie."

"You believe lies whispered to you from the enemy," Krecek pursed his lips.

"Who else am I to believe?" I said. "You? If anyone has been my enemy, it is you."

Krecek glared and I felt a crackle of power in the air. We

were both tense, waiting for the other to make some sort of move, giving an excuse to give in to our emotions. Krecek finally stood and walked across the room stiffly, staring outside through the window at the darkening sky without looking at me. "Others will be arriving over the next few days. Aral and a few of the newer wizards."

"You mean elementals?"

"If you wish," Krecek shrugged, but did not turn to look at me. "Some take offense to the term, so keep that in mind."

"Oh."

"We are here to assess your competence and control. I hope that you will understand when I advise against letting you rule your lands in any way but in name."

I found it didn't matter to me, except that it would disappoint Byrek if he thought it was any fault of his. "I never asked for this," I said, leaning back and closing my eyes. "Any of it. Advise what you wish."

What do you think will happen to you, if you do not rule?

I didn't care. I'd never exactly felt entitled to these lands, nor beholden to the responsibilities. If Byrek could run everything better than I could, well, that was fine with me. It was his home more than it would ever be mine, after all.

You're not concerned that they will imprison you, or worse?

No. I wasn't. I opened my eyes and looked over at Krecek, still gazing out the window. He already had me imprisoned within these walls. It was a luxurious cell, of course, but I'd never entertained the illusion that I was free to come and go or do anything without his or Byrek's consent. He wasn't going to kill me, at least. He'd said I could rule in name. That meant I would remain here, just as powerless as I'd always been. I was used to that. I could endure.

You were meant for greater things. These words were subdued, as if she had hesitated saying them to me.

Something interesting had caught my attention, distracted me from any response I might have given. Krecek had flinched when Nalia had spoken.

I think he's still afraid of me, she mused. *After all this time.*

I wondered if it was her in specific or any of the gods, but she gave no further response. He had shuddered and clenched his fists, and I nearly asked him why, but Byrek returned with his stern disapproval at our silence. He maintained a thread of meaningless dialogue through dinner, engaging Krecek and lightening the mood somewhat. However, when I was asked any question my replies were curt, and I pushed food around on my plate rather than eat it.

The moment the meal was finished I squared my shoulders and took my leave. "Rest well," I said as I turned and walked from the room.

He may have said something in return, but I was already gone. As soon as I turned the corner I kicked off my shoes and I ran to my room, locking the door behind me. I trembled as suppressed emotion overtook me. Memories had finally surfaced, playing before my eyes as vividly as if I were living them again. I stood against the closed door, leaning against it with my eyes squeezed shut and my hands over my ears. I could hear the final screams of my dead parents echo through my mind. I could feel the crushing pain and screaming abrasions from being thrown around and kicked and beaten.

Even Nalia was overwhelmed by the memories that flooded my mind. *Stop it,* she begged within at the height of my memories. It snapped me back into the present at once.

"Nalia," I whispered her name in near silence, wiping the tears from my eyes. Even that utterance of her true name sent a ripple of magic power to echo through the room. Her attention was sharp and focused as it was brought to bear upon me.

You've never said my name aloud before.

It was true. Her name had only passed my lips once. That had not been me, however. It had been her, using me as a puppet, wearing my skin and using me, but it was not me. It was a discomforting realization. I'd avoided her name, until now.

"Why did you want me to stop?" I whispered. "You've always seemed so amused by my pain and discomfort, entertained by my misery."

What something seems to be is not always what it is. Oh, there have been times where your petty problems seem so small as to be laughable, but despite your pain you usually refuse to suffer.

It took me a bit to understand what she meant by that. I'd always hidden my emotions deep inside, avoiding them because they were, and always would be, too much for me to cope with. I thought as I struggled to shove them aside more completely, and I realized.

"You feel whatever I feel. Every hurt. Every pain."

And every pleasure, she added. *Not that you've allowed yourself much of that, either.*

"What call have I had for pleasure?" I laughed just a bit, but it was without mirth.

She was right. I hadn't spent my entire life depressed and dwelling on every unfortunate event, but I hadn't sought out the things that brought me joy. From the perspective of a goddess who must have reveled in indulgence, my life would have seemed stark. My greatest moments were those brief glimmers where I forgot my constant fear. I'd never been particularly close to anyone, even Master Tennival and Ysili. I'd never let go and given in to a night of wild abandon. I'd never fallen in love, or any of those thousands of other things poets extol.

You're still young. You will find these things someday.

It was some comfort. I nodded and picked myself up from

where I'd crumpled on the floor. I undressed slowly while I mulled these things over. My suffering had been shared. I'd hurt her by being in pain. I set my beautiful gown aside with a wistful smile, thinking of how my greatest pleasure in the last five years had been in finding something beautiful to wear. How silly my life must be. How small.

I washed my face and brushed out my hair, staring into the mirror. I usually avoided my reflection when I was undressed. My chest was hairless, but flat enough that there was no mistaking me for a girl without the ruffles and frills I hid beneath. My shoulders were broad and my dresses had to flare at the waist a great deal in order to balance them. My skin wasn't as pale as Krecek's or Ysili's, but it was perhaps paler than anyone else I'd seen with an olive complexion like mine. It wasn't fashionable to be dark skinned, but no amount of avoiding the sun would ever bring me to what society considered ideal. My hair, however, granted enough of a contrast as to still make me a striking figure. It had been curly when I'd been a child, but now the black tresses were perfectly straight. It didn't matter most of the time since I wore it styled like a proper lady, but here in the dim light of my room, stripped of all my artifice, I was just a frail boy with a too-pretty face.

I turned away abruptly, pulling my hair back into a ponytail at the nape of my neck, deciding I couldn't stay in my room a moment longer. I found pants in my wardrobe and threw them on quickly. The thought of wearing one of my dresses rubbed my already raw emotions, making my heart constrict. I needed out of this room, away from the disguises and the layers and the barriers that I wore every day. My usual clothes were overwhelming, my own room was stifling, and even my very own skin was uncomfortable to bear.

The corridors and halls were left alight for my guests, but

brightness did not suit my mood. I walked out to the garden, feeling like I could finally breathe when I saw the dark vastness and bright pinpricks of light that was the night sky. One of my predecessors, or perhaps Byrek himself, had grown a rather simplistic hedge maze. It was tall enough to block my view of everything but the sky, with plenty of twists and turns to hide in, but not so labyrinthine as to present any hazard of getting lost. In the center was a reflecting pool, and tonight I went straight toward that rather than one of the hidden dead ends. The pool allowed just enough space that I did not feel enclosed or trapped. When I reached the reflecting pool, I knew I'd chosen the perfect spot for my mood. The sky was at my feet as well as overhead, and I walked out onto the calm surface, leaving not a ripple in my wake. I was perfectly balanced with eternity above me and below me. It didn't take much magic to let the shallow water be untouched by my presence upon it. I just let the magic happen and became one with the darkness for a time.

I stood there, staring up into the void, trying to shut out every thought that threatened to come. I was still overwhelmed by sadness and I tried to let that sadness drift from me into the darkness. I don't know how long I stood in that spot, hoping for some sort of release. It was for nothing. The ache that surrounded my heart would not be appeased.

I slid to my knees, turning my eyes downward to the reflections beneath me. Still, there was nothing. No answer. No release.

Nothing.

I heard a sound and ripples scattered the stars beneath me. I went perfectly still, holding my breath, scrambling to retain my peace of mind.

"Who are you?"

The words were barked at me as if I were the intruder here.

"Leave me be!" I tried to sound commanding, but my voice came out in a raw whisper. My pain was so close to the surface still. I glared, trying to warn off the intruder.

Krecek strode through the shallow water, intent. "No. Who--"

He reached for me and I felt like a caged animal. I was tense, ready to spring at him, to fight him off physically if I had to. My hand shot out to deflect his, to push him away and open an escape, but he easily grabbed my wrist and pulled me off balance. The magic I'd so casually used to remain untouched by the water was stripped from me in an instant. I splashed into the water, sprawling awkwardly at his feet. He pinned me down effortlessly, all the while maintaining a slightly puzzled, curious expression.

"Agrad?"

PART NINE

The surprise in Krecek's voice stunned me into momentary silence. Finally, I nodded. Who else would have been here, in my garden, in the middle of the night?

"I didn't recognize you without your finery," he chuckled, releasing me and stepping back, unconcerned with the water soaking into our clothes in the chill of the night air.

I closed my eyes, despising him for my humiliating defeat on top of everything else. I lay still in the water, half-heartedly hoping that it would turn suddenly deep enough to swallow me whole and hide me. "What are you doing here?" I moaned.

"It's always been my favorite place on your estate," Krecek said. "It reminds me of old friends and places I used to call home. There was a reflecting pool similar to this at--never mind. You didn't ask to hear about the past."

I sat up and I looked up at him and began to wring the water out of my ponytail. "All I wanted was to find some peace." My eyes itched with threatening tears.

"As was I," he said. "This is a perfect spot for it, most of the time."

"I've never found it here. I doubt it can be found at all."

Krecek sat down before me with a nearly apologetic smile. "I didn't expect you to be here," he said. "I certainly didn't expect you to be half naked and looking so very unlike yourself. I thought you'd be holed up in your quarters, avoiding me."

"If I'd been smart I would have," I said. My flowing gray pants were clinging uncomfortably to my legs, and I picked at folds and wrinkles in distaste. "No one ever comes out here."

"That's one reason I enjoy it." Krecek looked thoughtful for a moment. I could see the moment he decided to continue talking, and his voice was gentle when he did. "This was one spot that was truly Davri's. When he died Byrek told me he could never bring himself to return. Every Verwyn since has found solace here. I should not have been surprised to find you here." He hesitated just a bit longer before adding one more thing. "I should have left you to it."

I silently agreed, but the damage was already done. My emotional state was cracking at the edges, and his kindness was not helping in the least.

"Agrad," he said, moving closer, "you won't be able to avoid me forever. We used to be friends. We used to be closer than anyone else. Davri was--"

"Davri is dead," I interrupted. "And you've given me precious little reason to tolerate you, let alone be your friend."

"I am not who you think I am," he said, gently touching my arm with his cold fingertips. "I am not your enemy."

"You are," I whispered harshly. "You k-killed them. You said you were my friend, and you killed them, and you-you h-hurt me." The tears were coming, along with sobs and trembling and everything that accompanies such overwhelming pain.

"Oh Agrad," he sighed, looking tragic. "I wish I could have spared you all of that. More than you can know."

"I hate you," I said without conviction. "I hate you so much I could die." The words only hurt me further, tearing my raw and aching emotions into chaos. "Everything about you." The tears finally flowed, and with them a low keening as words lost their ability to express the depth of my suffering. "I hate it." I'd searched for this release alone, but only found it now as my greatest enemy sat before me as witness to my greatest moment of weakness.

Krecek held me, consoling me and whispering gentle words as I wept. In turn I clung to him as a lost child would, sobbing into his shoulder. I hated him more for being there at my weakest. I wept for my parents in the arms of the one who had killed them. I cried for the friends I'd lost on the shoulder of the one who had taken them away. I hated him so much it consumed me like the black night around me, but the darkness could not be maintained.

"If you need to hate me, then hate me," he whispered at one point. "I understand."

He sounded as heartbroken as I felt. My chest took a sudden, involuntary but tiny breath, akin to a sob. I had to hate him, didn't I?

Eventually I fell silent, sitting in perhaps a foot of water, ripples spreading from me with every breath, making the sky tremble around me and setting the stars in the heavens to dance. It was so very bright, in a way. This velvety blackness that was torn by a million suns around which many millions of planets like this one turned. It was something Nalia had shown me once, to make me feel small. It had worked for a while, but then I fell into the wonder of it all.

Just like the darkness had consumed me tonight, but now I felt the wonder of so much light.

I dipped my hands in the water and splashed my face to wash away the tears. Krecek helped me stand, keeping an arm around me when I stumbled, supporting me all the way back into my room. I was so tired that I let him help me change into dry clothes, and I stayed with him while he did the same. I must have looked pathetic, because he guided me to bed and sat with me, stroking my hair while I curled up against him.

"I'll hate you again in the morning," I said. "I'm just too tired to right now."

"I'll give you reason to hate me in the morning," Krecek said with something that sounded like humor, but also weary resignation.

"Don't," I said, closing my eyes at last. It was the last I remembered of that night. I may have hated him, but something inside me whispered that I needed him. And I could never hate him as much as I hated myself for just how good it felt to be held by him that night.

In the morning I was alone with my anxieties. Even Nalia was silent, though her pensive mood tinged my own thoughts as I went about my day. Byrek and Krecek were locked away in some room together, either to reminisce or to plot against me. Neither would surprise me.

Two carriages arrived later that morning and I met Shaelek Eudwyn and Modarian Lorwyn at the gates. My restlessness had driven me to slight impatience, but neither of them seemed to mind. The carriages were parked and we walked the rest of the distance together as if we were old friends. I wanted to warm immediately to Modarian as I realized I recognized his carriage and colors. A closer look confirmed that he was the other wizard I had met in my childhood, the one who had given me coin for simple directions. He was the one who had left me the book of simple spells, who had hidden me from the rest. I wanted to thank him. He held back and let the other dominate the conversation, however.

"I've been eager to meet you," Shaelek said with a bright smile and infectious enthusiasm. She was nearly the same height as I was and muscular, wearing clothes for comfort rather than appeal, and walking like a natural warrior. My first impression was that she could break me in two, but her easygoing nature invited me to relax in her presence. "We're nearly the same age, and I've heard about the missing Verwyn

as if he was my long-lost brother for as long as I can remember."
She winked.

"Just Agrad, please," I said. "I didn't know who or what I was
for so long that it's hard to think that this Verwyn person they
go on at length about is me."

"Well, don't worry about all that," she said. "It's quite a lot to
adjust to, even being taught everything from childhood.
Modarian and I are both elementals as well, so we know a bit
about how hard it must be."

Modarian grumbled. "Shaelek, don't be vulgar. We've got just
as much right to be called wizards as the ones who fought in the
Arcane War. More, perhaps, since we've had this power our
entire lives and they did not."

Shaelek rolled her eyes. "Don't listen to him. He's old. He's
one of the first elementals to have been born. And you can't take
offense to me using the word if I'm one as well, Modarian
Lorwyn! It's not an insult if we say it about ourselves."

Modarian looked mildly irritated, but simply shook his head.

"Krecek did warn me the term could be offensive," I said
neutrally.

"That's sweet of him," Shaelek said. "I wouldn't worry about
it, though. I think it's a badge of pride, personally. It sets us
apart and lets the world know that we're meant to have this
power. Modarian will get over it eventually. Now, tell me every
detail of what it's like to have a normal life, especially in a city
like Cairnborough. Did you have many friends? Did you get to
buy your own clothes and cook your own food?"

It startled me that she was interested in such mundane
details, but as we entered the foyer I began recounting some of
them. Modarian hesitated a bit and then joined our conversation
with questions of his own. I was surprised by their enthusiasm
and the nature of some of their questions.

"I didn't think I could get away with using magic," I

explained after she'd asked about how I'd kept my room tidy without a maid or valet. "I was afraid I'd be caught and killed if I did. So, no. I just picked up as I went along. I didn't have much in the way of possessions to keep tidy after all. It wasn't hard at all."

"I'd be a mess without my maid," Shaelek said with somewhat of a dramatic flair. "I never have any time for details like that, and there's always so much on my mind at one time or another. It's a relief to leave the little things to someone else so that I can concentrate on what's important."

Modarian shrugged. "I prefer doing whatever I can for myself, honestly. It is not an onerous task to tidy as you go, and menial tasks help me think."

"Exactly!" I smiled at Modarian, glad to find common ground with him. "I couldn't maintain this entire castle and keep up with my studies or all of the practice I must do, but picking up after myself makes me feel productive and helpful."

"It just seems pointless to me," Shaelek waved a hand dismissively. "What did you do the whole time, though? For money, I mean. Was it hard to live with so little?"

I looked at her, puzzled. "I had everything I needed. I always had enough, and just a bit more. I modeled for an artist, Master Tennival. He was very generous. Toward the end I was earning nearly a gold favor a year! I didn't know what to do with so much."

Shaelek and Modarian exchanged a look. "That's all? One favor? For an entire year?"

I shrugged. "It was more than enough for me. I never missed a meal, and I could buy a new dress whenever I wanted. I once bought six dresses in a year. I felt guilty for being so indulgent, though." They were still looking at me amusedly, but I understood why. The currency all had reasons for what they were called; nubs for being small, wheels because one side had lines that looked like spokes on a wheel, stars because one side had a star. Favors were different, though. There was no depiction or consistent description for them. Gold favors were extremely rare, and there was a personal irony because they were a literal favor owed by a wizard. They were worth one hundred silver stars, and if I had saved up enough of the silver coins I could have petitioned any wizard of my choosing. Of course, I had never wanted to. Why would I want to bring such attention to myself?

And now, of course, I would never need that sort of currency. I could literally commission my own once I was granted full power, with my own profile stamped upon them, and keep them like a miser or spread them far and wide until they meant nothing at all. Most people could not afford to use the coins as anything but currency, but someday it would be expected of me to grant such favors as currency demanded.

"I still think Master Tennival was being stingy with you," Shaelek said. "Wasn't he? I mean, so many people every year hand those to me that I wonder. I've started taking some out of circulation, just for privacy. And I've heard that Krecek hands out the least of them all, but the economy in Ceolwyn is still very strong."

"You'll find your balance," Modarian assured her with a pat on the shoulder. "The previous Eudwyn was a bit, shall I say, overly generous. Removing a few will probably help a great deal."

New favors hadn't been minted in Verwyn in a very long time, I mused. In all this time, there had only been a handful of years, a decade or so at best, for the favors to be brought to an actual wizard. Byrek admitted that he had, on rare occasion, granted them himself. I suspected most favors in Verwyn were actually foreign. I'd never heard of anyone in Myrenfeld possessing one, but people there had bartered more than they'd spent.

"Well," I said softly, "do either of you have advice for me, for when I have to do that sort of thing?"

An uncomfortable silence fell for a minute before Modarian shook his head. "Shouldn't you worry about getting past the next few days before you consider how you want to run the economy? My advice won't change between now and then, if you still want it when this is over."

Shaelek gave me an apologetic look before she spoke. "He has a point. It's been very nice meeting you, Agrad. I look forward to getting to know you, but it's been a long journey. We'll see ourselves to our rooms. They'll be the same as the last time we were here."

"Oh, of course," I said to their retreating backs. Their abrupt departure stung and left the rest of the day sour. Tsevric Aledwyn arrived that afternoon, but I did not feel up to socializing beyond welcoming him to my castle, and he seemed inclined to keep the encounter just as simple. He informed me that Aral would arrive the next morning and she would be the last one to bother to show up.

So, that was it. Those five were to determine my fate. I spent the rest of the day with the sinking dread that it had already been decided.

Aral arrived in the middle of the night and disappeared into a meeting with the others before I woke up. She joined me for lunch and looked me over without betraying any expression for an unnerving amount of time.

I inwardly sighed and offered as much of a smile as I could. "Hello, Aral. I'm sorry I couldn't have welcomed you properly."

She shrugged and sat down casually. "I wanted to avoid fuss and formalities. This isn't the sort of thing I ever thought I'd have to do, and I would like to just get it over with. How have you been, Agrad?"

My food stopped interesting me at all. "Byrek has kept me very busy. I haven't had much time to be anything."

"You've been lonely enough to consort with the enemy, from what Krecek has told us." A plate was set before her and wordlessly she was served. Aral ignored the matter except to start buttering a slice of bread. "You have no idea just how dangerous that is."

"On the contrary," I said. "I think I know more than you do. She wants me dead, and she wants her revenge as much as she wants her freedom. I am not exactly willing to grant her any of those, and with that understanding we have managed to grow civil."

"Do you even know which goddess you have within you?"

"Yes," I said. "Do you?"

Aral stiffened. "I was there. I watched her die, and I was glad of it after what she had done. I suppose she has not told you any of that? It's not something you will find in any history."

I shook my head, frowning. "It's not a subject that has ever come up."

"Just know that I will never forgive her," Aral said. "And as long as she has any power over a mere child like you, I can't trust you."

"I'm an adult now," I snapped, peeved.

"You are a child," Aral enunciated each word precisely, nearly turning each word into its own sentence. "I am three hundred and seventy-four years old. Krecek is at least a century older than I am. Byrek taught our fathers and their fathers before them. You are barely into your twenties. From the perspective of the rest of us, it's amazing you're not still spitting up on a bib."

I stood and walked away, refusing to prove her right by screaming a denial.

Paltry numbers, Nalia rebutted silently as I walked. *She's still young enough to think her precious numbers mean a thing, but gods have known since the world was young that numbers are not age.*

"I don't understand," I whispered to myself. "Why wouldn't the number of years you've seen be the same as your age? That doesn't make any sense. Isn't that the very definition of age?"

Numbers measure time. Time itself is, in this particular measure, linear and rigid. It indicates your potential for learning, but it may have nothing to do with what you have learned. You've had more experience and more chances to grow than that wizard gives you credit for.

"So, I'm not really a baby, like she said?" The thought made me a bit smug.

I wouldn't go that far.

Well, of course. It only made sense. I'd have to be old and ancient before I'd be taken seriously, and by that time the others would be older and even more ancient. It was hopeless.

You're still thinking linear. Time is a measure of what happens when, not what you've experienced and how you've grown. How you fill that time is fluid, and within you is the power of the goddess of all magic. Time is something I could bend. Something I could break, if I wished. It amazes me how much you limit yourself.

"I'd call it restraint," I said, but it wasn't. "Fine, it would be restraint if I had the faintest notion of how to do all of those things." I stopped, leaning against the nearest wall with some expression of exasperation.

I could teach you.

"I can't trust you." I closed my eyes. "You would see me destroyed to win your freedom. I rather like being alive and not condemned for something I had no choice over."

I had no choice, either. Her tone was thoughtful and more

sympathetic than I had ever known. *I think I would not be averse to making the best of a bad situation. I have had over three centuries to mull this over.*

"How do you mean?"

I grow tired of dying, Agrad. Every death of a Verwyn has been my death as well. If I could assure my freedom with your death I would take it, but I am beginning to think that that is impossible. There was a hesitation in the stream of her thoughts and then I felt some emotion leaking from her that seemed like hope tempered with a hint of trepidation. *I would rather work together, if you think we could.*

She wouldn't have offered if she thought it was impossible. Either that or she had reached a point of desperation. I couldn't think of anything to make her feel desperate, however. Was she offering because I was young and impressionable? Or could it be that she'd seen something else in me? There was no way to know.

"I still don't think I can trust you." I said.

I'm not asking you to trust me. I'm asking you to learn from me. You could be the most powerful wizard of all time.

"That's great for me," I said hesitantly. "What do you expect out of it?"

Peace, she said, and her mind seemed completely open to me for a moment, enforcing her sincerity.

Just peace. It was a motive I could understand. It was an option to ponder while I paced the halls and my captors decided my fate.

I looked around the room, feeling uncomfortably on the spot now that I'd finally been invited. Two of the original wizards and three elementals of various ages looked me over,

156

scrutinizing me like some sort of a bug. They'd asked questions, so many questions, about such inconsequential things, until I felt ready to scream. Then, after what felt like forever, came the thoughtful and judging silence.

Aral's mind seemed to be already made up. She was looking around the room at everyone else, frowning, shifting impatiently. Her eyes did not meet mine the entire time. Whatever she had in mind, I had a feeling it would not be to my benefit.

Tsevric was still as stone, eyes either upon me or upon the ground before his feet, clearly weighing his thoughts with care. He hadn't asked many questions of me, and I'd started taking a bit of a liking to his silence. Now, however, it was getting a bit unnerving. I had no way of guessing what sort of a conclusion he might have come to about my future.

Shaelek nudged Tsevric's meaty arm and gestured toward Krecek for some reason. Tsevric shrugged his broad shoulders and gave a half-hearted nod a moment later. Shaelek then looked at me, looking both worried and guilty until she realized my eyes were upon her. She met my eyes and smiled reassuringly, but she looked away too quickly and began to tap her fingers on the table.

Modarian watched her, looking more thoughtfully at her than he did at me. I didn't think he'd needed to think about his decision much either. He didn't look guilty, though, or impatient. He was watching in the way that I was watching. He was reading the decisions unfold upon their faces just as I was.

And then there was Krecek. I was reluctant to look at him for even a moment. The questions he'd asked had been the most searching and the most personal. He terrified me more by the moment, and when I finally met his gaze his smile was almost smug.

"He isn't ready," Krecek stated abruptly, ending the silence. "I think we can all agree with that."

"Byrek has done a much better job than I expected," Aral said.

Tsevric nodded, stroking his beard as the thoughts clearly still played about his head. "A very fine job, indeed. It is not the elf's fault that Agrad's training has been so stunted."

"I'm less worried about his training," Modarian said. "What concerns me, and should concern the rest of you, is his lack of confidence and maturity."

"He's been damaged," Shaelek said, casting an accusing glare in Krecek's direction. "He fears us and resents us, you know."

Krecek held his hands up in a gesture of surrender. "This is not the time or place for blame. What has been done has been done, and all we can do is figure out how best to handle the situation now."

Tsevric leaned back, eyes moving to look upward. I waited for him to say something, but no words followed his motion as I'd thought it would.

"I'm not placing blame," Shaelek said after a few moments, almost peevish and certainly aggressive. "I simply think it's clear as to who should shoulder the brunt of the responsibility in this matter."

"It certainly wouldn't be you," Aral drawled, leaning forward in her seat. "You've just managed to get your own feet on the ground, Eudwyn. We wouldn't want to shake up your precious routine just as you've found it."

Shaelek turned bright red, reaching to her side as if to draw a sword that wasn't there. Aral's chin lifted and her eyes narrowed, daring the younger girl to come at her. I thought they would fight for a moment, until Modarian put a restraining hand on Shaelek's shoulder and shook his head.

"I agree with Shaelek, threats aside," Krecek said, once the tension had lessened. "The conspiracy began in my country, under my watch. I am the one who trusted Torba and Fadal. I am the one who found them again, thanks to Donab, and I am the one who--"

Krecek's words ended abruptly as his gaze fell upon me. Torba and Fadal. My mother and father. I felt the blood drain from my head, and I realized I was trembling. I hadn't heard their names in so long I'd almost forgotten them.

"I think Agrad should stay with me," Krecek said, voice devoid of intonation, face devoid of expression. "He will be under my supervision until such a time as I see fit. I will be responsible for mentoring him, as well as--"

"No," I said, standing on unsteady feet. "No, not you. Not you!"

"As well as teaching him some self-control," he finished.

"I won't go anywhere with you!"

I was ignored as the others nodded, murmuring in agreement.

"Hopefully," Krecek added in a softer tone, "I will be able to use this opportunity to make reparations for the past. Things can't go on like this."

"You don't believe him, do you?" I was looking around the room on the verge of panic, looking for one dissenting opinion, one inkling of an idea that would spare me from this proposed hell. "Please! He's...he's a murderer.... He...he murdered...my...my...."

My words fell on deaf ears. The room cleared and only Aral had made any attempt to console me or calm me. She stood before me and put a hand on my cheek as a mother might do, and she shook her head. "It's for the best, Agrad." Her hand trailed down my cheek gently just before she walked away and left the room.

I sat down heavily in the nearest chair, staring straight ahead.

I floated in numb disbelief.

They couldn't do this.

I was an elemental. I was one of the most powerful beings in the world! Who were they to tell me what I could and could not do? Who were they to decide? A mere handful of my peers! Didn't they understand that Krecek was my mortal enemy? That couldn't be safe! That couldn't be right!

Krecek cleared his throat, reminding me that he had not yet left me. He watched me with that unnerving lack of expression until he knew he had my attention.

"I'll tell Byrek to pack your favorite dresses. We should leave tomorrow."

"Leave?"

Was that my voice, sounding so broken and vulnerable?

"You have no choice, Agrad. It's been decided. You can't stand against us all, not if you expect to ever have your freedom again."

My freedom.

I'd never have freedom again.

When the silence stretched too long Krecek simply left me alone in the room with my thoughts.

If only he'd known what they were.

Where will you go?

There was no fooling Nalia. She could feel my need to flee as if it were her own. We were both terrified to be so completely in his power. We couldn't let it happen.

We couldn't.

"I don't know."

PART TEN

Byrek was supervising the packing of my items when I returned to my room. He had set aside a dress for me to travel in that was comfortable and thankfully easy to move in. I nodded in approval and sat on my bed, watching as the life I'd built here was so swiftly cleared away and placed in a chest and a couple of bags. I hadn't made an impression on this place at all, I realized as the last of it was packed away and everyone but Byrek left.

"I suppose packing away one elemental's belongings has become a commonplace event," I said.

Byrek had started to leave, but he stopped and turned to look at me instead. "Too commonplace," he agreed simply.

"I want to be the last," I said. "Packing. Exile. It just seems so wrong, like an insult to the Verwyn name. I know I didn't seem too invested in my position, but now.... I don't want to be erased so easily. Not after so little time."

He looked me over and finally nodded with the slightest of smiles. "I'm glad you've started to feel like that. You came here so certain that you were only Agrad, and that's all you had to be." He gestured around us, smile growing as he did so. "You're accepting that you can be Verwyn as well, without losing yourself. You'll return to us."

"You're staying?" I hadn't thought about if he would stay by my side, or what he would do if I left. He'd become like my shadow, or my other arm. I wasn't sure if I could do this without him.

"I've run the country of Verwyn longer than anyone else has. It's nearly as much mine as it is yours. Don't worry, it's in capable hands."

I felt awkward for a moment, but I gave in to an impulse to hug the old elf. "It's a relief, but I think I'll miss you. I didn't realize I would."

He patted me on the back and pulled away. "Then work all the harder to return. This is your home. This is where you belong. When you're ready, no force in nature will be able to keep you away."

I nodded, comforted by his words, smiling despite my pain.

There was a knock at the door, interrupting anything further. Shaelek stood in the open doorway, shifting uncomfortably from foot to foot.

"I'll be leaving immediately," she said. "I just received word that there's a storm brewing in Eudwyn that I need to take care of personally."

"I'll alert the stables," Byrek said, hurrying from the room.

Shaelek moved to follow, but I hurried to stop her. "Wait! Do you have time for a word or two?"

"I'm not changing my mind, my vote, or my advice, Agrad Verwyn. I have reasons for what I said in there, so don't start trying to persuade me." She kept walking, refusing to even look at me.

"It's not that!" I hurried behind her, nearly running to catch her elbow and get her to pause a moment. "Please. Before you leave, I wanted to ask you something. This might be my last chance."

Shaelek stopped abruptly, searching my face closely before finally nodding. "Go ahead, but make it short."

Short? I flailed my arms a bit, trying to think how I could condense all the things I needed to know about being an elemental into what she might agree to as short. "I, well, okay. You're the only elemental I've met who really seems willing to talk to me. So I'll just ask, and if it's rude, impolite, or too abrupt, just keep in mind you're the one who told me to keep it short."

She rolled her eyes and snorted in good humor. "Go ahead. You have until I reach my quarters."

What was the one question I wanted to know from her the most? I thought a moment as we started walking once again. "Am I really the only one like this?"

"Like what?" Shaelek returned impatiently. "Remembering your parents? Being given a chance to be normal? Dressing as the wrong gender? If it's that last one, believe me I've been thinking a lot about it for myself. Dresses are so cumbersome and get in the way. I don't know how you can stand them."

I smiled. "No, none of that. You'd be striking in a suit, though."

"I would, wouldn't I? Maybe I'll try it. I could cut my hair short and carry a sword, and no one could tell me not to."

"Why would they?" I hesitated a step. "I've never had anyone tell me not to, or so much as give me a strange look for dressing however I want."

"You're very pretty, Agrad." Shaelek stopped in the middle of the hall, looking at me quizzically. "I don't think you realize quite how pretty. When you wear a dress you look like a lady of status and power, very proper, and beyond question. I was told that you hired a tailor to make your dresses, so of course he knew the truth and would never be so uncouth as to question you. A tailor is a professional, after all. As for wizards and elementals, we simply don't care about such things as what you wear. All we care about is if you're sane and able to do your job."

"Oh." I hadn't really thought of that. Did I never attract scorn before because no one had guessed my actual gender? And now, simply because as an elemental, I was above the common reproach?

"Still, I think if I wore pants from now on, it wouldn't cause

163

too much of a stir. Not just because I'm an elemental, but because I truly would look stunning, don't you think?"

"Isn't that what I already said?" I smiled weakly. "But, back to what you said before. About me being sane. Does that mean you think that I'm not?"

"I don't know," Shaelek said, turning and walking once again. "I just know that you don't act like the rest of us. Not that we have a uniform set of behaviors. I think that each of us are eccentric at most."

"What about--" I hesitated over the words slightly, walking half a step behind her. "What about, well, that I talk to--"

"That's just the wizards being a bit paranoid, if you ask me." Shaelek shook her head. "All of us, sometime around puberty, start hearing hints and whispers in the backs of our heads. We're trained to ignore it, or just not to talk about it, but every elemental hears the voice of the source of our power to some degree or another."

"How did you find out that the others do as well?"

"Modarian," she said, a hint of softness and caring creeping into her voice as she said his name. "He mentored me, and he seems to have a knack for knowing things that no one else does. I asked him when I first had troubles with it, because the whisperings that came to me were so dark. He was kind and explained that much to me, so I would know I was not losing my mind. I'd started having nightmares full of death and dying, and he let me know it was only natural since my house, Eudwyn, gained power from the god of death."

"I'm sure," I said, hesitating as we reached her door. "It's been difficult enough with Nalia existing within my own mind. I can't imagine what it would be like with Baedrogan--"

Shaelek cut me off by clamping a hand over my mouth. "Don't say his name," she hissed between clenched teeth. "No one is supposed to know that name. How do you know it?"

My eyes went wide in a rush of instinctual fear. She looked so very dangerous in that moment, as if I'd undone something that had held her darker side at bay. Had I broken some sort of control over what she had within her, even momentarily? "I won't say his name again," I said, pulling her hand away carefully. "I'm sorry. I didn't mean to upset you."

She glared at me, eyes narrowed down to slits. The helpful caring she'd projected all along was gone utterly, and I felt like I was seeing the real her for the first time. "You're just like that bitch of a goddess," Shaelek's voice was full of hate. "She deserved what Davri did to her, and she deserves to suffer with an ignorant weakling like you."

I could only stare in shock as she entered her chambers, slamming the solid door behind her with a resounding thud.

That last bit was pure Baedrogan, Nalia said, and her mental tone sounded equal parts exasperated and amused. *He hated me by the end. Hadn't spoken to me in a century or two, except to tell me to piss off. I gained more worshippers, more tribute, and more supplication from mortals trying to thwart him than anything else, and he always somehow blamed me for that. It's just as well that girl is leaving since she won't help you as long as Baedrogan whispers in her ear.*

I nodded, looking at the closed door a moment before walking away. My feet carried me to my garden, in search of privacy to think that over. "It gives me some answers, though," I said out loud when I was certain that I was alone. "It may be taboo to talk about where our powers have come from, but we're all like this. It's not just me. It's not just Verwyn. Every elemental is born hearing voices of the gods, whether they'll admit it to others or not."

That's not all of what you wanted to ask her about, is it?

"No, it's not," I said. I found a bench and sat down next to a hyacinth bush, breathing in the sweet fragrance. My fingers played gently along a row of the flowers as I put words to the mystery that still bothered me. "I've been having visions, like memories, of things I think Davri may have done. Before I upset Krecek further and ask him, or anyone else who knew Davri, I wanted to ask if that was just another aspect of being what we are."

I've wondered that as well. It's not just Davri that you've had flashes of memory from. It's the others that came before you, as well. I thought the visions might have leaked from how close you and I are becoming, but the memories you've seen from Davri are beyond my experience, from a time before he killed me. No other Verwyn has had visions such as that, though.

I stared at the flowers, poking the yellow pollen and pinching it to spread a streak of it across my finger. "They might be delusions of an overstressed mind," I said softly. "Or perhaps Davri and I share a soul, and these things are carried along. I'll have to find someone else to ask, though. Not Krecek. He'd keep me prisoner for all eternity if he had proof of my insanity. I'd rather die and take my chances on haunting the next Verwyn."

I'd rather avoid that option. I meant it when I said I'm tired of the needless, repetitious, painful death.

"It's not exactly my favorite plan," I chuckled softly.

Then pretend to be morose and say your farewells to this place. We'll leave with Krecek and vanish on the journey.

I nodded. They'd left me no choice but to run. I'd only cooperate long enough to find the right moment.

The morning was overcast with a heavy mist in the air. It wasn't at all accidental or coincidental; Nalia and I had worked on it before we'd retired for the night. I was sure that Krecek would realize it had been my doing, but equally sure he would not realize the reason behind it. He would probably attribute it to an echo of my mood. The lands were tied to the wizards who ruled them, and sometimes even the weather was a slave to our whims.

Byrek said his farewells to me with more kindness than he'd ever shown me before. I gave him a tight hug and he whispered in my ear that I would return. His kindness brought tears to my eyes and I released him to turn and wipe them away quickly with the backs of my gloves. I'd been dabbing at tears all morning, truly torn by the thought of leaving. I hadn't realized it before, but this was only the second place I'd ever felt was home.

I entered the carriage quietly, closing my eyes as Krecek said his own farewells. I wanted to shut out what was happening to me, but too soon Krecek was beside me, handing me a handkerchief without a word. We began to move at once, and as I took the handkerchief he looked out the window as if to give me privacy for my suffering. I whispered a thank you and dried my eyes, then stared at the square of cloth I'd set on my lap. Silver and blue. Like the uniforms of his attendants. Like the suit he wore.

Like the soldiers we'd played with when I was a child.

We were silent for at least half the day. The clouds darkened and the mist turned into a gentle rain.

"If it weren't for this rain," Krecek said, "we could stop to eat."

"The rain suits my mood," I said. "Have your men set up a pavilion if you're hungry or too impatient to stop somewhere more convenient."

He looked at me with a touch of irritation. "As you wish." He called out instructions to the driver to stop so they could set up for lunch. He hopped outside to help, which shocked me.

"I could run right now," I whispered.

While he's out of the carriage and probably expects you to

try? He's giving you an obvious opportunity, testing you. Don't fall for it.

I nodded in agreement. Nalia's caution made sense. It was too obvious a chance, which meant he was confident I would not get away. I watched impatiently out the window for a moment and then stepped out and let the rain fall on my face. It felt soothing, and standing felt so good after such a long ride. I found a tree for some privacy, catching one of the coachmen track me and confirm the idea that they expected me to run. I tried not to think about it as I relieved myself, returning quickly so as not to cause alarm.

When I returned the pavilion was set up and we had a small table to sit at. I felt magic in the air and wondered how much of the setup had been done with a wave of Krecek's hand. The food was real, but magic had obviously been used to heat it to a pleasant degree. I sat down in silence, picking at my food while thoughts ran through my head. He'd set this up so effortlessly.

"I lived in a cave for weeks, once," I said. "It stormed nearly the entire time. It wasn't a gentle rain like this, either. I gathered my own food from whatever I could find. This seems too easy. Too soft."

Krecek closed his eyes and took a deep breath.

"The inconvenience of a little rain is nothing," I continued before he could say anything. "Not when you think the alternative is death."

"You're not facing death," he said with long-suffering patience.

"A fate worse than death!" I protested.

"Agrad," Krecek said. "Shut up."

"No." I pushed my food aside. "I don't think I will. I was a child. I was terrified of you! I—"

"You still are," he said, speaking over me, shutting me up. "I don't have the patience for this right now. This was not my first

168

choice of action, making you a prisoner in my lands like this. You're still a scared little child, only instead of cowering you are trying to shout me down. You're trying to tear me down just to salve your fears. Believe me, you have time to take this all out on me later." He casually took another bite of his food, watching me dispassionately while he did. "For now, I'd just like to get this journey behind us so that I can deal with more important things. Such as if I'm going to have to kill you."

"What?" I stared at him in horror, unsure for a moment if this was some disturbing joke.

"I'd rather not. For the duration of the journey, I'd appreciate it if you'd not try to make an impossible decision easier."

He set his plate aside and stood, walking toward the carriage while the footman and his guards finished their own meals.

I followed him, catching myself twisting the fingers of my gloves in a nervous gesture. We stood beside the carriage in the light rain and I forced myself to stop fidgeting. It was difficult.

Krecek leaned against the side of the carriage and looked up at the misty gray clouds. "I am an enemy of the gods. We may have won that war, but so far as I am aware there was no truce called at the end of it and I cannot tell what side you are on. The more you speak with her, the more I wonder if we truly are fated to be enemies." He sighed wearily. "I rather hope we are not, though."

"Who else was I going to talk to these last five years?" I started pacing in irritation. "Byrek rarely has time to say a word to me that isn't related to teaching and training. Don't get me started about everyone else at the castle! It was always 'yes, sir' or 'no, sir' or 'let me get Byrek, sir'. That was it! For five years!" My voice cracked on the word "years" and I threw my hands in the air. I was growing too emotional. I walked around to the other side of the carriage and climbed in to wait so I wouldn't be seen if I started to cry.

I was given the time I needed to calm down. I stared out the window at nothing until Krecek entered and we were in motion again.

"It was only five years," Krecek said gently.

"That's nearly a quarter of my life."

"Oh," he said gently. "It's easy to forget from my perspective. I forgot how long that would seem to you. Give it time and you'll make the same mistake someday." When I looked, the expression on his face was a sort of wry, self-mocking amusement, and I wondered at what might be behind that.

"What's done is done," I murmured, turning away once again.

The silence fell between us again, and despite myself the clouds began to thin and the rain began to dry. It was growing difficult to maintain the gloom necessary. I was too weary to go on with my resentment.

"You can always speak to me, if you've been lonely."

I turned in surprise.

"You've made peace with a god," he said. "Perhaps you can make peace with me."

"With *you?*"

He nodded, meeting my eyes directly and deliberately. "If you don't want to talk, you could listen. I have centuries of tales I could share with you, and some of it may contain wisdom."

Listen to him. Gain his trust.

I nodded slowly to him, but Krecek had pulled away as Nalia had spoken, almost like a flinch in slow motion.

"Can you really tell when she speaks to me?" I asked, bothered by his response.

"I can," he said. "It grates on my nerves, like an insect's buzzing. You've allowed her to grow too strong--"

"I didn't," I cut him off. "She's been this strong ever since Cairnfeld. I'll accept that I'm responsible for that, and it's a

170

terrible mistake that I made, but it's done and cannot be undone."

Krecek looked alarmed. "She's not as strong as she was that day, is she?"

"No!" I put a hand on his arm to assure him. "No, she can't just take over my body the way she did. I still have to be vigilant, but she doesn't have that much power over me."

"I'm amazed you're not dead."

I nodded. Honestly, so was I. "It was a very close thing. I still know that she would rather see me dead and her free. I think I might feel the same if I found myself trapped in someone else's mind after being brutally murdered by the same person. I am not the one who killed her, though. She feels what I feel, and I think she has been learning empathy by looking through my eyes. She said that she is weary of tasting death, every death that every Verwyn has faced. Gods were never meant to die. I have begun to suspect that every Verwyn, perhaps even Davri, willingly died to make her suffer."

"Davri may have," Krecek murmured. "The rest, well, their reasons were their own. A few, I fear, she may have driven insane. It's what worries me about you, and about how much of a hold she has on you."

Wait.

"You think she drove them insane?" I frowned as the implications rolled through my mind. "You lied to me? You know that she spoke to them, too?"

He held up his hands in a placating gesture. "I've been thinking about it only since you mentioned it. It's what brought me to the decision to remove you from power. I'm not sure we can ever trust you."

"What will you do with me?" My budding anger had transformed almost immediately to fear.

"We can't kill you," Krecek said. "We can't know if it will

weaken her again, or give her the power she needs to break free at last. Does she even know?" He shook his head and answered his own question. "No, either she doesn't know, or she knows that it would weaken her further. Otherwise she would have driven you to death long before now."

I swallowed around a lump in my throat.

"I want to speak to her."

My blood went cold and I pulled away from him. "What?"

"Is it possible? Can you let me speak to Nalia?"

PART ELEVEN

I woke up in an inn.

Specifically, I woke up in a strange bed with sounds of bustling activity somewhere nearby. Krecek was seated in a chair beside the bed, watching me warily and perhaps impatiently over the top of a book. There were smells of freshly cooked food, and smoke from a wood fire burning in the fireplace. The décor conspired to be homey and inviting, but it lacked any personal touches and was both too worn out and too clean.

I groaned softly, upset at the missing time. A glance at the window confirmed that hours had passed, since it was fully dark outside. I sat up slowly, carefully.

"What have you done?"

Krecek set his book aside and moved to sit at the edge of the bed. "I needed to know--"

I glared, edgy that he felt so comfortable with our proximity. "After all the effort, all the lectures, EVERY SINGLE TIME I have been told to stay in control, not to trust her, not to give her any advantage, and you undo that in an instant! What sort of game do you think you're playing with me? I am not your toy! I am not your plaything! I am a human being!"

"You are a wizard," he said. "You are by no means a mere human."

"That isn't even an issue!" The nonchalance of his reply bothered me deeply. "You had no right to do that, to set her free, to break my control without my consent, wizard or not. You claim that she is the one who is the enemy, but you are the one throwing me into situation after situation where rights as a wizard, as a human, as a sentient being, are completely discounted. You had no right doing this to me."

"You're right," Krecek said. He reached over and placed a hand on my arm. "I miscalculated, made a mistake. Better me than someone else, however."

"Someone else?" I pulled my arm away roughly. "Who else? There aren't many in this world who know the names of the gods, and most of those are craven echoes of old clerics lurking in shadows who do not have the power to invoke her over my will! None of them could begin to guess which goddess lives within me."

"Aral knows. So does Byrek. Naran. Raev. A scant few trusted others. It was a situation I was uniquely qualified to deal with, more so than even any of them."

"So I'm vulnerable to people I haven't even met. Perfect," I said bitterly. "I hope whatever you learned or gained or accomplished was worth it."

"As do I," Krecek took my hands and searched my eyes. "How do you feel?"

Why did he keep touching me? He'd started doing that in the carriage. Reaching for me. Touching me. I couldn't understand why he would be the way he was, cold and cruel and unapologetic, but still reach out to me and touch me when no one else ever had. What was worse was he did it when I needed to be touched and reassured the most.

"I don't know. Awake," I answered him, somewhat flustered. "Rested, I suppose. I'm fine, aside from the missing hours. What did you talk about for so long?"

"I'm not sure you'd understand."

"You mean you won't tell me," I frowned.

"Not at all," he said, lips twisted in wry amusement. "She spent a great deal of time insulting me. My betrayal of her, personally, was second only to Davri's. We also conversed in depth about the nature of magic, the consequences of being what we are. The past. The future. All the many things I've done wrong. Assumptions I've made. False conclusions I've come to."

"In so little time?"

He laughed. He actually laughed, letting go of my hands and sitting straighter, more confident and more relaxed. "I'm sure she could have continued, but we had much more to cover." He sobered. "We fought over what to do with you. Despite what she's told you, she wants you dead--"

"I know that," I cut him off, rolling my eyes. "I know it better than anyone."

"How do you handle talking to her, knowing that?"

"She just wants her freedom," I said, feeling very small when I said it. "Unfortunately, it just happens to come at the cost of my life, and I'm not eager to give it. It's nothing personal, though. As far as prisons go I may be bordering on pleasant, but I am still her prison. I get the impression she would rather like me if not for the situation. We've called a truce, because she's tired of so much death, but I still know..." I paused and looked him over for a moment. "She doesn't hate me nearly the same as she hates you."

"No, I'm sure she doesn't," he said. "I'm sure she adores you, next to the feeling she harbors for me."

I looked at him in silence for a moment, curious at the haunted expression in his eyes. He was looking away, his emerald eyes focused upon nothing. It was as if he saw the past so vividly that he could no longer see the present. Without thinking, I found myself speaking. "Why did you do it?" I felt a shiver of fear to hear myself ask, unsure how he would react. I couldn't help myself, though. I had to know, and this could be my only opportunity. "Why, all of you, why did you kill the gods?"

"Freedom," he said softly, eyes still focused on the past. "And power, I suppose. That's the only simple answer I can give you.

We all had our reasons, but for me it was freedom."

I blinked in surprise. That wasn't the answer I'd expected. "What do you mean?"

"I'm sure it's impossible for you to imagine," he said, shifting further onto the bed to a more comfortable position. "You have no concept of what it was like before. The gods ruled every aspect of our beings and shaped every moment of our lives. To some people it was a comfort. Their lives were predictable, routine. Safe. A few of us even found it so, until events pulled that safety out from underneath us. Many others found it overwhelmingly stifling and stagnant. It was something that had to happen, and we just happened to be able to do it."

Krecek was right. I couldn't imagine it. All I'd heard were stories of how the gods had fixed things, helped people, and kept watch over their mortal creations. They ran everything, created everything, answered every prayer--and as I thought that, I realized I couldn't reconcile that idea of benevolence and altruism with what I knew of Nalia. She was the antithesis of all the tales of old I had heard of the gods. The thought did not sit well with me.

"I thought the gods did good things for people," I said. The doubt had crept into my voice, though.

"The fairy tales they tell today," he said, "have nothing to do with the reality of yesterday. The gods were petty beings with great power. Yes, much like the wizards of today." He rolled his eyes with good humor, and I found myself smiling despite myself. "They demanded worship and tribute. They demanded sacrifices. They demanded--everything. Complete and unquestioning obedience, for a chance, just a chance, that they might look upon you and judge you worthy of their attention and perhaps their aid. I don't know that we're any better, but I'm certainly happier with the state of things."

"That's awfully selfish, isn't it?"

He shrugged. "Yes, it really is." Krecek leaned back on his elbows and he stared upward at the ceiling. "None of us started out selfish. Well, I'd never thought of myself as particularly selfish, at least. We all thought we were doing great good for the world, not just for ourselves. No matter what good you do, though, you cannot make everyone happy. I've tried, others have tried. I have the power to place everyone I meet in a protective bubble of happiness for the rest of their lives. Half of them would thank me for it and worship me. The other half would hate me with the blackest resentment their souls could muster, and those are the people I would probably like the most."

"You like mean people who hate being happy?"

"I like people who think for themselves and want to make something better for this world than what they see. I like people who will argue with me and challenge me, instead of blindly accepting what they're given." He sat up straight again, looking at me intently. "Try it yourself. Do nothing but good for others, with all of your power and all of your might. You'll be resented and cursed by someone within a month. They'll raise armies to destroy you inside of a year."

"Why would they do that?"

"There are so many reasons I couldn't begin to name them all. Envy. Greed. You might help someone that another person hates. You might be blind to the suffering of one person while you're busy helping another. You might judge one person as more worthy than their neighbor, and gods help you if you happen to be right. No one is more dangerous than a sinner, and they're more than happy to seek revenge for a slight. Even if you were perfect and somehow avoided those pitfalls, achieving perfect fairness in your tireless effort, you've only scratched the surface of what you'd be doing wrong. People are not puppets. They won't dance around like you want them to.

They don't even want to. What if you help someone who did not want any help? What if they'd like to find out if they can do it on their own? What if someone sees that you're willing to help and decides they don't have to think or grow for themselves because you'll always take care of it? They'll become a perfectly happy lump because they know you've got infinite resources to spend on making them happy, wasting their entire life and all their possibilities and potentials. Trust me. Do some good, for those you love, for those you trust, but be selfish. And if anyone's earned the right to be selfish, it's me."

I shook my head sadly, but he gave me a look that bid me to remain silent. What could I really say after that? His words were so cynical it was painful to hear.

"No, never mind all of that," he said as he sat up once again. "I've seen too much of this world to live with blind hope and there are times I regret that. If you want to believe in people, do that. Take a chance. Have some hope. Get your heart broken for yourself, and become whoever you're going to be because of it."

"I don't think I have much of a choice in that. I'll be who I end up being in the end anyway, no matter whose advice I do or don't follow." I pinched a piece of fluff off the blanket, tossing it away after squishing it between my fingers for a moment. "Not that I'm convinced I should be listening to your advice. You're full of contradictions. Are you always this helpful?"

"I try not to be," he said, shaking his head. "Giving advice makes me feel old."

"You are old."

"Don't tell anyone," he said with a wink. "I think I've got them all fooled."

I giggled despite myself at the absurdity of it. As if anyone didn't know despite his appearance just how old he was. As if anyone couldn't tell by just talking to him.

He laughed as well, which made me laugh a moment longer

than I'd intended, but it wasn't something that could be maintained long because of who we were. He looked sad when the merriment ended, and he stood to pour us each a glass of wine. Krecek drank thoughtfully while I stared into the glass, bothered by the deep red color. When I took a drink I was surprised at the bitter, dry flavor of it, but there was something that lingered on my tongue afterward that prompted me to drink more.

"Naran started it all," Krecek said softly, staring across the room at nothing as he spoke. "He doesn't know it, even today. Aral spared him from that much, and rightfully so." He paused just a moment for a little more wine. "Master and Mistress Tennival, Aral and Naran's parents, were struck by an illness. It was a malady that would surely kill them, but they went to a temple of Garatara, the god of health and healing."

"I know who he is," I interrupted. "I...when I was hiding, a couple took me in who were—"

"Priests?" he finished for me. "Yes, I know. Did they teach you the names of all of the gods?"

I nodded.

"Then you know Garatara is still alive, though somewhat quieter now." He set his glass down and sat down next to me again. "The temple that Master and Mistress Tennival went to did not help them. The high priest they spoke to was not what he seemed. We do not know which god he actually followed, but he said that to save them the gods demanded a sacrifice of their youngest child. Surely not too high a price to pay, he said. But, their youngest was their only son, and they'd had difficulties enough conceiving the two children they had. Aral was nearly a master mage, but her brother was still a child. They sent Naran to Anogrin to be raised by her, and they gave themselves to death once he was away.

"Aral was beside herself with grief. Her friends helped her to

179

maintain her studies and research by watching over Naran as well, taking everything in turns and turning him into yet another project for them all. He didn't suffer for their attentions, though they were all young mages and given to irresponsibility at times. One of them, Davri, was quite devout. He was hoping to become a priest of Nalia himself when his magic studies were finished, and I was quite encouraging. That is what I had once done myself. We'd met that way, since he went to the temple and he had many questions to ask. We spoke together regularly about his prospects for priesthood and the nature of magic.

"Naran asked to see for himself what Nalia's temple was like. Innocently, Davri took Naran with him and they were stopped as soon as they entered. Naran had been marked for sacrifice."

"But, you said his parents died!" I protested.

"They did," Krecek said. "It didn't matter. He'd been marked without them knowing; his blood belonged to the gods. A high priest saw it and didn't hesitate to accept the boy as a sacrifice and started to drag Naran away. Davri was paralyzed with indecision for a heartbeat while he battled between faith and compassion. When he confronted the priest it escalated quickly. Words turned to violence, and in the end the priest was lying on the floor in a pool of blood, and Davri had grabbed Naran and run from the scene.

"A war that brought dwarves, humans, elves, goblins—all mortal races together, all started over the life of one human boy. Such a humble beginning. Such a simple mistake." He finished his glass of wine and poured another in silence before he continued. "I found out about it shortly afterward, of course. Every priest was sent to look, and since I knew Davri so well the magic helped me find him easily. He was waiting for me in Aral's dormitory. Naran was crying in a corner while Aral and Davri tried to protect him. One look into the child's eyes and I knew my days of blind faith were over.

"Truth be told, I'd seen it happen before. I'd heard of mistakes being made and sacrifices demanded that were unreasonable, but this was the first time it was made personal to me. I worked what magic I could to help, and I taught Aral and Davri magic usually forbidden to anyone not a priest so that they could hide. So that they could save Naran's life. Davri and Naran went into hiding. In the meantime Aral petitioned every temple, every priest and priestess, everyone she could find to spare her brother.

"For my part, I spent a week in fear that my lapse of faith would be discovered and my own life would be forfeit." He took a large drink of wine at this point, and then continued in a hushed tone. "I thought there was no way the goddess I had followed so faithfully would be blind to my betrayal. Nothing changed, though. The gods were not paying attention. For all our prayers and supplications, they did not actually care. Even when I saw Nalia take physical form for a new priest's initiation to the temple, blessing and accepting him, she didn't even notice me. She didn't care. The gods were so powerful that they could not imagine a reason to do more than accept the accolades given, and grant the occasional boon as whim took them."

He's wrong, Nalia's voice whispered into my mind. *Though, he is also right. I did notice. I did not care.*

I jumped a bit, startled. She'd been so quiet that I hadn't realized she'd been listening at all.

"I can imagine what she told you," Krecek said, frowning a bit. "I did learn some things later that—no, that's a tangent for another day. What I found out later isn't part of the story as it happened, and those were my thoughts at the time. I saw that the high priests were acting on their own whims, putting their own self-comfort above all and using religion as a shield to hide behind. I saw for myself, once my eyes were open, how corrupt we had all become, and how unquestioning the masses were because the gods were presumably on our side.

"In the meantime every attempt Aral made to save her brother, the only family she had left, fell on deaf ears. She was admonished to reveal his location, but for her safety even she did not know. To further confound things, every magic the priests could employ failed for some unknown reason." Here Krecek paused, smiling. Clearly he was to blame, or knew who was. "It was almost a year before a particularly unscrupulous high priest said he would do what she asked, if she traded her favors with him. She gave him an evening, giving up her innocence for him, and in return he denounced her publicly, dragging her through the streets for all to see her shame. All of Anogrin heard within hours the story of her being a wicked temptress, not to be trusted, not to be given any aid. And, of course, her brother would not be spared.

"That high priest died soon after, and I took his place.

"The irony, of course, was nearly suffocating. In faithlessness, through faithlessness, I'd finally obtained the position that should have represented my ultimate faith. To top it off, the one thing I wanted most to do as high priest was the one thing I could not do. My predecessor had been so thorough in his character assassination of Aral that if I'd so much as made the attempt to save her or Naran I'd lose my priesthood at best. In all likelihood I'd have been killed alongside the both of them.

"Thus the conspiracy was truly born. Most of what happened after that point is in the history books. We spent five years building our numbers, gathering those we could trust, killing anyone who would betray us. Too many of us had too much to lose. We saved what we could, as well, but when Anogrin was razed and the libraries sacked--"

"I thought the library was saved ahead of time!" I interrupted, trying to remember old lessons and stories I'd been told.

Krecek shook his head. "Byrek and a few others saved what

they could, and Raev Baelwyn still has the majority of what they saved, but a great deal was lost. Anogrin had been a shining host of all knowledge, and by comparison but a handful of the old texts remain. It was war, though. Some sacrifices had to be made."

"You make it sound like losing a few books was more tragic than all the people who died."

"In a way, perhaps," he looked thoughtful, cocking his head to the side a moment. "If someone spent their entire life in the pursuit of some skill, and their only legacy was left on pages that are now gone forever, it is as if that person has died twice." Krecek sighed softly. "The books were a tragedy, but... It's the children. The children who died bother me the most..." He trailed off, looked at his empty wine glass and just set it down.

"There is one thing I wanted to tell you that you will not find in any historical account. It was not exactly common knowledge, except among those of us who became wizards. The gods were betrayed by their own, or we never would have succeeded.

"Agrad, no other elemental knows what I have said. Only those who were there know how it truly began. I will not swear you to secrecy, but I do ask that you use your better judgment on how and to whom you choose to reveal any of this. I feel I owe you this explanation, and I hope you will respect what it means."

I nodded, eyes cast downward as I thought that over. "You don't want Master Tennival collapsing under the weight of guilt, real or imagined or exaggerated. Am I right?"

"Bless your compassion," he said with just a hint of a wry twist to his lips. "It is a concern, but you'll understand in a moment. We were aided by Baedrogan and Agruet."

"The gods of death and of deception," I murmured aloud, and then my head snapped up, eyes meeting his urgently.

"Shaelek?"

Krecek nodded solemnly. "Nalia told me what Shaelek told you."

Whatever they started with our death, with the war, is not over yet, Nalia said.

I conveyed her words to Krecek, and then I added a worry of my own. "She told me that Modarian and others heard from the gods as well."

"She would know," he said. "Lorwyn has possession of Agruet's power. Modarian Lorwyn is rather close with Shaelek, and they've both taken an interest in you. I am beginning to think I may be the aberration in hearing nothing from Fotar, rather than you for speaking to Nalia. I may owe you an apology."

"Only one?" I didn't bother hiding the bitterness in my tone.

"Much more than just one," Krecek said.

I didn't know what to say to that. I bit my lower lip, fidgeting. How much could I get him to apologize for? What was he actually sorry for? What if it was for all the wrong things? He might--

"I am certain my transgressions do not warrant an acceptance of any apology, however."

"I don't know," I said. I wanted to be honest, and he looked nearly as vulnerable as I felt. "Letting me return home would go a long way toward forgiveness." I tried to keep hope from my voice, giving him a half smile to show that I knew the probability was slight.

"In good time," he said. His smile was small but genuine. "I beg your indulgence for a while, so that we can find out what Shaelek and Modarian might have planned. I no longer know for certain if we are on the same side. Agruet and Baedrogan were our allies in the war, but we fought against Nalia and the others. If we fought with her on our side, would they become our enemies? I don't want to force their hands too soon or reveal my own intentions."

"I'll be forced to be your prisoner for no reason at all, then?" I wasn't happy with the idea.

"No," he said firmly. "You are new to the necessary obfuscations that staying ahead of an unknown enemy entails. I need to keep you safe and maintain the façade of normalcy until I know where the others stand."

"That sounds devious," I accused him. I struggled to keep a frown on my face, but my eyes probably twinkled with mirth despite it.

"I told you years ago that I cheat," Krecek said, amused. "This is but one example of why."

The words were a splash of cold water over my heart. The reminder of those days before my parents' deaths destroyed my sense of humor. I turned away from him, cursing myself for letting go of that pain for even a moment.

"I'm sorry," Krecek's voice was soft. "I never meant to hurt you."

"You killed my parents. Apologize for that."

"I can't," he said. "I can apologize for handling things poorly, for not preparing better for what may have gone wrong, but I cannot apologize for their deaths. You will never understand, but it is a thing that needed to be done."

I didn't say a word. He was right. I would never understand.

The mattress shifted, and I heard him walk toward the door. "Get some rest, Agrad. We still have a long journey before us." He left the room and I sat there for a very long time, so conflicted that I almost felt numb.

"I'll help you," I said as we both entered the carriage in the morning.

Krecek simply nodded in reply. We rode in silence. I would glance at him briefly, but I never knew what to say. I almost felt bad for him, because he was obviously conflicted. I wanted to know more, but a horrible thought occurred to me. If he'd had no choice but to kill my parents, what if it was because they'd done something horribly wrong? I wasn't ready to face the thought that he might be justified, that my parents may have deserved their fate, but I'd have to face the possibility if I would ever forgive him for their deaths.

No wonder Krecek did not ask my forgiveness.

I fingered the pendant of my necklace absently, distracting myself with other thoughts. I wondered if any enemy of Krecek's was actually an enemy of mine, and if that included my parents. I simply didn't know enough. Well, I thought, I knew that Master Tennival had been like an older brother to me for a very long time. I decided to start my allegiance there and figure out later where that would actually put me.

We hit a particularly large bump in the road and I jumped a bit in surprise. I laughed nervously at my reaction and placed my hands demurely in my lap in the hopes that I might not reveal my every thought by my bearing.

Krecek glanced over at me with something like fondness. "It surprises me," he said, "how you remind me so much of Davri, and yet you are completely and utterly the opposite of how he was in just about every way."

"I'm sorry," I said, and I could have kicked myself for it. I wasn't sorry. I was proud that I was so completely myself. I cleared my throat and added, "I mean to say, in what ways am I different?"

"Davri was bold and brash. Confident, or at least he pretended to be. He flirted openly with anyone who interested him, and no one could fault him for it because he was just so charming." Krecek reached over and patted my hands. "You may be none of those things, but you're as clever as he ever was, and at least as stubborn."

"That's it?" I shooed his hand away from mine. "Clever and stubborn?"

"I wasn't aware that you were fishing for compliments," Krecek said.

"No!" I shifted in my seat uncomfortably. "Why would I do that?"

"Well, I'd hoped. It will be difficult to work together if we can't even joke around a bit."

I felt flustered by his answer. "It's been so long since there's been any levity in my life that I think I've forgotten how."

"I'll help," he said, and his smile was unbearably sweet in a shy sort of way. "I know the past contains much that can't be forgiven, but if we could set it aside…"

Krecek trailed off, frowning as if distracted.

I heard thunder in the distance.

I nearly jumped from my seat. "I didn't do that," I growled the words, putting my hand upon the carriage door as if about to jump from it to stop whoever had upset the balance of my country.

"Wait!" Krecek's voice was commanding, giving me pause. He poked his head out, and before he could shout a command the carriage was already beginning to slow. Without even a glance in my direction he opened the carriage door and climbed up a series of handholds as nimbly as any driver I'd seen.

I heard no voices, no exchange of conversation, as the carriage slowed to a stop. Impatiently I opened the door myself, balancing on the foot rail and holding onto the door, waiting for it to be just slow enough….

Someone stood in our path.

It was a huddled figure, dressed in rags, looking like an old beggar. Our driver looked irritated as he held the reins tight, but Krecek looked almost scared.

"What are you doing here?" he demanded as he climbed down and jumped to the road. "There are two of us! We can stop you if you try anything!"

The figure looked up at Krecek, and when I saw his face I felt sorry for the old man. He looked lost and confused. "Try?" His voice carried strangely over the increasing wind. "What would I try, Uncle?"

Careful, Nalia warned as I hopped out of the carriage. *That is Garatara. What could he be doing here?*

I nodded, watching silently.

"Please," Krecek approached slowly, "let us pass in peace. We have business elsewhere."

"I'm looking for something," Garatara said. "Help me find it."

I was feeling uneasy. The storm was growing around us. I didn't feel right about it, and the harder I tried to still the weather, the stronger the storm grew.

Garatara is not causing this storm.

I started looking around for someone else. Garatara was the god of healing, of course. I knew that. The god of storms was Kedaran. I knew his name, but that wouldn't help me find him if he was the one causing this.

"They promised me!" Garatara began shouting. "There was something, and they promised me, and now where did they all go? Where are you? You are not Fotar! What are you?"

"Agrad!"

I shook my head. "There's someone else here!"

He nodded, backing toward me slowly. "Will Nalia help you if things go bad?"

"I don't know!" I started coming closer to him. At the same time Nalia was assuring me that yes, she would help. She was just as worried as we were at the insane look in Garatara's eyes.

Someone suddenly stood between us. Someone else was behind me. Before I could think to fight or defend myself there was a great rush of air, a flash of light, a deafening roar of sound, and finally a great nothingness engulfed me.

PART TWELVE

Eventually I awoke. I was in a dark room. The air was heavy and hot, smelling of dirt and dust. I used a touch of magic to illuminate my surroundings. The room was small and completely bare.

What was the point of this? They had to know I could escape. Locking me in a room was only irritating me. It took only a thread of power to unlock the door and nothing kept me from stepping outside of it except my own curiosity. I left the door open and sat in the center of the room, waiting, baiting them, whoever they were. It may have been cocky and foolish, but I was certain I wasn't in any real danger. I was an elemental after all.

I didn't wait long.

"The door is wide open!" It was a woman's voice, and it echoed strangely. "Tell him to get in there while I..."

Whoever was speaking had been walking away, the voice growing too low for me to understand. Moments later I heard someone approaching and finally the door was opened further.

"Lord Verwyn."

I started with surprised recognition. Could it be? "Master Kavidrian?"

My childhood tutor nodded, setting down a tray between us. There was a cup of water and a small bowl of something that looked completely unappetizing.

"I'm supposed to sit here on the floor and eat like this?"

"They are waiting to see whose side you're on, first."

"I'm curious to know that, myself." I took a sip of water. It tasted metallic and a bit like dirt. "Right now I am on my own side."

"What of the goddess within you?" Master Kavidrian gave nothing away as he waited for my answer.

I narrowed my eyes in suspicion. How did he know her gender? What else did he know? "She's on her own side as well."

"She's always been on her own side," he said with a sly grin, as if revealing we were co-conspirators.

"How do you know?" My fists were clenched at my sides. This turn of conversation was worrying me a great deal. I'd always looked up to Master Kavidrian. I'd had no idea he was still alive, so I hadn't thought of him except the way I had as a child. It made me feel strangely conflicted to be in his presence now.

"They told me who she was."

I frowned. Past tense, as if she was completely dead. Neither of us particularly cared for that. "Who's behind this? What do they want? What am I doing here?"

"I can't tell you anything, Lord Verwyn. It may seem like I have freedom here, but I am as much a prisoner as you." He bowed his head, shrugging just slightly. "All I know is that they are gods, and they have been talking about you."

I frowned. "First wizards, now gods." I threw my hands in the air in frustration. "What's next?"

"I would not ask if I were you." He glanced at the door, then back at me. "There are so many things you don't yet understand. Things I don't understand. Stay here. I'll return when they let me."

Master Kavidrian stood and walked out the door, closing it behind him.

No questions answered. Just vague threats and more questions I wanted to ask.

I left the door closed this time, and I waited.

Eventually I conjured my own food and water. I used the slop they had left me as the basis for the spell, but I turned it into something palatable. This way I would not waste energy by eating purely from my own creation. It was something Byrek had explained to me when I'd mentioned how I had survived as a child. I had no idea what was actually in the food and water they had brought me, so this way the food would not just be tasty, but it would be safe as well.

I sat a while. I paced around the room a bit. No one came to see me until Master Kavidrian brought me another meal.

"Is this lunch?"

"I have no idea. There are no lights down here unless you make your own. No windows. It would be supper for me, but I'm only basing that on the last time I slept."

"When will I get some answers?"

"I just gave you one."

"I meant about why I'm here!"

He left without another word, his eyes darted around the room in fear.

It wasn't long after Master Kavidrian left that I decided I was tired of this. It was time to find someone else who would talk to me. The door had been left unlocked, and an empty hall stretched out either way before me. After a moment of hesitation, I went right. Neither direction from my door looked different from the other, turning after a few paces either way. I followed it around the corner, which brought me to another right turn and a right turn again. One more brought me back to where I had started with no visible deviation. The hall appeared to be a square around my cell.

I frowned, backtracking that path with more care, touching the outer wall as I looked for something I may have missed. Some hidden panel or anything that would open up in another direction that would lead somewhere else. The walls were solid. Plaster, trim painted white, murals on the wall that didn't mean a thing to me. They weren't particularly well done, but they weren't terrible. They seemed to tell some sort of a story, something that I thought I should have known.

It is the history of the creation of Kayan.

How the gods had created the world? I stopped in my tracks and then returned to the spot right outside of my door. That's where it looked like the story began, with darkness broken by glittering stars that faded into light. There were six figures. Three women, two men, and one shadow figure that stood off alone while the others waved their arms around a sphere.

The shadowy figure disappeared from the mural after that. One of the women whispered to the four others and each, in turn, took a part of Kayan and created the immortal intelligent races. Imps danced in the fire first. Elves hid in their world of trees next. Then there were fairies. Finally the merfolk were created, and we reached the first corner.

I did that, Nalia said. *I tricked Fotar into thinking he needed to have a race of his own, better than the trees, the birds, the fish. Better than anything we'd all created together. I helped him, and then I helped Egridaea create the elves. I helped Bogradan create the fairies. I helped Atherva create the merfolk. I tricked them all, so that their favored creations were all my creations as well.*

I glanced behind me and looked at the mural again, putting names to each of the figures now except that shadowy one that had only appeared once. I felt like I knew them. They were old friends and comrades. And they were all dead.

"What about humans and dwarves and hobgoblins and, well, everything else?"

I helped make them all as well, but not until later. There were the five of us, and also chaos who kept to herself.

I nodded and looked at the story unfolding on the next wall. There were more gods in this image, all of them doing their own thing. They seemed to have traits in common with the other gods and goddesses, but it was nigh impossible to tell how one related to another. "Your children?"

We all had children. Together, alone…we were all each other had at first, and once our immortal creations started multiplying we simply wanted more of us to take care of the little things. My first children were twins, sons, and I had no idea what would become of them. Baedrogan was a strong boy from the start, with clever eyes and a keen perception my brothers and sisters feared. Agruet was quiet. He was small. He was a manipulative bastard, just like his mother. No, better than I was. I resented him and he knew it.

Around that same time Deyson and Brennan were born, taking the light and the dark and giving them a purpose and a time. Deyson was a brilliant girl, enthusiastic and sweet, blinding everyone with her brilliance. It was natural that she would become the embodiment of the sun, and her brother Brennan was happily the moon to balance and reflect her.

I think the idea of a day and a night gave Baedrogan the idea that eventually defined him. If these things should have an end, if day needs to lead to a time of rest, then so should the creatures of Kayan. Even those we never meant to die could do so, because he thought everyone deserved an end to look forward to.

It upset my brothers and sisters, but I praised him. I encouraged him. It would give us room to keep creating. We could fill the world many times over, and there would always be room.

I interrupted her. "Right here the darkness and the figure of chaos returned. Is this Agruet here?" I pointed at one of the young gods, looking into the darkness…and the darkness seemed to have nebulous eyes that gazed back at him.

Yes. That is supposed to be him.

The mural showed Agruet talking to Baedrogan after looking into the darkness, and then death came to the world. The goddess of chaos followed them around from that time onward, sometimes beside them, sometimes lurking hidden, in every image of them I could see even down to the next wall.

She's responsible? Nalia's mental tone came across as irritated. *I had no idea.*

I nodded, tracing my fingers over the wall, across some of the pictures. These were stories, mythology that had been lost in time with the death of the gods. Who had put them here, and why?

The next wall showed how the other intelligent races were created, how humans had tried to rule all other races and had been given the shortest lives of all sentient creatures. They were violent, but clever. They had children at an alarming rate.

I had nothing to do with the creation of humans, Nalia mused. *Baedrogan, my own son, collaborated with Vaederan to create an intelligent race that would be driven more than any other by the forces of birth and death. Human fertility was Vaederan's cruel joke to choke out the better races, while Baedrogan kept their growth in check by giving them a life span closer to that of a beast.*

I sighed. I could understand her resentment of humans, since most of the original wizards had been human. Understanding did not make her words irritate me less, however. I turned my attention to creatures beneath the surface, formed from rock and loving nothing more than plumbing the depths of the land and pillaging every secret contained within. The dwarves were short and compact, but powerful and curious. They found a gem they called the Skystone, and proclaimed its beauty was enough that they need never turn their eyes again upon the sky. They said it was more beautiful than Deyson, the goddess of the sun. Deyson was furious when she heard this and cursed their entire race. To this day they would turn to stone so long as sunlight touched their skin.

The goblins were purely Kaskal's idea, Nalia's inner voice had tones of amusement and grudging admiration. *Some stories claim that I had a hand in their creation, but that was just a rumor I had my own priests spread in a fit of envy. Their ability to put things together in shapes that move intricately together seems magical, but it is almost purely mechanical. Their understanding of physics and--* Her mental musing cut off suddenly. *I'll explain science to you some time after you have actually mastered magic. Who knows what you'd blunder into if I tried to fill your head with both at the same time.*

"Could you refrain from insulting me, at least for the duration of our imprisonment? We might actually be in danger, and I'd hate to accidentally stop defending myself. We might both get hurt."

Nalia's amusement grew at my statement, appreciating the wry humor, but she did not reply. Instead she drew my attention to a part of the mural where a new god and goddess had appeared.

When Thar and Brin came of age things became very interesting. The humans, as you saw, had already had their wars of conquest against the other races, but now there were a pair of gods to guide, instigate, and control war. It was pure chaos at first, and they took to their roles with unrestrained bloodlust.

Then Atherva begat Hastriva and they both took an instant like to her. She inspired loyalty from Thar and Brin in a way I still don't understand. It wasn't a sexual attraction, as far as I could tell, since they seemed more absorbed in each other than anyone else in that respect. Still, they would do anything for her. She tempered them and gave them purpose instead of letting them run loose bringing about endless death and misery.

We've come back to the door and haven't found a thing.

She was right. The murals had distracted us from a thorough search, but I was willing to bet that there hadn't been some hidden door or passage that could be found without magic. "Could it be an elaborate illusion?"

Give me power enough to look and I'll tell you.

I bit my lip in hesitation, but I couldn't see the harm. I nodded and let her look, feeling at the same time she did that magical illusion was all over the halls. Knowing it did not help us find a way out, however. We followed the corridor around one more time, ignoring the murals as we walked past them. It lead us to the door again and I walked in, at a loss as to what else to try. The room was as good a place to regroup and think as any.

As soon as I passed the threshold, I realized I was not alone.

PART THIRTEEN

The original six gods painted in the halls had all been pale except for one. It was something I'd been keenly aware of since I had dark skin and black hair, and my eyes were a bright shade of brown. Some of the younger gods had been painted darker as well, but the shadowy figure of the goddess of chaos had been the darkest of them all.

When I saw the woman in the middle of the room, my first thought was that this had to be that goddess. Her skin was a much deeper shade of brown than mine was, and her hair was a shade blacker than night. Her eyes were solid black, making the light reflecting upon them seem like stars glowing from deep within her.

She didn't look how I imagined a goddess would, though. She was tiny, for one. Hunched over with a twisted foot, leaning heavily upon a thick staff, she looked more like a beggar than one of the gods. Then again, I'd thought the same when I saw Garatara standing in the middle of the road.

"Come here and sit down," she said, sounding like both and invitation and a command. "I brought you here because I don't know what to do with you, child. Something's got to be done."

I approached and sat politely on the floor, waiting for her to join me in silence.

"It took you long enough to get here," she complained as she lowered herself to the floor. There was a cadence, a rhythm, to her words, and they were said in a melodic, almost sing-song manner. "You're more patient than I was expecting. Well, patient, or just stubborn. I can't tell which, yet."

"I've been told both, by different people," I shrugged. "I'm not sure which I am, myself."

She smiled just a touch. "That does not help me in the least to decide what I am going to do with you."

"Why would you need to do anything?"

She didn't answer. She just looked me over thoughtfully, starting to frown as time passed. Finally she nodded as if she had come to some sort of conclusion. "I am who you think I am. Yda, she who is the mistress of the void. She who creates and destroys. She who is the darkness, she who shames the light. I am Chaos, mother of all, mother of none."

I suppressed a shiver. "I'm surprised you told me your name."

"You have to call me something," Yda smiled slightly once again, and I wondered if that was as far as she ever would smile. "Mortals have this need to name things, and Nalia would have told you eventually."

I never would, Nalia said. *I wouldn't risk summoning her. Inviting chaos is never without risk.*

"Well spoken, sister," Yda said, startling me by replying to the voice I thought only I could hear. "Teach this boy, this vessel of yours, to fear me as you fear me. As all of you have always feared me."

"Why?" I asked, the word coming out without thought.

"Such a simple word for such a complex request," Yda looked amused. "Why do they fear me? Why do I want them to fear me? Or why do I want you, specifically, to fear me? Fear is powerlessness." She paused, cocking her head to the side in thought. "No, it is the knowledge of just how powerless you are. They could never stop me, the other gods. They could not control me, they could not predict me, and most of all they could not understand me. Without those things, they could never be certain that their plans would go the way they wanted, and what is more terrifying than that, to a being with such great power?"

I could understand that. With all the potential I had, I was still powerless in most everything that mattered. Powerlessness was the root of every fear I'd ever had. I'd done so much, pushed myself so much further than I otherwise would have, because of that fear. I'd forsaken my power, run from every comfort I had, kept my best friends at bay, kept from getting close to anyone, just because I was afraid. Because I knew I did not have the power I needed to stop the things that would hurt me, like losing my family, losing my friends, losing my home...

"Why do you fear me, though?" Why else would she kidnap me and keep me trapped?

"Fear you?" She laughed. "Oh, no, this is just my unpredictable way of saying hello. You should see the lengths I go through to say goodbye."

That was a lie. I was certain of it.

"You clever child." Her eyes were like onyx, glittery and black, looking me over like lifeless things that moved and shifted but housed nothing living within. "No, I'm not afraid of you, Agrad Verwyn. Not by far. An orphan who makes enemies of everyone who tries to help him? You'd destroy yourself before you'd manage to inconvenience me. I should kill you now just to not have to bother with you later."

I was suddenly beset by agony, radiating from my center with such intensity that all I could do was scream. I couldn't think from the pain, hands clenched in useless fists, curling up around myself with tears streaming down my face. I gasped for breath at some point, I'm sure of it, but the silence that followed meant nothing because the sensation of pain was so intense. As soon as I had the breath, I began to wail again.

It felt like I was being pulled apart from the inside, something just behind my navel being pulled through me and out. I couldn't let that happen, whatever it was. I refused to be unmade. I looked up at Yda as if a dying animal might, full of feral fury and primal need, ready to rip out her throat if need be to bring this to an end. I felt something, I can't explain what, sort of move within the landscape of my mind, and the pain ended as suddenly as it had begun.

I whimpered in relief, unashamed of the helpless sound as my whole body began to tremble.

"Killing you might not be my best decision, however," Yda said as she began to stand once again. "It would not solve my problems, and Nalia would just come back eventually. No, I need you out of the way, not dead. I'll think on this some more."

I just panted for breath as I watched her leave the room.

I've never felt such pain, Nalia seemed as weary and tired as I felt. *It felt like she was trying to unmake our very souls.*

I couldn't think. I curled up and concentrated on simply getting through the next breath until the memory of the pain gave way to sleep.

Something rough and wet was being brushed across my forehead. That was the only thing that confused me about waking up. I didn't wonder where I was, or what had happened, or why I felt so completely miserable over every inch of my body. The only mystery to me was why something rough and wet would be brushed across my forehead while I was laying helpless in this gods forsaken room.

It felt like either a sponge, or a coarse cloth. The hand guiding it was being as gentle as could be, but that could not change the texture of the thing. I cautiously opened my eyes a sliver, regretting it immediately as the light seemed to stab into my head. It was enough to confirm my guess that it was Master Kavidrian who was attending me.

"Lord Verwyn, how do you feel?"

"Like...last week's refuse," I whispered in return. My throat was raw. My voice, rough. I would have cringed at the sound of it, but that would have taken energy.

"You're lucky," he said softly, with a considerable amount of compassion in his voice. "You're alive, and you weren't driven completely insane. I've seen gods come away from her with less than she left you with."

"I'm not the first she's captured?" I tried once again to open my eyes, to gauge his reaction, but the pained squint I managed did not reveal much at all.

"No," he said. "I'm fairly certain that I wasn't even the first. This prison feels old, though it always looks new. It's worn at the edges, like a place that's been lived in for so long that the small things have fallen to the side."

"What do you mean?" I tried to sit, but midway through the motion I thought better of it. The memory of pain still burned in my belly enough that moving from the floor would have to wait. I would rest, and be grateful that the pain in my head was at least starting to fade.

"There's not much I can actually tell you, Lord Verwyn. If you find it for yourself, I can't stop that, but there are things she can do to a mortal that she would never do to a god."

"I understand," I said softly, closing my eyes and trying to relax and forget the pain.

The silence crept on for a bit, broken by the sound of water being sloshed around in a bowl followed by droplets falling into it. Master Kavidrian was attending to me again, just as gentle as before. I wondered what he thought of me, and why he had ended up here. What did I know of him, except that he had been my tutor once upon a time?

"Do you remember me, from when I was small?" I asked, simply tired of lying there in silence.

"Of course," he sounded amused that I would ask. "I knew who you were even back then, Lord Verwyn. How could I not when you were so talented, and so very stubborn? Just like my father had been."

That statement seemed like such a non sequitur to me, but why would he throw that in unless it meant something? "Your father?"

"The previous Lord Verwyn," he said. "It's why I was sent to find you, and to keep you from harm."

I opened my eyes and looked up at him. "But your name is Kavidrian." I blurted the statement without thought.

He nodded, looking slightly amused. "Kavidrian was my mother's last name. Verwyn belongs to you and you alone. It's not a name that will be passed to your children, should you have any."

"I hadn't even thought of that," I said. "It's not a subject that's ever come up before."

"No, I imagine not." He dropped his sponge into the bowl of water and leaned back. "How's your head?"

"Better," I said. "Don't change the subject. Tell me more."

"More of what? My father?" He looked me over for a few moments, shrugging when I gave a slight nod. "Doran Verwyn was powerful, and quite insane. I was a mistake, and he did not make any pretense of saying otherwise. He saw to it that I was educated, clothed, fed, sheltered. I did not stay with him in his castle, though. I saw him at Nightwatch and Dawnsday. Sometimes on the lesser holidays, if he wasn't too busy. It's not as if I could be his heir, so I became an afterthought. When he went off to war and died my life remained much the same, though with a few gifts less, until your parents stole you away and disappeared."

"How could they have stolen me?" I shifted to my side gingerly, trying to find a position that was slightly more comfortable. "I was their child. It was their right."

"That's not how the other wizards see it," Master Kavidrian shook his head. "Any other child, perhaps, but not an elemental. Or do you prefer wizard?"

"Elemental is fine," I said impatiently. The title didn't matter to me. I wanted to know more about the things no one had ever told me before.

"Lord Verwyn," he started with a frown, "you don't seem to understand the gravity of what happened to you."

"Just call me Agrad," I said. "You were my tutor; you're not some stranger." I held his gaze until he nodded. "What I understand is that my parents raised me, and you invited Krecek over for a visit that ended with my parents getting killed. I've learned that there was more to it than that, but details have been deemed too unimportant or too distracting to share with me."

"I can't tell you what happened after the night your parents died," Master Kavidrian said. "There was an explosion, and I woke up here. As for what happened before, well, that is a difficult subject. My father was dead for years before you were born, of course. That's how it works.

"I was a student at the university in Anogrin, sponsored by Lord Ceolwyn. I had seen your parents, was one among many to congratulate them on your birth, but it meant little to me until the news spread that you had disappeared.

"The speculation was immediate. At first it was thought that a rebellious element, perhaps old priests, had stolen you to raise you as a weapon against the wizards. It would mean yet another war, another way for Verwyn to die and take another few wizards with him. It was alarming, but seemed to many of us just another twist of the status quo.

"Lord Ceolwyn quietly asked for volunteers among the students to look for remnants of the old ways, for bands of priests and worshippers of the Old Gods, so that we might find you. I felt I owed Lord Ceolwyn a debt for sponsoring me, and so I volunteered, but he didn't have me search. I waited with him until word came back that you had been found, not with seditious rebels, but being quietly raised by your own parents.

"I was there when the news came in. Lord Ceolwyn was beside himself with fear. Instead of being trained by well-meaning idiots, you were not being trained at all. At any time, anything could happen, for any little reason, while you had no idea what sort of power you held. Again I volunteered, and this time Lord Ceolwyn agreed to send me to watch over you. I was accepted as a tutor and scribe in Lesser Stonegore when you were two years old.

"It went well, until Master Ceolwyn decided it was time to intervene and bring you home."

"So my parents are dead because I decided not to go with him?" I asked in a small voice. I'd known. I'd had that thought from the day I woke up in Myrenfeld, but I'd never given voice to it before. It was my fault they were dead. The weight of it was suffocating.

"No," he said softly. "It's not something so simple that blame of any sort can encompass. There are always turning points in every life that can lead to one outcome or another. Most of all, you cannot blame yourself. You were a child. You did what you thought was right. It is others who committed wrong."

I didn't know if I could believe him. The idea that I was to blame took ahold of me. My chest hurt, but my mind went numb, overwhelmed.

"I have to go," he said, straightening. "I've been in here too long as it is. I'll return later with food." He gathered the bowl and sponge in his arms as he stood. "People cannot be blamed for the actions of others. Wizards are people, elementals are people, and I'm beginning to think gods are people, too. Don't blame yourself for what others have done. Even they had their reasons."

I heard him, but the words meant nothing to me. It was just too much.

I had pulled myself together by the time Master Kavidrian returned. The food was the same unappetizing slop, and again I changed it with magic before I took a bite.

"Have you seen anyone else here?" I asked.

"Of course," he answered, eyes shifting around as if afraid he'd be caught. "You, and a few of the gods. A few guards that I suspect may not be mortal. There have been other prisoners here, as well."

I felt hope surge within me. "Was anyone else from Lesser Stonegore taken here with you?"

"No," he said sadly. "I'm the only one. Everyone else is dead."

"How? Who killed them?" If Master Kavidrian was here, perhaps that meant that Krecek had not destroyed the town. Perhaps Yda had.

"There was a flash of light and I found myself here. I found out later that everyone else had died."

"That's not what I asked," I protested, but he was already leaving. I followed him to the door, but by the time I reached it he was gone.

"How do I get out of here?" I murmured the words aloud in frustration as I walked the circle of the hall yet again.

The pictures on the walls had changed again, showing some

small drama about humans and Fotar, and harnessing the power of his flame without his consent or control. Everyone knew how that one ended, with an artist named Alon appeasing the god of fire with flattery. He never forgave mortals for using his power, but thanks to Alon, fire could be used for great things so long as we were careful. That was the essence of the story, I think. It's one I never cared for, especially now that Fotar was dead and fire hadn't changed in nature at all. Perhaps Alon had been a real man, but I always suspected that this story was not entirely the way mythology had remembered it.

Why aren't you using magic to leave?

"I don't know how!" I glared crossly at the depiction of Alon bowing down to a smug and gloating Fotar, since I had no way to direct the glare at Nalia herself. "If I knew what magic to use to leave, don't you think I'd have done that by now?"

You could teleport. Simply leave. You don't know how, but you can do it.

"If I don't know how, then how can I do it? That doesn't even make any sense."

I can teach you. It's not easy, it's exhausting and it upsets the natural balance since you have to cart around your physical form, but you can do it. I used to do it all the time.

"We could have died at any moment, and you decided to turn it into a lesson?" I was too irritated at this thought. "Teach me how. I want out of here as soon as possible."

You're ready to leave your old tutor behind to his fate and the wrath of chaos?

Oh. "I couldn't take him with me, you mean?"

Not with the command of magic you have right now, no. Perhaps with time. Perhaps with practice. Yda will not give you either, if she knows what you intend to do.

"Why did you bother to bring it up, then?" My exasperation knew no bounds.

To make you think. To make you realize you have resources beyond your own feet and eyes. This hall is an illusion, and you've been going around it for days.

She was right. I didn't like it, but she was right. "What else should I do, then? Start blasting down walls?"

It sounds like a good start.

I didn't know why I was here, though. I would never find out if I simply left. On top of that was the memory of Yda's attempt to kill me. Just the memory of the pain still made me tremble. It made me think I should return to the room and wait for Yda's return. I quickened my pace down the hall, opening the door--

A stranger stood within the room, and the room had changed entirely. The door looked the same from outside, but within the walls were covered in pictures that moved and spoke, fifteen of them that looked like the bare room I'd been in, and several halls with different murals, starting with the one of the creation of Kayan, of the world.

Master Kavidrian was in one of those pictures, humbly mending a shoe.

"I don't understand," I said, taking a step further into the room.

The young lady within calmly spoke into a tube. "Prisoner three has escaped. He has entered room twelve." She then turned to me and smiled. Her hair was as dark as mine, but her skin was like a porcelain doll's skin. "Lord Verwyn. Please wait here. You will be returned to your room shortly."

"How did I get here?"

"Please, Lord Verwyn. Just wait here."

"No! How do I get to that room?" I pointed to the room Master Kavidrian was in.

"You can't," she said.

Already I was puzzling it out, though. The murals in the halls were the key. They weren't randomly changing; they were indicating that I had been going into different rooms that mostly looked the same. This wall's pictures were arranged in a pattern, four corridors and then a room at the end, which must mean whichever one was in the middle. I'd been making only right turns as I wandered, so if I went left then perhaps it would take me backward, to the story of Ceraan and Agruet; the goddess of memory and the god of secrets.

I was already running down the hall before I'd fully figured it out. Now that I knew the secret I could feel the deception built into the magic of this place, the slight incline of the hallways and the distortion of the space it occupied. It nearly made me dizzy when I realized it, but I didn't have time. I had to ignore my vertigo.

"Master Kavidrian!"

He looked up at me in surprise as I crashed through the door. "Come on! I'm getting us out of here!"

"We can't," he said, shaking his head and backing away. "I can't leave, she won't--"

Master Kavidrian's voice cut off suddenly with a choked cough.

He began trembling.

He hit the floor and began to writhe.

I couldn't move fast enough. His skin distended, and there was this sound. This wet, sickening sound, like slurping and tearing. He--it seemed like he exploded in a great spray of blood.

Yda stepped out of him, as if shedding some bloody disguise full of bone and meat. "Leaving so soon?"

I'd been rushing to Master Kavidrian's side, to help him, to kneel down and do something, and I wound up on my knees before the dark goddess of chaos, wearing my tutor's blood and bits of his flesh.

I may have screamed. I may have gagged. I'm not sure what I did, exactly, but stare in horrified revulsion. I know I wasn't thinking clearly. Still, one thought rose to the surface. She had tried to do that to me before. That's what she had tried to do.

The thought was followed by one word.

Run.

"You're clearly not going to be swayed to my side," Yda said, taunting.

I was turning, springing to my feet, and dashing toward the door all in one motion. I had to get my distance so I could think. I had to get away from her so that Nalia could help me get away. Teach me what to do. At that point I was nearly willing to let her take me over entirely if it would just help us to survive.

I didn't have time to make that thought known.

"If you're not with me, I can't have you wandering around freely."

Yda's voice was right behind me, and I felt as if she could reach out and touch my back, grab my hair or my skirts, pull me back and steal my hope. She was a goddess. Her twisted foot and hunched back meant nothing. She could be anywhere.

Anywhere.

I stopped short before I ran into her, materializing right in front of me.

We were in a vast and rocky desert, halls and rooms banished to their alternate realm or whatever distorted space they belonged. Perhaps we had been squished flat within the bolder to our right, or maybe we had shrunk down small enough to fit into a grain of sand. Perhaps we'd been no real place at all, just a construct of magic.

This, though, was real.

I scrambled away, dress tearing as a branch from a bare but green tree grabbed hold with its thorns. Every plant here was sharp and vicious, leaves turned into spines that looked ready to rend flesh. Some rocks were worn smooth by time, but most were jagged and just as dangerous as the strange-looking vegetation. Beneath the blistering sun I could see no animals, but what sort of animal would venture forth in this heat?

I dodged at a sudden urging, feeling air rush past my head as some invisible projectile had been hurled at me. A giant tree-like cactus was hit, falling towards us swiftly, and with every bit of concentration I could muster I deflected it from my path. My shoes were made for softer paths, not these points and edges. I ignored the pain. Internally I chided myself for noticing discomfort in the face of death.

Wind was blowing around me, picking up speed as I ran with everything I had. The pointy spiny cacti and trees and bushes were thick, and the wind bent the weaker ones into my path, but again I ignored the pain.

The air grew darker and for a moment I thought it would bring relief from the searing heat. I thought only that it could herald rain. I looked up at a wall of dust and sand bearing down upon me, so tall it touched the blue sky, and it swallowed me whole. The tatters of my dress were pulled violently from my body, except for scraps of cloth that had maintained integrity. It felt like I was being pelted with tiny shards of glass from all directions. I heard Yda's laughter echo around me, her magic seeking to tear even the flesh from my bones.

"I will bind you, blind you, make you helpless as a babe!" My magic was being ripped from me as well. Every bit of me was being torn apart, shredded into nothing, beaten by whatever the wind was picking up....

"NO!" I coughed as the sand entered my lungs, scraping raw my tongue and my throat. My defiance was all I had left. This woman, this goddess, could not beat me. Could not destroy me. Could not end me, no matter what she threw in my path.

An explosion grabbed the world and shook it like a child's toy, bringing me to my knees, and a familiar sensation came over me. When my parents had died, I had felt like this. I tried to blink, tried to open my eyes, but the heat was too intense and I could not see a thing. I gasped for a clean breath of air and felt the ground rush up to meet me.

Part Fourteen

I heard a door open and close, followed by the excited chattering of a young man. "Is he awake yet?"

The young man was shushed by someone else, and I slowly became aware that I was awake. It hurt to breathe, but my lungs filled and depleted relentlessly. I thought about calling out to the voices I had heard, but all that escaped me was a raspy sort of moan. It was less a protest of the pain that overwhelmed me than it was an attempt to make them, whoever they were, aware of my state.

"Either you woke him up, or your timing is incredible." That was a woman's voice, but there was something strange about it. I thought about turning my head to look, but I wasn't curious enough to muster the strength it would take. I didn't even open my eyes.

"Are you okay?"

"How are you feeling?"

I sighed. I'd survived. I couldn't remember what it was I'd survived, exactly, but I was relieved nevertheless.

"Thank you," I whispered. I didn't know who or what I was thanking. It didn't have to make sense. Awareness slipped from me, but I was just relieved it would not be for the last time.

The next time I awoke, I smelled food. I felt something brush against my lips and I opened my mouth, drinking something that tasted like weak broth. I opened my eyes slightly to see a small woman hovering over me. Literally hovering. She moved away and I heard the clink of silverware being set down, and then she reappeared.

"Good morning," she said. "How are you feeling?"

I took stock of myself. "I don't hurt as much as I did the last time I woke up."

She smiled at me. "That's good to hear. Do you remember what happened to you?"

Did I? The first thing that came to mind was darkness and sand. "I'm not sure. It's hazy."

"It'll come to you," she said. "Don't worry too much. You were, as my people say, 'slippery and gibbed,' when they brought you to me. Humans tend to forget something that traumatic for a while. I expected you to be dead already, to be honest."

"It takes more than that to kill me," the words came out without thought.

She hummed thoughtfully in reply, looking me over. "You heal fast, for a human. Are you human?"

"I think so." I thought I was, but I wasn't entirely sure.

"You're not sure?"

It was a good question. I was fighting back panic as I realized just how much I didn't know. I tried to sit up, but I was tied down and bandaged all over. "Where is this? I--I can't remember anything! What did you do to me?"

The tiny flying woman scowled. "I didn't do anything to you but heal you. You were found at the side of the road. I heal people, I don't rob them of their memories."

I took a deep breath and forced myself to calm down and think. "I'm sorry," I said. "You were feeding me something. I suppose if you were the one that did this to me, you wouldn't be trying to keep me alive, right?"

"Unless I meant to torture you," she said, and then she held her hands out as if to take back what she'd said. "No, it's only a jest. I have a terrible sense of humor. Most of the time I'm healing the horses, and they don't care what I say."

I relaxed. I nearly laughed at her joke, but my chest hurt too much to try. "It's fine," I said. It took no effort to smile, at least. "I appreciate what you've done for me. Whatever it was you had to do…"

She shrugged. "You were covered in residual magic when you were brought in. I nearly choked on it. I couldn't tell what it did to you, though. Aside from flaying you and breaking nearly every bone in your body, that is."

"That's why I'm tied down?"

"Yes," she said. "To give your bones a chance to heal." She looked me over one more time, flying over me to take thorough stock. "I never would have thought it, but I'll be unbinding you tomorrow. Remarkably fast, for a human. You should rest now. Sleep is good for healing. If you awaken and need me, I'm Tarela. I will be here."

"Thank you, Mistress Tarela." I was feeling worn out from all the talking, and the sheer effort of being awake.

She giggled. "That would be Betain. Tarela is my given name. If you're in pain, Tarela is quicker to say than trying to be formal. What about you? What can I call you?"

I opened my mouth to answer, but I couldn't find an answer. I didn't just not know where I was or how I got here, but something as simple as my own name was gone as well.

"That too?" Tarela sighed. "I'm sure it's just a bump to the head. It will come back to you in time. Rest and give your brains a chance to heal as well."

"Thank you," I said. The thought that I couldn't remember anything about myself at all was a miserable and lonely one. I heard a door open and she flew away to greet the new arrival. I took the opportunity to rest, falling back into a deep and troubled sleep.

At night Tarela surprised me by being able to change her size to something closer to human. She explained that it was the magic of her family, and that every faerie family had a different magic aspect that could help them. I fell asleep again before she said much more than that. In the morning I finally met her assistant, a young man named Fereth. His hair was black and curly, clinging to the top of his head like a bird's nest. His skin was paler than mine, though, and his eyes were a bright and brilliant shade of green. I trusted him immediately, liking his enthusiasm and warmth.

"I'm assisting for the season," he said as he introduced himself. "It's part of my apprenticeship at the stables. I have to know how everything works."

"His father, Fanrin, runs the stables," Tarela said. "Fereth here will probably take over, at least if Fanrin has his way."

Fereth scowled a little and changed the subject. "We're replacing all the bandages today, right?"

Tarela nodded, already set up and ready. "Go wash up and start a fresh pot of water to boil. I'm not entirely certain I prepared enough bandages last night."

"Just hit them with a clean spell," Fereth grumbled as he walked out of the room.

"The boy has a good heart," Tarela said. "He just has many things he would rather do at any given moment. He daydreams, and he's almost obsessed with the past, but he'll give his last nub to a stranger without a second thought."

I smiled. There were worse traits to have as a young man. "How long will you be teaching him?"

"He just started with me not too long ago," she said. "I'm sure he'll be the one assisting me the entire time you're here."

Silence followed while she flew around and prepared. I sighed and slid into a half sleep while Tarela and Fereth worked on me, keeping silent so as not to distract them at any point. I was worried at the sheer amount of questions about myself I could not answer. Who am I? Where do I come from? What happened to me? Tarela had said that it would come back to me over time, but I was impatient and worried.

"Sleep now, stranger. You're healing swiftly. That's all you need worry about for now."

Her words were like a blanket. I was comforted by them, and slept.

"How often do riders come through here?" I asked Fereth a few days later, after I'd gained more strength. He'd been talking to Tarela about the stables, horses, and a rider coming through in the middle of the night, until she flew out of the room to check on something. It was the only thing I could think to ask to fill the silence.

"Not that much, usually," Fereth said. "Maybe once a month or so. The last few weeks have been crazy with messengers, though. Something's going on."

"What do you mean?"

Fereth sat down beside me. "Well, when I was little, I remember riders coming through, um, every week or so. That was normal, until they announced that Verwyn had been found and would be learning how to rule his country. Then, for the last few years it was about a month or less. I guess Ceolwyn and Baelwyn didn't have as much to talk about once Verwyn was found. See, we're along the message route between them. There are six stops where riders can refresh their horses, and three

217

where they can pass off the message. Grennenburgh is the third stop. That's us. We don't have a relief rider waiting, but we've always got a horse ready."

"We used to have a relief rider," Tarela said, flying back into the room with a blank piece of paper. "Every stop did, when the Verwyn child first went missing. That was before your time, Fereth."

"Really?" Fereth said, looking both hopeful and disappointed. "I wish I could have talked to one of them. I'll bet they've got wonderful stories. Now they all just ride through."

Tarela nodded, picking up a pencil and a writing something while she spoke. "The last time I saw Lord Ceolwyn with my own eyes was when they were keeping a rider at every stop. It was but a few weeks after the Verwyn child was stolen, and a rider came in from a different road than usual. He was badly burned and barely alive. He was brought in to me, and thank goodness it was at night. I was able to grow to your size and attend him on my own in those first crucial hours before Ceolwyn arrived."

"My father told me about that," Fereth said. "The horse was a yearling, chestnut, and also badly burned. Missing a lot of hair. Said he'd never encountered a smell so foul or disturbing before. Every rider here took off in the night, vowing to outdo each other in getting the news directly to Ceolwyn before the night was through. I guess one of them succeeded."

"They'd had to have used better than the usual messenger spells," Tarela said with a shake of her head. "Anogrin's too far for any of them to have arrived that quickly. Ceolwyn had to have found out some other way. However he did, it was luck that he arrived when he did. The man was beyond my skills to help any further, but Ceolwyn healed the man with a wave of his hand. The amount of magic it took literally blew me backward into a wall, and I watched silently from that point on.

"The rider sat up immediately, gasping as if waking from a nightmare. He said he'd found the Verwyn child, but the child's parents were mad with fear. The rider had tried to soothe them, but the moment he suggested they return to Anogrin they cast a spell that set him ablaze. He cast his own spell to quell the flame, but the heat remained, consuming him and his horse as his horse ran blindly in terror. That they found our town before the burning devoured them both was a miracle."

Tarela paused a moment, and even her wings stilled to further the solemnity of the silence that fell. When she began again her voice was heavy with remembered emotion. "I don't know what sort of monsters Verwyn's parents were, to do something so terrible to a man doing his duty. I've heard some defend them as simply parents doing what any parent would do to protect their child, but that goes beyond any cruelty I've ever seen before. People accuse wizards of being aloof, cold, and even cruel, but after that night I can't believe it. Ceolwyn embraced the rider as if he were a brother, comforting him as the memory of the pain he'd been through overwhelmed him. I'd never seen such a depth of compassion. It made me think that it must be very lonely to be a wizard. All anyone sees is the vast power, the show and the flash and the spectacle. No one sees the person behind the position."

"It does sound lonely," I said, not understanding the flash of empathy her words brought to me.

"That's what she just said," Fereth said, snapping me out of my melancholy. "Anyone can be lonely, though. Everybody walking around, thinking someone else has everything going so well, but everyone's got their problems. Not just you, or powerful wizards, or orphans, or homeless wrecks found at the side of the road."

"Oh no, I just realized," I said, a bit startled. "If I don't know who I am, and I don't know where I live, I'm homeless unless someone recognizes me."

"You just worry about healing," Tarela said sternly. "We'll worry about finding your home, or finding a new one for you, once you're back on your feet."

"I'll never be able to repay such kindness," I said.

"Don't worry," Fereth laughed. "It's a busy town. They'll find a way to put you to work, and you'll earn your keep and then some in no time at all."

Tarela cleared her tiny throat. "There are spell pages to put away and bandages to clean and herbs to hang to dry and..." She ushered Fereth out of the room, still listing chore for him to do.

I sat in silence, mulling the conversation over in my head. Try as I might, it felt like I'd found a puzzle piece with no puzzle. Something about the conversation somehow felt personal to me. The harder I tried to figure out why, though, the faster the feeling slipped away.

The day eventually came when I was well enough to take care of myself. A week after that Tarela agreed with my self-assessment.

"You still haven't recovered any memories," she fussed over me, flying from one shoulder to the next as if looking into my ears would give her the answers we both craved.

"Nothing," I said. "If it's not from a bump to the head, perhaps it's magic. If that's the case, the spell will break or it won't, and sitting in here taking up space won't fix it any sooner. You've done your best."

"That's the problem," Tarela sighed. "I said your memories would come back, but you don't even know your name. If that's from a spell, it's a mighty powerful one. I'd just like there to be more that I could do."

Fereth walked in with a sack. It was pitifully small, for all that it contained the only items I had left in the world. They'd provided me with two suits and a shift I could wear in privacy, for comfort. The clothes itched on my healing skin, but they fit well enough and they were better than the scraps of cloth I'd been brought in with.

I opened the sack and sighed. "Buttons, a necklace, and bloodstained rags that look like I rolled in a child's sand box."

Tarela nodded. "It's what you looked like from head to toe when you were brought in. Sandblasted until you were bleeding all over. There's no sand like this anywhere I've ever been, though. It's red by itself, that's not just the blood."

"Then I'll have to earn enough money to travel until I find a place with red sand," I said. "And hope I don't run into whatever attacked me."

"You could stay here," Fereth said, hope in his eyes. "It's peaceful here, mostly. You won't get attacked like that again."

"I might," I said. Why not, if I could find a way to earn my keep? Eventually I'd want answers, but there was no rush. I pulled the necklace out of the sack. "Was this in the tatters of a pocket?"

Tarela shook her head. "You were wearing it around your neck. It looks delicate, so I thought it might be some sentimental keepsake from someone you once loved. A wife, a mother, a fiancée."

"My mother, perhaps," I said. That word at least stirred feelings within me. The necklace didn't make me think of a woman, though it seemed to be made for one. "It's not even scratched or tarnished. Did it cost much to restore?"

"Not at all," Tarela said. "This is elvish craftsmanship. It may be dainty, but it's enchanted. You'll never need to have it repaired. I thought you knew."

"Elvish?" I tried to think about what I knew of elves. "They don't just give things like this away, do they?"

Fereth was inching closer now to get a better look at the necklace, and I couldn't blame him. What kind of person had I been to have such a thing?

"It can also never be stolen, only given," Tarela explained. "Whoever gave this to you must have cared for you a great deal, or owed you their life. That, or they did not know the value of what they were giving. Elves keep to themselves, so anything of theirs that makes their way to the human population is extremely valuable. Even a spoon crafted by an elf would be...coveted."

"It's probably the best clue I have to finding who I was," I said as I put the necklace on. I would keep the necklace, sell the ornate buttons, and discard the ruined fabric they were attached to. It would give me a start in my new life.

I frowned, absently extending the wick on the lantern as I took hastily scribbled notes and turned them into the minutes of the last town meeting. A town as small as ours did not have a printing press, so my duties as the assistant scribe were varied and seemingly endless. I was less than impressed with the penmanship Mistress Greta had when rushed, but she was quick and accurate even if it did take me a bit of time to decipher her scrawl.

Just two more pages to go, I thought with an internal groan. She was quick, accurate, and entirely too thorough for my taste. She always used six words if only one word would do. I thought from time to time that she was trying to impress me, but it honestly lead more to eyestrain than admiration.

There was a tap at the window just before my door was thrown open. "Come on, finish in the morning! You can waste the Master's oil some other night!"

I looked up and grinned. Fereth was there, older and taller than when I'd arrived. He'd become my first friend, and it was a friendship that hadn't waned when I was no longer a novelty that may spill untold secrets at any time. His lessons with Tarela had come to an end, but he used the knowledge he'd gained to help his father in the stables. It wasn't his ideal job, but as the oldest son it was what was expected.

"I'd just have a miserable time, knowing what awaits me in the morning," I said, rustling the offending pages toward him.

"Mistress Greta again?"

"Who else?" I sighed and set the pages down.

"All the more reason to spare your eyes for a time."

I looked at him skeptically. "Who bribed you into interrupting me?"

"Bribe is such a weighty word, full of meaning that lends itself to negativity. It suggests underhanded dealings and payoffs behind closed doors among those lacking morals."

I raised a solitary eyebrow.

"Mistress Elliniva may have offered me a thing or two if I persuaded you to linger in the great room longer than usual this evening," Fereth drawled, pacing his words slowly for effect.

I sighed, dusting and then clipping my page on the line next to the others to dry. I finally blew out the lantern and stepped out of my small office. "A thing or two?"

"Nothing like that!" he protested hastily. "History books and old letters she found in her grandfather's shed when he died."

Boring things full of useless information to most boys his age, perhaps. Fereth had told me time and again that the girls in Grennenburgh were shallow and flighty, and he would rather fill his time with more fulfilling pursuits. His insatiable curiosity had strengthened our friendship, since it was something we had in common. Sadly, it had long ago driven away most of the girls despite his status as the son of the most influential man in town.

"Did she say what she wanted with me? Elliniva struck me as singularly uninterested the last time we shared company."

Fereth shrugged. "She said the great room, not a cloak room, so my guess is she wants to be seen in public with you. Perhaps she's out to make someone else jealous."

It seemed a well-reasoned conclusion to make. I had been extremely popular among the women at first. The mystery of my origin had drawn them in, but none of them stayed interested once it was realized that my memories would not return easily or soon. They were pleasant enough diversions to be had, but no one grew special to me, nor I to them.

I shook my head and smiled a touch. "I'm sure she'll let me know when we get there."

A comfortable silence fell over us as we walked, until a moment before we arrived.

"By the way," Fereth said, standing before the door with a smug grin on his face. "I do know what she wanted. Since no one knows what your naming day was, we thought we'd make up one of our own." He pushed open the door and waved me in.

Most of the town was there, with a veritable feast set up in my honor. Usually a naming day was something small, something quiet for a family to celebrate when a babe had proven healthy enough to live and the parents felt it safe to give a child a name. There was a small celebration of life, usually private, every year after that. Before the Arcane War it had been the day a child was presented at a temple and every year expected to return to give thanks for another year of life. That practice had fallen to the wayside for obvious reasons.

"We've been calling you Lanrin long enough, so we've all decided to name you officially, until such a day as you remember the one you had before. We all want you to think of us as family, for as long as you need one."

My eyes stung at the corners, and my vision wavered a bit. It took me a moment to find my voice. "Thank you all," I said, putting a hand on Fereth's shoulder as I looked around the room. "I couldn't ask for a better family, for as long as you can all stand to have me."

Laughter and cheers followed. They threw me a party I'd never forget, with stories and music and great conversation and even better food. Everyone had brought a bit of something to share. Mistress Greta handed me a complete, and less chaotic and wordy, version of the minutes I'd been transcribing earlier.

"I have a feeling I've been set up," I said as I looked it over, shaking my head.

"We've been planning this for a week," Greta said, grinning. "Thosak had the idea and a few of us may have taken it over to a bit of an extreme." She gestured across the room to her husband, who was talking to a few others.

I couldn't contain my grin. "I will need to find a way to repay him, some day. It is a wonderful gift."

"Think nothing of it," she said. "You're an easy man to work with, and our sleepy little town has quite enjoyed having something new to talk about. You're a welcome distraction, and a good man."

I was overwhelmed. The sentiments of all who attended were the same, making it the best night I've ever had. I was not haunted by memories or chased by worries. They made me feel at home, finishing the night with a handful of the most creative people in town making up silly backgrounds for me, each more outrageous than the next. Fereth was crowned the winner, claiming I had been a tree until being cursed by an errant surviving god in the throes of madness, to be a human. I could never do justice to the way he had told it, with gestures and asides and different voices. It had all of us laughing by the end.

It was then that Fereth became enamored of telling tales to an audience, and began to fancy himself a bard. I encouraged him, to his father's dismay, but once he had a taste for it nothing could have stopped him. He was born to be a bard and a troublemaker. My part in it was incidental to his eventual success.

The entire time I spent in Grennenburgh, not knowing a thing about my past, was peaceful and pleasant. I wondered why my memories wouldn't return, but it became a passing curiosity. It fell into the same sort of daydream as finding the perfect woman and having a family.

Perfectly safe. Perfectly mundane. Perfectly normal.

The perfect trap.

PART FIFTEEN

The apple tree was by the road; fair game to anyone brave enough to climb it to reach its fruit.

"Lanrin, I've got another," Fereth said as he grabbed a low branch and scrambled awkwardly up onto it. "You were a High Priest of the Old Gods, and when they died you were put into a magical coma. A wizard found the temple ruins you'd been sleeping in, but he didn't know you were trapped there, and he blew it up!" He paused, leaning against the trunk as he clapped his hands together for emphasis. "The explosion broke the spell and you barely survived. The magic overloaded your brain, erased everything, and here we are. Did I get it this time?"

I laughed, craning my neck to watch his progress. "No, I don't think so. I woke up familiar with at least some history of the last three hundred years. Eventually you'll stumble on the truth." I watched him climb along the limbs of the tree to get to the best apples. "I only hope I can remember it if you ever do come up with the right story."

Fereth laughed as well. "Okay. Here, catch this." He dropped an apple into my hands and I slipped it into a pocket. "There are some better ones just a bit higher. Two for you, two for me, one for Mother, and—"

He broke off right about the time I was about to ask him to be quiet. I'd heard something unusual in the distance, and he must have seen what it was. He leaned forward and nearly fell in his attempt at closer look. He dropped two more apples down to me and climbed down in silence. "It's a carriage," he said. "Red, yellow, gold. Those are Baelwyn's colors, and that's no courier. I'll bet it's the wizard himself."

He took one of the apples from me and slipped it into his

own jacket pocket while we ran back to let everyone else know what he had seen. I had no idea what to think, since we were in Ceolwyn lands and another wizard was approaching. It was about midday, so perhaps he was just traveling through. Still, seeing a wizard traveling through or stopping, it was unusual enough that it couldn't go unnoted. I was ready to call out to the first person we saw, but I hesitated over what to say.

"Inspection! Tell the stables!" Fereth's voice carried and soon people were crowding their windows or busying themselves with previously procrastinated chores and duties. He then stopped and turned to me, catching his breath. "It might be a false alarm, but it's better to be prepared." He leaned against the wall of the nearest building and gave me a quick grin. "We only get this kind of excitement once in a lifetime. Usually they're too busy for surprise visits, but all the old folks like to tell us about one that happened twenty years ago, or fifty, or whenever."

I heard the rumbling of the approaching carriage again, and there was no doubt it was slowing down as it approached. My heart beat faster. Despite the love of the townspeople toward Ceolwyn and despite their reverence for wizards, I was terrified. I hadn't realized I would be. It just came from deep inside and I froze in place, watching the carriage approach as if trapped in a nightmare. The wheels trundled to a halt just a few feet away and Baelwyn stepped out.

The first thing I noticed was that he looked familiar. His nose was a bit too prominent and hooked for his face, but he was tall and looked more like a king of legends than a scholarly wizard. He wasn't just tall; he was round and looked strong and habitually jovial. His eyes swept the activity around him, taking it all in instantly, and I could see the calculation in his eyes before he allowed himself to relax and smile. "Just like I left it," he said to the coachman who was tending to the horses. "How long has it been?" He turned his head toward me and Fereth. "Young man! How long has it been?"

"Um, twenty years, I think?" Fereth stammered at the sudden attention. "It was before I was born, Lord Baelwyn."

"Of course, of course," the wizard smiled and kept looking around. His dark eyes finally met mine and he did a double take. "Do I know you?"

"I—I...don't think so," I struggled to get the words out, stammering worse than Fereth had. I knew to the core of me that I did know him, but my memories remained stubbornly silent. He was a part of my missing past, and I nearly forced myself to ask him, to admit to him about my forgotten memories, but my terror would not be conquered so easily.

"No, of course not," Baelwyn laughed. "Come! Drink with me and fill me with tales of what I missed since I was last here. It seems I have time to kill before Ceolwyn's inspector arrives."

"Fereth can," I said, gesturing to my friend. "He knows a lot of history. More than I do." I almost told him I was new to the area, but that irrational fear continued to hold my tongue.

"Very well, Fereth. You tell me everything while my new friend and I drink to your health and long life." Baelwyn ushered us into the inn with him and ordered enough mead for him, me, and his servants. Nervous townsfolk made nervous gestures and murmured softly among themselves about horses and wondering how long this visit would take. The entire event seemed to have all the excitement and anticipation of Nightwatch to everyone but me. For myself, I drank half a glass of mead straight away to calm the terrified tremble of my hands.

Fereth did his best, embellishing only a little to keep his audience interested in what mostly amounted to the day-to-day business of a largely unimportant town. The two visits of Ceolwyn were glossed over, since Baelwyn nodded and gestured impatiently as if he already knew all there was to know of those incidents. They'd been his couriers, after all.

Finally Fereth came to my arrival, nearly three years before. He mentioned my lack of magical ability, but my possession of quick wits, impeccable manners, good taste, and unusual degree of literacy. He mentioned my mysterious amnesia, and Baelwyn grabbed my head in his gigantic hands and peered deep into my eyes. I felt his magic probe my mind, surprisingly gentle and leaving behind an impression of care and compassion as his presence receded.

"There's something in there worth knowing, and something keeping it all blocked up and hidden. If it's magic, it's something I've never seen. Then again, I am hardly a healer, or the sort that people would bring such problems to." He shook his head and released me. "I am sorry that this is something I cannot fix. A couple of my brethren may be able to find something I cannot, and may even be able to help you regain your memories, but that is beyond me. What did you do, anyway? Were you in a fight with another wizard and lived to forget the tale?" He laughed and patted me on the shoulder kindly and with an unexpected gentleness.

"If I did I wouldn't know," I said, slowly relaxing around this giant of a man.

"If you crossed any one of the other wizards to the point that they would do something like this I doubt you would be sitting here," he said with a twinkle in his eyes. "I have an extensive collection of books in Plath. I rescued them before the razing of Anogrin some, oh, three hundred and some years ago. I'm sure one of them will have some hint about how to cure your memory."

I stammered over an answer, but Fereth's enthusiasm overshadowed my hesitation.

"Books? Three-hundred-year-old books?"

"Oh no," Baelwyn said. "They are much older than that."

"Older?" Fereth looked stunned and excited. "May I go, too? Can you tell me what everything was like back then? Oh, please."

Too? I hadn't agreed to go. I wasn't sure I wanted to go at all, some small sense of dread of being taken by a wizard reared its head and roiled my gut. I wanted my memories returned, more than anything, but the thought of leaving this comfortable life was suddenly unbearable.

"If the two of you would like to accompany me to my home, I would be delighted to have company."

For Fereth's sake I nodded. It would be a dream come true for him, to be able to learn more about the past.

"I would be honored," I said, trying not to show any hint of my irrational fear. "Thank you for your concerns."

"I love a good enigma," Baelwyn said. "It will be my pleasure to host you and your friend."

Baelwyn's carriage was surprisingly comfortable. We left early the next morning, having to rush to explain to everyone that our absence was at the invitation of a wizard. No one could argue with that, though my fellow scribes looked put out by the extra work they would now share. Fereth's father was less than happy, but a wizard's wish was law.

The early hours inspired a long stretch of silence as the scenery passed us by. Well, it wasn't much for scenery, to be honest. There were trees, there was the road, and on occasion we would reach the crest of a hill to see the trees from a slightly different vantage. The road itself was rocky in many spots, which was an interesting change from the deep ruts in the rest of the road. The condition of the road was less than ideal, which made the comfort of the carriage worth remarking.

"Lord Baelwyn, you said yesterday, when you arrived, that you were going to wait for Ceolwyn's inspector," Fereth said suddenly as midday approached. "Yet suddenly, we're leaving just as fast as you could usher us from town."

He made the words sound spontaneously thoughtful, as if it were something that had just occurred to him. I could tell from how his hands were clenched, however, that Fereth's question had been an act of courage. It was a detail I had forgotten. It raised my own fears anew.

Baelwyn nodded. "I have an idea of who you may be, my friend." He looked me directly in the eye as he spoke. "I am not certain, but if you are who I think you are, you are many times more important than any inspection."

"How important?" Fereth said.

The wizard looked us over closely. "Imminently important. If I'm wrong, of course, I'll return you to Grennenburgh in comfort with a golden favor each."

"What if you're right?" My voice was softer, shakier than I'd expected. I cleared my throat. "You don't think I'm some sort of a criminal, do you?"

"You are in no trouble," Baelwyn said. "You may not be happy if I am right, but you are in no trouble."

I wasn't sure if the dread I felt was fear of false hope, or fear of whatever he thought I would not be happy about. "It would be good to know, though."

"If I am wrong, I will have stirred up trouble in your soul for no reason," he said solemnly. He then rapped on the roof of the carriage. "We should take a break, stretch our legs, and perhaps eat a bite."

The food was good and the company was jovial, but I still felt a sense of unease. Baelwyn and Fereth conversed with ease and enthusiasm the rest of the day, but I was wrapped up in my own thoughts. I stared out at the landscape as the trees grew sparser and the land lost its rocky outcroppings and breathtaking vistas. My thoughts were running through the same circles, over and over, always coming back to the beginning as I realized I did not have enough information to decide how this should all make me feel.

There had been a feeling of recognition when I first met Baelwyn that I still didn't understand, but my fear did not seem to be tied to him as a person. It was the idea of him being a wizard that inspired that thrill of fear. I knew it didn't make sense to fear someone with such a joyful personality and generous spirit. I liked Baelwyn in a way that I genuinely wanted to be his friend. I wanted him to like me in return.

A large tent was set up as twilight came upon us. I'd half expected Baelwyn to have a tent of his own, but his bedroll was no different than anyone else's was. He did not hold himself above anyone else, and his infectious smile was as generous to me as it was to servants who looked like they had a mere handful of years before they retired. They all spoke as if they were members of a large family, happy to be together and help each other, each to their own ability. His coachman was named Alador, and his footman was named Erador. They were brothers, and they addressed Baelwyn by his given name, Raev. As the evening grew into night and the conversation became more natural, I found it hard not join in with the same comradery.

I eventually lay down upon my own bedroll and stared up at the darkness of the tent's roof. All my thoughts had finally run their circles to a conclusion. When I set my feelings of fear aside I found several sound, logical reasons not to run away in the dark of the night. Baelwyn didn't seem at all malevolent in his intentions. Secretive, yes, but not malevolent.

Even still, I fought with myself to stay with them through the night. Something within me urged me to run away and not look back. It was a gamble to go with this wizard. Despite his assurances, I was trusting someone who I did not know with my fate. He may have lied when he said I was in no trouble. He did not seem to be lying, but my unreasonable fear persisted and made me wonder.

My fear built within me and told me to run. Leave Fereth behind and just disappear.

I couldn't.

A bemused part of my mind wondered, as if the words had come from another person entirely, when I had ever been concerned for hostages in the past.

The thought made me dizzy and faintly sick. Fereth was my friend, an innocent I could not abandon. I had no idea what sort of person I used to be, but at this moment I was a man of honor. Besides that, I thought to myself, Fereth had the makings of a great bard someday. If I left him now, he would come up with some wild tale that would haunt and embarrass me years from now. I couldn't have that.

The fear kept me from sleep, but reason kept me from running. It was a long and uncertain night, but at daybreak I felt content with where I found myself.

Baelwyn was even more relaxed and gregarious when he saw me in the morning light, and I was sure I caught him sighing in relief. "You looked like you were not so sure of staying with us," he said in a moment while the others bustled around us, breaking camp. "This morning you have the look of a man who has made up his mind. You have no idea how good that makes me feel."

I smiled in return. "I just want answers. If you have them, I'll conquer any fear."

"I could assure you that you have nothing to fear," he said.

"Proof will convince you better than my words could, however." He turned to help the others with their work. No pretense, no magic, but plenty of muscle and sweat.

He was clearly a man of action. I would indeed see his proof in the end.

By nightfall we were nearly to the lowlands, the mountainous region of Ceolwyn mostly behind us.

We drank that night, and I learned songs they both loved. Fereth's songs were ones I'd caught him humming or whistling before, but his father had discouraged outright singing. It was probably in a futile attempt to keep him at home and keep the rest of the town from encouraging his lofty dreams of becoming a bard.

Baelwyn's songs were bawdy for the most part, and I assumed they were as ancient as he was. When sleep came upon everyone I joined in, and in the morning we felt an ease around each other that surprised me. I didn't know what sort of fate I was headed toward, but the journey was becoming oddly joyous.

The foothills gave way to expansive grasslands with occasional trees that poked out as an afterthought. The roads were flat and well maintained, and we saw other travelers more often. Baelwyn told us when we crossed the border to his lands, and I felt my mood lift as we did so.

"How soon will we arrive at Plath?" Fereth asked, hanging out the open carriage door as if he meant to climb to the top with Alador.

"Perhaps this very evening," Baelwyn said with a smile. "The city is near the border because it is a trade hub with the rest of the countries under wizard rule. To the other side of my lands is the great desert of Navrihal. Beyond that, elves, and beyond their lands is the frozen wastes."

I could almost remember looking at a map that showed these things. The frozen lands of the north. The great expanse of forests where the northern elves lived and let no human tread without permission and strict supervision. To attempt otherwise was met with a swift death. South of that was the Great Chasm, then a vast desert wasteland called Navrihal. It was a place where subversives were exiled, and where primitive people somehow thrived outside any sort of rule outsiders would understand. The rest of the continent was the domain of the wizards, and beyond that...

"I never thought about your lands being on the border of Navrihal," Fereth said. "Do you have problems with exiles or savages trying to sneak in?"

"Savages?" Baelwyn raised an eyebrow. "Those are my people. I was born in the desert to a tribe of traders and nomads who were as civilized as any who live under wizard rule. My people may have different hierarchies and moral codes, but we are not savages."

Fereth looked terrified, and understandably so. "I didn't know! That's just...it's what people say. I didn't mean to offend. I had no idea."

"Obviously," Baelwyn said. His tone was wry and he looked more tired than offended. "I am no stranger to what is said in insular and homogenous communities. I just wish that these were things that were not said. All the powers of a god, and still I am mocked by sheer ignorance."

"Can't you do anything about it?" I asked.

"What would I do?" Baelwyn shook his head. "I could cast a spell to erase the very word 'savage' from language, but another word would take its place. I could command people in my own kingdom to never say such things under pain of death, but that would only prove them right in their hearts. If I turned people into mindless slaves to my will, I would be worse than the gods we deposed. Perhaps someone who did not earn this much power the hard way, who did not see why the war was begun, would have fewer qualms. I hope I never see a day where that happens."

"You teach all the Elementals not to abuse their power, though," Fereth said. "Don't you?"

"We try," Baelwyn said. "Learning from others is not the same as living the lesson yourself. And, of course, there was the Verwyn child who was stolen from us, and has again disappeared. There is no telling what he has learned, or what he might do." He glanced at me and then quickly looked away, out one of the windows.

My blood ran cold. "Is that what you think?"

Baelwyn looked me over, but he held his silence.

"Do you think I might be him? Do you think I am Verwyn?"

"I can't be certain," he said. He paused, looking pensive and drawing out the silence for a time. "Verwyn disappeared months before you were found in Grennenburgh. The timing does not disprove the idea, though your lack of magic should. However, I met Agrad Verwyn once, just after he came of age. I carried him from a cemetery to my carriage because he was unconscious at the time. I had a very good look at his face, and you remind me of him, but older."

"An elemental knocked unconscious?" Fereth said. "What happened?"

"It was eight, almost nine years ago," Baelwyn said. "On Memory Day."

"The one where everyone fell into fear and sadness?" Fereth interrupted. "I was little, but my parents told me about it. They said no one could explain it, but it hit everyone all at once, and it was all anyone would talk about for years."

I tried to remember. I know I would have been old enough to remember something like that, but it eluded me the same way every memory did. I shrugged, frustrated at yet one more thing that was locked away from me.

"Yes, that is the one," Baelwyn said. "An explanation would have caused people more concern than a mystery, so none of us explained what had happened. Not publicly." He took a deep breath and leaned back in his seat. "If most people in this world knew just how dangerous a young elemental could be it would cause panic and mistrust. That day, we had come together to honor Memory Day in our own way, and we had planned to bring Verwyn into the fold at last.

"Kaelwyn's brother had been mentoring him for us, keeping an eye on him for years and letting him lead a normal life. We had tried to bring him to us before, but that ended poorly. So, rather than scare him and have him lose control of his magic, we left him alone until he came of age. Kaelwyn herself made contact with him, but we overestimated his state of mind. He tried to hide from us, but he did not know how to control his magic. He tried to make himself insignificant so that we would not notice him, and it worked at first, but it worked too well. The magic took a life of its own, and it projected his emotions across the entirety of Kayan.

"It could have been worse. No one died that time. Still, a colleague of mine had to knock him unconscious in order for us to undo what he had done. We hold the powers of creation within us, we have the powers of gods. Each of us are capable of great wonders, but also of greater atrocities."

"What do you mean by 'that time'?" I asked.

Baelwyn's expression softened. "If you are not actually Verwyn, you have no business knowing what it is. If you are Verwyn, I will not burden you with knowing of such a tragedy.

I'm sorry, my friend. I should have said nothing."

The capital city of the country of Baelwyn was Plath; a sprawling city that looked like it could be packed away and moved with very little notice. It wasn't that there was a lack of permanent structures, but that there was a plethora of portable ones. Wagons and tents dominated the outer layers of Plath, with merchants calling loudly and colorfully for attention. No, they didn't use course language; they were not crude at all. They were flowery and poetic, and more than once I found myself craning my neck out the carriage window to follow what they were saying.

"These are just the merchants who gather here and on occasion leave," Baelwyn said, chuckling in clear amusement as Fereth and I stared at the chaos around us. "These are your 'savages', Fereth. They are simply nomadic people with no roots. I don't even know where it was I was born. My mother, father, and older sister were all of differing opinions. These people know my heritage and stay here longer than in most places, so that this has become almost a new homeland for many of these folks."

"You're right, though," Fereth said. "They don't seem savage at all to me. Just loud. Very loud."

"I never imagined a place like this," I said. "There's so much going on all at once, everyone trying to get attention all at the same time."

"It's like a hundred circus troupes met up with a hundred traveling actors and they're trying to sell you everything they've ever seen," Fereth added.

Baelwyn nodded, looking satisfied. "Just wait; this is still the edges of town."

As we traveled into the center of the city the buildings appeared more stable, but no less colorful. The palace where we were being taken was surrounded by a low wall that showed the colorfully painted walls and the garden statues that towered higher than anything else in the city. The statues slowly morphed into new shapes as I watched, from towering trees to giant interlocking rings and finally to human-like figures that resembled our host. My eyes were so stimulated that I'd been tempted to shut them at times, yet I did not want to miss a thing. It was a relief when we were finally ushered inside the palace proper.

Fereth and I shared a guest suite. A bath had been drawn and fresh clothing set aside for each of us before we'd even reached our rooms. It was a pleasant surprise as we entered, and I relaxed immediately into the luxury of washing off the grime of travel. It wasn't until we were in the sitting room, clean and waiting to eat, that Fereth finally spoke.

"Do you think you might be Verwyn?"

"I'm trying not to entertain that thought," I said. "The idea scares me. What would it mean if I am? What will they expect of me, especially without magic?"

"Don't you think they'll return your memories before they expect anything of you?"

"Probably," I said, "But do I want them?"

"It's all you've wanted for years," he said. "Why wouldn't you?"

"Everything Baelwyn said on our way here," I said slowly, putting to words a half-formed dread. "I've been so happy in Grennenburgh. If I'm Verwyn, I'll be leaving that behind for—"

There was a soft knock at the door and many servants came in with several small plates of food. Both Fereth and I were thoughtful as we ate, silent in the face of eating before others.

The servants seemed to be gauging our reactions to each dish, immediately taking away any we weren't pleased with, giving us a moment with any we seemed indifferent to, and taking special note of any that made one of us nod or smile. On top of that there were small glasses of wine, beer, and some of the cleanest water I had ever tasted, and our preferences were gauged on those as well.

"At this rate, I won't ever want to go home," Fereth said once everyone had left. "To think, this is only one city. What must the rest of them be like? I want to see them all. How can I go back when there's so much to the rest of the world?"

I smiled at him, understanding how he felt, but still feeling trepidation. "I'm sure they're all wonderful in their own way."

We'd known each other for three years. He saw through me instantly. "Lanrin, what's wrong?"

"If you never return, that's all there is," I said. "You travel, you see everything, and it's amazing. If I don't return, it will be because I'm a wizard. It's a lot to live up to. If you do something wrong, your family will be concerned. If I do something wrong, entire countries might be endangered. On top of that, it's Verwyn that I might be. Of all the wizards, why Verwyn? Tragic. Cursed. I don't know, Fereth. If you hadn't wanted to come here so much, I'd have been happy to just stay at home and be a scribe the rest of my life."

Fereth reached over and placed a hand on my arm and he smiled. "You'll be powerful; you'll be able to do whatever you want. I've seen who you are without being all-powerful. You are a good person, and I can't see that changing no matter what you are, or what you find out about yourself."

"You know more about Verwyn than I do," I said. "Do you really think that's true, with all you've read and all you've heard?"

"I know who you are," he said firmly. "I believe in you."

If he had faith in me, I vowed to myself to live up to his expectations.

PART SIXTEEN

A few days later I was in the library, staring at the book before me more than actually reading. My mind drifted easily and played with a thousand thoughts before I could remember that my eyes were skimming over words without giving them meaning. I felt as if my thoughts had become the city outside the walls of Lord Baelwyn's estate, flashing color and sound before me and then fading beneath the flashy onslaught of the next.

I was probably Lord Verwyn. The thought would flash before me, but without context or knowledge, or even magic, the idea was adrift, imperative but unable to take root. It came to me dozens of time, shouting like an undisciplined child, and then running before the repercussions could begin to unfold.

This was invariably overshadowed by the next thought; all too soon I would know of a certainty if I had inherited the troubled position of that particular elemental. Baelwyn had said that Ceolwyn would probably arrive within the day, and he above all other wizards would know beyond doubt if I was Verwyn. Again, it flashed before me with blinding realization, but again, without supporting thoughts to sustain it.

The questions that haunted me were unstoppable and varied. I kept coming back to the first two distracting thoughts though. I sighed and rubbed my eyes, turning back a page to find the last paragraph I had paid any attention to. Another page, and as I reached the last paragraph I remembered reading, I heard voices coming from down the hall.

It wasn't a new or unusual occurrence here, but I closed the book and sat back. I wasn't accomplishing anything, sitting in front of a book and failing to read. There were too many distractions, inside and out. I leaned back in the chair, closing my eyes and listening as the sound of voices came closer.

"She used the candles, keeping the curtains drawn all day."

"Candles?" a second voice replied, sounding scandalized. "Even if she can't cast, there are lamps all over the place if the light of the sun was too much. I should know since I have to fill them every day."

"Candles are for common folk who make their own," the first voice said in an irritated tone. "She said it was because she was sick, but if you're sick why would you wander around a room lighting ten or more candles in the middle of the day? I think she was just trying to be difficult."

I smiled to myself a bit at the mundane conversation between the women walking in the hall, thinking of how life went on despite my distraction and dilemma.

The conversation in the hall died suddenly as a third set of footfalls echoed down the hall. Once again it was not an unusual occurrence, but this time (as every time) a knot of apprehension settled in my stomach. I held my breath until I heard the soft murmur of conversation again, retreating down the hall. I opened my eyes and reached for the book to put it away, but a soft sound caught my attention. I looked up toward the doorway to see someone standing there, watching me.

The first thing I noticed about him was that he was undoubtedly a half elf, short of stature and fair of color. The second was that he wore blue and silver, colors I'd seen displayed so often in Grennenburgh. I knew at a glance he must be Krecek Ceolwyn. I set the book down slowly and carefully, wondering if I should recognize him, or if he should recognize me. My hand trembled a bit, and to hide the motion I rested it on the book's cover and took a deep breath, waiting.

"Agrad?"

It took a moment to force a reply from my lips. "Am I?" My lungs emptied in a great surge that started as a relieved sigh, but ended in simple shock.

"Undoubtedly," he said, walking toward me, touching my arm as if to assure himself that I was, indeed, real.

"If you are Lord Ceolwyn, you would know better than I would. I can't remember a thing." I sat there, watching him look me over, at a loss as to how I should react or what I should do.

"Yes, I really am Krecek, and you really are Agrad Verwyn. I'd recognize you anywhere; I've been looking for you for so long." He had hold of both of my arms now, and he stared into my eyes intently. "Even with short hair and without magic I'd know you. I am amazed you're alive, after what happened the last time I saw you. You don't remember a thing? Not even that?"

I shook my head. "I don't remember a thing, but the mention of it scares me. What happened? Can you fix this? Can you help me remember?"

"Normally I wouldn't have a doubt that I could. There's not much I can't do." Krecek took a step back, shaking his head. "When gods are involved, things grow a bit more complicated. I can feel the magic that's locked away who you are, and I can tell which goddess it was who did it."

"Oh." It was a hard idea to think about. I was so close. I knew who I was now, but what if the knowledge would do me no good? An elemental without power, without magic, and without even the training to govern his own country.

"Don't lose faith, yet," Krecek said with a small, reassuring smile. "It will take time and some effort, but I think it can be done. I've done the impossible before."

I relaxed, finally allowing myself to be hopeful.

Dinner that night was a small feast. It was served in Baelwyn's private chambers to keep me from being overwhelmed, but the amount of food and drink that was brought to us was a clear indication that we were celebrating. I ate silently while Baelwyn and Ceolwyn exchanged the sorts of words that only the oldest of friends could, starting stories only to be told that the other had heard it a century ago.

"Who is this other young man?" Ceolwyn said at one point, looking at Fereth curiously. "Do I know you?"

"N-no, Lord Ceolwyn," Fereth stammered, surprised. "I am Fereth Taden. My father runs the stables in Grennenburgh."

Ceolwyn thought about that for a moment. "I've met your parents, then."

"Did you notice his eyes?" Baelwyn said, straight faced.

Ceolwyn looked closer, raising an eyebrow.

"Don't they look familiar, somehow?"

Ceolwyn gave Baelwyn a dirty look. "They look like the eyes of anyone descended from elves."

"But this one is from your own country," Baelwyn said, grinning. "It calls to mind that night--"

"No," Ceolwyn said. "It does not."

"Are you certain this boy might not be a descendant of a by-blow from--?"

Ceolwyn frowned, and Baelwyn cut himself off with his own laughter.

Fereth was blushing a bright shade of pink, but I found myself laughing as well. Even Ceolwyn began to laugh, shaking his head. "I suppose I cannot be entirely sure," he said ruefully as the laughter tapered off. "It's been a very long time since those days, though. Responsibility has caught up with me and made me a responsible and almost respectable figure."

"What a terrible fate," Baelwyn raised a glass as if his words were a toast, and he drank deep.

"Don't believe this gluttonous wretch," Ceolwyn said, putting his hand over mine so I would not join Baelwyn in a drink. "He'll have you thinking I wenched my way across half my country in the early days."

"You mean to claim you did not?" Baelwyn chuckled and refilled our glasses himself. "Look at that face of his, my friends. Krecek would never have a cold or empty bed, if he allowed it. Human women swoon at the sight of him, but he claims he would sleep with his books instead. In fact, a great deal of men would stand and volunteer for the position of bed warmer, if he gave them the chance."

I choked on my wine. It wasn't shock at the notion, but surprise that his words had seemed to answer my own thoughts. Krecek patted my back while I choked until I waved him off.

"Nearly any human would entertain the thought," Krecek said, rolling his eyes. "That's the problem. Humans. Even immortal humans eventually die, or their hearts turn elsewhere."

There was a long and mournful pause, while the two wizards looked at each other, sharing something I could not understand.

I watched them, taking a deep drink of my wine. "Surely not every human is fickle," I said softly, hating to intrude.

"No, of course not," Baelwyn said. "Our friend, Krecek, has just seen too much that has been painful. He has currently forgotten how joyful life can be if you let it."

"I'm sorry," I said, putting a hand on Ceolwyn's shoulder. "In fact, I'd like to apologize for all humans who have wronged you."

He looked startled, as if I'd just done the most absurd or unexpected thing ever. "How much wine have you had?"

"I don't know," I said. "Enough that I can talk without getting so very worried about what I'll say?"

"In that case," Baelwyn started. He ended the sentence by refilling my cup, which made Ceolwyn smile.

"Oh no," I said. "I won't be able to stand if I drink much more. I have a feeling this wine is horribly potent, more than any we had at the inn. Even now I might not be able to make it to my own bed."

"Nonsense," Baelwyn said. "Tonight, we are celebrating! The wine will help us relax and forget the long road."

"You traveled by carriage," Ceolwyn said, leaning against my shoulder. "I was on horseback. Three days. And, I did not bother to sleep." He looked at me with a mischievous grin.

"Are you trying to kill more of my horses?" Baelwyn drew himself up with a look of anger on his face. "I've warned you!"

"I switched them out properly," Ceolwyn protested, straightening as well to match Baelwyn's posture. "I used magic to keep them fresh as well. When I arrived in Grennenburgh I was an entire week behind you. The very hint of finding Verwyn again was worth all the magic I could muster to know for certain."

"Why?" I asked. "You didn't have to push yourself so hard. It could have waited a few more days so that you could travel in comfort, couldn't it?" I took his hand to show my sincerity, and apology, that he put himself through that just for me.

"I've been searching for you for years," he said. "Nearly all your life I've been searching for you in some way or another, for some reason or another." Ceolwyn was looking deep into my eyes, and between that and the wine I was feeling very lightheaded.

"Well," Baelwyn said loudly, drawing out the word for nearly a minute. "It could have something to do with Krecek feeling responsible for your latest disappearance. Oh, and the one before that. And the one before that."

"Raev, please," Ceolwyn said with a sharp look at the other

wizard.

"It is your fault," Baelwyn said.

"I hate you with the blackest hate of the darkest forest for the brightest fire some days," Ceolwyn said, eyes narrowed. "It's not as simple as blame and fault and sure, Verwyn was my responsibility at the time, and my custody for his own good, but there were things going on at the time and we will talk about this later, once Verwyn has his memories back."

It honestly took me a while to remember that they were talking about me. "So, you think I'll remember it all someday?" My words were remarkably unslurred, and I congratulated myself silently.

"I'll need to bring you all the way back to Anogrin, finally, but yes. I can return your memories and your magic, if you are certain that you still want them. I think I like you better like this. Sane. Rational. Normal. And not at all trying to get yourself or someone else killed."

"Powerless?" I suggested the word with a frown. "Because that's my least favorite part. I look at you and you have all this sort of power. Because you're nice. And you're so...soft..."

I slid down onto the floor under the table and I rested my head on Ceolwyn's lap.

"I suppose I was wrong. I should have offered more water and less wine," I heard Baelwyn's words as the world went dark around me and then I stopped paying attention to anything but how comfortable I was for a very long time.

I relived all of those memories vividly when I woke up, groaning softly to myself at how embarrassing my actions had been. I didn't suffer a hangover, but I was suffering for my actions nevertheless. I pulled the blanket over my head and hoped against hope that Fereth would be kind enough to leave me alone until a decent hour.

"Are you planning in hiding in my bed all day?"

I sat bolt upright and stared in shock. Oh, no, no, no! I didn't remember this at all! Had I fallen asleep under the table with my head in Ceolwyn's lap? How had I gotten from there to here?

Ceolwyn was smirking at me from the side of the bed, and I must have blushed to my toes. "I didn't realize where I was."

"It's not the first time we've found ourselves like this," he went on. "Though, you were a bit more snuggly last night than the last time we shared a bed."

My cheeks were suddenly hot enough to catch fire. "Just how much--?"

Ceolwyn shook his head. "You were too drunk to make it to your own room. I thought, perhaps, you were trying to gather too much courage. I know why you have wanted to run away from us, why you are afraid of us, and why you feel so conflicted right now, even without your memories. You hated me, Agrad. With very good reason. When your memories return, you will see."

"I can't imagine that," I said. "I like you. There's something about you that makes me want to be close to you. I don't want to hate you."

That made him pause, but he still did not turn around to look at me. "If you don't want to, then don't. No one will question you. You're a wizard, Agrad, and you were born with more power than any of us. No one will force you to hate me or even so much as look down on you if you don't. I will not hang on to hope until your memories are returned to you, though."

He walked out and left me alone.

I hadn't unpacked a thing, but I still found myself putting items in my trunk as I prepared to leave. I'd been given new clothes to befit my station as a goodwill gesture from Lord Baelwyn. We'd stayed only one week and I was frowning as I wondered how everything was supposed to fit. Some things, like the rare tea grown only in Lord Baelwyn's private garden, or the wine that had been bottled during the Arcane War, could be shipped to my estate along with any other belongings I could live without but did not want to discard.

"You're going to need a new trunk and your own carriage, at this rate," Fereth said next to me as he scanned everything I had laid out. "Why do you want to take it all with you? It's a bit much."

"Everything over here I'll be sending off," I said, pointing to the right half of the bed where I'd spread things out. "I don't think there's any help for it, though. I'll have to unpack so that I can pack again. You realize that the contents of this trunk represent my entire life since I was found in Grennenburgh?"

"That's it? They packed it all in that little trunk?"

I shrugged. "It wasn't even completely full, and I've more than doubled it in a week with gifts I'm not sure I even want. They're nice enough, but what am I going to do with a bag of spices blended just to season an animal you can't find outside of dwarven tunnels? Do I have a trade agreement with the dwarves where I can even get a silver-spotted giant salamander? Or is it going to sit in my kitchen until the flavor has been leached away by time?"

"It's still incredibly valuable. If you don't have a trade agreement, maybe you could trade it to the dwarves for something else?"

"That's not the point," I frowned. "Some of this is fantastic, but I feel like it's not really mine. It all belongs to some wizard named Verwyn I barely know a thing about. How can that wizard be me? Even the clothes are too soft and too finely crafted, even though they fit me like nothing else ever has. I'm wearing the clothing of a madman, sending a madman's gifts to his home of madness, spending time with a madman's friends as if they were my own. The more I hear of Verwyn, the less I want to be that man, but they keep handing me these things in his name as if to appease one of the wrathful old gods."

Silence fell between us as I moved a few precious items, mostly clothing, from my trunk to the pile of items to be shipped to my estate. I moved a book from that pile and set it closer to my trunk, but I didn't quite set it within yet. It was a volume of history, and I wasn't sure I wanted to read it on the journey and find out more of what atrocities had been committed in the Verwyn name.

"You are not a madman," Fereth said at last, sitting down on a clear spot on the bed. "You won't become one, either."

"You've heard the stories and the history." I sat down next to him, staring across the room at nothing at all. "You know it all better than I do, even."

"You are who you are, Agrad."

He hesitated over my name, still trying to call me Lanrin, and I knew that's all he saw me as still. I would always be the man found at the side of the road, helpless as a kitten, harmless as a newborn babe.

"If you're afraid of who you might become, just make the decision not to be that person."

"As simple as that?"

He nodded and patted my knee. "Why wouldn't it be?"

"I don't know," I said, starting to feel confused. "What if I had my reasons for being who I used to be?"

"You probably did," Fereth said. "Won't you have reasons for changing, though? You're not--"

His words were interrupted by a knock on the door.

"Sir! Lord Verwyn!"

I recognized the voice of the maid assigned to our suite and shook my head as Fereth rose to open the door. I'd run out of time to hesitate over my decisions, so I explained to her which things would need to be shipped away and which things I wanted to go with me. Fereth disappeared into his own bedroom, leaving me to brood alone.

My doubts were not entirely overwhelming, but they weighed on my mind more and more as the time to leave drew closer. I wanted to be lost in the thrill of knowing who I was and knowing that I was powerful and would never have to scrimp and save for every silver wheel I earned. I wanted to enjoy the idea that my future was spread wide open before me, and I finally had all the power I could dream of and more. Of all the elementals to be, of all the people to be, I couldn't help but be worried at what a reputation I had inherited. It was simply overwhelming.

"Lord Verwyn," the maid interrupted my thoughts. "That book. Will it be going with you, or shall I send it ahead?"

In my hands was the history book I'd been pondering over so hard, trying to decide just how much of my own history I wanted to know before I could remember it for myself. I realized I'd been fingering the pages for some time while she'd finished packing every other item I hadn't yet packed myself.

I hesitated. I wanted to know what I would be facing in my future, but by the same token knowing it ahead of time wouldn't change any of the events and could never prepare me for what was to come. I opened it to a random page, staring at it a moment without reading a word while I thought.

"Send it ahead," I snapped it closed with a feeling of finality.

"I may want the perspective later, once the memories have settled in."

"Yes, Lord Verwyn," she smiled as I handed the book to her.

There was a certain freedom in making that one decision. I was going forward into the unknown. It seemed wondrous. I was going into a world of untold adventure, when all I remembered was a day-to-day life of insignificance. Even my fears were, momentarily, thrilling.

We went by horseback rather than carriage, possessions tucked away in rare magical pouches that held more than they looked like they could. They were extremely valuable, Krecek informed us with a laugh and a shake of his head. "I received the three of these as a gift of good faith during a treaty negotiation with one of the elven countries. It takes a hundred years to make each one, and craftsmen will only make one at a time."

"I suppose I'd better not get used to this," Fereth opened and closed the flap over the top of the pouch he'd been handed, sticking his hand into it and pulling it out with a look of puzzled wonder on his face. "These don't look like much for taking a century to make. You'd think they'd make these look amazing, not just like any ordinary pouch."

"They're not always given to wizards, or even mages. Some of them are given to ordinary people who cannot easily fend off the greedy. This way they are hidden from attention and do not look like anything a thief might be interested in."

I nodded. "That makes sense. They stand out a little bit from everything else you're carrying, though."

"I'm not at all concerned with thieves," Krecek said. "There aren't many out there who would have hope of accomplishing it, let alone eluding me afterward."

It should have been obvious to us that he would be so confident. With his power, both magical and political, who could get away with stealing anything any wizard cared for? I thought about it, wondering how much of a problem that might be. Would Verwyn's estate, my estate, be the most vulnerable to theft? Did certain wizards look out for each other? Since I'd heard that Ceolwyn and Verwyn had traditionally been allies, did that mean Krecek watched out for just this sort of thing when I was incapable of doing it for myself?

The journey was, despite worries and expectations, fairly pleasant and uneventful until we reached Ceolwyn lands. The weather had picked up and was threatening to storm, and Krecek looked skyward with an expression of irritation. "No delays," he said.

The wind immediately stilled.

"Did you do that?" Fereth asked with wide eyes.

"Yes," Krecek said. "We'll be in the mountains tomorrow, and the pass is difficult when windy and muddy."

"So, just like that," Fereth said with a wave of his hand, "you can control the weather? Just because you wish it or because certain weather would be and inconvenience to you?"

"Any wizard can," Krecek said. "It's easiest on our own lands. Sometimes it's too easy, and the weather will reflect our moods. I try to keep that in check, however. There's a natural system to the weather that I prefer not to change without reason."

"What's been happening in my lands since I left?" I had to know. "Do things like the weather fall apart without me, or will that natural system you mentioned take over?"

"You've never shown an interest in that before," Krecek said, looking pleased. "Things return to their natural state for the most part, but Byrek keeps most disasters at bay." He anticipated my next question and held a hand up to forestall it. "Byrek has been the steward of your lands essentially since Davri died, and has taught every Verwyn since. He is no wizard, so Raev and I help when he needs us, but he is a mage of enough power that he keeps things running. If it helps, we have only helped if lives are at stake."

"The two of you could do more than just help though, couldn't you?" I shifted in my saddle and my horse paused half a step in response. "The two of you, or Byrek even…against my will, you could destroy —"

"We could," Krecek cut me off before I finished. "Right now we could, and if you had command over your magic I, or any of us, could make things very difficult for you. I've told you, though, I'm not your enemy and —"

I guided my horse closer to him and put a hand on his arm. "Thank you."

His surprise was punctuated by a sudden gust of wind before he regained emotional control. He nodded and we continued on in silence for a bit before Fereth came up with more questions to fill the time. My friend was clearly delighting in having a wizard's undivided attention and took full advantage of it. I couldn't complain since all the questions he came up with were ones I was curious about, myself. Unlike the trip with Baelwyn, we conversed extensively and enthusiastically about history, the truth behind certain rumors, and just how magic worked.

We took our time for the most part, and we always had somewhere to stay along the way. We didn't camp outdoors, so sometimes we stopped early in the day and sometimes we didn't come upon the next town until very late at night. We rode through Grennenburgh in the middle of our journey and a few people waved, but the sight of Krecek with us kept anyone from approaching. I felt a pang and wondered if this was the last time

I would see the town. I would soon have a home of my own, and Grennenburgh was so far into another's country. I wanted to do something to thank them for taking me in and helping me when I had nothing, but it was a very prosperous town for being so small. I wasn't sure what I could do.

"I'm not coming back until I'm the greatest bard in the world!" Fereth yelled as we passed, and my concerns were forgotten as I laughed aloud. Others in the square laughed as well and then they returned to their lives as usual.

PART SEVENTEEN

The final inn we stayed at was an unexpected delight. News of our arrival had preceded us. We were greeted with warm baths, mulled wine, and hearty food, without needing to make a request. There were two rooms reserved for us, and before I was aware that any arrangement had been made I found myself alone in the larger room with Krecek.

I hovered near the door, unsure a moment until Krecek began talking casually as he settled into the room. "I will have business as soon as we arrive," he said. "I swear I will return your memory and your power as soon as I possibly can, however."

"It's fine," I said. "I've waited this long. A little longer shouldn't matter." I moved to the opposite side of the bed from him and sat down hesitantly.

"Everything will be different, though," Krecek said as he pulled out his night clothes and began to undress. "I'll be more formal, and I won't have time for your friend's questions anymore. I've got to set up an area where bringing your power back will be safe in case you lose control."

I hesitantly took off my shirt, getting ready for bed and thinking about his words. "I can imagine that is a matter of great concern. I've heard that my reputation is…" I hesitated, trailing off a bit and feeling a weighty silence hang in the room before I found my voice again. "I'll do my best to stay in control, however much that will help. I don't want to do anything horrible or disastrous. It doesn't strike me as the sort of thing I'd ever do on purpose."

"I know," Krecek said softly, pulling on his nightshirt. "There have been accidents. There have been mistakes." He walked over and put his hand on my shoulder, offering comfort and reassurance. "I'm not just talking about your accidents and mistakes, either. We have all made them in our time. Or, in my case, quite recently. Becoming what we are, after doing what we've done...there was no rule book. There are no guidelines or helpful suggestions about what to do when you've devoured the soul of a god. I used to have nightmares about that sort of power being possessed by a person who could not be controlled. When we lost you all my nightmares came true."

Learning about my history from others had given me an outsider's perspective. However, his perspective, the perspective of any of the wizards, was not one I'd really considered. I put my nightshirt on thoughtfully, mulling over his words, and finally nodded.

"What scares me," Krecek said, "more than you growing up with no training and no control, is the thought that there are still Old Gods out there. If we could do what we have done, so might someone else. We all made mistakes, and some of them earned us a reputation as bloodthirsty tyrants. What's to stop us, except each other? And I think that's what you have been doing. Well, Verwyn, not you personally. I've just never been able to ask."

"So, I've become the nightmare that keeps the others in line?" I shook my head, bemused. I opened my mouth to say something, some comment that his mention of Old Gods had tried to bring to the surface, but it faded too fast to hang onto. Instead I said, "That's quite a bit to live up to."

"There's more," he said. "I have been entertaining the thought that perhaps the Verwyn line has been riddled with death and war because something within your soul is watching. Keeping us in line, even when you can't remember that you're doing so. We'd talked about this just before you were taken from me, and

I looked into it afterward, but I had to be discrete. The gods we killed are not quite as dead as I'd supposed. We have their power, but it has come at a price and you have so far paid the most for it."

"What do you mean?" I sat down on the bed, feeling as if my knees had gone weak. "Does it have anything to do with my amnesia?"

Krecek sat down beside me. "Perhaps." He stared off at nothing, gathering his thoughts. "I can't be sure, yet. This goes further back than just recent events. When you were a child, you found your way to the city of Cairnborough. It was easy enough to find you there, but we could not risk frightening you into running again, or worse. We asked a dear friend of ours to watch over you until you came of age, and finally Aral Kaelwyn approached you on the anniversary of our ascension to power. We underestimated your fear, and overestimated how you would react to a wizard being related to Naran, the one who was watching over you."

"I've been told most of this," I said, feeling decidedly surreal to hear his point of view of things I already knew.

"Bear with me," Krecek said, smiling gently. "You said later that the spell you cast was to keep you hidden and beneath the notice of the rest of us, but I could tell as soon as I looked at you that it had weakened your self-control, your very presence of being. It may have made others in the world feel despair, but it nearly destroyed you. It released any sort of control you had over what remains of the goddess whose power your line possesses. She wore your skin like a costume and walked around like she owned you, and I'm not sure to this day how I managed so easily to drive her back and pull your awareness to the fore.

"I found out that after that event she spoke to you regularly. I thought at first that it was the incident that caused it. When you corrected me and told me that she had talked to every wizard in your line, and I began to worry. There was more going on than I had ever suspected, and before I knew what to do with the information I'd received, you were gone, kidnapped by one of the Old Gods..."

He trailed off into silence, and I didn't know what to say. Old Gods, voices in my head, spells gone awry, everything he said about what my life had been like scared me.

"I just wanted to warn you," Krecek continued at last. "There's nothing I can do. Once I return your memories, the goddess within you will talk to you again. She is part of what has been locked away within your mind. She is the most powerful of the gods we destroyed, perhaps the most powerful of all of them who ever existed. You'll know that immediately. I was one of her high priests before we betrayed them, and I think it would be her crowning achievement to finally see me dead for what I've done. I've given you ample reason to hate me as well, and when your memories are intact — "

"I don't hate you now," I said, reaching over and touching his shoulder, surprised at myself that I could be so bold.

He took my hand in his own, smiling sadly. "You will. When you can remember...it was horrific, and you were very young. All I will ask is that you find it in your heart not to kill me, and I won't expect even that. Your hatred and hers combined..."

"I don't want to kill you," I said, taking his other hand, holding them both as I thought of what it would feel like to embrace him and comfort him.

"I know," Krecek squeezed my hands as if they were a lifeline for a moment. "Right now you are happy, and you want to forgive." He let go and moved to his side of our large bed, climbing in and settling himself. "I'm not even old, for an elf. My father is barely considered mature, and he dances beneath the sun at the tops of the great trees. I didn't seek immortality, only change. Only justice. But even still, I am not ready to die."

"As long as I am still myself, I will not kill you. I swear." I laid down beside him, looking at him, knowing that there was a reason he had been close to every Verwyn before me, almost feeling a brush of familiarity and kinship with them all.

"Thank you," he breathed the words softly as if in a reverent prayer. "I believe you."

I believed it, too.

The following day went much as Krecek said it would. Our journey ended with a great deal of formality and throngs of people bowing down every street we rode through, culminating in kneeling when the gate to his castle closed behind us. Anogrin was a fortress city carved into the top of a mountain, and the palace that crowned it was solid and stark. Silver and blue were everywhere, even in the stone that shaped the city and the palace; true silver was used for nearly every piece of trim and only the people seemed to possess colors of their own. That impression remained with me until I saw one man among Krecek's personal retinue whose very hair and eyes were the brightest blue of all.

The blue man stared at me as if he knew me and wanted to approach, but instead he followed Krecek as Fereth and I were ushered to a suite of rooms of our own. Finally my eyes were met with colors more to my liking, with warm and inviting earthy tones highlighted with golden and green accents. I felt welcome and relaxed immediately, as if I knew these rooms from many happy times before.

Unpacking was done for me, and a bath was drawn immediately. Baelwyn's castle had been more ornate but relaxed. Ceolwyn's castle was stark and everyone within it was formal and efficient with every movement they made. Every face was neutrally set; every eye was either downcast or set upon their duty. Only one event broke their clockwork efficiency and concentration.

"Why have you set out a dress for me?"

They'd draped me in a long and delicate bath robe when I stepped from the water, and I'd thought nothing of it because I assumed the cold of the mountains called for more fabric. The dress draped across the foot of my bed was another matter, however. It was beautiful, and it did look like it would both fit me and suit me, but it was a dress.

All four attendants froze at once. One of them stepped forward, trembling slightly and wringing her hands. "It was all we had of yours. It's from when you were to visit before, but you never made it here. We did not know it would not be to your liking, Lord Verwyn."

"I packed a suit for my arrival. That lad over there," I gestured across the room to the young man who was helping the three ladies. "He just put it away. It may need freshened, but it should be suitable."

They scrambled to obey, acting as if I'd threatened to murder them for their mistake. I was bemused, but I was hardly angry. I'd been told a few times that I had the sort of face that would be fetching on a woman, but I hadn't expected something like this. I was pulling my trousers on as I thought of what the maid had said.

"Did I really wear dresses?"

No one looked up or answered. The magical sack that Krecek had let me borrow was emptied and all of my possessions put in drawers or wardrobes or on shelves. A fire had been built and was burning well in the fireplace, and as soon as I was dressed my valet and everyone else in the room quickly left. I settled into a plush chair and relaxed at last, putting aside all thoughts of what was to come. It was a rest I felt I'd earned.

Supper was just as formal and rigidly structured as settling into my room had been. A strict hierarchy seemed to be observed by everyone in the room, placing me to Krecek's right and Fereth somewhere further down. The table was large and long and the food was plentiful and delicious. It was the warm and heavy sort of food that I always appreciated on a cold night, and I enjoyed the rich flavor after traveling so much on food that sacrificed taste for portability.

Mid-way through the meal I wondered if the food was so rich because the chef had hopes of putting some meat on Krecek's bones. If so, it was a lost gesture. Even from my position to his right I barely had a chance to say a word to him as business and politics monopolized his time. He had barely a taste of each dish over the course of the evening because he was either listening intently or talking the entire time.

"Is it always like this?" I asked of the man to my right.

He looked at me, a bit startled, and then grinned after a moment. "It's a slight bit busier tonight, Lord Verwyn."

"So, word has gotten around that I'm here?" I smiled.

"Of course, of course," he said. "The anticipation has been building for a week. We have all been excited to hear you would be here at last, Lord Verwyn. You've been the most popular topic of conversation since your disappearance, and even for a wizard you are a legend."

"I had no idea," I said. "I've been somewhat detached from it all, I suppose."

"May I ask," he began, but I interrupted him with a shake of my head and he immediately looked abashed. "No, of course not. I'm sure your travels have been of the utmost importance and secrecy."

"It just does not seem to me to be suitable dinner conversation," I explained. "I've grown tired of repeating myself, for now. I do not even know who you are, sir. I have only just arrived, after all."

His face grew flush with embarrassment. "As always, I assume too much. I am Gadin Hart, my lord's own appointed mayor of Anogrin."

"It is good to meet you, Mayor Hart. I found your city to be beautiful as we rode in, and I'm sure we have you to thank for such a warm welcome after our journey."

"I merely coordinated with the guard," Mayor Hart said modestly. "It is the people and their love of Lord Ceolwyn that provided such a grand greeting."

I nodded, gesturing to him to continue as I could tell he desired. I listened to him as I nibbled at the next course of our meal, glancing at Krecek now and then to see that he remained busy the entire time. Would I have that to look forward to when I returned to my position? It was a daunting thought.

Conversations died down around us eventually, and I was startled to feel a hand on my shoulder. "Gadin, my friend, please excuse us. I've decided to walk Agrad to his room myself." I looked up to see Krecek standing beside me, a preoccupied look upon his face.

"Of course, Lord Ceolwyn," Mayor Hart said, wiping his mouth as he stood, and then bowing to us both. "It was an honor to meet you, Lord Verwyn."

"You as well, Mayor Hart," I said as I stood.

Krecek took my arm and we walked from the room in silence. All eyes were upon us as we left, and I was relieved as we reached the stillness of the hall outside. "Something urgent?"

I asked as we walked.

"No, not at all. I was simply tired of listening to complaints and requests, and I thought you would appreciate a respite from Gadin's incessant ramblings."

"He wasn't so bad," I said. "So long as he was talking, I wouldn't have to answer questions, or reveal the depth of all the things I don't yet know."

He chuckled and shook his head. "Gadin does love the sound of his own voice, and he spends most of his days listening more than being able to talk." We walked down the hall a few paces before he sighed. "I will give you your answers as soon as I can," Krecek said softly, "I just need time."

"I know," I said. "I do trust you."

"It's so odd to hear you say that," Krecek said. "It's something I wish I could get used to."

"I don't know what will happen," I said, "but I won't forget this. New memories will not erase the kindness you are showing me now."

He smiled just a bit, and we continued our walk in silence until we reached my suite.

"Rest well and be at ease," he said, opening the door for me. "I will see you at supper tomorrow."

I fought against a surprising urge to kiss him on the cheek and, flustered, I hurried into my room with a quick and possibly confusing reply. I closed the door, leaning against it hard. Where had that come from? Why would I have such an urge?

My visit here suddenly seemed less like a boon and more like the beginnings of madness.

A week passed, and every evening at supper Krecek offered

an apology for delays. I smiled and accepted this every single time, saying that I understood how busy he must be. The words began to wear thin as his excuses grew into a second and then a third week. He was always busy, always looking into one thing more, always needing to spend his attention on something new that had come up. On the fourth week he disappeared without a word.

"He was called away on an urgent matter this morning," Mayor Hart said. He took Krecek's place at the head of the table and attended to what business he could while I silently listened. He handled everything efficiently and in the way I thought Krecek would have, but I quickly grew bored with it all.

After two nights I began to take my meals in my room, spending most of my days reading or talking about matters of no real consequence with Fereth. He'd become popular with the young women at the castle, never lacking for company at meals or even just a stroll around the grounds. We talked about love and simple pleasures and sudden passions, but I was content to browse Krecek's library while my friend suddenly bloomed into a vibrant and confident young man in the presence of so many appreciative young women. He started out unsophisticated and easily flustered, but the women tutored him eagerly in the social roles and expectations of castle life.

"You seem to be a natural," I commented casually over tea, a full month after our arrival. I was growing anxious, but I could not complain about the hospitality we'd been shown even in the face of the absence of our host.

"Oh, hardly," Fereth said, rolling his eyes. "I am still tripping over my tongue and saying all the wrong things, but the ladies here are gracious enough to be forgiving."

"Be confident," I said, leaning back and smiling. "That itself will go a long way. I have heard that you're quite talented on a harpsichord, and that goes a long way toward impressing others as well."

"You heard about that?" He looked startled. "My mother taught me to play it, and a few other instruments, when I was younger. She said that a man who knew more than just horses would be more interesting. My father discouraged music in the house, and the instruments were put away as I grew up, but my fingers seem to remember enough. I suppose this is the sort of thing she meant, though I always saw myself entertaining my own children, not random ladies of the court."

"The maids have had a lot to say, too, when they think I'm not listening. I'd like to hear you play some time, though not over tea." I added that when he looked about to stand up and drag me to one of the harpsichords that could be found in the castle. "This is a time for relaxing, for both of us."

"I appreciate that," Fereth sat back and sighed. "I enjoy these afternoons with you, but I did not expect that we would share so many now that we know who you are. Has there been any news of when Lord Ceolwyn will return?"

"Not that I've heard," I said, suppressing a scowl. "I'd hoped you would have heard more than I had, from one of your ladies or such."

"Not a word, not a murmur, not so much as a rumor," he said. "How long do you think we'll be here, waiting like this?"

"I can't do a thing until Krecek returns," I said. "My magic is locked away wherever my memories are, and I'm not much of a wizard without either. You can leave whenever you want, but I'm afraid I'm completely at his mercy for now."

"I won't leave without you. I've never seen so much nor lived so well, and I am not eager to return home to the way things were. I'm doing what I want, finally. I'm meeting new people and learning new things. I'm telling stories, I'm singing songs, and there are no demands on my time that I don't make for myself."

I set down my teacup and looked at him closer. "You aren't homesick at all?"

Fereth shook his head. "I'll have plenty more stories to tell when I finally do return, but I'm not ready for that yet."

I nodded, but I didn't know what to say. I didn't know what it was to really be homesick, but I felt a vague craving for something familiar. Yet, it was a craving for something I'd never known in Grennenburgh. Perhaps I would know it soon, if Krecek ever returned.

"He'll be back," Fereth finally said, setting down his empty cup and standing. "You won't be trapped here forever."

I knew he meant that as a closing statement to our conversation, but that brought up so much that I couldn't hold in. "Are you sure, Fereth? Krecek told me he's worried I'll try to kill him. The other day Mayor Hart let slip that before I'd disappeared, I'd been given to Krecek's custody. Considering my age I can only assume that the others had found me incapable of ruling my own country. You have heard the same stories of my past that I have. I wouldn't trust the person they talk about, the person I used to be, to rule anything. I'm afraid of who I was. Fereth, this is insane. I don't feel like someone who could do any of those things, so what will I become when I know why I did them?"

Fereth sat back down, leaning forward. "The memories you made while you lived in Grennenburgh will still be your own. You've learned and you've matured, right? You don't have to give that up and be someone you don't want to be."

"Perhaps," I said. "If I'm afraid, though, I'm sure you can imagine why Krecek has not been in a hurry to change things back to the way they were."

He nodded, thoughtful, until the silence grew unbearable for us both and he took his leave.

I paced, thoughts awhirl with doubts and worries. Eventually

I decided to relieve my restlessness by walking aimlessly through the halls and corridors. I was tired of the same four walls, the same walk to dinner or the library. There had to be something new to see around a new corner or down an unexplored corridor. If I got lost I would ask someone's help, but the decorations were varied enough that I was confident I could return by finding some familiar painting or sculpture.

I gasped. Something had gripped icy fingers around my heart and squeezed.

I stopped, deeply afraid. This sense of dread was familiar somehow. Something from my forgotten past, perhaps? It was as if darkness would swallow me whole, but the halls were well lit and I saw daylight through a casement nearby.

I walked toward that light as if it were a lifeline. The sun on my face was an immediate balm for my soul. I stood, looking out at the view for a few long, rejuvenating minutes. The air was fresh and soothing, and there was just a hint of a cool bite and the earthy smell of harvest to it. I loved it, dismissing and forgetting my momentary fear as I looked out over the gorgeous mountainous landscape and terraced farmland, with their magical canals running upward from the lake in a valley below. One talented farmer seemed to be irrigating his crops with an unnatural rain cloud that hovered exactly over the crescent of his property, and I remembered what Krecek said about not wanting to use magic to control the weather too much. Surely something so small wouldn't affect much, but I mulled the thought over in my head a while until the crescent shaped cloud dissipated.

Eventually I turned around, looking at the hall I found myself in, and I was delighted to find it full of beautiful works of art. The first one that caught my eye seemed to be that of an adorable young girl. Her black hair was done in pin curls and the top was tied back away from her face with a bright yellow ribbon. Her dress was a rich golden color that flattered her lightly tanned skin. She was laughing and seemed to be caught in the act of dancing in a field of flowers. I could feel my muscles ache in sympathy for the child who had to stand in that pose for so long. The girl's eyes were a bright and vibrant shade of brown that seemed achingly familiar to me. My eyes were drawn to the pendant around her neck and I knew then that this was not a girl. Those were my eyes, and that was my pendant, the very pendant that I had been wearing when I'd been found. I sympathized with the aches of holding that pose because I'd felt it once, years ago.

This was the secret of how the wizards had found me as a child. I didn't look so much like a girl anymore, but I was sure that I could have passed for one with little effort. But, why?

I looked at other paintings along the hall, looking for more like this one. I found Krecek and Baelwyn in a few of them, but I did not see another of me until I turned the corner. It was the very spot I'd been overcome by fear, but when I looked at the painting I could not figure out why. I was older in this one, holding a parasol like a proper lady, blushing just a hint and smiling as if I kept some great secret. Was it the secret that I was a boy, perhaps? Or the secret that I was a wizard?

Whoever the artist was, he was good. All the paintings seemed to have been done by the same hand. Every image seemed as if they were about to take a breath or blink if I would just watch patiently enough. It wasn't the hint of reality that proved to me the talent of the artist. These were not mere portraits. They told stories and made a person wonder what else was going on, or what had just happened. I wondered at my own apparent mystique as a child, wondering if I'd truly appeared this way to others or if the artist had added something more that somehow wasn't there.

Either was amazing to me. I noticed the subtle way the body

was shaped, the almost unnoticed clues that this was me dressed as a girl and not just a girl's body with my face. The position of the elbows, the shape of the neck, the set of the jaw - I wondered how well I'd known the artist. I didn't think those were details the average person would notice, so rather than just being a model for him I must have learned from him over a period of time. I was about to move on to another painting to see what other details I knew to look for, and how they would strike me, but I saw someone.

The man with blue hair stood at the corner.

"There you are, Agrad," he sighed in relief. "We were almost afraid you'd disappeared again."

PART EIGHTEEN

I took a step forward, toward the man with the blue hair. I wanted to grab him by the shoulders and look into his eyes. I knew they'd be the same brilliant shade as his hair. "Do I know you?"

He looked startled for just a moment before he turned and ran back in the direction he had come. "Lord Ceolwyn, I've found him!" he called out. "He's this way!"

I started to follow, but he had run quickly. The commotion amused me so much that I waited and listened to the fuss being raised. A few minutes later Krecek approached, his relief was so obvious that I laughed aloud. "I've waited here a month," I said. "Why would I run away today?"

"I wasn't sure what to expect upon my return," Krecek said, starting to chuckle as well. "I suppose it has become habit to call a search."

The laughter we shared was not long lived, but the anxiousness I'd felt was forgotten over the course of it.

I finally gestured at the painting I was waiting in front of, buoyed with delight. "It's me," I said. "Who is the artist?"

"A friend," he said.

"He's remarkably talented," I said. "Did I know he was your friend? Wait, no, of course not," I added as soon as the question was asked. "I wouldn't have trusted him if I'd known. Is he the one who watched over me when I was young? When I lived in, what city was it, Cairnborough?"

"Yes--yes." Krecek was shaking his head, amused and slightly flustered. "Agrad, you are the most random person at times. Yes, all of these were painted by Naran Tennival, the man I told you about on our journey here. No, you had no idea he was a friend of ours. Also, hello, it is nice to see you again, and I would like to apologize for my sudden and unexplained departure."

I laughed again. "I skipped that part, didn't I? You must have been braced for me to be angry."

"Fereth said that you had been frustrated earlier. When no one could find you in your usual haunts--"

"I know, I know," I said. "I was upset, but, well, you caught me a bit distracted. And, after all, you do have a country to run, not everything is about me, so..." I shrugged. "I've given it some thought. Returning my memories doesn't sound like a light undertaking."

"It's not," Krecek said, growing immediately somber. "I'm ready now, but I have to admit I dread the prospect. It's been such a relief having you here, seeing you relaxed and at peace for once. I know that you're growing impatient, but I don't want to see you lose the light in your eyes that you've gained."

I actually blushed, feeling warmth spread through me from the way he looked at me. I felt strange desires build in me that I'd easily brushed aside or ignored before. I cleared my throat and looked away, questioning my motives. I couldn't want to kiss him now. I couldn't want to run my fingers through his hair just to see the contrast of his pale tresses against my darker skin. I shouldn't want to gaze into his eyes to see if an elf's eyes really did contain the secrets of the forests. Most of all, I should never want to know if he felt the same. He was the only person I'd felt this strongly toward, male or female, human or otherwise, but it was stupid to even entertain thoughts like those when I didn't truly know who I was or how I would feel about him once I did.

"The sooner my memories are returned, the better."

"One more day," Krecek requested softly. "Let me rest from my journey."

"Tonight," I said. "After dinner. I need to know who I am,

before I do anything I'll regret."

He hesitated still, looking down the hall at nothing. "What sorts of regrets?"

Could I say it? Did I dare?

I didn't trust myself to speak. Instead I took his hands in mine and leaned closer. I'm sure I telegraphed my every intention clearly as I bent to kiss him. As scared as I was, and as much as I hesitated, I gave him every chance to pull away before our lips met. I'd meant it to be brief, but his hands were no longer in mine. He was holding me close to him, kissing me in return in a way the girls from Grennenburgh never had. I wasn't coaxing a response, convincing a skittish girl that an intimate kiss would be a pleasure. We were kissing like equals, both of us eager from the very start until the end.

"Those sorts of regrets," I whispered, when I finally could.

"Were I a lesser man," Krecek said breathlessly, "I would take advantage of you, string you along, and offer excuses while I keep you happy and imprison you here."

The way he said it, I almost wouldn't mind it if he did. Almost. I was afraid, deeply, of what I would think of my actions once I remembered why I hated him.

"I won't," he continued, "but I'm a greedy enough bastard that I'm never going to forgive myself for this." He took a step back and took my hand, leading me somewhere. "I'll do this right now, but only because waiting makes it harder to face what is to come."

We reached his laboratory after many twists and turns and two flights of stairs. My stomach was tied in knots from the building anticipation. He sat me down in a plain wooden chair in the middle of the room. The rest of the room was full of items that sparked or spun, glowed or danced, attracting the eye and evoking the imagination, but this was a plain wooden chair with no padding for comfort, no carving of ancient runes, nothing that stood out about it at all except for its plainness in a room of spectacle. He circled a black cord around me and the chair, crossing the ends, and a feeling of lethargy came over me when the circle was complete.

"That is to keep you relaxed," Krecek said, patting the back of my hand reassuringly. "If anything goes wrong you'll be able to shrug it off with some effort, and I won't be able to force my will upon yours. Still, it will keep you from doing anything violent if a particularly disturbing memory surfaces."

"Like what?" I asked. It took effort to talk, but not too much.

"Like the time I beat you unconscious on Memory Day to save your life," he said with his back to me. I could hear the regret in his voice.

"I heard about that," I said. I wanted to let him know I forgave him, no matter how difficult it was to speak. "You did what you had to."

He looked over at me with a look in his eyes that stopped me cold. "Or that I killed your parents."

That troubled me. "No one told me that," I said. I wanted to be angry, or hurt, or sad, but it struck me as something far away and long ago that happened to someone else. "That might be harder."

Krecek winced and turned away again. "If I could only indulge in the absolution of an apology," he whispered. I heard him clearly, but I don't think he meant for me to. Even without the spell, I couldn't have thought of a reply.

He walked to one wall and placed a hand on a symbol there. At each corner and the center of each wall there were more symbols, and he walked around the room and touched each. When he reached the first one again they all glowed with a soft blue color. At the same time my skin felt cool and awash with a tingling sensation. I felt energy building within the room, making my breath catch a bit in my throat. I felt lightheaded and giddy, though physically I still couldn't muster the will to move.

"Are you ready?" Krecek walked over to me, looking into my eyes to make sure. "Good." He took a deep breath and placed his hand upon my forehead. "I name myself Ceolwyn, possessor of the power of Fotar, once the god of fire and flame. The power I possess is my own, and with it I name thee Verwyn."

A shiver ran through me, accompanied by an overwhelming sense of déjà vu. I knew I'd heard words like this before, and I was on the verge of remembering.

"Verwyn, possessor of the power of Nalia, goddess of magic. Cast off the spell of the Old Gods and remember who you are."

My mind filled at once. My skin crawled beneath his hand, and despite the spell that kept me subdued I struggled to contain myself. I had to maintain control. If I didn't--

I felt the goddess awaken as well and could feel her desire to be released. She was fully aware at the invocation of her name. I made a small effort to keep her at bay, but the influx of memories tripped me up. The pain of it all was immediate and fresh. I curled up around my thoughts, withdrawing, giving in to her promises of peace if I would just give her this small amount of time.

"Agrad!" There was panic in Krecek's voice, but it sounded as if it were miles away.

"No," I felt my lips move to form the words, but my voice was not my own. "Give him some time to recover, and the two of us will talk."

Nalia said more, but I wasn't there to hear what the two of them talked about after that. My consciousness seemed to shift to another place suddenly, some place warm and cozy and familiar. I sat upon a plush couch, the crackle of a fire blazing in a fireplace beside me soothed me, and even the scents were sweet and inviting.

"So. It's finally you."

That's just what I needed. Another voice inside my head.

Whoever it was chuckled, and I could feel that his intentions were benign. "Relax. The spell awoke me, but soon enough I will be a part of you. I prepared this spell centuries ago, just so I could talk to you before that happened, Agrad Verwyn."

"This room is of your choosing?"

"Of my choosing and of my design," he said. "I knew this would be your favorite room of the palace. It was my favorite as well."

I looked around, realizing why it was so familiar. It was a small study near the library, though I'd taken out the desk and replaced it with a couch within my first year living there. The chair that had been there already was comfortable enough that I'd left it, but I'd never used it. With just that minor change it had been my favorite room to find peace within.

"The couch is a good choice, but I still love this chair. I'm glad it has survived."

I could see him now. He was tall and lanky, and I supposed he was the reason all the doorways and ceilings in the castle had been so high. His skin was as pale as the pine wood that had been found throughout Verwyn castle, and his hair was even lighter, more like ash than what I usually thought of as blond. His eyes were the same bright brown that mine were, though, which I thought was a delightful coincidence.

"You're Davri," I said, certain of his identity as soon as the thought had occurred to me. I'd seen him so many times in Master Tennival's paintings without realizing who he was, but now I had no doubts.

"Yes," Davri said, sitting down with what seemed to be a relieved smile. "It's so good to meet you at last."

"You've been waiting for me?"

"In a manner of speaking," he said with a shrug. "I've been

waiting for you, and this moment, since the day I died. I've known it would come since I became a wizard and saw with awakened eyes just what the true nature of magic is. Do you remember?"

I nearly scoffed and said of course not, for that was his memory and not my own. I did remember, though. I stared at him in shock. "Yes, but how?"

"The memories belong to Verwyn," Davri said. "Krecek named you Verwyn, specifically, and as such his spell unlocked not just your own memories, but all Verwyn memories. I knew from my visions of the future that if Krecek ever had need to cast a spell to recover memory it would be because the Old Gods had made their move against the wizards, and I had to ensure that I would be their target. Well, Nalia needed to be their target, to be exact. And that brings us to you."

I felt dizzy despite not having any real awareness of my body. "That's why you died? That's why you declared war on other wizards, killing your brethren, spilling the blood of your allies —"

"To save the world." He got up from his chair to sit beside me on the couch. His touch seemed solid, though he was dead and I was still inside my own imagination.

Or was I?

"Davri, is this real?"

"Yes and no," he said. "The perception of it seems real enough, but it's just a bit of magic. Impressive, isn't it?"

"I wouldn't think something like this could be possible," I said. "The very idea would have been beyond my imagining."

Davri shook his head. "Don't start doubting yourself. I had a lifetime of magic training, but you've had a lifetime of learning self-reliance and survival. We have both, now. You are everything that I was, and I am everything that you are. Don't waste this gift. I gave my life so that we would have the best

279

chance possible. Never be modest. You're a wizard."

It was something I'd needed to hear. I'd always doubted myself, and always let others intimidate me. I was a greater wizard than any that had ever lived, and I had Davri's wisdom and knowledge to augment the lessons I now remembered from Byrek. I could do anything.

"Even Nalia can't stop you now," Davri said, leaning close. "The body is yours, and with that the power is yours. She may try to trick you into surrendering it, but she cannot keep it from you, now or ever." He smiled and caressed my cheek, looking into my eyes gently and proudly. "You may not have to worry, though. She likes you. In fact, she likes you enough to have forgiven me."

I was surprised he would think that. "She always told me she would kill me to get free if she could."

"That was before the gods made a move against her," Davri said. "She's been, well, sort of locked in this imaginary room with me, and with all of your predecessors. It's given us all time to come to terms with what happened, and with what is to come. You have choices to make now that will decide the fate of the gods, the wizards, and the entire world. You must finish what I started, and you are the only one who can."

I thought about it, realizing through his memories and visions that he was right, and the thought terrified me.

The spell faded and I quietly absorbed more memories, becoming just as much Davri as I was Agrad, realizing so many things about magic I'd never been able to understand before. I understood how the wizards had come to power, going so much further than just what textbooks said, and even further than what Krecek had told me. Aral and her brother had been catalysts to the ultimate conflict that had brought about the death of so many of the gods, but Davri had known things that none of the other wizards had realized. He'd had visions from a very young age, and he'd grown up as friends with some of the very gods they had killed.

That last revelation would have come as a shock to me if it hadn't felt so much like a memory of my own. Davri had kept so many secrets, and that was a concept that was not alien to me in the least. He'd been more gregarious, outgoing, and had known so many good friends that it was hard to integrate certain aspects of his life into my own, but those were external differences, and differences of expression. On the inside we were not so different that I could not understand his motivations, or felt like I had to second guess every decision he had made. They were things I could have done, or would have done if I'd been raised the way he had.

With Davri's memories came more knowledge of Nalia. The hatred she'd felt toward Davri had been white hot and destructive as the burning center of an exploding star at first. His betrayal of her had been particularly personal, for both of them. Davri may have been a human mortal, for the most part, but in his veins beat the blood of a god. It was the result of a casual tryst generations before, which was the source of his extraordinary talent and innate power with magic. He had not been sure which god had dallied with a mortal, but Nalia had known. As soon as Davri had trapped her, she had known she had been betrayed by her own blood.

When Davri had killed her and taken her power, he had seen a vision of the nature of magic and the world these gods had created, and the truth of Yda's nefarious plan. Unlike the other wizards who had hidden from the knowledge and rejected the personalities of the gods they stole their power from, Davri had deliberately awoken her and used her personality and knowledge to come up with his plan. He had to fight against her to implement it, to start out with the idea of awakening the other gods within the wizards, until she realized that his plan would lead to their deaths. She saw her revenge on the horizon and was almost gleeful in her enthusiastic assistance.

It had taken centuries for her bloodlust to abate, but eventually Nalia grew tired of death and tired of dying. I knew this from thoughts she had shared with me before I'd lost my memories, and I put those thoughts in perspective with what Davri had known. I slowly came to myself, aware of Nalia talking, but retaining none of it while I mulled over Davri's plan and all of the new ideas I had with all of my new memories. There were so many things I could do, if I just had the time to do them.

Time.

The thought struck me with disturbing certainty. Yda had been watching me. If she did not know already that I had regained my memories, she would realize it soon.

I've missed you, Agrad. I've missed being you.

Nalia's voice within my mind was soothing with its power and assurance. Without a fight at all I was myself again, aware and looking around the world with my own eyes.

Krecek had unbound Nalia at some point. I was leaning against a stone battlement overlooking the castle and all of Ceolwyn's lands. It was dusk, the sun had clearly set some time ago, but there were deep rose tones to the sky near the horizon still. I was startled that so much time had passed, but not as startled as I was to feel Krecek's arms around me. I stiffened and he released me immediately.

"You seem to have made up with your goddess," I said, straightening my clothes and brushing them off for effect. I wasn't yet sure if I hated him and the thought of his touch, or if

I was jealous.

He took a step further back from me and turned away. "It's not what you think."

"It doesn't matter what I think," I muttered. Looking around me at the growing darkness reminded me of my sudden new priorities. "I don't even have time to figure out what I think in this case."

I knew what I had to do.

I had to scare the living hell out of him, convince him that his nightmares had all come true.

I had to betray his trust before he'd even given it.

Yda was watching.

I leaned close, almost whispering in his ear. "I have an army to raise."

"What?" Krecek's eyes grew wide with fear.

"I have a war to fight." I took a step back, grinning wickedly to add to the effect.

"Against who?"

I laughed, taking one more step back. "Davri's madness is full upon me, and this time I shall not be stayed. Prepare yourself for battle."

"Gods," he gasped.

"They know what you've done," I watched him quiver with fear. "They come for you, and for us all."

I turned abruptly and stalked away, leaving him to his fears.

PART NINETEEN

I threw open Fereth's door without knocking, catching him in the arms of a young woman who was giggling and whispering something in his ear.

"Fereth, I'm leaving."

I turned and walked to my room without another word. I heard Fereth follow me, but I strode too quickly down the hall to invite conversation.

There was no sound of alarm being sounded yet, but I could feel whispers and spells being raised against me. I threw open the door to my chamber and grabbed one item from within.

"Lord Verwyn?" Fereth said, hesitating in the doorway.

"You may call me Agrad." I almost said Davri. I lifted a hand to my forehead, trying to concentrate on the present. "If you're coming with me you don't have time to pack. We leave as we are or we'll never make it out of here without a fight." I was eyeing the nearest window. It did not swing open, so I would have to use magic to remove it as I left.

"You have your memories," Fereth said.

It clearly wasn't a question, but an observation. I nodded and grabbed a pair of heavy winter cloaks from my wardrobe. They were old, but they would do. I'd left them...Davri had left them behind long ago. It was amazing how much of him lived on in this room.

"I will stay by your side for as long as you can stand me."

I tossed him one of the cloaks. "We'll have to fly." I held out my hand and he took it. The window blinked out of place just before we would have hit it, and it returned to its position a moment after we passed. I could feel Fereth flinch, clutching my hand tightly, but I didn't let that distract me. I pulled us through the air, faster than any horse could travel, and that brought my mind to where our next stop should be. Grennenburgh.

With the decision made I rode the wind like I'd never done before. I laughed at the sheer freedom of it, remembering the days when I was young, running away from Krecek, living in a cave like some wild thing, not appreciating the freedom I'd had. In minutes I'd covered more ground than a horse could have in hours. In half an hour I'd landed just outside of Grennenburgh, exhilarated and anxious. It had been so long since I'd done magic of any sort. I rubbed my aching arms and Fereth did the same. It was a quick way to travel, but it was tiring, uncomfortable, and it left a streak of magic rippling in the fabric of reality bright enough to be a beacon to anyone with magic sense at all.

"Home?" Fereth looked around, shivering a bit and struggling to keep his teeth from chattering despite the heavy cloak. "What are we doing here?"

"I rather not fly the entire way to Verwyn," I said. "We'll need to convince your father to give us his two best horses. I have things to accomplish between here and there that must be done in secret, and I think you might freeze to death before we arrived."

"Why are we in this much of a hurry," Fereth asked, "leaving without food or favors? I'm sure Lord Krecek would have given you--"

"No," I interrupted him quickly, walking into town. "After what happened he would not give me a thing."

"I was afraid of that," he muttered. "What did you do? You didn't kill him, did you?"

The thought made me chuckle. "Kill him?" I shook my head, grinning. "He still lives, unless I frightened him to death. I told him to ready for war. I can't explain more than that. You will have to trust me and what you know of me."

"I don't think I know you that well," he said with a sigh. "I never would have guessed you'd do this."

"You're wrong, my friend." I hesitated, stopping in my tracks to look Fereth in the eye. "You know me better than anyone. You have seen me more purely myself than anyone still living. You said so yourself. You were right."

It caught him by surprise, but he nodded after a moment of deep thought. "Okay. I trust you."

I grasped his arm in appreciation, and we headed to the inn. Fanrin, Fereth's father, was regularly found there even into the darkest hours of the night. On top of that, our appearance would cause a stir, and that is exactly what I wanted.

There were general cheers of welcome as I opened the doors, and I let Fereth answer questions as he saw fit. Fanrin sat at his usual table, and I joined him before he could make a move to his son. "We need your help," I said as I sat. "We need horses. You can demand payment from Ceolwyn, and if he refuses to pay go to Verwyn. It's an emergency."

Fanrin's face turned red and his eyes narrowed. "What have you got my boy involved in, Lanrin? Who do you think you are to come in here and make demands of me like this?"

"We're on wizard business," I said, "and it must be the two of us because we are complete unknowns in their political world at this moment. It will not remain so for long, but we will be safe as long as we keep moving." Fereth joined me at this point and began nodding to assure his father of the validity of my lies and half-truths. "I could leave Fereth here, or he could return to Anogrin with welcome arms if he wished, but I would feel safer with him at my back. I trust him, and him alone, with my very life. You've raised a good boy."

He took his time answering, looking me over carefully, not fully convinced. "What's going on, really?"

Fereth leaned in close. "We can't tell you, and we're in a

hurry. You've seen enough messengers through here over the years to know what it's like."

"You are no messenger," Fanrin growled in the back of his throat. "You are my son, and you have made your mother sick with worry."

"If I were lying," Fereth said with growing impatience, "I'd have spun some fantastic tale of our great peril and dire need. This is more urgent than that. And Mother is not sick with worry. I've been corresponding with her and she would have said something."

Fanrin started to say something, and I wondered what the truth of it could have been. Instead he grunted and crossed his arms over his chest. "When this is over, you will have to return here at once. Promise me."

"I promise," Fereth bowed his head, but it was obvious even to me that he did not mean it.

"Not you," Fanrin's lips twisted in a half-smile. "I know better than to trust your word when you don't wish to give it. Lanrin," he stared intently into my eyes. "I want you to swear to me you'll return him home when your business is through. It's the price I demand for my horses."

"I swear it," I said with sincerity. "He will return here as soon as this crisis is over, and I will make sure of it."

Fanrin looked satisfied and we shook on it. He then led us out into the darkness, toward the stables. Fereth fell into step beside me and groaned. "Agrad, did you have to swear it? And so specifically, too! 'As soon as it's over.' Bah."

Fanrin missed a step at the sound of my name, but Fereth did not notice. I watched Fanrin closely, to see if he would renege upon our deal because of who I was. He continued on.

"Yes, I had to swear it unless you wanted to be left behind." I smiled to reassure Fereth. "I need your help, and I need his help. I need to conserve my magic. Since I need a horse to travel, and you know horses better than I do, I need you by my side."

Fereth shrugged, but otherwise did not answer.

"I'm an orphan," I pointed out in a low murmur. "I watched my parents die, and I remember it now. Trust me; if you do not return here whenever you can, you will regret it. Someday there may not be a here to return to."

He remained silent, but I could see in his eyes that he was taking what I'd said to heart. Maybe Fereth couldn't understand what I meant, but it was important to me that he at least think about it. Wordlessly he caught up to his father and they walked side by side, and just as silently they readied two horses. They worked well as a team. It may have been wishful thinking, but Fereth seemed a little warmer toward his father than he had been before.

Fanrin gave him some coin and pulled him aside for what I learned later was a warning against meddling too closely with wizards, and with me in particular. I'd refused to eavesdrop, but I would have agreed if I'd been privy to the conversation. I'd begun second guessing my decision to bring Fereth along. If I'd left him with Krecek he would be safer than he would be at my side. Anywhere was about to be safer than near me, but if I left Fereth behind I would not be able to look at him with my own eyes and protect him and see that he was safe.

I didn't want to leave behind another friend. I'd done it too many times already. For once I wanted to be selfish and have someone by my side who wanted to be there with me. He was seventeen, barely a man. I was taking him away from his family and a secure future. I was dragging him into dangers unknown and a battle I already suspected would become a thing of legend. He didn't have my magic, my power. There was no guarantee I could keep him safe. There was no guarantee my vow wouldn't be fulfilled by bringing home his lifeless corpse to a town that had trusted me and given a stranger a place to belong. I knew how selfish I was being, but I wanted him here. More than anything, more than ever before, I needed a friend.

I kept my silence when I finally got on my horse. Fereth followed without hesitation. We rode through the night and at daybreak we stopped to eat. I was going to conjure something, but he surprised me with some food he'd been given at the inn.

"Mistress Wedra insisted when I said we didn't have time to stay for a drink," Fereth explained as he opened the sack she had given him. In it was bread and dried fruit and hard cakes that would sustain us for a few days. "It's the same kind the couriers carry with them, she said. I think she wanted to give it to you herself, but you were preoccupied the entire time."

Wedra had been the first girl to catch my attention and spend time trying to get to know me. She worked hard at the inn, and had looked after me even when we'd agreed that romance just would not work between us. It was sweet of her, and I almost regretted that we hadn't tried harder at a relationship, but I knew that it was for the best.

"We're going to Cairnborough first," I said, rather than comment on where the food had come from. I had to put Grennenburgh behind me for now. "From there we'll travel through Verwyn lands, but they've spent more time being ruled by Ceolwyn than by me. That could be tricky if he's angry with me."

"Why exactly would Krecek be mad at you?" Fereth said around a mouthful of bread. "What did you do?"

I thought a moment. What had I told him last night? Not much. "I warned him of impending war, though I did say it in such a way as to imply we may be on opposite sides." I tilted my head to the side. "I may have mentioned madness, and I do have Davri's memories as well as my own. Yes, there's a very good chance he may be angry. Or afraid."

"I'm sure he thinks you're going to kill him," Fereth said,

seeming somewhat amused by that idea.

I nodded.

"Well, you're not going to. Are you?"

I paused to take a drink of water, still mulling over my answer. "I don't think so. It's not my primary goal, at least."

"You're not sure?" Fereth stared, dropping the remainder of his bread onto his lap in shock.

"I haven't entirely decided yet." I began packing my portion of the food away, no longer hungry. "I don't want to, but at the same time I do. I love him and I hate him. He's hurt me more than anyone else, and he took away everything I had three times in this lifetime alone." I felt the shadows stirring, listening in on my answer. "He's also been generous to me, and helpful. I'm not sure if I can forgive such an enemy, but I'm not sure if I can help myself."

"Then why go to war at all?" Fereth looked agitated.

"Because a war must be fought, and then I'll know which side I'm on." I wasn't entirely talking to Fereth. I was casting doubts in words that would surely reach Yda's ears. I could not say that aloud, though. "Do you still trust me?" I looked at Fereth in earnest now. "Or, do you wish to return to safety now?"

"I don't like what you've said," Fereth spoke slowly. "If I don't come with you, though, I'll never have a chance to change your mind."

I nodded, relieved though I could not show it. "When I've made it up I'll let you make an effort to change it," I said softly.

We continued our journey in silence the rest of the morning. When we did converse, it was deliberately over matters of no consequence.

I used my magic sparingly, but I did use it to aid our journey. I didn't need sleep, so I kept watch whenever Fereth reminded me that he still had to, and the horses needed regular rest. The nights may have been long and boring, but I had many things to think about, so it was not time wasted. The conversations as we traveled were sparse and our pace did not encourage much depth or great meaning in what was said. We traveled hard and fast, and I was vigilant and wary the entire time.

Our arrival in Cairnborough went mostly unnoticed and completely unremarked. We were two travelers just like many who came and went from the city every day. I took us to a decent inn where I knew we would be both comfortable and not taken advantage of. If it had just been me, with no horse to care for, I would have returned immediately to where I had lived before to see how things had changed. I wasn't sure about taking Fereth to the seedier parts of town, however. Not yet. Not until I knew who I was dealing with.

I knew which door to knock on, at least. I didn't return to where Ysili and I had lived together, most boarders there would have moved on by now. It was a haven for children, not adults. I knew where we would have been welcome had we stayed another year or so, though.

"We have five arrows and three spells aimed at your heart," a gruff voice intoned from the other side of the door. "You've come to the wrong place, stranger. Just forget you found yourself here and turn around."

"I'm looking for Bledig," I said quietly, leaning close to the crack of the door so my request would not be heard by anyone passing by.

The door closed without another word, and I waited. I wasn't afraid of their spells and their bowmen. I'd found all the real threats before I'd knocked, and protected myself from it as well. My real concern was that I'd be turned away without being given a chance. I was patient, though, and they would not want me to stick around and call attention to their door.

The door finally opened without an attack and I walked inside. The room within appeared empty, but I knew we were not alone.

"Where did you hear that name?"

I smiled. "I knew him when we were children. He invited me and a friend of mine to live at Mistress Relata's, and we probably would have died without his intervention. It was a terrible winter."

I heard whispers and then a pause.

"He said he does not know you."

"I am Agrad, but he would know me better as Ysili's lady," I said, letting my voice carry with confidence this time, echoing through the empty spaces. "Would it help if I wore a dress to prove who I was?"

"Put this on," I heard Bledig's gruff voice this time, and a dress was tossed from the shadows and into my arms.

I took off my coat and shirt without hesitation. I looked over the dress and shook my head. "It's not as elegant as any I used to wear," I said. "It's pretentious and tries too hard, with ruffles and lace in all the wrong places for the effect I used. Also, yellow was never my favorite color." I pulled it over my head, buttoning up the back and tying the sash in the back with practiced ease. I softened my voice, spoke just a bit softer and higher. "All things considered, does this bring back the right memories?"

Bledig stepped out of the shadows, looking me over with a scowl. "Oh, it's you. I'm disappointed to find out that you're not actually a girl. How have you been, Agrad? How is Ysili? And what in the name of the gods are you doing here?"

"The name of the gods?" I repeated as I unbuttoned and untied the dress. I chose to ignore the first two questions. This was not a social visit. "An interesting phrase we all use and think nothing of it. Bledig, my old friend, I've come to offer work. Honest work, I'm sorry to say. If I need to I'll mint as much coin as you require. I kept to myself and you never knew who I was. I am Agrad Verwyn and I was hiding from the other wizards. That part of my life is through, and I am finished with hiding. I've come to pay you to start a war."

The room exploded with voices, some crying out, some murmuring, but it seemed that everyone present had something to say.

"The offer is open to anyone who cares to join me, of course."

"So it's true," Bledig said, tilting his head back to look me in the eye. "Verwyn is insane."

I shrugged as I put my shirt back on. "Perhaps. Teaghan down the lane was insane, but you still accepted the odd job from her."

Bledig laughed aloud then, and it was as rousing as I had remembered. "Come with me, Agrad. We will discuss this business venture. You've lucked into knowing the leader of this den of thieves, and I'll see that a fair deal is made for all." He crossed his arm over his barrel chest and nodded. "So, a war you say? I've always wanted to start of one of those."

PART TWENTY

In one afternoon I had the beginnings of my army. When I returned to Fereth I was almost sheepish to announce my success, because it had been so much easier than I expected.

"They remembered me," I said with a bit of a grin. "When I told them who I was, who I really was, they were excited. They want a chance at being part of something bigger than just this town. They want to help."

Fereth teased me with a chuckle. "They don't just want golden favors falling from the fingertips of a wizard?"

"Money might be part of their motivation," I agreed, "but I knew it would be. I've been where they are. They know there's no guarantee that I'll survive to pay them, or they'll survive to get paid, though. They really want a chance to do something more with their lives."

"Are you going to meet more of them tonight?"

I shook my head. "I have somewhere else to go. An old friend I want to see."

Fereth nodded, looking around the room as if for something to do, but we still only had the clothes on our backs and whatever we'd been given in Grennenburgh. He shrugged, sitting on the simple wooden chair that had been absently shoved toward the corner of our room, a seeming afterthought to comfort.

"Come with me," I said after a few minutes of contemplation. "You'd like him." Truthfully, I just didn't want to go alone. I was nervous about taking such a risk.

"Okay," Fereth said.

"Good." I headed to the door.

"What, now?" Fereth stood quickly to follow.

"Yes, before I change my mind."

"I thought he was an old friend." Fereth frowned as I locked the door behind us. "Why would you change your mind?"

"It's complicated," I said, walking quickly so it wouldn't seem odd for me not to meet his eyes.

"I shouldn't be surprised by that," Fereth said. "Nothing having to do with wizards seems to ever be straightforward."

"No, I suppose it isn't," I muttered under my breath. "I wish I could explain. I'm not sure I can even think to myself what my real motives are, let alone tell someone else. I want to see him, but I don't—" I cut myself off with a shake of the head. Let Fereth think that was the end of my sentence; that was fine.

I walked without hesitation to the house I'd spent so much of my adolescence in. The streets were all as familiar to me as the rhythm of my own heart. I thought I could walk them, find my way, even if I were asleep. At the same time a completely different landscape filled my head, overlaying the familiar city with a town called Hodarian's Bay that had been eradicated centuries ago. The rubble from that town had provided the stones that had given Cairnborough, and Cairnfeld, their names.

I stood in front of the house at last, taking deep breaths to steel my nerves. I forced myself past the gate, thinking of how this house sat on the space that was once my good friend Raev's house, back when I was Davri. I'd hidden there, underground, toward the end of the war. Raev had a shop on this spot, this very spot—

I walked up to the door and knocked, feeling eyes searching for me, eyes of darkness as the sun began its descent. I waited, impatiently shifting from foot to foot.

The maid answered, and I saw in her eyes that she recognized me immediately. "Master Tennival!" she called out.

She didn't let us in.

I fingered the hem of my sleeves, unable to stand still as a rising sense of anxiety filled me. I thought about turning away before he could get to the door, but I found it in me to wait and hope that the searching darkness would not find me first.

The maid suddenly stood aside and the door opened further. Naran Tennival hadn't aged a day. It was the first thing I noticed as soon as my eyes fell upon him. "Agrad?" He looked me over and I could see him waste no time coming to a decision. "Come in. Quickly."

I nodded, hurrying inside, not saying a word, filling even my thoughts with anything irrelevant and inane I could think of, just to be sure. As soon as I'd realized where this house was, I'd had to suppress my growing hope. Fereth thankfully took my lead and hurried in without a sound, and once the door was closed I breathed a sigh of relief.

"Master Tennival," I said. "The wards are still here! I can't imagine a greater stroke of luck." Yda couldn't notice us unless we spoke her name. I could even feel Nalia relax at last. She had been doing her best to be quiet, both to give me a chance to adjust and to keep Yda's attention from us.

"Aral and the others set the wards when Raev took her in," Tennival acknowledged. "She renewed them when we built this house. How did you know?" He looked into my eyes. "The last thing I had heard about you, you had lost your memory."

"I've finally become Verwyn," I said. "When my memory was restored it restored all of my memories. All the way back to Davri."

Tennival held up a hand. "Knowing Davri, I'm sure there's a fascinating story and urgent necessity to all of this, but first things first. Lord Verwyn, you mustn't call me 'master' anymore. You're a wizard, and not in my employ or under my authority at all. I am Naran, or you can leave at this moment."

He sounded weary, and he gestured for me and Fereth to follow him.

"Then don't call me 'Lord Verwyn'," I protested. "And about the wards, we need to talk. This is urgent. We need to--"

He cut me off without even looking at me. "I also refuse to talk business or war or anything more serious than my next painting so soon after you walk in my door. The agents of chaos are not descending upon my doorstep, so you will at least join me for supper and engage in a little bit of socializing. You were more polite the last time I saw you."

"I was bedridden the last time you saw me," I said with a frown.

He ignored me and walked into the sitting room, gesturing for us to be seated. "Supper will not be finished for a little while still. Please relax and try to remember your manners. You have yet to introduce your companion."

I stammered, flustered at being treated like this. It just didn't seem right, but I couldn't exactly command Naran to obey me.

"Master Naran Tennival," Fereth said formally, stepping in front of me and cutting me off, "I am Fereth Taden, from Grennenburgh. It is a great honor to meet you. The ladies in Anogrin spoke very highly of your talents, and did indeed show me some of your greatest works."

"Yes, Krecek has talked me out of a few pieces I regretted parting with," Naran said. "He has always had a good eye for beauty."

"Indeed," Fereth said. "I do hope you will forgive my companion for his poor behavior. He does not mean to be rude, but I am afraid he has lost touch with what civilized manners are in our long and wearying trek. The road forgives rudeness that the rest of the world does not."

I was shocked into speechlessness.

"I do understand," Naran said. "This is my home, however. I

---

will remind even gods and wizards that I am the end all and be all within these walls. You wouldn't believe how many times I've had to have this very talk with my own sister, of all people."

"Sister?"

Naran nodded at Fereth. "Aral Kaelwyn. Lovely woman, very sweet, but very driven. She is the reason I have had to put my foot down and establish such rules."

"I see," Fereth said. His voice gave away his surprise, but he recovered well. "I can imagine that every wizard must think their every word is the most important thing ever uttered. After meeting only three, I have developed that impression."

"All of them are the same," Naran said. "It got old very quickly. It's good to remind them that politeness has a purpose. Barging into a man's house at all hours without so much as a hello is unacceptable. They are people just as much as the rest of us. Their greater power doesn't change that."

"To be fair," Fereth said at last, "The forces of chaos are, indeed, bearing down upon your door. A good supper does sound lovely, however."

"A good crisis is always better on a full stomach than an empty one," Naran mused, considering. "In that case, even news of the forces of chaos can wait.

I fell into sullen silence while the two of them chatted about inconsequential things until it was announced that supper was prepared. I followed them into the dining room, growing more irritated by the moment. Naran waved away the help and closed the doors, finally giving us privacy to talk.

"Agrad," Naran finally said as he sat, "Are you going to tell me what brings you here? Or are you going to continue to sulk?"

"If I weren't so desperate for your help I'd indulge in wallowing," I grumbled. "I'm still considering leaving the two of you to share jokes about my shortcomings while I go alone to save the world."

"He didn't used to be so dramatic," Naran said to Fereth.

"It's a recent thing," Fereth nodded. "I'm still hoping he will come to reason again."

"Reason?" I pushed my plate away from me and stood, too anxious still to eat. I decided to work out my nervous energy by pacing. "I wish I had the luxury of reason. I felt her eyes searching me out, even as I knocked at your door, Naran. It won't take her long to realize where I am, and wonder what I could be doing here when I need to convince her I am on their side."

This finally captured Naran's full attention. "Her? You mean...chaos herself?"

I nodded, enjoying his discomfort.

"You want to try to trick her? That's your brilliant plan?"

"It's the central part of it," I said. "We need a battle, a large distraction. Naran, I said I have finally become Verwyn. I am not the simple orphan boy you took in. I'm not just Agrad anymore."

Naran nodded. "You mentioned memories all the way back to Davri. He was like a brother to me. He saved my life. He kept me safe."

"He was at your side for years, taking you in the same way you did for me," I said softly. "He took you to the dwarven lands. The two of you spied on priests and governors, keeping track of their travels for the dwarves by day. I remember. I close my eyes and I see their great caverns myself, smell the stale beer in the air, and hear their bawdy songs and ribald jokes. I remember the Arcane War, I remember starting it when you were still a child, and I remember seeing it through to the end because I could not stand to see one more innocent wrongly sacrificed for gods who could no longer remember that they gave us the ability to care. I remember Davri and Aral begging

Krecek to spare you. I remember how you cried to see how much the war had changed us, once Byrek brought you out of hiding at last. I am dramatic right now because Davri was dramatic. And Davri was dramatic because he knew from the time he set eyes on you that the fate of the world was at stake. It is just as true now as it was then."

The silence that followed my speech lasted just enough to grow uncomfortable, and I fidgeted, wondering if I should continue, but unsure what to add.

"Drama," Fereth broke the silence, nodding sagely as if he'd said something profound. "If the world has been in peril this long, it will hold for another hour."

"It will," I admitted with a weary grin. "However, I'm honestly terrified. She who gives me my power, the goddess of magic, is also terrified. Realizing there's a chance we could win just solidified how many, many more chances there are we could all lose, and the entire world be unmade."

"Unmade?" Fereth took a sip of wine to clear his mouth. "She--whoever she is--can do that?"

I nodded.

"She who is chaos," Naran said before I did. "If the circumstances were right, if she drove enough of the remaining gods into madness, she could undo everything the gods have done, and them along with it. Oh, it would free the first ones. The gods of earth, fire, air, water, and magic would be free from their deaths, reborn from the primal forces that shaped them in the first place. Everything they've done, everything they've accomplished, would be thoroughly destroyed, however."

"I don't want that." The words that came from my mouth were not my own. Nalia was speaking directly to my friends, directly through me, for the first time ever. She used an ancient spell to put weight to her words, so that neither of them would doubt that the words were from a divine source. "I want to live, but...not like that. Never like that."

I shivered, wondering if it was okay to let her do that, if it was okay to feel so much as if she was a part of me that her speaking with my voice had almost felt natural. She felt my concern and she shared an apologetic thought with me, but it didn't quell my concern. If I lost track of the line that separated her identity from mine, who would I be? What would have been the point of the Arcane Wars to begin with?

Naran went pale, his hands clenched in white-knuckled fists before him. I sat down next to him, wanting to reach out to him, to let him know she wasn't taking me over. To let him know he had nothing to fear. But I couldn't be sure if those words were a lie.

The silence stretched, but finally Naran took a deep breath. "What do you need me to do?" he said. "I want to help."

"I don't have much to ask," I said. "I wanted to ask you to convey a message to your sister, but not so soon that it seems to be from me."

"Convey a message?" Naran laughed bitterly, taking a drink of wine before rounding on me with a sudden anger that caught me off guard. "I'm nearing four hundred years, and you just want me to convey a message to my sister! I'm an artist, not an imbecile! Centuries of being treated like a pampered child, protected from my own folly so that I can't even suffer a paper cut! I have to put up with it from Aral, but I will not put up with that from you! I am capable. I am useful. I am intelligent, and observant, and I am so tired of being put to the side so I can be comfortably safe."

I nodded, miserable and guilty because of all the things I could not say.

"If Davri took some oath to protect me the way the others did, that ended with his death. I was your mentor, and I was your friend. You owe me more respect than that, Agrad! I can't stand back one more time and wait for things to happen. I know this is all because of me. It started because of me. Aral tried to keep it from me, but I know what happened. I was there. How could I not know all this time that I started the war, and that the gods died just so I wouldn't be put to death? How many times has Verwyn died or been killed, while I sat in this beautiful prison and waited for everyone I have known to die before I did? Thank the gods, living and dead, that I never fell in love and had a family to share in my curse! Would Aral even let my children become adults before she preserved them for eternity? Put me in danger! Let me know, for once, what is going on! Let me get involved! Let me live!"

I hadn't imagined or suspected for a moment that Naran had felt this way. I wanted to correct him, tell him that it wasn't his fault, that things would have happened the way they had without him, eventually, but I wasn't sure. He may have been right. "If I bring you into this, Aral will be against me. I will need her help."

Naran's lips twisted into a sneer. "Without me, she won't even know. I'll make sure she's on your side."

I shook my head. "I had another plan before I came here. It won't be as easy, but it could be done."

Both of us watched each other, stubborn and silent, but he had me at a disadvantage. The chances my original plan working were so slim that I knew it was just another Verwyn suicide mission. Another war that would end in death and tragedy that would undo everything I'd accomplished in this life.

I reached over and took Naran's hand. "You're older than me, wiser than me, and cleverer by far. Yes, I have Davri's memories, but I am still me and he's still dead. I owe you a chance at glory if that is your wish." I sighed heavily. "Your sister will never forgive me."

"It's unusual for you to put so much weight on the opinion of any other wizard," Naran said, beginning to smile. It made him look more like the man I used to know. "That is why you were bedridden the last time I saw you, isn't it?"

"A lot has changed," I said. My heart constricted as I thought of what to me was the biggest change. I'd fallen in love with Krecek, and declared war on him the same day I'd declared my feelings. It felt so unreal to have these thoughts here, of all places. "I can't afford to run scared this time. I have to act, not hide."

Fereth leaned forward. "So tell us," he said. "Trust us enough to tell us what's going on! You're driving me mad, keeping everything such a tight secret."

Naran nodded in agreement. "You've got to trust someone. You can't be everywhere at once, wizard or not."

"If I can trust anyone," I said solemnly, "It is the two of you. Just trust *me* enough to tell me if I've forgotten something, or left anything out. If there's something I can do better, let me know."

"Of course, of course," Fereth said, and Naran nodded as if impatient for me to get to something he didn't already know.

"I'm going to invade, and occupy, Cairnborough."

Fereth was stunned into silence.

It took Naran a moment, but he leaned forward. "Well," he said. "You have my complete attention."

Before the Arcane War, the town of Hodarian's Bay had been a somewhat small and unassuming place. There had been the usual traffic since it was in an almost ideal spot off the ocean, but the local mermaids had discouraged a large and stable population. The colony that had lived in the waters of the bay proper had been territorial. If they did not approve of someone, that person would find living off the shore almost impossible.

The war had changed that. The entire mermaid population of the bay had been slaughtered in the final battle, along with nearly every other mortal in the vicinity. From the ashes and beside the graves grew a town that quickly became a great city. Almost immediately the wizards wondered which of them would take jurisdiction of that place, and just as quickly decided it should be none of them.

What I was proposing went against one of the first, and one of the only, agreements that all wizards had made.

I spent an hour letting my friends know most of what I had planned. Naran had a few suggestions, especially with resources I'd had no idea he would have at his disposal. By the time I reached the final stage, the final secret of my plan that would change the balance, both Fereth and Naran were scowling.

"I don't like it," Naran said after a pause to absorb the implications of what I'd just described.

"Well, I hate it!" Fereth said, crossing his arms tight over his chest. "It's an abomination, and--"

Naran raised his hand and Fereth held his tongue. "We don't have to like it. There's a lot of risk, but it may be his best chance of saving this world." He looked like he almost wanted to add something, but instead he seemed to change his mind with a smile. "It will probably work, but the others will never forgive you. You don't expect to live long enough to see their wrath, though, do you?"

"I'm not making any plans for next Nightwatch," I said with wan humor. "I offer my apologies in advance if I am unable to bring presents to either of you. I would prefer to live, of course."

I would like that as well, I heard Nalia's voice within me. I felt warmed by her agreement.

"No, sorry, I can't forgive you in advance," Fereth said. "You'll just have to survive, and make sure the presents you give are worthy."

"I'll do my best," I said, with half a smile.

Awkward silence followed for a moment.

Naran cleared his throat. "I will wait three days after you leave," he said, speaking clearly and changing the mood in the room. "I'll ask my sister here in such a way that it would be natural for her to bring either Krecek or Raev along. I pray that it will be Krecek, but either one will suit our needs."

I nodded, squaring my shoulders and straightening my back. "We should leave now. We have a room nearby, and I have friends to consult with before we leave town."

"Stay here," Naran said. "Have them come here, meet with you here where you can plan freely. Nothing will seem amiss since we are known friends. You will be able to rest soundly, and it may be your last chance to do so."

"We have horses already stabled," I said, "and rooms we've already paid for. We don't have much coin upon us…"

Naran interrupted me with a withering look. "I have room for your horses, and Byrek will reimburse me for any amount of coin you require from me. Do you have any other objections?"

"We'll stay," I said. I hadn't wanted to argue in the first place. Truth be told, this was perfect. I couldn't think of any place I'd rather be.

A great deal was planned and accomplished in the days we spent there, but the details of planning and coordinating are not what sticks in my memory. The three of us, whenever we could, spent time talking and sharing confidences that may not mean a thing to the course of events, but meant a lot to us at the time. One last time I modeled for Naran, even while discussing matters of import with the underground element that would be the first ranks of my secret army. For me it felt good to be still, to model, to do something to familiar.

None of the others, or Fereth, could sit still long enough to pose the way I did, but Naran used that masterfully. The painting, which he put the finishing touches on after we left, was come to be known later as either "Shadows of Greatness" or "Shadows and Greatness." It was of me, seated at a table with papers scattered about, concentrating as I listened to ghostly images of those who planned with me. It was a great work, and instantly popular among those who recognized the ghostly images…but I get ahead of myself.

My heart was heavy with the surety that none of this would happen again. I wasn't sure if it was an echo of Davri's former talent for premonition, or just an unshakable fear of the dangers to come. I tried so hard to enjoy every moment to its fullest. We sang and we spoke and Fereth learned some of the most embarrassing episodes of my adolescence. It was an amazing time, and it ended much too soon.

Part Twenty-One

T he painting will be my excuse to invite my sister and others here," Naran said as we stood in the foyer on the morning of our departure. "It needs just a few details more. Three days."

The door was opened for us as we approached, and I felt exposed immediately. "I look forward to it," I said warmly.

As soon as the door opened, and I could feel Yda's attention seeking me out, I was convinced that my plan would end in my death. Even if I succeeded, I couldn't see a way out. She would not attempt to render me harmless again, since the first time had not worked. I decided to meet my end with my eyes open and with all due deliberation. Yda and her plans be damned.

I guided Fereth through Cairnfeld on our way out of town, but I resisted the urge to stop anywhere. I knew that Davri was buried there now, and with his memories it felt strangely like knowing I was already resting in my grave. I could not stop the morbidity of my thoughts until Fereth started to sing.

It's something I realize I haven't touched upon here. His stories had been what impressed me the most, and what brought us together at first, but I've done him a disservice to neglect his talent at song. There had to be magic to it, though I never had the presence of mind to check. He had no great talent, though his voice was pleasant to listen to and he never failed to be perfectly on key. I've heard others sing as well as him without causing any great stir, but Fereth brought all eyes to him the moment his words turned to song.

He sung earnestly and with passion, even on that cold and misty morning as we rode past graves that meant so much to me. I felt myself soothed and even encouraged as we began our ride. If he did these things without magic, I would pay dearly to learn how.

We crossed the border into the country of Verwyn well before we stopped for lunch. I could feel a difference in my power and my awareness of the land around us. We were retracing the path I'd taken with Ysili when I was younger. I hadn't known at the time that the town I'd left had been such a comfortable haven because it had been on my lands. I'd barely suspected I might be an elemental at the time.

We stopped at every town, speaking of war, of conflict, of things to come. In each town I let Fereth speak a little more, and a little more. I was their lord and their wizard, but Fereth's oratory talent was growing every day, and he was more persuasive than me by far. All he needed was my endorsement and my presence, and with it he stirred the hearts of everyone who heard him.

He stood with me and spoke of me as some hero who had been raised as one of them, and who would fight for them. The version of me that lived within his words was some great leader reincarnated to lead them to glory at the end of some righteous battle they would be honored to lay down their lives in. Apparently, I was amazing. I'd never known.

It continued until the last day of retracing my previous path. We stood outside of Myrenfeld and I paused by the sign and dismounted. "Full circle," I murmured.

"What is this place?" Fereth asked.

I shook my head, unsure how to answer at first. Without another word I took in the magic around me and used it to change the nature of my clothes. In a moment I wore a dress as elegant as any I had worn before, and a hat that would disguise my lack of hair. They would recognize me here, looking like this.

"It was a home, for a while," I finally said. I used my softest and gentlest voice, as I'd learned to do as a lady. "They will know me here."

I walked on foot to the center of town, feeling too large as landmarks I'd known as a child failed to loom over me. Fereth followed, guiding both horses while he watched me closely. I did not turn to look, but I could feel his eyes upon me, and the eyes of so many people from windows around us. Nothing much had changed, except the faces around me were older than I remembered.

I walked to the small market I knew would be set up, where the people would be meeting and haggling and exchanging the gossip for the season. Fall harvest had been good to the outlying farmers, from what I could tell of the activity around us. I wandered around and simply looked at first; I was drinking in the sounds I'd never realized I'd missed. Everyone knew everyone else here. The market square was more of a tradition than a necessity. Trading could have been done directly, but they enjoyed the spectacle and celebration. Like their version of Dawnsday that had scared me as a child, the autumn market was a ritual event that could not be missed.

From all around us there were excited calls of, "Young miss! Young master! Come and look!"

"Young miss! See here!"

"Young master, look!"

It wasn't as stunning as Plath, but it warmed my heart.

Finally, finally, I walked to one stand and said hello.

"You look familiar."

I smiled and curtsied just slightly. "I lived here as a child."

The man stared, dropping the large squash he'd been showing off a moment before. "The girl the priests took in! They called you Eria!"

"Indeed," I said.

"Priests?" Fereth looked amused. "Well, that's ironic, isn't it?"

I laughed. "I prefer to think it fortuitous, for them and for me." I returned to the farmer selling his wares and leaned closer. "Do they still live here?"

"Of course, of course," he said. "They still look for you and wonder why the gods took you from them."

"The gods did not. The wizards did." I dispelled the magic that had turned my clothes into a dress, and I stood before him as who I am. The street grew eerily quiet at the sudden display of magic. I smiled to myself and raised my voice to be heard by them all. "Tell the people their wizard will see them in the town hall tonight. And tell my foster parents that I have returned, in the gods own time."

"Y-you-you're Verwyn!" he stammered, pointing. "Lord Verwyn was their little Eria? I--" He stopped a moment and then dashed off to do as I'd asked, and the square virtually cleared as people hastened to spread the news of my return.

I laughed and clasped Fereth's shoulder. "Exactly as I'd hoped it would go!"

"Didn't you look around? This is a town of god-worshippers. They have priests! How are you going to convince them to follow you into war against gods who still live and who, you might remember, are trying to kill you?"

"If I can't," I started, and then allowed my voice and appearance to shift, "I will." Nalia finished the sentence. "I've been waiting for a chance to do this for hundreds of years."

Fereth stumbled backwards, falling to the ground and scrambling away in fear. "You're not an elemental? You're not a wizard? You're a god?"

I'll admit to being amused by scaring him like that, but I returned to myself before he could scramble backwards into the horses and spook them. "I'm still me. Just me. Just Agrad." I bent down before him and offered my hand to help him up. "She is helping me now, but that is all. I'm not a god, just a wizard. I'm still your friend."

He hesitated a moment more before finally accepting my help to stand. "You've changed. Agrad doesn't seem to be much like Lanrin was. You act like a wizard, not a person. You show off. You boast. You scare people. Sometimes you scare me."

"I'm sorry," I said. "It's one reason I need you, to remind me of who I am. It's also why I asked you to trust me, because I can't always act the way I want to. I've learned from you how to act larger than life, but perhaps it's a bit too frightening considering just how much power I do have. You'd think that being a wizard would mean I wouldn't have to bluster and bluff. You'd think it would mean I could master the world and everything in it. It's what I used to think, when I did not know who I was. Yet here I am, terrified because there's something I'm not sure if I can do, and if I fail it could destroy you, people like you, the whole world, and everything I love that's in it. I do love this world, and the goddess who gives me power loves it, and Davri loved it, and none of us would want to see it ended."

"So, you are on Lord Ceolwyn's side?"

I cast my eyes downward and began to walk. I wanted to tell him plainly, but I still felt the darkness and the chaos at my heels, watching my every move, listening for every whisper. "I don't know. It is not yet time to find out."

"I'll just keep trusting you," Fereth said after long consideration. He met my eyes, and I silently thanked him for his doubts that kept me from going too far.

"Are you sure that's wise?"

I knew that voice.

I turned around quickly, heart racing, searching for the source of the voice.

"I once trusted Agrad Verwyn and I was betrayed. Discarded like an old toy."

He was still wearing the uniform of a palace guard for

Ceolwyn. He was taking slow, cautious steps toward us, searching my face and expression carefully, and I met his eyes, bluer than any shade of blue. He'd grown up strong and with an expression of determination and defiance so etched in his countenance that I could only assume it was what he wore most often.

"I saw you," I said. "I did not know who you were, but I saw you, Ysili. I know who you are, now."

"You've never known who I was," Ysili said as he walked up to me, stopping an arm's length away. "Not now, and certainly not then."

I covered the rest of the distance without hesitation, despite the stiffness of his bearing, and I embraced him almost violently. "You were Krecek's slave and creation, weren't you?" I whispered in his ear, knowing immediately that I was right. I took an almost immediate step back and looked into his eyes. "You were my friend, and I owe you my life. I would have become a wild and savage thing, hiding in that cave the rest of my days. I'm glad you found me then, and I am glad you have found me now."

"I was sent to follow you," Ysili said. "What do you hope to accomplish, stirring the passions of your own people like this? Another war? Another grand death for whatever plan the Verwyn line has worked toward? Is there even a plan? Death after death after death, because that's all Verwyn knows how to do."

Even his anger couldn't quell the joy I had in finding him again. "Come with me and find out."

He took a step back and held a hand before him to stay me. "They've been taken into custody. Rhada and Goriath Brinn, the two who took you in when you were little. You have a hostage, and now Lord Ceolwyn has two."

"That's a bit extreme," I said, confused. "I didn't know Fereth meant so much to Krecek."

"I am simply here to deliver the message," Ysili said, verging on another step back.

"Ysili, stop," I said, taking half a step forward. "Why are you acting afraid of me?"

It was his turn to look confused. "Afraid?" He took a step forward. "I'm not afraid, I'm angry! You're the one who should be afraid! You have more enemies than allies, Agrad."

"You speak for yourself, don't you?" I said. "You're telling me that you're my enemy, aren't you?"

"You left me!" Ysili looked angrier than I expected he would. "I had to go back to him, and now I'm playing soldier as if this is the life I would have chosen for myself! I'm not one of the castle guard because my Lord trusts me, but because he knows my loyalty is assured by force! Do you really defy him and the other wizards? Answer me, Agrad!" He grabbed me by the shirt and shook me, as if his answers could be obtained with violence.

"I defy everyone and everything," I said, looking into his eyes. "Come with me and I will give you the power to do the same."

I lifted a hand to touch him, to cast a spell that would free him from magic compulsion, but he pushed me roughly to the ground. He seemed as surprised as I was by his success, but before I could pick myself up and try again he had run away. I stayed where I was, sitting on the ground, legs splayed awkwardly before me as I watched him disappear around a corner.

A moment passed before I let Fereth help me up. "That could have gone better," I said, dusting myself off.

"Who was that?" Fereth asked.

"The only other real friend I've had who is still alive," I said, sighing.

"You do have other friends, surely. I mean, Krecek was your friend, wasn't he?"

"Nothing ends a good friendship like a declaration of war."

"Nonsense," Fereth said with a lighthearted grin. "I'm sure he'll forgive you in no time!"

"If both of us happen to survive, perhaps." I chuckled at the thought. "I'll apologize for trying to kill him, he'll apologize for killing my parents, and we'll kiss and make up over a nice bread pudding. Very realistic scene you've painted for me, there."

"Oh no, not bread pudding," Fereth said. "That dreadful mush is no good for an apology. Surely two wizards such as yourselves would splurge on something exotic, like chocolate, if the pirates haven't killed off the supply lines again."

"I could ask him to accompany me to the south, so we don't have to worry about pirates at all. What a date that would be."

"That's the spirit," Fereth laughed. "Nothing says, 'I'm sorry for my murderous intent,' like a journey somewhere exotic."

"And chocolate," I corrected him. "The chocolate is the most important part."

"I thought that was a given," he said.

"I'm glad we have my apology planned," I said. "Now we both have to survive the war."

"Details."

Fereth's speech that night was subdued, considering the loss and anxiety spreading through Myrelfeld at the loss of their priests. I was anxious as well, but Fereth still roused the spirits and inspired everyone to fight. They had more of a stake in the resolution than any other town we had visited. I felt connected to every one of them in our shared anxiety over Rhada and

Goriath's fate.

It was dark out, but Fereth said he felt restless and I was feeling the same. Knowing that my foster parents were captured because of me had caught me by surprise. Seeing Ysili, and seeing his reaction to me, went beyond surprise. My concern was growing because Krecek seemed to control everyone I cared about except for Fereth. By this point he would have Naran either near him or near Aral. It was part of my plan, but it made me uneasy. I was trusting that he would agree with my plan, and I had no way of checking. I couldn't tell if he was protecting them for me, or holding them hostage against me.

Eventually we made camp and Fereth fell into a fitful sleep. I lit a fire to keep the encroaching cold at bay, and I simply stared into it most of the night. This would be our last camp before we reached my castle. Just this one night, and then by tomorrow evening I would be home, and I would be able to sleep at last.

Two figures sat down beside me. I'd felt their approach and had been considering how to deal with them. I could have hidden from them, but I wanted to meet them away from the palace and prying eyes. Now was a better opportunity than I could expect later.

"How is the Enchanted Path these days?" I asked as the two wizards got comfortable. The Enchanted Path was a secret I'd learned from Davri that had once been used by only the most powerful mages, and never alone. It was a nightmarish mirror of our own world, with perils that could make even wizards uncomfortable, but it could shorten travel time between two places a considerable amount.

"Surprisingly wet," Shaelek said, shaking off her cloak and spraying droplets around us like rain.

Modarian was more circumspect, simply tying his cloak around a tree branch to drip dry where it hung. "It's worse than usual," he said. "If we weren't trying to reach you in secret, and

315

quickly, I'd have suggested some other way. I'm not looking forward to the return trip."

I looked them over, noting that Shaelek was wearing a suit. It was a good look for her, as I'd known it would be. Modarian hadn't changed at all, and he sat beside me as if we were comrades.

"It's not that bad," Shaelek said, rolling her eyes. "We're wizards. It's not as if going home will put us in any real danger." She sat down on the other side of the fire from me, keeping her distance. "Are we socializing first, or are we getting directly to business?"

"Business," I said. "If I remember right, the last time we spoke you had some unflattering things to say to me. We can decide, once we know where we all stand, how much we can stand each other."

Modarian tried to hide a smirk behind his hand. "Well said. You've grown up in the last few years, Agrad."

His words would have been flattering, once. Now, however, I was looking at him for motive and screening his words for flattery. "What is your game," I asked, "what are the two of you playing at? Whose side are you on?"

"I'm on my own side," Modarian said, sounding weary. "I have been since the day I heard the voice of Agruet within me, and he showed me those things that nearly drove Davri insane."

I stared at him in shock. Of course I knew what he was talking about. "The Void. You've stared into The Void?" It even made Nalia shiver to recall.

Modarian shook his head. "Not directly. I just know what Agruet showed me. It became so intrinsically a part of him that any wizard with his power, or any descendant of his, wouldn't be able to escape it."

Shaelek sighed. "I have a memory of a glimpse of it, and even that is enough to haunt me. As far as I know, the three of us are the only ones now alive who know what it's like, what it means."

"Isn't it ironic that Nalia now sits here knowing what started the conspiracy to kill her?" I mused. "She was born in that Void, but she never returned her attention to it."

"It was meant to be," Modarian said. "Agruet makes sure that I know things. Secrets even the two of you don't know. I am still myself, but I know what he planned, and what he still is planning. He was a trickster and a manipulator, and I can't stand those things, but...the longer I know him and live with him, the more I understand why."

I closed my eyes and relayed some words. "His mother says he was once a very serious lad..."

"Her son says she was an insufferable bitch who needed to be taken down a peg or two, which is why she was the brunt of most of his jokes, pranks, and conspiracies."

I didn't want to laugh, but it bubbled up despite myself. "I can't argue," I said. "She probably deserved it. She doesn't think she did, but as someone she once tried to kill..."

Shaelek chuckled. "The three of us, around this fire," she said. "It's too much. You know now that the goddess of magic was the primary target in the Arcane War. You know the role the god of death had to play for it to be possible for her to die. Yet, here we are, and the two of you are speaking as if the gods were here themselves, bickering once again."

I noted how she avoided the names that Modarian and I were unafraid to speak. "There's one important difference now," I said. "She knows what drew her sons away from her now. She knows what Davri saw. She knows why the two of you did what you did, and she can't hate you for it."

Shaelek spit. "Don't talk to him through me as if I don't exist. I don't care what the war was fought for, or about. We're all pawns of greater forces. Those two gods are merely the first who realized it."

Modarian nodded. "She is not Baedrogan, and I am not Agruet, any more than you are Nalia."

I nodded, but I gave him a very curious look. When he said her name it didn't give her power, or even stir her awareness the way it usually would. "How did you do that?"

"It's one of Agruet's secrets." Modarian didn't even pretend not to know what I meant. "I can speak the name of any god and they won't be aware. I could never have—I mean, he could never have helped coordinate events in the Arcane War, otherwise."

I nodded in understanding, both at the events of the past, and his slip in saying he had done events that the god had done. He understood how sometimes the line between us could blur, but in the end we were still a separate person apart from that god. "Can you teach me?"

He shook his head no.

Shaelek snorted. "I've asked him myself, more than once. He's just as stingy with his secrets as Agruet was." She was free with that name, I noticed. How curious.

"Have all elementals, or wizards, gained something from their gods?"

"I'm not sure," Modarian said. "Verwyn hasn't demonstrated anything spectacularly more impressive than any other wizard as would befit having the ultimate power over magic."

I shrugged. "Nalia wasn't particularly interested in helping any of them."

Modarian smiled. "Krecek hasn't shown any extra talent or affinity with fire. Quite the opposite, he seems to have an aversion to it. Aral and Raev haven't shown any particular extra gift, either. Aerek Lychwyn seems haunted, and at times fearful. However, that could be because he is the only full-blooded elf among those of us who have been reborn, rather than because

Lychwyn gained power from the god of nightmares."

"That's all?"

"Maeloth Shaiwyn's power waxes and wanes with the phases of the moon," Shaelek said with a shrug.

"That seems to be all," Modarian said with a tone of finality. "We've drifted into socializing, and we have no idea yet where you stand."

The message seemed plain to me. He would not answer any more questions unless I chose his side.

"She who is Chaos has also seen into The Void," I said cautiously. I did not want to accidentally invoke Yda.

"Yes," Modarian agreed. "She is the only one who can enter it unscathed, but she is not The Void itself."

"I know what Davri saw," I said. "I remember all that he knew. I know what side the two of you must be on because of what you know."

"We have worked with Yda," Modarian said solemnly. "But we are no longer on her side."

I looked into his eyes and I saw something beyond truth. Something almost beyond knowledge. Davri's vision had changed the course of history, but it was only a portion of what Agruet had seen. I knew I was a part of that vision. Yda's birth, and the birth of the gods, was a part of that vision. Yda's ultimate intentions for the world, and for all of creation, were a part of that vision.

"I'm on my own side," I told Modarian. I knew he would understand.

"Whose side is Nalia on?"

I let her answer for herself. "I'm on my own side as well," she said through me. Looking at Modarian through Nalia's awareness was overwhelming for a moment. I'd never known it was possible to feel so much regret. She withdrew into herself quickly, not wanting to face my sympathy, and not wanting to share the reason for her pain.

"So are we," Modarian said, and I could tell that the words were coming from Agruet.

No further words were necessary. I added a log to the fire, stoking it to ensure it would be warm for Fereth's breakfast. The three of us sat for a while in silence. By dawn they were gone.

Part Twenty-Two

It was dark again by the time Fereth and I arrived at the palace. The guards were surprised to see me, but it seemed that Byrek was not. When we reached the courtyard he was directing people to take our horses, draw warm baths, prepare some food, and whatever else he felt the need to have them do for my return. I wasn't particularly interested in the details.

For the moment, I was only interested in him.

Davri's memories nearly overcame me from the time I spotted him in the oversized doorway. They'd loved each other so very much. I almost wanted to cry for the tragedy of their too-brief affair, but instead I jumped from my horse without a thought and ran up to the elf and felt foolish for the way I'd nearly kissed him.

Byrek was caught completely off guard for just a moment, but he grinned and grasped me by the shoulders. "Welcome home, Master Verwyn. I didn't realize you would miss me so much."

"I didn't either," I said in all seriousness. "There's so much to say, so much to catch up on, and I don't even know where to begin." I embraced him tightly, holding him as a lover would, holding him the way Davri once had, because I just needed that one moment to put the ghost of feelings I'd never had behind me.

I was surprised he didn't stiffen or pull away, but instead he held me just as close, just as warmly. When we finally parted he looked at me quizzically. "You look at me the way Davri once did. Did you somehow become him when you disappeared?" He reached up and tousled my hair playfully as if I were a child.

"That would make things easier," I said, taking a step back and combing my fingers through my hair. I noticed it was getting longer and wondered if I should cut it or let it grow long again. "No, I didn't somehow become Davri. I'll explain once we're a bit more settled." I paused and gestured to Fereth, who was walking over to join us at last. "This is my friend, Fereth. Let him stay in Krecek's room. I'm feeling wicked and irreverent, and it will do me some good to feel like I've indulged in some harmless rebellion. Fereth, this is Byrek Arsat, the true lord of this house, the power behind my power, and he'd have been a wizard himself if it hadn't been for our friend, Naran."

"I'm not so sure of that," Byrek said with a raised eyebrow. "I'd like to think I'm smarter than the rest of you were."

I began walking, leading us all in the direction of my chambers. "Someone had to be the voice of reason, I suppose. Just do me a favor, and don't start up again right now."

"Why?" I heard him increase his pace to catch up with me.

"Oh, you don't want to know what he plans to do," Fereth said.

"Let me guess," Byrek said with droll humor, "it's reckless and going to get him killed."

"Oh, it's worse than that," Fereth said.

"Well, that's a twist," Byrek said. "Every Verwyn ever has done the same thing. Honestly, I'm getting used to it. I think I'll name the next Verwyn child Reckless."

"I'll bring you with me," I said over my shoulder, looking at Byrek. "Fereth, you can keep this place running while the two of us go take care of my plan, right?"

"No!" Fereth said, eyes wide. "Don't joke about that!"

"Just tell everyone no," Byrek said to Fereth. "I haven't had a break in nearly thirty years."

"I'm telling the two of you no, first!"

"You're off to a good start," I said, grinning. "I'll give you a few days to get settled and practice saying no some more before we leave."

"What if something goes wrong?" Fereth protested.

"Something always goes wrong," Byrek said, shrugging.

"You can't do this to me!"

I laughed. "I am a wizard and this is my domain. I'll do what I want."

We parted ways at that point so that Byrek could show Fereth to Krecek's suite. I went to my room and looked around, amazed and comforted at how familiar it was. It hadn't changed a bit since the last time I left, but it had changed dramatically since Davri's days. I bathed and slipped into more comfortable clothes, relaxing more than I had since the day Raev found me.

There was a knock at the door and Byrek entered without waiting for an answer.

"If I die," I said, "I'm coming back as a girl just so you'll have to give me privacy."

Byrek shrugged. "That wouldn't stop me," he said. "Don't dig your grave over vain hopes."

I smiled, and even Nalia chuckled, but I knew he had come with a purpose. "I can't give you all the answers you wanted," I said, setting aside levity for honesty. "When Krecek returned my memories I gained Davri's memories as well. It was a powerful spell. That is all."

"I know," Byrek said. "You're warning me that Davri is dead, and will always be dead. I buried him myself; something you've been spared. I'll never look at anyone and think that he's been brought back. Even now, death does not work that way."

I nodded.

"However," he said quietly, "you have his soul. I know you do, and every Verwyn has. It is tied to the power of the position, and the soul of the god that provides it. I've done a lot of research into this."

"I can imagine," I said. "It must be hard to see a part of someone you love return, making the same mistakes over and over again, suffering for them without end."

Byrek nodded. "It's a comfort to me, though. I can be here for him, even though he doesn't realize it in quite the same way. You're the closest I'll ever get to knowing if he's appreciated all that I've done."

I walked over and gave him a hug. It's what Davri would have done, and it warmed me to do it as well. I would never be able to replace Davri for him, but I could offer him comfort and understanding at last.

People began to gather, forming an army in a surprisingly short amount of time. Veterans of the last war, the one that Doran Verwyn died in, were put in various positions of authority. They were training and leading the young men and women who were ready to lay down their lives for their lord. Sadness touched me, knowing the weight of what they were facing and the horrific probability of their young lives being cut short. I had to remind myself that they either faced the chance of death and dismemberment or the certainty of the entire world being erased. Some would die so that all might live.

It was not the only thing to haunt me as I planned the invasion of Cairnborough. Fereth thought he knew the worst of my plan, but I hadn't told him all of it. I played with the idea more and more of leaving him behind for the crucial final step and taking Byrek in his stead, as I had teased when we first arrived, but I knew I would need someone there. Someone to keep me grounded and sane.

My army had a month and a half for training. I had a month

and a half of planning and coordinating. It went by impossibly fast. The day before they would begin their march I was wandering around, overwhelmed that I had run out of time and excuses. I steeled myself and sought out Fereth, finding him in conversation with Byrek. "Shall I come back later?" I asked.

"We were just discussing history," Byrek said. "Or, as I think of it, things I saw happening in my youth."

Fereth blushed. "I didn't mean to imply that you are old."

"No, no," Byrek said, giving Fereth a droll look. "We elves have come to expect impertinence from the short-lived child races. Especially humans."

I chuckled softly, shaking my head. "I hate to kill this mood, but I have one last thing I need to do, and I did not want to do it alone. Would you both come with me?"

Fereth nodded immediately.

"You're going to Lesser Stonegore, aren't you?" Byrek looked at me with a guarded expression, betraying nothing even when I nodded in reply. "Do you know what to expect there?"

I took a deep breath, nodding. "I...I know it was destroyed."

Byrek walked over to me and put a hand on my shoulder. "I'll go with you," he said.

I didn't trust my voice to reply, so I nodded again and took a step back. In the last few weeks Nalia had taught me how to open a space between spaces, a portal that would take us from one place to another as quickly as taking a step. "I've never done this before," I warned them before I silently invoked the magic that would tear a hole through the fabric of reality. It glowed with colors that shifted and glimmered at random.

Their eyes went wide in surprise, but I didn't wait to watch their reactions. I stepped through first to make sure it was safe. I came out the other side unharmed and took three steps before the impact of my surroundings hit me.

It was, of course, worse than I had imagined. My feet

crunched on charcoal and ash as I entered the hellish landscape. The air held a hint of smoke and rot. Everything was silent and undisturbed as if a glass bowl of immense size had been erected over it to preserve the destruction I had wrought.

It had been me, not Krecek, who had destroyed the town. Some part of me had known all along, but I'd never been able to think about it directly. The knowledge had been too big. Too terrible.

So terrible it had struck me dumb.

Are you sure you want to do this? Nalia's concern flowed through with her words, and I took strength from it.

"I'm sure," I murmured. "We'll need every advantage."

The others walked through behind me, but I did not turn to look. One of them gasped, probably Fereth, but I didn't move.

"I did this," I said, staring at the destruction. "Didn't I, Byrek?"

He was silent a long time before he answered. "You didn't know any better," he said, which was confirmation enough. "You were just trying to survive."

We had arrived just outside the house I had lived in. I didn't recognize it except for the feeling that this was where it once had been. There was a crater where my parents once had slept—where they had died. I walked through the skeletal beams and supports jutting out of the ground, blackened and broken from fire and explosion, until I was at the edge of the small crater. I knelt, touching the ash that lay on the floor, feeling the powder between my fingers, wondering how it all made me feel and coming up with no answer.

"I lived here."

Byrek put a hand on my shoulder, and I looked up into his eyes to find compassion and understanding. Fereth was walking around as if he were lost, trying to make sense of the corner of a door, or the melted glass of a window that I'd helped my mother enchant on our last Nightwatch together. There was a shadow on the ground from where I think my bed once sat, where I'd so long ago heard arguing, heard screams, in the middle of the night.

I finally stood and began to walk through the town where the ghosts of buildings stood in my mind. In reality it was all bones. Bones of houses, bones of family, bones of friends. Bones of two strangers who just happened to be in the wrong place at the wrong time, traveling with a wizard trying only to save people from the very fate that had befallen my town.

Byrek and Fereth followed me silently and I showed them what had been home. I showed them the dried bed of the stream I played at and hid beside, where I first played soldiers with Krecek. The smooth rounded rocks lay at the bottom, completely exposed now that the grass had been blasted and burned away.

I pointed out the homes of friends, the common school house my friends had attended without me, and the small store that bartered more than it sold. There was the enforcer's office. The stone and iron still stood, but in spots it had melted or cracked from the intensity of the fire. I stopped in the middle of town, overwhelmed by so much destruction and so much residual energy that I knew to my own bones was the result of my grief and fear at seeing my parents dead.

In the center of it all I began to chant. Nalia told me what to say, told me what the words meant, and I repeated it exactly.

"What are you doing?" Fereth asked in alarm.

I ignored him, unable to stop once I began.

"Those words are words no mortal should be able to utter," I heard Byrek explain in a hushed tone. "I've heard that language before, when I was a child." He paused, listening intently, before he explained further. "It is the language of the gods. The language of creation and destruction. I can't tell what he means to do, but whatever it is is supposed to be impossible."

I knew exactly what I was doing. Byrek was right that it should be impossible. But I had Nalia's power within me, and her full cooperation. I knew what I had to do.

I had known before I arrived what must be done.

This was the source of my nightmares. The very reason I had been unable to sleep while we journeyed, after Nalia and I had conceived the plan.

One could say I was playing at being a god.

The bones of my childhood friends began to quiver. Invisible forces of magic knit those bones together, giving them the semblance of life. The small skeleton of a child was the first to approach us, and though he had no face I knew he was Garim. He must have died above the store his parents owned, which sat just a few feet away. He was bones and magic, but I could see his soul, a restless spirit that had been tied to this town by the power of my innocent childhood grief.

Others came, and I knew them all.

I'd killed them all.

They saw me and they wailed in their grief, knowing after all this time that they were dead. Realizing that I was not among them. I closed my eyes and my chant became a shout as I raised the shattered bones of my parents, though I was not the one who killed them. It was more difficult, but it was Nalia herself who pulled the extra power from the universe and forced reality to comply. I called them forth and they cut through the milling skeletons around me. They were the first to bow before me and call me their master.

Fereth stumbled away and I heard him retch from the other side of a pile of rubble. Perversely, I was grateful for his humanity at this moment, for as I looked at the defiled corpses of my childhood I wondered if there was anything left of my own. For myself I felt nothing but a distant fascination and satisfaction for what I had done. It was the worst abomination seen upon this world since the creation of the wizards in the first place, but in order to win I needed such a horror.

Your feelings will return to you later, Nalia whispered within. We go to war. There are further atrocities to witness. You can be ill and hate yourself when it is over.

I nodded and looked out at the undead surrounding me, and I smiled at them as if they were alive. "I've missed you all," I said kindly. "None of us knew this could happen, or the circumstances of my return, but I ask of you all to help me. A war is coming, and I need you all by my side."

They pressed closer, touching me as if I were some sort of hero. I knew they would gladly follow whatever order I gave.

Part Twenty-Three

At my command my army of abomination dispersed, traveling to Cairnborough in shadow and secret. To the side, Byrek helped Fereth clean himself up, giving him a skin of water to rinse his mouth out and casting a spell to freshen his clothes.

I walked over to them, standing a moment at a loss for words. They clearly shared my unwillingness to break the silence.

"I'm a monster," I said at last.

"No," Fereth protested weakly.

I stared at him. I was grateful that he would try to protect me even now, but I knew he lied.

"Perhaps," he amended after a moment looking around. "I don't know. That was--"

"Disturbing," Byrek finished for him. "What were you thinking?"

"I thought about warning you," I said.

Fereth looked at Byrek for a moment, then at me. "Were you afraid I'd try to talk you out of it?"

"Afraid?" I laughed without mirth. "You would have. Either of you could have." I took a deep breath and let it out slowly, my shoulders slumping. "I wanted to be talked out of it. I didn't dare say anything to anyone at all."

"It's something that Davri would have done," Byrek said. "He would see the necessity of things and keep them to himself. He would do what only he could have done, even if it killed him inside."

I couldn't breathe. He was right. I winced a little at how transparent I was to him.

"It's not an accusation," Byrek said. "I think you've gained, or at least learned, one of his strengths. You do what must be done. It's a decision I couldn't have made, wouldn't have condoned, but it might give you your victory."

Fereth nodded. "Besides that, even monsters need friends."

I could have cried if I'd been able to feel. "Thank you."

"Are you going to be okay?" Fereth asked.

"I don't know," I said. "We'll find out when this is over, I suppose."

Fereth nodded and then looked around. "Will anything ever grow here again?"

"I doubt it," Byrek said before I could bring myself to answer. "The area is cursed. Perhaps my brethren could convince the land to produce once again, but only once the souls of those who died here are at peace."

"I'll have to survive long enough to bring them that peace," I said, finding determination and a cause to survive this battle.

We sat in silence, each of us with our own thoughts for a while more, and then I opened a way for us to return once again. Byrek hastened through. For all his patience and love, this place had offended his delicate elf sensibilities long enough.

Before Fereth stepped through he turned to me. "Was it beautiful?"

I nodded slowly. "It was…home."

I whispered the last word, catching a fleeting glimpse of the emotions I'd hidden from.

I could never return.

With alacrity I stepped through, breathing in the clean air of my palace, shutting the rift closed on Fereth's heels.

It took time for me to recover. I couldn't close my eyes without seeing it all again, shivering until Nalia chased the visions away with harsh words. *There is an army of living men who need you! You can be human later.*

She was right, and I hated her for it. Uniforms had been made for me, and I put one on like a shield against my own guilt and fear. I walked out to the encampment that now spread as far as my eyes could see.

The men, and not a small number of women, came to me and cheered for me. I smiled and waved and shook hands. I encouraged. I laughed at jokes and listened to concerns.

I forced myself to forget the darkness I'd created.

"It's my wife, Lord Verwyn," a man before me stumbled over his words. "She is with child--"

"It's fine," I said, smiling. "I asked for volunteers. If you wish to be by her side, you may go."

"No, my Lord!" He looked distressed at the very thought. "She asks for your blessing, she asks to name her final child after you, and she asks your forgiveness."

"Forgiveness?" I stopped in my tracks, looking at him closely. "What is your wife's name?"

"Eleneh, my Lord."

How could I forget Eleneh? For one night she'd treated me like a child of her own. She'd warned me before she betrayed me, for the sake of her children. I reached into my own pouch and pulled out a coin, a gold favor that had been struck in Davri's time, and handed it to the man. "She has had my forgiveness since the day I crossed your threshold. Your whole family has my blessing. I would be honored if she named a child after me. Though it was only one night, she did kindness to me to last a lifetime."

He looked stunned, eyes going from the coin to my face and back again.

"Lord Verwyn!" We were interrupted by a shout.

I frowned, seeing a veteran who was also a bit of a spellsmith and an inventor who had wanted my attention for days. I dismissed Eleneh's husband and turned to the veteran with a frown.

"I've told you. We are not throwing metal pellets at the enemy through your long tubes. I don't care how fast--"

"It's not that, my Lord!" he said urgently. "It's an elf claiming to be from Cairnborough."

"Northern elf, brown hair, smug?"

"Yes, Lord Verwyn."

Paelloret was here at last. "Bring him to me immediately."

It was time to put my plans into action.

The invasion of Cairnborough went largely the way I had planned.

My friends underground had slipped sleeping potions into the evening meals of the city guards. A scant few had bought or brought their own food, and all but a handful of those had surrendered easily when presented with superior numbers and hard steel. One man and his compatriots had sounded an alarm spell that roused some of the citizenry, but it was too little and too late.

Cost of life, minimal. Structural damage, none. I couldn't have hoped for a cleaner initial victory.

Cairnfeld had never been built to withstand an attack by a wizard because we had all agreed from the start to let the city remain neutral territory. I'd known it would be easy.

This was just the declaration of war, not the war itself.

I stood, apprehensive, while the conflict began to arise. There

333

was rebellion among the citizenry, of course, but it was quelled one outbreak at a time. I had spellsmiths and mages in every section of town trying to manipulate the general atmosphere with feelings of contentment and peace. It was a tricky sort of magic, and prone to backlash, but I would not have to employ it for long. I just had to keep things calm until the other armies arrived.

That did not take long. From the roof of the courthouse I could see the pass that opened to the northeast, to the country of Ceolwyn. I watched it every day, and I saw the first signs that the army approached even as one of my generals climbed up to inform me of the impending conflict. Three armies were marching through the pass, one more was said to be approaching along the coast from the north, two were a week away to the south, and more wizards and their forces were sailing in by sea.

I didn't stand in their way. I wanted the conflict and the war that was sure to come.

"Keep eyes open for priests and gods," I said softly, staring at the pass and watching the armies come.

"The armies we see could attack at any time," General Falgoran said, full of bluster and bluff, apprehensive of every sneeze or twitch.

"They won't," I said. "Not yet. Krecek doesn't know what to expect from me. He'll wait, take our measure, and request parlay before he thinks to attack."

"We won't attack them first, before they gain more strength?" the general asked.

"No. It's not yet time."

"Are you waiting for the gods themselves?" General Falgoran scoffed.

"Yes," I said. "They'll come."

On the third day fighting broke out in the streets in earnest. It was a good diversion. I saw it for what it was, however, as did my highest ranking veterans. They sent a portion of the fighting force immediately, with mages to support them. Most were held back, waiting for the real attack.

It never came.

Instead, Krecek and a handful of his guard approached. They walked on foot to the outer wall and waited. I saw that Ysili was among them.

I saw that my foster parents were not.

Part Twenty-Four

N aran joined me as I stalked through the streets to meet Krecek and his entourage. "He'll expect you to meet him in kind, person for person."

"I'm not doing this for him," I said, glancing at Naran. "Between the two of us, we're a match for whoever he has along."

"Us?" Naran gave me a strange look. "You, me, and where are your guards? Where are your allies? I'm an artist, Agrad."

"You're the one who wanted to be involved," I pointed out. "Well, now you're involved. I have Davri. I have Nalia. Now I have you. What more do I need?"

"A semblance of sanity?"

"Oh no," I said, responding seriously to his droll humor. "That is the last thing I want at a time like this. I need to seem thoroughly insane."

"Congratulations," Naran said. "In that case you've won."

I laughed, feeling giddy as Krecek came into view along the deserted lane. "Are you going to follow my lead? Or are you going to ask him for asylum?"

"Can I ask him to send you to an asylum?"

"No."

"Can I just recommend it?" Naran paused, pretending to cringe in fear at the glare I leveled him. "Suggest it heavily as an option?"

"Is it too late to trade you for your sister?"

"Oh, that's a low blow from you. I think I'm wounded."

I laughed louder this time. "Of the two of you, she's actually fought in wars and has possession of an army."

"Perhaps," he quipped, "but I am ever so much more

attractive."

We were still laughing as we approached Krecek and the others.

"Either you truly have lost your mind," Krecek called across the space, "and it is somehow contagious, or you don't understand the gravity of what you have done."

I began to compose myself. "I understand exactly what I have done," I called back to him. "I'm standing before you, winning a war you're not even fighting yet!"

"Don't worry," Krecek said, his voice going softer as we approached each other. "You won't have to wait long for that."

"I know," I said. "I'm glad you're here."

"You're glad?" Krecek looked momentarily enraged by the idea. "I haven't come to fight on your side."

"You've come to fight," I said. "That's enough."

"I've come to talk you out of this!" We were close enough now that Krecek grabbed my arm and pulled me aside. "Is there any way I can talk you out of this madness?"

"If it's madness," I said, "then you know you can't talk me out of it. Feel free to try, but I am not the one who declared this war. You are."

"You truly are mad." He looked hurt, confused, and deeply afraid. "Is this how you mean to justify my end? Is this why you mean to kill me at last?"

"Come at me and find out," I said.

"Damn it!" he yelled. "I did not ask for this!"

"You did, though," I said, and one more time I took Nalia's form and spoke with her voice. "You did, my priest. You, and Aral, and Davri. Have you lost your nerve, priest? Are you unable to see this war through to the very end?"

Krecek was outraged by the shift. "You dare become her--" He cut off his own words, looking intently over my shoulder. "You were right," he said, countenance shifting to calm so quickly it seemed as if he'd donned or discarded a mask.

I knew what to expect. Immediately I tore open two portals to safety.

"Run!" Krecek and I yelled in unison to our companions.

"Through the rifts," I added, pointing.

Krecek's guards all ran through the one nearest them, except for Ysili. He followed Naran, watching me with defiance in his eyes.

It didn't matter to me.

They were safe.

"You should go, too," I said to Krecek softly.

He shook his head, and I felt him gather power within him to defend us both, if need be. We stood side by side, waiting.

The weeping god I'd seen so many years ago, Garatara, was standing to the side of the road. He was dressed in rags, looking like a beggar. He approached slowly.

"You're a wonderful actor, by the way," I said while we were still assessing the situation, measuring Garatara's mood and waiting for him to do more than shamble forward.

"Really?" He asked, taking a step back and guiding me to do the same. "You're terrible at it. We're trying to fool gods, not doddering grandparents."

"I'm not sure I can tell the difference," I said, gesturing. "You've had much more practice at deceiving gods though, haven't you?" I couldn't tell if the words were my own, but I think they were Nalia's. I could feel both bitterness and admiration for him emanating from her.

"We all do what we must," Krecek said. "You should be grateful for it now, Nalia. Now that we're on the same side."

Garatara looked up suddenly. "Nalia?"

Hearing this god say her name while I used her appearance and her voice was a frightening thing. It gave her more stability and control. For now I knew I was still me and could wrest control from her with an effort if needed. It was as if his word had wrapped a rope loosely around my waist. It could become binding, but it was not yet so.

"Nalia, I found you. They told me you were dead, but I did not believe them. I never believed them. You're not dead, are you?" Garatara, the god of healing, wore the countenance of a befuddled old man, lost within his own mind and trapped in the past.

"I am dead," she answered him, taking a step back and holding tight to Krecek's hand. "I am still here, but I died long ago."

"I don't understand," Garatara said, relentlessly shuffling forward. "I found you. You are here. If you, of all the gods, can die... If you can die, why am I still here?"

"I don't know," Nalia said. She truly didn't. She'd been dead before any other god had arrived to fight to free her, before any other god had died, and before the survivors had broken free. The urge to walk over to Garatara and hold his hand, to tell him everything would be okay now, was nearly overwhelming. "But who would dare kill the kindest of us all? The mortal races feared most of us, but they loved you. They adored you. I would have died to protect you." I held tighter to Krecek's hand, to hold me and Nalia back from running to the poor god's side.

Garatara fell to his knees. "Are you a ghost? Did you die to save me? I don't want you to die for me, go back and change it."

I grasped his hand tighter yet, and his grip increased as well.

"No," Nalia said. "I died for petty revenge and greed. You never could heal the selfishness and corruption in my soul."

"We have souls? Like mortal things?" He sounded broken, confused, but somehow hopeful.

Nalia began to nod, but a chill rode in on the back of a sudden breeze and gave the three of us pause. Yda stood behind

Garatara, stood him up like a puppet and whispered into his ear with all the intimacy of a lover. The smile she gave me and Krecek was sultry and smug.

"You don't have to listen to her," Nalia said calmly.

"Do you deny what Yda says?" Garatara's eyes narrowed. "The one you cling to is one of those who murdered you. That mortal killed Fotar, did he not? Are you a traitor? Is that the corruption that sickened you?" Madness blazed anew in his eyes.

"I was the first one to be betrayed!" Nalia shrieked.

"I WAS!" Garatara shouted her down, echoing words that Yda had mouthed a moment sooner. "The end began in my temple, and I would have died that day as well if not for Thar and Brin! You—you deserved to die, Nalia!"

I took control of myself back, fighting harder than ever to do so. Nalia's anger and having her name repeated so many times had given her more power, but it was still my body. It was still my life.

I uttered words in the dark and ancient tongue of creation, and from the very ground climbed the bones of my childhood. Every man, woman, and child who had died in Lesser Stonegore pushed and clawed their way from beneath cobbled streets and any free patch of earth to reach the surface. Any near enough to Yda grabbed her, though even I could not say if they sought to pull her down with them or simply use her to pull themselves up.

Yda screamed. It was the first time either Nalia or I had ever seen her so affected by anything. As skeletal fingers clawed at her clothes and at her flesh, the goddess of chaos was actually afraid.

"You should leave while they're distracted," I murmured to Krecek, slowly letting go of his hand.

Krecek nodded, backing away from me at first, his face an

echo of Yda's horror. "You did this? You brought forth this abomination?"

"Yes."

He didn't say another word. He just left through the rift I'd left open after his companions had run, and I closed it behind him.

I looked at Garatara. "Come with me," I offered softly. "I'll keep you safe. I'll keep you sane."

"Abomination," the god echoed the last word Krecek had said.

"No more so than the entirety of my life has been." I turned my back on him, following the path between me and my own rift, listening to the sound of Yda fighting off the undead as I walked away. A moment later I was in the safe room where I'd set up the rift, and I closed it behind me.

I was alone in the room. The others, Naran and Ysili, had left and closed the door behind them. I sank to my knees, just breathing, just being alive for a little while longer. I could question my morals later. I could pull myself together and be strong in a moment. Right now I was exhausted, and lucky to be alive.

Or, was I? I concentrated, sitting more comfortably on the floor so that I could just think. Was it actual luck that had saved me? Just what did it take to actually kill a wizard or an elemental? Davri knew. Every Verwyn had known and had taken the secret to the grave. It was in that mass tangle of visions that Davri had seen in his life and in those first moments of becoming a wizard. I just had to find the right —

"Lord Verwyn?" The door to the room was thrown open, shattering my concentration. "Lord Verwyn! You're safe! There are — there are horrible reports of the dead rising! The men are in a state of terror, and some have run for their lives!"

I balled my hands in fists, frustrated to be interrupted, but knowing I had to reassure my people. "I'll take care of this," I said, shrugging aside my weariness to do what must be done. "Send out the message that the skeletons will bring no harm. They serve me. And bring the generals to me at once."

Before the young soldier left, I saw the word in her eyes. Abomination. It was as clear as if she had spoken it. Instead, she just turned and followed orders, swallowing her fear to do what must be done.

I forced myself to do the same.

I had five generals, and what that meant as far as the size of my army I had no idea. I had a few hundred skeletons, and they were the only ones who would actually obey me or listen to what I had to say. The generals were necessary for organization and communication, but they had opinions of their own. Opinions that would not be swayed by the orders of a baby-faced child who had not yet demonstrated that he could end their lives with no more than a gesture or a glance.

I took a deep breath to settle my thoughts. Anger and frustration would not win this war. I needed a level head.

I walked into the command room to wait. Byrek was the only one there at first, and I told him what had transpired.

"She was afraid?" he asked, just as astonished by this detail as I was.

I nodded. "They reached for her and she recoiled in terror. I don't know what it means, but it's a tool I intend to use against her."

When the generals arrived he spoke for me. His experience and his years had earned him respect that I had yet to achieve, as far as they were concerned. Soon, they were current on the latest developments.

Byrek and I only disagreed on one thing.

"We shouldn't fight Krecek's forces unless they attack us first," I said firmly. "No surprise attacks. Nothing that could be seen as underhanded. If they attack my special forces, do not attack them. Only if they make a move against living, breathing targets." Special forces. That's what Byrek had decided to call them, because calling them undead or skeletons was distasteful or unprofessional.

"I thought your plan was to maximize the distraction factor," General Falgoran said, leaning forward. "We're here to fight a war, not play nice with the enemy."

"Ceolwyn is not the enemy," I said.

"That's news to us," General Zarah said. She had a wide face and a ready smile, but I hadn't seen it from her in weeks. These days her brow was furrowed or her eyes narrowed as she did her best to stay five steps ahead of the situation. She hated surprises.

"That's what I went out there to meet him about in the first place," I said, frustrated. "Keep up with current events. Our enemy is, and always has been, the goddess of chaos."

"How are we supposed to fight gods?" General Zarah demanded. "That's something that wizards do, not the rest of us!"

"At any point in the last few days," I said, "did you even once look at Cairnfeld? Are you familiar with it at all? There aren't twenty cairns there. There are thousands. They died fighting against gods, fighting for what they believed in. That war is still being fought. I need each and every one of you, and Ceolwyn's soldiers, to be able to fight against whatever forces the gods bring to bear. I do not want any lives wasted under my command fighting against people we have a chance of fighting with."

"Since you're suddenly interested in taking charge," Byrek said in carefully neutral tones, "why don't you tell us how?"

"I don't know!" Why were they suddenly against me, just because I wanted them not to kill Krecek's people? "Just don't fight against people who aren't our enemy."

"Are we to just surrender, after all your plots and plans that put us in this gods-forsaken town in the first place?" General Falgoran decided he couldn't be left out of the spotlight any longer. "I'm sure our spoils of war include at least a crate of white linens. We can go to war under a blank banner and cry for them to lead us!"

I leaned forward to make an impassioned rebuttal, but Byrek placed a hand on my shoulder and shook his head. "Just let us do this the way it needs to be done," he said. "We understand the realities of war. I've fought in enough of them. You don't understand what you're asking."

"I know exactly wh—" I stopped myself, standing and turning away. "Fight under whatever damn banner you want, for whatever cause you feel like. I need some air." I left without another word. The room had fallen silent behind me.

PART TWENTY-FIVE

A t the top of the building was a roof terrace. It was modest, with a handful of chairs taking up most of the space, but no one else was there and I found that to be its best feature at the moment. Oh, yes, it had a beautiful view of the bay, but that wasn't important to me. A chance to think was all that mattered.

I wasn't sure how I had so completely lost control of things. My instructions had been simple. There was no reason for this insanity. It was as if I'd asked them to behead their own children, the way they'd reacted. It didn't make sense.

I took deep breaths, closing my eyes. It was hard not to worry, but this part had been mostly Byrek's plan, not mine. He could lead them better than I could at this point. I knew from Davri's memories how old Byrek was, and I knew that he had fought beside every other Verwyn since. The generals of this army trusted him and answered to him.

"You look overwhelmed."

I should have been startled by the suddenness of hearing someone up here with me, but I wasn't. I didn't recognize the voice, and when I opened my eyes to see who had joined me I felt calm at the stranger's presence, as if I'd known her my whole life. I felt as if she belonged here on this terrace much more so than I did. In fact, I opened my mouth to apologize for intruding on her peace before I remembered that no one had been here a moment ago.

"Who wouldn't?" I asked instead.

"I think that was the point."

I looked at her askance.

"You didn't realize yet? I'm sure Nalia would have realized it by now."

Her words pulled at me with power when she said Nalia's name, and I realized belatedly that this was a goddess. "Nalia lets me figure things out at my own pace. I'm still young, and still learning, compared to the rest of you."

"Oh, of course," she had the decency to blush. "She who is chaos has regained some of her concentration, and she is most wroth with you. Her hands were all over the reactions of your generals. I am surprised you didn't realize."

"Given time and a bit more concentration, perhaps," I said, bowing my head to her to acknowledge that she had bested me. "Thank you. Your insight is very helpful."

She smiled, and I felt buoyed and hopeful.

It's just her magic working on you, Nalia said. She seemed irritated and amused, but there was another feeling mixed in that I did not immediately recognize. Tender and protective. I struggled to put a name to it, and finally came up with maternal.

"Who are you?" I looked at this goddess in something like wonder. "I thought all of the gods were against me, but you are looking at me with kindness and treating me almost as a kindred soul."

"You know my name," she said. "I heard it on the air when you learned it for the first time and I wondered if it would be a boon or our bane. I think you wondered the same."

I thought for a bit, struggling with what I knew of the gods, before I realized who she must be. Hastriva, goddess of peace, daughter of Nalia and Garatara. My eyes widened, wondering what that would mean. We were facing against her father, while I held her mother imprisoned. She may be the goddess of peace, but she was goddess. How could she possibly be on my side?

"Have you decided yet," I asked. "Boon or bane?"

Hastriva shook her head. "You try, Agrad Verwyn. I have

seen just how hard you try. I can't yet tell what you are trying for, however."

"You will probably find out at the same time that I do," I said. "I can tell you what I want, though."

"You want peace," she said, smiling. "I can feel that much in you. It calls to me and makes me second guess all the things I once wanted to do to you. It bewilders me too, however. You want peace, but you work toward conflict. Perhaps that's why the three of us have chosen to champion your cause, if just for now."

"Three?"

Hastriva nodded. "I wanted to hate you. The gods of war wanted to crush you and make you suffer."

"I was vulnerable most of my life," I said. I wasn't afraid or resentful. In a way, I think I understood what she meant and why she would think that way. "What stopped you?"

"Another of our diminished number persuaded us to watch and wait, to see if you were worth hate. It was a tense night, when you we finally found you, small and alone. We had found you only after the wizards had, though we had looked just as hard. It was exceptional magic that had protected you; your parents were very skilled and very protective. Yet, suddenly you were there. A child. We watched over you after that. Do you remember the names of the priests who took you in?"

Surprisingly, I had to think about it. They had been in my thoughts every day, but somehow their names tried to escape. "Rhada and Goriath." I thought harder, trying to remember. "Their last name. It was Brinn, I think."

She let that sink in, waiting patiently for me to make a connection.

Memory returned to me of the day they had taken me in. They moment they had introduced themselves. Goriath had introduced himself as Brinn first-- "Thar and Brin," I said, eyes widening with realization. "They were the gods of war."

Hastriva nodded. "I kept my distance, but they are more aggressive than I am. They needed to see and shape events themselves. They raised you the entire time you were in Myrenfeld, keeping you hidden to keep you from growing afraid. They were concerned at first, of course, because we all know what my mother's potential is, and that her power was given to you. Thar and Brin gave you a distraction from your pain, gave you something like a home, and gave you a disguise from the wizards and from the pain that was too much for such a young child to deal with."

"I had no idea," I said, unsure if I should be embarrassed or just grateful. "They said I was like their lost daughter."

"They did have a daughter, once," Hastriva said with quiet pain. "She's dead now. Stealing you from the wizards, even for just a time, gave them their own revenge and sense of closure. You were a very sweet child. They taught you more than they intended because of that, including our names."

"I almost wish I'd stayed," I said. "I only ran away because I wanted to protect them."

It did make more sense to me, now. They'd called me Eria, given me a name and an identity separate from what I'd known, as a disguise. They'd told me they were priests because if they'd told me they were gods I'd only have been afraid. They may have taught me priestly magic because they'd never taught any other form of magic to a mortal before, or perhaps because they were testing just how powerful I was. And, of course, Nalia couldn't have told me who they were because she'd been dormant in my mind until I was old enough for our minds to begin to understand one another.

She smiled and touched my cheek. "A very sweet child."

I smiled, buoyed by her praise.

Hastriva sat back and looked at me for a few moments more.

"The gods are divided on where we stand in your war. Not just this battle, but the whole of it."

I nodded, grateful not to be alone, but not surprised that there were more who stood against me. "Are you really here to help me?"

"Thar and Brin have been at your side," Hastriva said, "fighting for you all this time. It's my turn, though you may not like what comes of it. Peace always comes at a price."

Naively, I thought any price would be worth paying. "I will appreciate your help, however you can deliver it. You and any other of the gods who survive, if they are so inclined. I have no animosity toward the gods."

"You may not," she said, "but I am sure that other wizards still do."

"There are only three of them left," I said, "and I don't speak for them. Only me. I'll bring an end to this war, no matter who I have to fight. Wizard or god."

"This is why I'm not at all certain you are trying for peace. You may want it at any cost, but I am not sure I see an end to any wars to come for you." Hastriva shook her head, giving me a sadly sympathetic look. "It's one of the things we like about you."

I looked at her, confused, as she faded away. Did she take me for some warmonger, or just someone that misfortune would always seek? Even to wizards and elementals, gods were confusing beings.

She had been gone for only a few moments when a cacophony of whistles and sirens rang out, met with shouts and marching feet. The call to arms had begun, and it was nearly time for battle to be met. The terrace seemed as good a vantage point to fling my spells from as any. Battle casters of varying ability peppered the ranks of the troops, adding spells to the strength of weapons and bodies in the oncoming clash. They still bore my colors, but I had my doubts of who they fought for.

It didn't matter. I suppose it only mattered that they fought. All of them, no matter who they fought in the end. I had Yda's attention. I had my war.

In a sudden gust of wind and magic thick enough to make my skin tingle, Modarian Lorwyn's forces came to port and joined the fray, catching everyone by surprise. He'd used illusion to mask their progress, I could tell now. I stared in disbelief for only a moment before calling down the stairs for a messenger. The generals were informed post haste, and when I went down to see their reactions I heard all I needed to.

"Good! We can use the help."

"Fresh targets!"

"More help!"

"Kill them all!"

"At the least he'll make for a good scout."

Disgusted, I left the building to join the fray. I saw two men, both in the pale blue and blood red from Kaelwyn's forces, fighting each other ten paces from the door. I had no doubt, as I felt the forces of chaos rise, that this was being repeated throughout the city by members of every army.

I stopped no one. I was thankful that the brutality had stopped short of looting, but considering what I knew of the underground I knew it was only a matter of time. "Is this what war is?" I asked a man in Krecek's blue and silver, but he looked at me as if I were mad and continued chasing down three men who wore no uniforms at all.

Men and women in gray and black began joining from the west, surprised at first as they took in the scene, but one by one

Lorwyn's army fell apart and just attacked anyone they saw. I tried to lift the spell as I walked, and an island of calm and confusion followed me where I went, but I could only make it spread so far. Men and women rushed to me, throwing themselves at me to kill me, but they reached my influence and stopped cold. It happened so many times I began to find it ridiculous, almost humorous. It was fantastic, until the first arrow reached me and pierced my arm.

I stumbled and nearly fell from the sudden force of it. I felt tremendous pressure before I felt the pain, unbalanced and confused before I realized I'd actually been shot. I took hold of the arrow, making it vanish from existence, but I did not have time to heal the wound. It burned when air met with where the arrow had been, but I ignored the pain and continued. Other arrows were shot at me, but none caught me by surprise again.

I continued on to Cairnfeld. There was power in those cairns, and I meant to use whatever I could of it. My throbbing arm had given me focus and determination. I'd left the building bemused and irritated that all had succumbed to Yda's power so easily, but now I was growing angry.

My undead creations were still hiding, but I could feel their desire to aid me. I paused a moment and invited two of them, Enforcer Longbar and Master Dayle, to walk with me and protect me. With them by my side it felt easier to keep chaos at bay, and I reached the low wall at the edge of town faster than I expected.

"Hey, little girl!" The tone was teasing, and the voice familiar. "Mind if I go your way?"

"Ysili," I cried out, relieved to have found him. "I didn't expect to see you here."

I'd been holding my arm, keeping pressure on it and trying to hold in the blood, but I held out my hands in welcome when I heard him. My left hand was stained red, but then again so was the white sleeve that covered my right arm. I looked at both and shook my head, dismissing it. It was merely flesh. Inconsequential.

More men had rushed me, attempting to kill me, and some of them wore my own uniform. I gestured for Ysili to hurry, to reach my side and my circle of calm.

"Are you okay?"

I nodded curtly. "I'm an elemental. It takes more than this to kill me."

Ysili approached and took my hand, looked at my arm. "Of course it takes more than a blooded arm to kill you. It would take something more like this."

Calm as ever, he grasped my arm and turned, sliding his sword into my exposed gut.

I stared into his blue, blue eyes, searching for something, but only seeing my own surprise echoed back. He pulled the blade out and stared at the blood upon it, tossing it aside and raising his hands backward as the men I had freed from Yda's influence cried out and ran to my side.

I was too shocked, too surprised, to stop the skeletons at my side. They fell upon Ysili, ripping out his throat even as one of my soldiers impaled the man who had once been my friend.

Ysili collapsed onto the cobblestones, first his knees, then his back, finally his head, and every moment felt like an eternity where I tried to reach out to him, to save him. In truth it was but a moment, and before I could register what had happened, before I could even begin to feel my own pain, it was too late to save him.

I fell to my knees, shoving everyone away as I crawled to Ysili's side and held him. His eyes focused upon me, head bobbing as if he was trying to take a breath, and his ravaged throat spurted and gurgled.

I wanted to ask him why, but there would never be an

answer. I would never know. I brushed his beautiful blue hair out of his face, and closed his eyes.

"It was one of Ceolwyn's men! They've attacked us!"

I glared at the woman in her gold and green, disgusted. "They've been attacking us all along, as we have been doing to them. It's all fallen to hell already. Look around you and see what Yda has reduced us to!"

She did as she was told, inhaling sharply. Ysili was not the only corpse around us. Outside of my circle the fighting continued on without reason. And, with the pain and the grief, that circle was rapidly dwindling.

"I don't understand!" she cried out. "There's no reason to who they fight! I must stop this." My circle slipped ever smaller, past her, and she turned away from me. "I will make them stop this madness!" She ran away and rejoined the fray, succumbing to the madness.

"It takes more than just this to kill an elemental," I whispered. I didn't understand, but I didn't have time to understand. Sitting on the ground, cradling his corpse, would not bring my friend back. It would not bring me answers. Gingerly, I stood and began walking once again. There were other graves that called to me. I would make one for Ysili soon enough.

I walked through rows and rows of small cairns, knowing their number was about to grow once again. I nearly stumbled, again and again, but I would lift my head up and look across the field, looking at the larger cairns in the center, forcing myself to take another step. Innate healing had already begun, but the pain was intense. I closed my eyes to catch my breath, and when I looked up once again I saw figures standing near the cairns.

"If we don't hurry it will be too late."

I looked beside me, seeing Modarian practically carrying Krecek to the center of the field just a few paces to my left. The difference in their height could have been comical, if not for the burns and blisters on the half-elf's skin, or the bloody and tattered clothes that Modarian wore.

"What happened to you two?" I looked them over, noticing more and more injury as I stared.

"There was an explosion," Krecek said with a rasp to his voice. "One of my own guards set it off."

"My shipmates turned on me and began throwing rocks," Modarian said. "It took me a bit to realize why. What happened to you?"

"I was shot," I pointed. "And stabbed. And avenged, gods be damned. They killed Ysili." My face puckered and fresh tears stung my eyes.

"They?" Krecek looked at me, alarmed. "Who killed him? What happened?"

I gestured to the skeletons, my guards. "Enforcer Longbar and Garm Dayle's father, here. I was too young to know Master Dayle's given name." I chuckled, just a touch, and the pain was exquisite. "Ysili stabbed me. Seemed as surprised as I was." I began to walk again, small steps, but I couldn't give up. "I thought there were others. Do either of you know where they are?"

Krecek coughed for a minute, but they kept up with me easily despite it. "Aral," he gasped, and coughed again.

Modarian patted Krecek on the shoulder. "Aral was taken by surprise, hit in the head with a mace. The last I heard, Raev was looking for a healer to tend to her, but it was impossible to find anyone not touched by the madness."

I nodded. "Will he join us?"

"He might," Krecek said, finally past his coughing fit. "Tsevric and Charsa may be close enough to join us and help, but they have six armies to fight through first."

I barely knew those names. I thought hard and finally

recalled which wizards they were, Aledwyn and Jaelwyn respectively, as I took another step forward. I'd heard their names when Byrek had taught me.

Modarian gasped suddenly, as I was trying to puzzle out any other memories I might have of other elementals, and my train of thoughts was lost. I looked at him and then I followed his shocked gaze to the center of Cairnfeld. We were close enough to make out the figures standing there now.

One of them was Naran.

PART TWENTY-SIX

We hurried. Despite injuries that would have killed most mortals the three of us walked as fast as we could to the center of the field. I heard shouting, but I couldn't make out what they said yet. I couldn't lift my head to watch and walk at the same time. I was staring at the ground in front of my feet, looking up only when I paused to catch my breath.

"Name of the gods!" I heard Modarian exclaim.

I looked up, fighting to focus my eyes. We were so much closer, but still so far away. I had been trying to heal myself as we walked, trying so hard to use magic to make this easier. Garatara had mastery over all healing magic around him, and he knew that this was his greatest tool to fight us. The pain was nearly unbearable, but I told myself it could have been worse. I still healed faster than a mortal, at least. I still—

I stumbled over a rock at the corner of a cairn while I was trying to make out what had stunned Modarian so much. I fell to my hands and knees, jarring my injuries and causing them to bleed more. Muscles that flexed and tensed to brace myself, to catch myself, caused more injury. I gasped at how intense the pain was. My eyes flew wide open, my mouth fell agape, and I must have made some sort of sound odd sound. It felt like a scream, but it sounded more like a kitten caught beneath the wheel of a carriage.

Modarian and Krecek continued without me, their urgency growing. Others were coming, but it wasn't enough. I knew it would not be enough, because Yda's hold was too great. I could almost hear her laughing on the wind. I balled my hands into fists, dirt and bloody mud trapping itself in my grasp. I was calling the undead to me, to protect me, to stop whatever it was that was happening where I could not reach. In doing so I felt the restless dead beneath me, laying unsatisfied and unfulfilled from the final day of the Arcane War, so long ago.

With my blood mingled into their dirt, they stirred on their own and I could feel them begging to be released. I could feel them begging to be of service once again, to defeat the gods who had wronged them. All they needed was my word, and without thought I gave that to them.

Stones were pushed away from every lesser cairn in the vast field, and I lay my head down upon the dirt to rest. I wish I could take credit for thinking of such a brilliant strategy to chase Yda away, but in honesty it was done without thought. It was nearly done against my will. A whim, a thought, and a connection with their bones. That was all there was in raising this great and terrible army of undead.

I closed my eyes, using my strength to take just one breath. Just one breath more. I concentrated on that now with all the effort I had used to take each step just moments before.

Just one more.

The dead milled around me, pausing in my presence before they continued on in their purpose. I wasn't healing like I thought I should. I was sweating and I felt cold. If I could sleep, if I could only sleep, this would be over. I could surrender to Garatara, and then I could sleep at last. Fight another day.

It was so tempting to accept that thought. I would not die. I could not die. Not from this. My surrender would be a sweet respite. I could come back, older and wiser, with perhaps a better plan. Yes.

"I," the syllable formed on my lips. "Sur." I panted, losing track of my intent from pain. "En." It slipped out in a gasp, but I couldn't get further.

Mustering the presence of mind to talk brought back every

reason, every vision of Davri's, which told me I could never give in to Yda's plan. I took a deep breath, rallying what strength I had left.

"No," I breathed. I would not surrender. I gathered the last of my strength.

"Garatara, I pray to thee," I whispered words I'd learned as a child that I thought I would never say. It sounded like supplication, like prayer, but it was magic that would circumvent even his will if he was not paying attention. If he was distracted enough by denying healing to too many others. "Grant me thy healing power, not just to bring wholeness to my body, but to my soul and to the souls of those around me."

I breathed.

At first I couldn't tell if I was growing numb, or if healing had begun.

The pain was receding and my mind began to clear. That was all that mattered.

"Hastriva," I began to pray once again, clinging to hope that this was working. "I pray to thee. Bring an end to this battle, please."

She knelt beside me, putting one of her hands upon my shoulder gently. "I am. You've helped. You've driven Yda away for now. Come with me and behold the fruits of your labor."

I was sitting in a chair, wrapped up in a blanket, my wounds bandaged tight and protesting the sudden change of position. My first thought was to wonder at the facility of Hastriva's spell, and how swiftly it had been done. It was a thought I brushed aside as I took in what went on around me.

We were within the circle of cairns erected for the gods. Fereth and Naran stood there, and Fereth had been crying. He was setting aside the suit that Naran had worn earlier, while Naran was pulling on a strange old robe I recognized only from ancient illustrations. It was simple and bared his chest. The fabric was a deep and dark red that I had seen too much of already today. It was the same color of the deep red blood that was meant to be spilled upon it. It was garb worn only by those who were to be sacrificed, back in the days of the gods.

Fereth turned with a dagger in his hands, trembling as he held it out. "Don't do this, Master Tennival," he begged. "Please. They'll never forgive me for helping you with this. I'll be cursed the rest of my days."

"The gods will protect you," Naran said. "The wizards will forgive you in time."

"They won't," Fereth sobbed as he spoke. "Agrad will hate me."

"This is more important," Naran said. He was perfectly calm.

Fereth closed his eyes and composed himself. "Sorry. You're right. One life, to save many. I'm sorry." He held out the blade, hands open this time so that Naran could grab it.

I tried to protest, to get up from my seat, but I was still too weak and dizzy to do more than moan pitifully.

Hastriva leaned close to murmur in my ear. "You prayed for peace. The price for it is very high."

Naran and Fereth heard us, freezing where they were for a moment, both looking guilty to be seen in this state.

"I can't do it!" Fereth dropped the dagger, looking for an escape, but there was a ring of undead around us now. They watched and waited. Fereth stood, frozen in terror and indecision, torn between two sorts of impossible horrors.

"I will," Hastriva strode forward. "Naran Tennival, your soul cannot rejoin your parents. Baedrogan is dead." She spoke of the god of death, dead himself and trapped within Shaelek. "You understand this, but still offer yourself as a sacrifice to Garatara, god of healing?"

Naran looked over at me in weary apology before he knelt before her. "I understand. It is a sacrifice long overdue."

"No," I said. "No, no. Not you, too." I couldn't watch this, but I couldn't look away. I searched for Modarian, for Krecek, but they were still so far away. I thought I even saw Raev, running with his impressive bulk and bowling down any obstacle in his way, but everyone was just too far away.

"Tell them I am sorry their many sacrifices were in vain," Naran said to me, looking at me as Hastriva pulled his head back and aimed the dagger true.

I closed my eyes as her arm came down. Many long heartbeats I hoped, I denied, I told myself that as long as I kept my eyes closed then what I'd heard had not happened. It was a hollow sort of a sound, wet but hollow. I couldn't stop hearing it. I wanted to. I tried to close everything out, but I couldn't keep my eyes closed.

Garatara had appeared.

Hastriva was whispering in Naran's ear as she pulled the blade from his chest. There was so much blood, so very much blood. Garatara stood next to them, helped Hastriva lower Naran's body to the ground. He touched Naran's blood and looked at his daughter with something that seemed to be confusion.

In his presence I was healing swiftly now. Too late I found the strength to pull myself from the chair, hitting the ground but still crawling forward. Too late to save my friend. Always too late to save anyone. I reached Naran's side, grabbing him, listening for any whisper of breath, feeling desperately for a heartbeat.

"Are you satisfied now?" Rage momentarily took me, now that I had a target for it. I grabbed a rock, throwing it at Garatara and hitting him above his ear. "Oh, some god of healing you've become. Nalia is ashamed of you! You let him die! He was my friend, and you just let him die!" I threw another, smaller rock, but I missed and I was finished.

"You let him die!" I sobbed. I curled up like a newborn, knees to my chest, arms wrapped around myself and my pain.

Garatara crawled to my side. "You," he whispered. "I know you." He knelt beside me, brushing hair from my face. His hands were gentle, and the madness I'd seen before was gone. "You are Agrad." He looked intently into my eyes, understanding coming into them the longer he looked at me. "This man is — no, was — the final sacrifice."

"He was my friend," I said, sobbing. "He was my mentor. He died so you would stop this, but you're not stopping a thing." I couldn't look at him. I wanted to wipe my tears away, but my hands were covered in blood. I couldn't tell whose it was, mine or his. Both, perhaps. It all looked the same. I couldn't stop staring at the blood, wondering, even when my sight blurred. "People are dying. My friends are dying. Everyone is dying and I hurt so much." I sobbed again and closed my eyes. "So much."

"I did this?" Garatara asked.

"Yes, father," Hastriva said. "Yda took your grief and twisted it. This entire war is a festering wound that you wouldn't heal."

I looked up in time to see her turn her back on him.

"I never wanted this boy to die," Garatara said. He was kneeling at Naran's side, and he lifted the body and cradled it like some doll. "I never wanted this sacrifice. I remember it now. His parents died so that he would live. That was enough. That was more than —" He broke off and looked at me. "He wasn't supposed to die." There was a mixture of horror and disgust on his face, and I couldn't help but sympathize. "Everything — all of this — just for this boy's death?" The horror of it was sinking in, and I couldn't help but empathize. "No. No, the reign of gods is better put behind us! Look at what we have done to our creation!" He cradled Naran to him like a child, like a doll. Then, Garatara laid Naran down before me, tears streaming down his face. "Look at what we've done, Nalia. We're better off dead."

The realization hit me that I was completely healed and I wanted to scream. NOW I was healed? NOW? The urge to laugh hit me like a wave of nausea. I screamed instead.

"Nobody's better off dead," I shouted. "Nobody! Naran thought he would be better off dead so that this whole stupid thing would be over, but dying didn't change anything! He's not better off! He's just DEAD!"

I don't know if he heard my words at all. Garatara was looking around, and he would keep looking down at Naran's staring eyes and then look around again. "We started this," he kept muttering as if Naran could hear him. "We brought this on ourselves." He arranged Naran's body into the semblance of peaceful repose and healed the wound in his heart, for all the good that could to. It was much too late. "If gods did this, I don't wish to be on the side of the gods. It hurts, Agrad. It hurts, Nalia. It hurts too much."

Before I understood what he was doing, Garatara leaned over Naran, and from there he just…disappeared.

"Name of the gods, what now?" I was too emotionally raw to think about it. Garatara was gone, but Hastriva was still there, and I could feel other powerful presences closing in on us. "How will his disappearing end this all?"

The sounds of fighting had finally stopped, though. Close by, I heard people exclaim in surprise, crying that they'd been healed. Even Krecek, as he came ever closer, was no longer burned and was running to us on his own. The undead were walking away, no longer feeling the urgent draw to battle and redemption that had helped me awaken them.

"He was insane," I said. "All of his words were just ravings of a madman. Weren't they?"

"A fair bit of it was," Hastriva said. "I don't think Yda's influence on him could ever have been undone, and he knew it."

Her words and tone confused me, though I could tell that Nalia understood something that I did not. There was finality to it, and she spoke of Garatara in the past tense. No sooner had that thought formed within me when I realized and became more confused. Just because he'd disappeared didn't necessarily mean he was gone, did it? Gods vanished and appeared in front of mortals all the time. I'd seen even Hastriva do it.

Yet I knew, this was different.

"Do you mean he's gone entirely?"

Hastriva came to my side, helping me to my feet and looking me in the eyes. "You of all people know best that one cannot kill a god. Agrad of Verwyn, you speak with Nalia because she is not entirely dead. She is only changed. Now, so is my father."

I looked at Naran hopefully.

Nothing. No sign of life. No breath.

"I don't know," Hastriva murmured. "I think he is there with your friend. I don't think Garatara would have healed the fatal wound unless his intent was to at least attempt to become one of you. Is there room for another wizard?"

PART TWENTY-SEVEN

I stared at Naran, trying to will him to life, though my magic would be of no more use to him than what was already coursing through his body. "We'll make room," I said without hesitation.

"You have your peace," Hastriva said, "but it is not a permanent one. Thar and Brin have foreseen as much. Worse is yet to come." She took a step back, distancing herself. "Keep your undead handy, Agrad. Your abominations and perversions of nature may yet save this world." She paused and cocked her head to the side. "Or condemn it. The future is always in motion."

Krecek had joined us, kneeling at Naran's side in shock, and I began to explain to him what happened. Modarian joined us, and Raev, and I had to start again, and again. Hastriva had disappeared, but no one else seemed to notice it, and it felt unimportant as I finally revealed the events of Naran's death to his closest friends.

Fereth cleared his throat, looking miserable and guilty. "I tried to stop him," Fereth said. "We'd been talking together when the fighting began. It made sense to me at the time, but I--" He stopped, shaking his head. "I don't know what I was saying to him, but he looked at me with wide eyes and said I was brilliant. It was something about coming full circle."

Krecek recoiled, taking a full step back with a look of horror on his face. None of us reacted much better, seeing what it meant with perfect hindsight that Fereth couldn't have possessed.

"A gorgeous woman appeared, and even though my mind cleared when she did, I couldn't say anything." Fereth shifted his weight from one foot to another, staring at the ground. "She asked him if he would do something. I think she said, 'Are you ready?' He just said yes. That was it. And the next I knew we were in his house, and he was handing me things and then we walked here. He was raving like a madman. He said...he said it would finally be over. I felt the bundle in my arms. The knife. And I knew what he meant, then. He told me...he said how it all began. Because of him. He told me everything while we were walking. The next thing I knew, the knife was in my hands. He expected me to do it. To kill him." He took a deep breath and looked around at us, wide eyed. "He begged me."

"And you would have, if you hadn't seen me?" I asked bitterly.

"Agrad, no," Krecek said, putting an arm around me. "Don't hold that against the boy. You told me that Naran's last words were an apology, that our sacrifices had been in vain, but I don't think any of our sacrifices were in vain. Especially his."

I leaned into him, unable to hang on to rage.

Raev gasped. He was bent over to pick Naran up, both arms scooped under the body. "Everyone, look."

I stared in disbelief, hope beginning to blossom.

"He's breathing," Raev said. "He lives."

My heart skipped a beat. "Thank the gods," I whispered. Krecek squeezed my shoulders tighter. Despite his enmity toward the gods, I knew he understood why I'd said it.

Among the dead, Ysili's body was not the only one I recognized, but it was the one with the most impact. When I saw him again it drained all the joy from me at once. Unlike Naran, there was no chance that he would return in any form.

Elemental

He was dead and dishonored, and I wondered if I'd ever know why. I'd always thought he was so loyal, and that he'd been my friend.

I knelt next to his body, covering his face with my own blood-soaked shirt and holding his cold and lifeless hand as I tried not to think. This hand that had tried to kill me. This hand that had once worked hard to give me food and clothing and shelter. This hand that had comforted me. This hand that had betrayed me.

Eventually Fereth found me and sat beside me. "My cousin, my mother's nephew. He was found—I knew him. He lived in Anogrin. He'd visit. We'd visit. My uncle encouraged me to be a bard. That's why you never met my cousin. My father didn't like his family after that. Still, he's family, and I feel like I should feel more, but I keep thinking. Ysili was your best friend, wasn't he? Here you are, and there he is, and I can't feel like some cousin I haven't seen in four years is anything next to—"

"You are my best friend," I interrupted him. "I knew him longer, but I've known you better. You wouldn't try to...to kill me." I looked at him, into his green eyes, searching, completely unsure. I felt as vulnerable as a child. "Would you?"

"Never," he swore, hugging me suddenly. "I couldn't imagine it."

I leaned against him, trying to cry and yet too tired to be able to. "I won't turn you aside. I won't question your loyalty. I won't, I swear. I won't drive you away like I did to him. I'm sorry. I'm so very sorry." I was babbling, and I knew it. I took a deep breath, trying to gather my thoughts. "I've done everything all wrong. My plan was to trick the gods into thinking I wanted to fight against Krecek, and they'd seen through it all along. It was hopeless. It was a joke. Everything went wrong. Bringing forth the dead was supposed to be my greatest weapon against those who would have betrayed me, but it all went wrong. It nearly killed me. I did everything wrong. And the first person I ever fell in love with is dead and he tried to kill me."

Fereth was shocked only at my last words. I hadn't meant to say them out loud. I'd never thought about love when it came to Ysili. I only realized it as I said it that it was true. I'd been in love with him once. So this is how that would end.

"It could have been worse," Fereth said, and I stared at him. Just how hard did he want me to hit him for saying something as trite and useless as that? "He could have killed you."

"He tried hard enough," I said as I stood and wiped off my hands. "If he had succeeded, it wouldn't have changed a thing. You and Naran would have gone through with the sacrifice and saved the day. Everything I did was for nothing."

"Well, at least you're not dead!" Fereth stood as well, crossing his arms in front of his chest and looking as belligerent as his father always had. "You're here, and I'm not all alone standing in the middle of a great field of carnage wondering how soon the gods would kill everyone else I've ever loved because I stood with you and defied them. I'm sorry you couldn't save everyone. I'm sorry that you couldn't save him. I'm sorry that you're suffering. But I'm not sorry that I am GLAD you're not DEAD!"

"Oh."

What else could I say to that?

"Exactly," he said, arms still crossed, waiting.

I sighed and stepped forward to thank him, or to apologize, or something in that range of things that I hadn't quite decided on yet, but someone nearby cleared his throat and we both looked over in surprise. It hadn't even occurred to me that anyone else might give us a second glance.

"So that was your grand plan?" Raev watched us with a wry expression.

367

"Every bit of it," I said, shaking my head. "Well, except for the part where...everything that actually happened. See, we were supposed to have the upper hand, lull the gods into a false sense of security, and actually have some sort of parlay before things fell apart. We were supposed to have all of our armies here, and functioning as armies instead of deranged mobs bent on self-destruction. More bluster and bluff and actual parlay where Fereth could be witty and I could be devious."

"More fire, more showy explosions, less actual death?"

I nodded.

Raev raised an eyebrow. "Where in your plans was the bit about convincing all of us that you'd gone insane?"

"Actually, I think that's the only part of my original plan that I managed to pull off," I sighed. "Without the rest, it didn't do much good."

Raev sighed and patted me on the back. "You did well, my friend. Without your undead to hold the goddess of chaos back this would not have ended so well. You survived. It is more than the rest of us expected of you. Now, we've got negotiations and celebrations and funerals to plan and attend and move on from. I have done this so many times. Too many times." He stared into the distance for a moment, and Fereth and I joined in his silence. He finally shook his head and smiled. "Come. We have much to plan and much to talk about with the others. There are treaties to draw up and new borders to define if we're to make way for another wizard."

"So, you think he'll wake up?" I said, barely daring to hope.

"He was dead, and yet he breathes," Raev said, looking to the sky. "It is not the way we became wizards, but I am glad of that and would spare him that experience. We will plan for it, and we will hope. He has been like a brother to me, as well."

I nodded, and the three of us walked to the center of town. As we walked I took Fereth's hand. I needed a friend--no. I needed Fereth, more than I'd needed any friend ever before.

PART TWENTY-EIGHT

The rest of the day was a blur. I remember bits of it when I try, but no matter how technically eventful the day was, anyone would be better served reading a history book than my account. I snuck off to go help prepare the bodies of the dead for burial, which was both gruesome and soothing. That is where Raev found me when Aral had awoken at last.

Eventually I sought her out. Naran had been carried to his house and placed in his own bed. Aral was kneeling by his side, eyes and nose red from crying. Some women cried beautifully, but Aral was not one of those. Her skin was blotchy and her eyes were sunken and bloodshot. Somehow I liked her better, seeing her disheveled in her grief. She was showing her vulnerability, and the last of my fear of her dissolved into compassion.

She sniffled as she looked up at me, and then she cleared her throat. "His pulse is even, and his breath has deepened. It's as if he were...asleep." Aral's voice cracked on the last word. "I've tried to wake him up. There's nothing I can do. I don't know if it's me, or—"

I knelt beside her and patted her hand. "He'll wake up when he's ready. We've all tried. It's not you."

Aral gave me a strange half-smile, and I noticed the corner of her right eye did not crinkle the way her other did. In fact, her right eye did not track with the other, and I reached out to touch her face.

She flinched, pushing my hands away. "Don't."

"I'm sorry," I said. I still wanted to reach for her, to heal her if I could. I couldn't bring myself to look anywhere but at where her face didn't move right.

"I'll be fine," she grumbled. "I was hit in the head with a mace, and if I weren't a wizard I'd have died from it. I don't know how long it will take to completely heal, or if it will. For the love of magic, stop staring at me."

"I'm sorry," I said again, standing and finding a chair a few paces away. "I thought that we had all been immune to the chaos, but not one of us thought to have defensive spells at the ready, did we?"

"No," she bowed her head and closed her eyes. "Even walking through the streets of Urdran, or even here in Cairnborough, on a normal day...even then I have defenses ready. It seems insane now that I did not today."

I nodded in agreement. "I was shot," I said, "and I was stabbed. I was distracted and I was weak when I could have made a difference."

"I was unconscious," Aral said, giving me that strange half-smile once again. "I win."

"I didn't mean it as a contest," I said, embarrassed. "Krecek was in an explosion, and Modarian was attacked as well. Raev was looking after you, and there must be a reason the others were delayed or distracted."

Aral nodded thoughtfully and walked over to sit in a chair beside me. "We're all lucky, then," she said. "Any one of us could have died, and we would have another elemental to train and worry over."

We both lapsed into silence after that, both of us hoping that Naran would awaken. Eventually though, I left. It was the middle of the night and thoughts were weighing heavily upon me. I wandered around the city, and I was not the only one. People were talking, crying, sometimes wailing in the street at their misfortune. I was surprised at the destruction. I wanted to help, I felt I had to help, but I was too exhausted to trust my control of magic to make anything right. For now, I just stared, seeing it all and not feeling a part of any of it. I saw Raev down one street, moving rubble from a collapsed home, but I turned away and kept walking. My feet took me out to Cairnfeld, feeling hopeless and alone. I'd reached my limits. Ultimately I was not a god. I was human.

I walked to the old cairn stones that had watched in silence as my mentor had died. I sat upon Nalia's grave, feeling her disquiet at seeing the resting place of her immortal remains. I touched the stones, feeling the jagged edges that had cruelly cut into my back so many years ago. I'd thought at the time that that had been pain. I'd slept for a week and thought that was exhaustion. If I closed my eyes I could see the fear and panic on Krecek's face as he did that to me. I could still feel Nalia's surge of hope that she could be reborn one last time and be freed from the prison that was me.

You are no longer a prison to me, Nalia's thoughts were comforting and kind. You are a gift. Everything's changed, and I am content here with you.

If I could have hugged her I would have. We were at peace with each other, though that had been unimaginable so many years ago. We both stared through my eyes into the darkness, at the dark patch in the middle of these graves, and we shared our horror at all that had transpired in this spot. That was the difference, of course. We had learned, over the years, to share. We'd shared pain. We'd shared fear. We'd shared our isolation. We'd shared hope. We'd shared love.

Love.

I leaned my back against the stones and closed my eyes. She loved as I did; foolishly.

She'd hated Krecek, but I knew she had also loved him. As did I.

I'd almost decided to kill him. The first few days after I'd regained my memories, until I found myself at Naran's door, I wanted to see him lifeless in my arms, at my hand. When I'd thought about my parents an undeniable rage would return to me, and along with it the knowledge that I could kill him. It consumed me at moments, crowding out all other thought. I loved him as much as I hated him, and Nalia did as well.

There were others that I loved without so much conflict, though. Ysili had been one of them. If I'd known a thing about love, if I'd stayed with him longer, I think he and I might eventually have been lovers. Maybe he'd have stayed by my side, if we had. Maybe he wouldn't have tried to kill me. Maybe he wouldn't now be dead. Name of the gods, the maybes running through my head were enough to cripple me!

Then there was Naran. I'd loved him as well, the way I'd have loved a father or brother. He'd been my mentor, my savior, and at the end my true friend. I worried about him so much now. Would he ever wake up? What life be like without him?

From the depths of my soul, one more face came to my mind. Donab Kavidrian. He had been my teacher, but part of my soul cried out that he was also like my son. I hadn't had time to mourn him when he died. No one had mourned him, ever. Yda and I were the only ones who knew he was dead. Weren't we? No, there were others there, in her impossible stronghold that was so alien to the world... There were others who would be aware of his passing.

I fell asleep where I was, thinking my deep and painful thoughts about love, revenge, and death. At some point I heard and smelled fire, but I also smelled food and felt a warm blanket draped over me. I stared at the small campfire through a half-lidded gaze, too weary and stiff to move. Eventually I moaned and I heard someone chuckle.

"I knew I would find you here," Krecek said, helping me sit up and handing me food.

Elemental

I picked at it in silence, and Krecek did the same with his. Eventually I set the plate aside and sighed. "We're alive," I said at last, voice still rough with sleep.

"So we are," he said softly. "I didn't expect to be."

"I'm not sure if I did, either," I admitted. I was still mostly asleep, speaking without thinking. "Killing a wizard requires another wizard's willing death. That's the cost of the spell every Verwyn has used, and why we are always so short-lived. We've never told anyone. I'm sure you can imagine why."

He looked so shocked, green eyes wide and jaw slack. He dropped his plate on the ground and made no move to retrieve it. "Agrad?"

I nodded. I remembered now. I'd known it, but Yda's blanket of chaos over the city had driven it from my mind and distraction had kept it from resurfacing until I'd had some peace. It's what I'd been trying to remember, a thought that had nagged me every time someone had said something about the possibility of my death. I'd known when I planned the battle that it could not happen without a spell that only the Verwyn line knew. A spell that was imprinted on Nalia's soul. A spell we had not invoked.

I felt like I was giving him a very personal gift, and it made me feel nervous and vulnerable. "The Verwyn line hasn't been suicidal. We've been murderous. It was Nalia's doing. She'd planned on Aral being next, and finally you and Raev. She changed the plan when I had reason to hate you, wanting you to be next and make Aral suffer longer, but I don't want to die. And I didn't want you to die. I've already lost too many —"

Krecek kneeled next to me and hugged me, letting me cry.

"I almost did it," I whispered against him, grabbing him close to me. "All the memories were fresh again, and I wanted my life as a nobody again so much that I was willing to die to find it. Nalia tried to talk me out of it, can you believe it? It was her

374

plan, but she couldn't do a thing to stop it once she changed her mind. It was seeing Naran that reminded me of all the good you've done. That's when I started this insane plan to try to save us both. To save us all."

He stroked my hair gently and thanked me, and eventually I felt calmer. I sat there, arms wrapped around him, head on his shoulder, listening to him breathe. We were both alive. It felt amazing.

I had a question racing through my mind though, and I had to ask it.

"Do you know why Ysili tried to kill me? I'd canceled the chaos around me, so he should have been released from its hold."

Krecek shook his head and sat back to look at me. "I don't know. It wasn't my doing."

It's not what I wanted to hear. It didn't give me any answers. Still, it laid to rest the last little worry I'd had that Krecek may have been behind it. He wasn't. I could feel it in his words.

I tossed the remainder of my food into the fire. I knew I couldn't eat more for now. "I'm glad it wasn't you. I suppose I'll never know what went on in his mind at the last, except that he seemed surprised. That's all I know."

"Could you bring him back, the way you've brought back the others?"

I shuddered at the thought. "No." It wasn't the strict truth. I could, if he desired to come back enough. I didn't want to touch that sort of magic again. "I just want to put the ones I created to rest, and then forget I ever learned to do such a spell."

"Oh good," he said with a sigh of relief. "I'm glad they chased Yda away, but I'll be relieved when they're gone. Their presence makes me ill."

"I know," I said. I paused though, looking at him curiously. "Aren't you afraid of summoning her, or getting her attention, by saying her name?"

"Not while your undead are milling around." Krecek grinned at me and stood, brushing himself off. "They bother me to no end, but I have to admit that they are convenient."

I stood as well and we returned to town.

We helped others as we walked. We cleared rubble or reunited loved ones whenever we could. We conjured food for those who needed it. Whatever we could do, we did. At one point I noticed Fereth slipping out of a dark building, and I almost called to him. Almost. He wasn't alone. Hastriva was behind him, and she wrapped an arm possessively around him before she pulled him back into the darkness. I heard playful laughter, and blushed when I realized what I'd seen between them. It seemed inappropriate, but it warmed my heart a bit to know that the horrors around us had not erased joy from the world.

The next day the new cairns were built and the dead laid to rest. A mass funeral was held, and every wizard who had managed to arrive attended to pay their respects. At some point a large cairn was raised on the spot where Naran had died. No one knew where it came from. It did not pulse with the same power that the others did, but it looked like all the rest.

I found Fereth at his cousin's grave, and I realized he was suffering over it more than he'd said before. I stood next to him in silence, waiting for him to be ready to talk. It took longer than I'd expected.

"I saw you with Lord Ceolwyn yesterday," Fereth said at last. His voice was falsely bright and cheerful. "The two of you work well together. Is everything good between you?"

"We're both alive," I said. "That should be answer enough."

Fereth rolled his eyes and then nudged my shoulder. "Not by far. The two of you should kiss, hold hands, do a little more, if you know what I mean."

I grinned. "Do you mean more, the way you were with a certain goddess yesterday?"

Fereth blushed. "She said there's nothing like being close to death to make you feel like celebrating life, and she taught me what she meant. I never knew gods and goddesses could be so kind."

"Be careful," I said gently. "She can be sweet, but gods are still gods. They're fickle and sometimes hurtful without meaning to."

"Like wizards?" Fereth teased, grinning.

"Yes," I said seriously. "You've seen what I am capable of, Fereth. I'm looking forward to a long and lonely life, where no one will understand me. You look at me at times as if I'm some strange creature from the blackest forests, and will destroy you at a whim." I had to hold a hand up to shush him as he tried to deny it. "I could. I won't, but I could. So can any god. She won't, but she could. She will never be your equal. Don't fall in love."

He stared at me, and I watched a dance of various expressions drift across his face. I recognized indignation and stubborn consternation, but in the end he reached resignation and I knew he understood. I hoped I'd said it soon enough that it wouldn't be too late.

Nalia, of course, hated that I'd said something like that, even as she understood why I had. *Let them fall in love if they want to!*

It was a mother's affection for her daughter. It wasn't a practical thought. There were too many obstacles to a relationship between a mortal and an immortal of any sort. Would Hastriva have patience for him? Would she be able to understand him and have compassion enough for him to understand him, to accept him, to love him, and to eventually let him go?

I know, Nalia's thoughts were pained and frustrated within me, but she understood.

"She told me her name," Fereth said softly. "I don't know if it means anything."

"You will have to ask her what it means to her," I said. "It gives you power, though. It gives you protection from certain things, and may attract her attention."

"It's not something I should use lightly, then?"

I shrugged. "If you ask me, Hastriva's name should be used much more often than it is. It would make the world a much better place."

Fereth looked shocked. "How do you know her name?"

"I know the names of all the gods," I said.

"Oh! Because of...her?"

I shook my head. "Nalia might have told me eventually, and please do keep her name safe as well. No, I was taught a long time ago. Modarian might know the names of all the gods as well, but he might not. Krecek knows, because he was once a priest. Aral was taught a few when Davri was still alive, but I don't know how many. I don't know if the other wizards or elementals know the names of any gods, even the ones whose power they possess."

"So," Fereth said slowly, "it's something that only priests and wizards might know, or might not know?"

I nodded. "It might mean she cares. It might mean she wants to keep an eye on you to see where your life goes from here. Then again, it might mean nothing at all." I shrugged. "It's hard to tell."

"Can I do magic with Nalia's name?" A mischievous glint appeared in Fereth's eye.

"A bit," I said. "If you kill yourself with it, I refuse to take the blame."

Fereth laughed for a minute, but it died when I refused to even crack a smile. The possibility was a remote one, but I wasn't going to tell him that. I was more than happy to let him think the consequences could be that dire.

"I'll be careful," he said at last.

"Thank you," I said, finally smiling. "Are you ready to go home?"

He shook his head at first, but it wasn't a very enthusiastic shake. "I want to see my aunt and uncle in Anogrin, first. I want to tell them what happened here, and see if they're as kind as I remember them to be. I have horses to return, but that can wait a little while longer. Unless you still need me?"

"You're welcome to visit me any time," I said. "As often and as long as you would like. There's much more out there for you, though. Meet people. Find adventure. Return your father's horses, and give him a handful of golden stars." I held out a small purse full of coins. "It should be recompense enough. Use the rest to buy what you need. Become the bard you've always dreamed. Just come back and tell me tales. That's all I ask."

He gave me a hug. "I will," he said, voice rough with emotion. "As often as I can."

I realized I hated goodbyes, but it was too late for that now. As soon as I let go I walked away, sorrow at my heels. I was through in Cairnborough, more than ready to leave everything I'd seen here behind. We'd won, I reminded myself over and over again as I walked. We'd won, and I'd survived.

Byrek waited for me, carriage loaded and horses impatient to be on the road. "Are you ready to return home?"

Home.

"Always," I said softly as I climbed into my seat. "Always."

ACKNOWLEDGMENTS

Wow, what a ride. This book was a monster to begin with, and it took a raid group to wrangle it into existence. In fact, some people who play World of Warcraft on Moonrunner will probably find some of the names a bit familiar. (I'm getting ahead of myself…)

First and foremost, I need to thank my husband. He came in half way through the process of my writing this, and he married me anyway. Richard, you've been my rock, even though you didn't have anything to do with the writing itself. (No, I won't put your name in comic sans in the middle of my acknowledgment page, no matter how hard you beg.) My family has put up with temper tantrums, late suppers, a dirty house, being ignored…wait, were those things they put up with from me, or things I put up with from them? Either way, this book wouldn't be the same without them.

Huge thanks also go out to my dad, for so many reasons. It started with instilling in me a lifelong love of reading and writing. He taught me to keep my feet on the ground but my head in the clouds, balancing all things. More than that, though, he is one of two people who has read every draft I've gone through in my quest to make this a story I am proud to share with others. He had suggestions and questions at every step, believing in me from the start.

Sabrina Zirakzadeh…you've been with this book from the very first words. This book wouldn't exist without you. Seriously. I may have had the first line in mind for a decade before we met, but it's because of you that I found the right story to go with those words.

Noelle Barcelo, I can't begin to express how in awe I am of the cover art you created for me. You've always awed me with your talents, and I am so very lucky that I can call you my friend. Thank you. Thank you. Thank you.

Sandra Leblanc, thank you for your proofreading and your instant enthusiasm for the project! I didn't have time to add all of your story suggestions, but believe me when I say I WILL expand upon the story in all those directions at some point. I want to know all of those things, too.

To my beta readers Cat Lynn, Em Joyce Ascano, Suzi Kilpela, Sabrina Zirakzadeh, Bryce Alexander, but ESPECIALLY Justin Davis...wow. I love you guys! Your unwavering belief in my ability to do this story justice kept me going, and your suggestions didn't just make this story better, but you all made me a better writer in the process.

I can't forget all the people who read and reviewed my fanfics when I started getting brave enough to share things I'd written. From the Star Wars Chicks, to CLAMPesque, and everyone who has stumbled on my stories in various places with the grace enough to drop me a line, thank you. My critics made me stronger, and my fans made me brave.

Finally, to my World of Warcraft family. Everyone I raided with/was in a guild with, thank you. The Night Crew, Serenity, Gods of War, The Browncoats, and a few more who escape me right now...you helped me raid this boss. My biggest shout out goes to MY favorite people on Moonrunner, Honored Exiles. We've been to hell and back in the last decade plus, but HE has always been my home when I'm in the game. You raided with me when I was a kick ass healer at the top of my raiding game, and you still bring me along now that I'm a distracted, filthy casual. I love you guys!

Thank you, everyone, for reading. I hope you have enjoyed this tale.

ABOUT THE
AUTHOR

Tam Chronin is a figment of the imagination, which might be why she lives there often enough to find her main characters and convince them to share their stories.

Before becoming an author she slayed trolls for many years in the wilds of the internet. She was occasionally granted the legendary weapon, Ban Hammer, to aid in this quest. It was a relief to retire from such harrowing adventures, but for a coin and a stiff drink she might recount them over a campfire.

She lives in Phoenix, Arizona, with her family, two parakeets, three cats, a bunny, a varying number of both fish and chickens, and a vicious attack tortoise who guards the back yard.

ALSO BY TAM CHRONIN

The Godslayer Series

Available now:
Elemental
The Arcane War
Abomination

Upcoming:
Graves of the Gods
The Madness of Verwyn

The Graceful Death Series

Everyone Dies Alone

Upcoming:
Zombies Half Price

Made in the USA
Columbia, SC
19 March 2022

57732321R00231